Deadly Rumors

By

Jeanne Foguth

Cataloging-in-Publication Data is on file with the Library of Congress.

ISBN: **978-0-9913338-1-3**

Chapter 1

"I can't believe you brought Grandfather." Kelsey crossed her arms over her stomach, feeling like the woman she'd trusted all her life had sucker punched her.

Martha made a helpless gesture, but a swell of voices from the crowd on the other side of the auditorium's thick curtain drowned out her explanation. They both looked at the curtain's stained back.

After the wave of sound subsided, Kelsey said, "How did he find out about tonight's rally?" She tried to keep her tone interested instead of accusing.

Martha gave Pearson Brady a significant look. "He phoned yesterday." Kelsey glared at the silver fox's impeccably tailored pin-strip suit. Kelsey sharply inhaled. "He invited Calhoun to speak along with you." Martha's gaze moved to her grandfather and softened. "The real question is how he managed to remember tonight's engagement for over twenty-four hours."

The last thing Kelsey's brother needed was their dementia-plagued grandfather stepping in to help campaign. "Does he realize this is Ramsey's campaign for Senate or does he think he's still in office and running for reelection?"

Martha made a helpless gesture. "All I know is that those two old coots can't stand the idea of a female doing a 'man's job'. The only thing worse is that you're doing so good."

Kelsey narrowed her gaze on her grandfather, whose bright eyes belied the fact that half of the time he didn't know what decade it was or who he was talking to. His decline had begun the day, perhaps even the minute her grandmother had died. Initially, she'd thought his mental lapses were grief induced, but it soon became apparent something drastic had happened to his once razor-sharp mind. "Has he taken his medication?" Martha nodded. Kelsey dared to hope that the evening could turn out well. "Perhaps it's a good thing Pearson called. If his mind stays on the subject, instead of waltzing off on a tangent, Grandfather's support would be the best assistance Ramsey could hope for."

Martha snorted. "You're the one who held his campaign together while he mourned." Kelsey blinked, at Martha's judgmental tone. It wasn't as if Rams could have campaigned from his hospital bed. In fact, it was a miracle that the freak accident hadn't killed him as well as his wife and daughter. "Of course, I'm still amazed that you did it."

"Did what?"

"Stepped in like you have." Martha gestured toward the curtain. "I know how much you dislike being the center of attention."

"You knew?" Kelsey asked. Martha gave a tiny smile as she nodded. "You realized public speaking has always been my worst fear?"

Martha shook her head. "Just knew how you

were raised to think men were kings and us women were peons." She narrowed her eyes. "How did you get past your phobia?"

Kelsey helplessly put up her hands. "Getting that jerk out of office is very motivating." Thinking of Marvin Frederickson, who had succeeded her grandfather, brought a wave of anger. "In the four decades he held the senate seat, Grandfather always put the voters first."

"He was – is - a good man. Some still think he should have stayed in office after your grandmother died."

"Well, he didn't." Instead, he had encouraged his assistant to run and once Marvin won, everyone in their family had been shocked over his change of attitude. Whatever else anyone could say, the man was a good actor.

Martha spat at the curtain. Within his first term, Marvin Frederickson switched parties and tore down forty-two years of policies her grandfather had painstakingly built to protect the people of North Carolina. It was time to get a MacLennan, who cared about the constituency back in office. She hoped the voters had figured out how two-faced Frederickson was. If the polls could be believed, Ramsey's percentage had risen nearly thirty percent, since the accident. She frowned. While she hoped there wouldn't be another fatal accident and she wouldn't have to wear black much longer, Abby and Jen's deaths had helped in an odd way. Voters were often fickle and the election was mere weeks away, how long would the sympathy votes persevere?

Probably not much longer, so anything could happen between now and then.

"Welcome, everyone." Pearson Brady's deep southern drawl seemed to ooze through the high school's thick curtain. "I've got an extra treat for you this evening. Calhoun MacLennan." Head high, her grandfather slipped through the gap in the curtains. A rolling thunder of applause greeted him.

"Now if he can just stay focused on the issues and remember Ramsey is actually the one running," Kelsey said.

Martha nodded. "I wonder why Ramsey didn't come, himself." Her brow furrowed. "He's been out of the hospital for almost two weeks, yet you're still filling in for him."

"He says he can't stand for very long," Kelsey said.

"And you believe that?"

Gooseflesh quivered over her arms. "Is there something I should know?" Martha shrugged. "What?" Kelsey demanded; daring her to articulate the rumors that the accident had either been a suicide or murder attempt. When Martha refused to say anything, Kelsey admitted, "I think he lost his center when Abby died. I think he's holds himself at fault for the accident." Her biggest fear was that her brother might be starting to slip away, like their grandfather.

"How will he be in office, dealing with big issues if he can't get past his own personal problems?"

Kelsey looked hard at Martha. "Believe me when I tell you that I know how fragile he is, but he's a

MacLennan and we recover." She had to believe that for everyone's sake. Six weeks ago, he was lying in the hospital fighting for his life; five weeks ago, she, her grandfather and Martha stood shoulder to shoulder at the graveyard. Tears blurred her vision and chocked her.

"I know." Martha squeezed her hand.

Kelsey swallowed. "Four weeks ago, Ramsey woke from that coma and faced the reality that he'd lost the two people he loved most and the fact that he might never walk again." She swallowed. "A week after that, he took his first step. He's conquering the physical stuff, it's just taking a little longer to deal with the rest."

"Maybe you're right."

"But you don't think so."

Martha shook her head. "I think he wanted to make the world a better place for Jen and without her to build a future for he's lost." Martha fixed her with a firm look. "And I don't think he'll recover from her death by the election, if ever."

"There are lots of other kids to make a better world for. They deserve a decent place to grow just as much as Jen did."

"I know that. And you know that. Perhaps Calhoun even remembers that, but, right now, I don't think Ramsey sees anything but his loss."

Kelsey hoped that she hadn't put aside her fear of speaking in public for all these engagements, just to have her brother lose to Frederickson, who seemed to be making every effort to return their district to the Dark Ages.

ooo

"So you're really going through with this." Quinn swiveled his wheelchair away from the row of black and white monitors and glared at him. Doran inclined his head, while he searched his best pal's worried expression. Quinn looked up at the van's ceiling. "Even though Wes hasn't given us an official authorization."

This wouldn't be the first time they had used unorthodox methods, so why had his partner suddenly gone soft? "We've never worried about having everything signed, sealed and perfectly punctuated, before." Quinn scowled. Doran added, "As long as every document is perfect when we present the case to the prosecutor, does it really matter if the timeline on when we begin as compared to our authorization is hazy? This time the red tape snarl is just a little worse because of the politicians involved."

"Why does he want us to slap this op together so fast?" That question had bothered him, too. Uneasily, Doran shrugged his shoulders. Quinn barged on, "How about why the only input we've had from Wes have been undocumented conversations over supposedly non-existent scrambled lines?" Quinn's mouth flattened.

A knot of dread formed in his stomach, but he played it cool. "So?"

"Something does not feel right about this."

Though a chill rippled over Doran, he tried not to show his anxiety. "Are you saying we should delay until the paperwork trail has all typos corrected?" Quinn shrugged. "How many times have we gotten ops stuck with red tape?" Quinn's brow furrowed.

While he mulled that one over, Doran added, "Wes asked us to expedite this, because his information indicated that they planned to make major changes shortly."

"My guts still don't like it," Quinn muttered. Doran swallowed as he recalled another time his best bud had an inexplicably accurate gut reaction and not listening had nearly cost him his life. "And I don't like the way you're ready to jump into this op, half prepared because someone who hasn't worked outside his cozy office in the last decade says we have some sort of unprovable deadline."

"Why did you wait until now to say something?"

Quinn's mouth flattened. "If you'd listen to me, you'd have heard reservations from the moment Wes mentioned that bogus deadline. You'll get yourself killed going into that shark's nest without full department backup."

Wes had called him earlier and said, 'I don't know anyone else I'd trust with this because the situation requires someone who isn't greedy enough to be bought – someone who wasn't afraid of the political clout – someone who doesn't think the damned MacLennan Family are saints.' Wes had paused to clear his throat. 'Someone who knows firsthand that gorgeous women can have hearts of a snake. Someone who can focus on the object instead of get distracted by a woman's charms.' Doran wished he felt as confident about his invulnerability as Wes obviously did. Doran sighed. "You don't have to back me up."

Back stiff, Quinn swiveled his wheelchair to the bank of monitors. "Guess it won't matter if we get killed, since I'm already half dead." Quinn's quiet proclamation raised the tiny hairs on the back of Doran's neck as it echoed through the surveillance van's shadowed interior. "I've watched you stare at the surveillance footage we got of her. Makes me think you're thinking with the wrong head."

Instead of pursuing the discussion and getting into a situation where he needed to lie, Doran plucked the photo of his kid sister from his wallet. Over the past decade, the paper had softened and Marnie's image had developed a wrinkle in its corner, but her big blue-gray eyes still looked trustingly at him and her senseless death still infuriated him. He smoothed out the wrinkle then slipped her memory into the pocket of his black T-shirt. Having her likeness next to his heart felt right; particularly tonight, when he began this operation. If children couldn't get the damned poison from parasites at the playground, then other brothers wouldn't be haunted by memories of funerals or sickened by the scent of lilies. Doran squared his shoulders and steeled his resolve, then he slapped his billfold onto the surveillance van's minuscule counter, next to his badge. The thump resounded in the tight surroundings with the finality of the jail-cell door he intended to slam on the MacLennans. "The flow of poison has to be shut down," Doran said.

Quinn grunted in agreement, but kept his attention on the screens. Doran lifted his chin; though the next phase of this operation wasn't officially signed, sealed and sanctioned, he'd come too far to quit. Tonight, he would set in motion a plan to gain evidence on the drug ring. Eventually, they should be able to collect enough evidence to convict the scum.

Doran looked over Quinn's tense shoulder at the infrared monitor, which showed a wide view of Kelsey MacLennan's house and garage, then he looked at the other monitors. There was no sign of life on any of the screens.

"What do you expect me to do with the information you and Wes gleaned on their cartel involvement?" Doran asked. When Quinn ignored him, he added, "I can't sit back and do nothing when we're so close to having solid evidence."

"There is no guarantee any of them will ever serve time. All they gotta do is figure out who else to nail and the fucking DA will roll over on his fucking back to give them immunity for their testimony."

Doran sighed at the way so many wealthy bastards got off scot-free. He shoved the palm-sized drill into his pant's pocket and deliberately secured the Velcro flap.

"Worst thing the damned politicians ever came up with was the fucking witness protection program," Quinn growled. "I'd like to know who thought that one up and if they really figured the slime-balls would go straight after they got the chance to build a new life." Quinn twisted a dial. Green tinged the shades of gray and reflected off Quinn's face, giving his rugged profile a sickly cast. Damn, he hated it when his partner started using the electronics to communicate his emotions.

Doran swallowed a Tums, hoping it would

silence both his qualms and his acid stomach. "The good thing about going after a high-profile family like the MacLennans is that they're too superior to choose the program and become nobodies. And, if Wes is right about their distribution ring being on the fringes of Ling's operation, we have the added bonus of knowing that Ling likes permanent solutions."

"Tell me something I don't know," Quinn snapped as he gave Doran a look meant to remind him that Ling also knew exactly who they were and wanted them to have a 'permanent solution'.

Doran ran his fingers through his thick, dark hair. Ling's pushers had spent over a decade lurking in schoolyards and getting kids hooked on poison. Wes believed the MacLennan political clout had protected the cartel for years, but beliefs did not get convictions, so he'd figured out a way to gain the evidence he needed for a jury and if the plan worked, all the key players would finally end up behind bars.

"You've spent most of the last decade trying to stop Ling and that slippery bastard keeps getting away," Quinn said. "Do you really think this cobbled-together op will finally give you vengeance for your sister?"

"This hasn't been about revenge in a long time."

Quinn glanced pointedly at the pocket covering Doran's heart. His fingers dug into the black leather arm of the wheelchair he'd been forced to rely on since their last encounter with Ling's alliance. His knuckles whitened. "You can't change the past."

"I'm not trying to." Doran adopted his most

14

conciliatory tone. "I want to change the future."

Quinn took a deep breath, then relaxed his grip. He worked the kinks out of his hands, before he tweaked another button. The image of the vine-clad front porch turned into angry slashes of sickly green and black, which rolled discordantly over the screen. If Quinn had doubts, why hadn't he spoken up sooner? Why continually claim to want a piece of the action, then wait until moments before they were ready to set their plan in motion to vent his doubts? As the silence lengthened, the pixels swirled faster.

Doran rubbed the knotted muscles at the back of his neck. "We can spend the rest of our lives following a narrow-minded interpretation of the rules or we can die infiltrating his local operation." Doran's right fist connected with his left palm. The smack echoed throughout the van like thunder. "The end justifies the means." Mouth flat, Doran fastened his night vision goggles around his neck and adjusted his audio headset.

Movements rigid with tension, Quinn calibrated an audio receiver. The call of a whippoorwill echoed hauntingly through the van. Finally, with nothing else to putter at, Quinn swiveled his wheelchair and faced Doran. "Ling's kind is why I signed on to begin with." He sighed. "It's still about the pushers, but now, I want revenge for my legs, too." Quinn bit out each syllable. "There hasn't been time to do a full analysis and there's only circumstantial evidence that the MacLennan chick is involved." Doran snorted. Quinn's eyes narrowed. "She's one hot number, and I've seen you watch her."

"I hear she's an ice queen. I'll probably get frost bite." Preferably while warming her from the inside out.

"More like she's discriminating."

"Meaning Lancaster is her lover?" Doran asked. Quinn shook his head. "I heard that rumor and I'll bet you did, too."

Quinn raised his gaze. "There's a world of difference between urinal talk, what's printed in the society column and a deposition," Quinn said. Doran snorted. Quinn's mustache quivered. "Dev, I feel like we're being setup, but I can't figure out by who. I don't want to think it's Wes, but who else could it be?"

Ling. Coldness settled in Doran's stomach. "What exactly do you suspect? That Wes is throwing us to the cartel so he can pocket the reward?" That Ling had made a trail he knew they would follow, so he could finally have the satisfaction of killing them?

"That much money can change values, particularly if you're living on a government salary." Quinn adjusted a knob. Kelsey's front porch replaced the rolling gray-green slashes.

Doran's gaze dropped to Quinn's once muscular thighs, which were now an emaciated ruin beneath his faded Levi's. Nothing had felt right since Quinn had shoved him out of the way of the bullet aimed at his heart. "If that's what is going on, it's my fault."

Quinn grunted in disagreement.

"No, it's true. I was young, stupid, egotistical and

gullible enough to believe screwing Pia would give me a gold-plated invite into daddy's little cartel." He sighed at the bitter memory of romancing a deadly viper like Pia Chen to get to daddy Ling. "I learned my lesson. I just wish you hadn't paid the price of my stupidity ... if this is a setup, I want you out."

"You need to quit beating yourself up. I was team leader, the whole fiasco was my fault."

Doran stared at Quinn, shocked that after so long, they were actually talking about the debacle. "I told you to fuck her. If I hadn't you wouldn't have been there and we wouldn't be analyzing the past." Quinn closed his eyes and rubbed his temples. "The MacLennan chick looks good."

Trust Quinn not to consider the price of being partnered to him and change the topic. "Not to me," he lied. Instead of being a hero and saving the life of the green recruit he'd been assigned, Quinn should have let him die for his stupidity. But, he hadn't. If he hadn't saved his life, he wouldn't have to live with the knowledge that Quinn took the slug meant for him.

Doran closed his eyes against the reality of Quinn's sacrifice and controlled his breathing. If Wes's plan proceeded as intended, they would save thousands of kids from the poison pushers spread over playgrounds. But if Quinn had a bad feeling about it, it could be a setup. "We have to protect the children Ling's cartel preys on," Doran repeated. "That takes priority over petty concerns like the depth of Kelsey MacLennan's involvement in her drug smuggling family's illegal operation or even if this a setup."

"I can't find a shred of solid proof against any of them."

"They've been smuggling for decades. Did you expect anything but rumors?"

"It'd be nice."

Doran sighed. "They're in the public eye so much that they've obviously buried their dirt deeper than most." He worked a kink out of the back of his neck. "Have we ever gotten a case laid out on a silver platter?" Quinn grunted. Doran added, "Everything points to their involvement." Now was not the time to run scared or think about the way Kelsey's blouse molded to her chest in the wind. "If we wait for incontrovertible evidence, the rats might spot us or worse, change their distribution network as a precaution and save themselves. Again."

"What if Wes relocated us here as part of his plan to offer us up to Ling? He could put his kids through college and still have enough left over to buy himself a tropical paradise with hot and cold running servants."

"Ling has been offering millions for us dead or alive for years. If Wes was going to cash us in, I think he'd have done it before now."

Quinn stared at the screen showing the side of the garage. "I thought I saw something move in that magnolia." He tapped some keys, centered on the upper branches of the tree, and then zoomed in.

Nice try at distraction. "What if we never get another chance like this? I'm not asking you to do anything, except run for your life, if your hunch is right. And just in case it's not, I'm going to follow through with the plan and gather the evidence we need." Doran grabbed the jar of camouflage paint. After a few deft movements, he checked his reflection in a blank monitor. His face looked as black as his hair, his clothing and the night.

The next monitor showed the surrounding shadowed woodlands. The trees seemed to reach toward the immaculate colonial, as if trying to wrap it in shadows worthy of a gothic murder story. Doran shook his head at the idea and turned his thoughts to the woman. "Anyone who would leap onto the campaign trail and crusade for her scummy brother the day after he put his kid and wife in the morgue is guilty as hell," Doran said.

"We don't have proof that he-"

"Christ, how much more proof do you need? Twenty-four days before the accident, the man insured them for ten mill apiece." Doran gritted his teeth. The contract Ling had out on each of them was only half that and Wes had stuck them in this backwater town after a dozen attempts on their lives. "Ramsey MacLennan is guilty as Satan and Kelsey crusades for him like he's Jesus H. Christ."

"You've always hated lawyers."

"You like him?"

"I like him better than Frederickson." Quinn had detested Senator Frederickson from the moment he entered the P.I. office the department had set up as their local cover.

"Hell, you like dog shit better than him."

"There's something fishy about anyone that smooth."

19

Doran nodded in agreement. "He's a lawyer and a politician, they're all 99.9 percent slick."

"I still think the new life insurance and crash were part of a murder attempt against Ramsey," Quinn said. "Or maybe whoever was behind it simply planned the accident as part of a smear campaign." Doran shook his head at his partner's naivety. "MacLennan was coming up in the polls awfully fast," Quinn persisted. "We both know there are a zillion ways to sling mud."

"So?" Thanks to Kelsey's campaigning, Ramsey MacLennan is skyrocketing in the polls.

"I never uncovered anything incriminating about MacLennan other than a couple typical scrapes when he was a kid."

Doran rubbed his temples. "All I need to know is that Ramsey MacLennan had a one-car accident with no witnesses less than one month after insuring his wife and kid for a fortune."

"Accidents aren't uncommon." Quinn's tone lacked conviction.

"What about his lame excuse?" Doran demanded. Quinn raised a brow. Doran mimicked the televised interview that had infuriated him, "The car swerved on its own to avoid a chicken." Doran shook his head at the sheer absurdity of it. "Chickens roost at night. If the fool had claimed it was an owl, it would have at least sounded feasible and I'd give him the benefit of the doubt. But a chicken?" Doran shook his head. "No way."

The speakers emitted a whippoorwill's mournful night song.

Quinn began to hyperventilate; his fast breathing

seemed to deplete the van's oxygen. Doran instinctively moved to help, then remembering the doctor's warning to let his partner handle the attacks, he clasped his hands behind his back. Until Quinn had begun life on wheels, he had lived as if he was indestructible. Now, a T-shirt with the logo 'Fragile, Handle with Care' might be more appropriate than the pale blue knit, which stretched over his muscular shoulders and biceps. Doran's nails cut into his palms as he forced himself to give Quinn the chance to control his emotions and tried to think of something to say. All he could think of was Kelsey. Smart. Beautiful. A genuine walking wet dream. "The woman acts like she's perfection personified," Doran said, "and you already found out that she's involved in all public aspects of her family's empire." Doran gave Quinn a significant look. "Everything you've discovered indicates she's involved in the corruption, too." He pulled on thin leather gloves, fisting his black-sheathed hand to adjust the fit. "I know in my gut that she's using her delivery trucks to move drugs along with flowers."

"I'd like more than rumors to base an op on."

"We'll get the proof with the op."

"Trent's informant swears that the drug lab is at their poultry factory," Quinn said. Doran snorted. Quinn glared up at him. "Why are you so convinced that the processing plant is located inside her lab?"

Because he wanted a valid reason to investigate her in exquisite depth. "Do you have a better explanation for why she has such a high tech security system for a greenhouse?"

21

Quinn shook his head.

"No one needs that kind of security for plants."

"My research indicates there's big money in hybridizing."

Doran grunted. "If - no - when, the plan works, she'll believe she needs help and I'll make certain she realizes I'm the one to protect her." Doran clamped his hand on Quinn's muscular shoulder. "Then, I'll get into that damned lab and videotape the operation for you. Will that be solid enough evidence?"

"I still can't figure out why you expect her to trust you just because she rear-ends you."

How many more times would he have to explain this? "She drives like a Sunday granny. The accident won't hurt her, but it will throw her off balance. She'll see the correlation to Ramsey's crash and figure someone is trying to kill all the clan. I'll make certain she believes I'm the only person she can trust to protect her. And once we're in, we'll get the evidence we need to nail them all." It would be simple, if he could ignore the other types of 'rear-ending' and 'getting in' that he'd like to do with her.

Quinn sighed. "Logic according to Devlin Doran." Doran turned off the van's interior lights and waited for his eyes to adjust to the darkness. Quinn exhaled and added, "Beats me how, but you tend to be right."

Doran gently cuffed Quinn's rock hard biceps, then stepped through the blackout curtain, put on his night vision goggles, then opened the van's rear door and stepped into the humid shadowy forest that cocooned the van from observers. After he moved across the desolate pavement, he ducked under the perfumed boughs of an ancient magnolia and became invisible to all observers except Quinn's infrared camera.

He stayed within the protective darkness and listened to the night. Then darted from shadow to shadow until he arrived under the old magnolia, which grew mere feet from the garage's man-door.

Through the night vision goggles, the shrouded setting looked like an open invitation to burglars. Gooseflesh rippled over his back as he weighed the possibility of a trap. Had Quinn's subconscious sensed something?

An owl's mournful tones echoed his thoughts.

Nothing ventured, nothing gained. Doran eased out from the heavily perfumed air, past the thick, waxy leaves and stepped over the dewy strip of lawn. When he inserted the lock pick, he immediately hit an obstruction. Employing a calm he didn't feel, he worked a broken key-tip out of the lock. Once it was gone, the catch clicked almost immediately.

Prickles of caution mingled with cold sweat. The only other time a deadbolt had been this easy, it had been a setup. A stealthy stirring within the magnolia's boughs revealed the watcher.

Clever place to hide.

Doran took a step backward and merged into the deepest shadows. He crouched motionless, every sense alert for an assailant, every muscle ready for combat.

Again, a rustling movement. What were they

waiting for? Reinforcements?

Doran peered toward the ambusher's hiding place, but only saw leaves quaking in the humid, unseen breeze.

In the distance, a dog howled. Roses, recently cut grass and moist earth scented the air. Occasional clouds shrouded obliterated the crescent moon.

His thigh muscles started to cramp. He tried to ease his position as he waited for the concealed onlooker to make his next mistake.

Time dragged on. "Dev-"

"Shhh." Though the sound was quiet as the breeze, Quinn instantly went silent.

This watcher was a pro. Doran should have expected Kelsey MacLennan to have at least one guard. Lord knew the family had enough money to hire a squadron of mercenaries.

Dampness saturated his socks and the knotted muscle in his right thigh got so bad he gritted his teeth to keep from groaning, but Doran remained still as death, senses alert for the tiniest sign.

Several feet up the magnolia, waxy leaves moved. Doran steeled himself for an attack, but as the branch shivered, a whippoorwill's mournful song resonated from the spot. Doran expelled his breath in an unintelligible curse.

"What'd you say?" Quinn sounded tense as his aching leg.

"Nothing." He kneaded his cramped muscle then stood. The bird's song quit. He hobbled out of the shadows, eased the door open and entered the garage's eerie stillness. "I'm in." Doran ghosted past a utility cupboard and a trashcan that smelled too pine-fresh for rubbish. Muscles protesting, he stooped to peer under the Mustang's chassis. He reached under and felt for the flexible rubber brake line, then squeezed his head and shoulders under. "They make these damned things lower every year." Quinn grunted agreement. Doran twisted his head until the clumsy night vision goggles focused on the brake line. Drilling the tiny hole seemed ridiculously anticlimactic. He repeated the process on the other front wheel.

"Nearly done," he said, as he slid under the rear. The ingenuity of copying the method her brother had used to fake his own crash should make her distrust her family, and everyone else that she had previously relied on. Except she'd trust the innocent stranger she rear-ended. He grinned as he drilled the fourth hole.

Abruptly, the overhead light snapped on and the main garage door began to rise. "What the hell," Quinn exclaimed.

It was a setup. Doran closed his eyes and whipped off his night-vision goggles. How could he have been so stupid? He should have sensed the trap. Should have confronted the lookout in the boughs. Should have listened to Quinn.

Damn.

A car's headlights sped down the peaceful semi-rural road, as he tried to push out from under the low-slung car, but something snagged his shirt and held him in place. Helplessly, he watched the car's headlights careen into the driveway. The light emphasized the incriminating drill in his hand and three pristine drops of brake fluid on the polished concrete floor. Doran squinted against the glare as the brakes shrieked and tires screeched on the asphalt.

Then, the engine revved and hurtled forward on a collision course with the Mustang. Damn, the driver must have spotted him.

Doran ripped his shirt as he slid out from under the car and scrambled toward the side door. Staying low, he used the Mustang for cover.

Brakes squealed and then the oncoming car skidded to a halt mere inches from the Mustang's rear bumper, its headlights centered on him.

Doran froze.

Rummmm. Rummmmm. Rummm. The motor revved.

The man door moved.

Trapped between two foes. Doran mentally kicked himself for wanting Kelsey so much that he'd jumped to accept Wes's pathetic plan. When it came to getting into that skinny redhead's pants, he'd acted stupid as a teenage recruit. He'd been so determined to get the plan started, that he'd given the unseen watcher with the phony birdcall time to set up this trap.

Varroom. The car surged backward, engine shrieking like a pack of starving banshees. Tires squealed as it halted for a moment, then it came forward. Again, it stopped mere inches from the Mustang's rear bumper. Trapped between the concrete floor and the chassis, he squinted at the red sports car, trying to glimpse his attacker. The bright headlights simultaneously masked the malicious driver and held Doran helpless as a moth in the glare.

Eeeeeeeeeeeeeeee, a fan belt wailed as the car vaulted backward. Brakes squealed, then the car rocketed forward, swerved to the right and came to a screaming halt in the vacant spot between the Mustang and the house.

With a whine, the garage door began descending.

Doran slid along the floor toward the Mustang's rear and the dubious safety outside the steadily lowering door. His torn shirt snagged on the mud-flap and he was yanked to a stop just short of his objective. He ripped his shirt free, but a quick glance told him the garage door would crush his torso if he tried to make it.

The other car's door slammed against the Mustang. Scents of stale cigarettes, whisky and Opium mingled with the garage's pine-fresh smell. Caught between assailants and a crushing door, Doran wished he'd brought his handgun.

The door settled to a stop.

With no real backup and no hope, Doran expected to feel a bullet's death bite any second. Wishing he'd carried a gun, he rolled over to face his fate. Too bad his last memory would be the sight of a six-inch-high metallic gold heel descending toward his forehead.

Doran crammed his wide shoulders and long legs under the Mustang. Again, his shirt caught on the frame. The gold clad foot landed on the pristine concrete, then the second foot joined it. The slim ankles wobbled. The shoe's flimsy diamond-studded straps hovered over candy apple red toenails. Odd garb for a mercenary, but typical attire for one of Ling's pushers.

Doran slid as far as he could under the rear bumper. Something thumped against the Mustang.

"Fucking shoes." The woman's voice sounded slurred. She shook her foot and fell against the Mustang. She gasped, then shook her foot until the golden spike-heeled shoe thumped to the floor. Two bejeweled hands landed next to the wobbly ankles. "Attack me, will you, you, you-"

Doran clutched his flashlight, ready to smash it into her face.

Long, glittery crimson fingernails clumsily worked at the strap of the remaining shoe. The woman belched loud and long; the wave of putrid air made Doran gag. She managed to rid herself of the second shoe while he fought nausea. The bare toes wiggled. His stomach twisted and he clenched his teeth against gagging.

Doran inched sidewise, toward the long expanse of shapely leg and peered upward. Wispy black lace underwear were visible beneath a miniscule red leather skirt.

Appalled that Zoë Lancaster, Kelsey MacLennan's housemate, had given him the fright of his life, Doran wormed his way under the Mustang's rear bumper and wished the car were higher. Zoë stagger-walked between her crimson Porsche and Kelsey's Mustang then tottered to the door connecting the garage to the house. She fumbled with her keys, swaying as she tried to line one up with the lock.

Abruptly, the door slammed open. Kelsey stood in the open doorway; hands on slim hips, her gaze snapping with fury. Doran froze, mesmerized by the sight of the way her sheer ivory silk robe molded to her form. "Where have you been?" Kelsey demanded.

"Missed me, huh?" Zoë staggered into the house, rubbing suggestively past Kelsey. "I love you, but you gotta quit locking that door." With each word, her voice receded.

Kelsey glared after Zoë with obvious malice. Doran watched, spellbound by his first glimpse of the woman showing genuine emotions. With no paparazzi to shackle her feelings, she seemed like a different person. An even more desirable person.

Anger apparent in every muscle, Kelsey stomped into the garage and studied the mustang's passenger door. "You disgusting drunken twit!" She stooped down. "You clumsy, drunken klutz. You will never park next to my car, again," Kelsey fumed. She stood up and whipped open the door to Zoë's Porsche. When she stuck her head inside the car; the ivory silk caressed Kelsey's bottom like a lover's touch. Doran swallowed to stifle his groan. She straightened, holding something small and black in her hand. As she closed the Porsche's door, Doran eased farther under Kelsey's Mustang. Her bare feet marched around the hood of her car. She stopped in front of the utility cabinet, whipped the door open and stood on tiptoe. The sensual line of her arch made Doran's mouth go dry. "Let's see you mess with my car, again," she muttered as she slammed the door.

Even her ankles looked sensual, as she tramped into the house. After the door closed and the dead bolt snapped into place, he counted to one hundred and tried not to think about how tantalizing feet could look. Then teeth clamped against the lingering memory of being so close to his prey and his body's intense reaction to her, Doran hastened outside. If he reacted like an oversexed teenager, tomorrow, Quinn would be right and he'd end up dead.

Chapter 2

Kelsey opened her eyes as the first rays of the coming day caressed her lashes. She rolled onto her back, looked up at ceiling's plaster swirls, then recalled the vow she'd made herself, so she sat up, grabbed the phone and dialed the weather line. "Possible pop-up storms this afternoon with highs in the 90's," said the recording.

She laid the receiver on her nightstand. "There! Let's see you get past the busy tone." Kelsey hummed a little victory song as she hopped out of bed.

Every morning since he had come out of his coma, Ramsey had phoned before breakfast and started her day out with a dose of gloom. As she showered and dressed, minute-by-minute forecasts whispered from the receiver. For the first time since the accident, she applied eye shadow without fighting tears as he relived watching the life ebb from Abby and Jen.

She'd loved them, too. Had he ever considered her loss?

Her morning cup of herbal tea tasted exceptionally fine. The sky looked particularly blue. Kelsey hummed as she watered the potted ferns on her front porch, then she settled into her car and fastened her seatbelt. As she backed out of the driveway her cell phone rang. "Good morning," she sang.

"There's something wrong with your land line," Ramsey said. Kelsey pinched the bridge of her nose to forestall the sudden headache. "I called in a service report for you." Ramsey's bellyaching tone made Kelsey want to roll down the window and throw her phone into the surrounding woods. Instead, she made a sound of solace.

"I wanted to make the world better for Jenny." Kelsey silently mouthed the words along with him. Did he realize that he said exactly the same thing every morning? She arrived at the busy intersection at the end of her road, stopped and glared at the heavy flow of traffic.

The election signs clustered around the stop sign caught her attention. Marvin Frederickson's sign had been placed directly underneath the stop sign. She grinned at the unconscious message. Maybe other drivers would catch the unintentional, but picture perfect meaning, too. Then, she noticed that Ramsey's MacLennan for Senate sign tilted like Pisa's tower and black tire marks marred the blue and white lettering. She shivered at how accurately its subliminal message mirrored Ramsey's situation.

"He sabotaged my car," Ramsey whined, "but I'll never be able to prove it." Was he right, or had he simply talked himself into believing it after so may repetitions? While she sympathized with his loss, every day, as she listened to his litany of misery, her compassion weakened. "You have no idea what it's like to hand upside-down from your safety harness and watch-"

"You act like you're the only one who ever loved Abby and Jenny," she snapped.

"-your child go white as she bleeds to death," he continued without missing a beat. "I've never felt so helpless." Kelsey's mouth flattened. Before she did something she might regret, she placed the phone on the passenger seat. "Abby tried to reach her, but-" Kelsey turned on the radio. "-she was too weak. You don't know what it's like to watch the people you love die."

Kelsey grabbed the stadium blanket from the back seat. Before she could talk herself out of it, she buried the cell phone under the thick blue and black plaid, held her breath and listened. On her radio, the Temptations were crooning an old song about imagination. Traffic was rumbling. A distant bird was singing. With a sigh of relief, Kelsey stretched the tension out of her neck, leaned back in the seat and closed her eyes against the sight of morning traffic flowing bumper to bumper past her road and let the music transport her to a realm of relaxation.

ooo

Doran's fingers drummed against his Suburban's leather clad steering wheel as he watched rush hour traffic speeding through the morning haze past the verge where he waited, engine idling, for his quarry.

He glanced at the clock on the dashboard. Kelsey was four minutes behind her normal routine. He plucked the transceiver out of his shirt pocket, and pressed the on button, but then he paused. If he called Quinn once more, he'd either look like a green recruit or the infatuated fool Quinn had jokingly accused him of being. He preferred thinking of himself as paranoid rather than infatuated. Obsessions made a person blind to danger; suspicion kept the senses sharp. He gritted his teeth against the suspicion that Quinn knew which head he was really thinking with. Doran clicked his phone off and slipped it back into his pocket, where it settled against his pounding heart.

Doran took a deep, calming breath, popped a couple Tums and leaned back against the cool leather seats, grateful that the vehicle's air conditioner filtered out the humidity along with the stench of exhaust coupled with the scent of cedar; typical aromas of a September morning in the Piedmont. After his late-night encounter with Lancaster, he didn't need any reminders of how awful the blend of sweet and sour could be. But he sure as hell was looking forward to his next look at MacLennan. Once Wes's plan got off the ground, they would get the evidence they needed to convict the entire lot of them.

"Dev, Trent – we're on our way." Over the radio, Quinn sounded like the confident man he had been before the bullet confined him to a life on wheels.

Finally! Doran touched the radio's send button, through the black silk of his pocket. For an uneasy moment, he wondered when he'd lost Marnie's photo. "Any reason for the delay?" Thankfully, his tone only conveyed casual curiosity.

"Normal routine, just behind schedule," Quinn said.

"Let's get this show on the road," Trent said. The receiver magnified the sounds of an engine being gunned and underscored Trent's impatience.

Now that the time had come, Doran wanted to get past this necessary step. Doran adjusted his headset as he looked in the Suburban's rearview mirror. About a half mile behind his Suburban, Trent's battered blue pickup bulled its way onto the highway. Horns blared and brakes squealed. Doran winced and lowered the volume. A yellow corvette swerved around Trent's old Ford and nearly had a head on with a white utility van. Trent's pickup fishtailed, then stalled, blocking all oncoming traffic. Tires screeched, but sounds of tortured metal didn't come. Instead, a discordant shriek of horns rose from the obstructed traffic.

"Good job," Doran said. "You'll get a bonus."

"Thanks, boss!" Trent said.

A breath later, the corvette rocketed past the Suburban.

Doran accelerated onto the road, then floored it to catch up with the Corvette. Over the headset, a faint voice shouted, "Git your damned rust bucket off'n the damned road. Git!" Trent, who enjoyed being the center of attention, even if it meant being the cause of hostility, started whistling a joyful tune.

Doran closed the gap between his Suburban and the yellow corvette. After he passed the intersection where Kelsey's mustang waited in front of Quinn's handicapped van, he slowed to fifteen below the speed limit and watched her mustang in his rearview mirror. Despite having an opening in traffic big enough for a convoy, the mustang stayed at the stop sign. What the hell? Dora took his foot off the accelerator and coasted, his attention on the motionless image in his rearview mirror.

Quinn's handicapped van crept forward. The mustang didn't move. "What's gives?" Doran demanded. "Is she turning left or something?"

"Blinker says we're going right," Quinn said.

The suburban slowed to a crawl. "Trent, hold the traffic."

"Roger that." His whistling became even jauntier.

If this doesn't work, I'll nudge her," Quinn said. The van's horn wailed long and loud. Doran winced and held the phone at arm's length. "That got her."

"Bummer, this was just starting to get fun," Trent said. The sound of an engine revving accompanied his remark.

"Trent, count to ten, before you let the traffic go," Doran said, "then keep it slow, like you're still having engine problems."

"Roger that." The background honking ceased. "My motto for today is: to be a leader with a large following, go five under the speed limit on a winding, two-lane road." Trent's cheerful whistling resumed.

Doran chuckled. "You're a regular contemporary Confucius." He glanced in his rearview mirror. The reflection showed Kelsey's mustang closing fast with Quinn's van far enough back to stay out of the coming crash. He tightened his seatbelt.

"Dev," Quinn said, "she left a big pool of brake

fluid back at the stop sign."

"Excellent." His tone conveyed confidence, but as he calculated the mustang's speed, his heart thudded against his ribs and he held the steering wheel in a crushing grip as she raced toward him.

ooo

Behind her, a horn blared. Kelsey opened her eyes and saw an opening in traffic. She floored the accelerator. One of her tires squealed as she surged onto Dunkirk. The mustang made a slight fishtail, but she corrected it. Gotta check the tire pressure.

"I just can't deal with this race without them," Ramsey whined. Kelsey glanced to her right. The phone had slid out from under the blanket. "I quit."

She snatched the phone as she floored the mustang to catch up with the big black vehicle in front of her. "I miss them, too," she screamed. "Stop acting like you were the only one who loved them." Ramsey audibly gasped. Her fingers clenched as she fought the urge to crush the phone. Sam Cook sang his version of what it took to make a wonderful world. Kelsey wished life were as simple as the oldies made it sound. "How come you were only willing to make the world better for Jenny?" The unexpected question thrown into the middle of Ramsey's rant extended his silence. "What about all the other kids in our district?" She used a kinder tone as she pressed her point.

"It isn't like that." Ramsey's contrite tone made her wince.

"Isn't it?" Kelsey forced herself to use a clam pitch. "Rams, think about that crash. You say you have proof that someone tampered with your car, but you're the only one saying it."

"That doesn't mean it's not true."

"I know that. I also know that Marvin had a lot to gain without you in the race, but surely he isn't the only one with a grudge against you."

"You think everyone hates me?"

"Everyone? No, but you're a district attorney. You put people away for years, if you win your cases and you don't exactly win friends even when you lose, because that means someone feels like you didn't get them the justice they wanted. Face it, there are a lot of people who might want you dead."

"I may not have the evidence, but I know who killed Abby and Jen. And without them, I quit."

She lowered her tone, "If you're right and you quit, you'd be rewarding Marvin for killing them. Do you want to give him the senate seat?"

Ramsey exhaled noisily. "It doesn't matter any more. I'm quitting."

"You're ahead in the polls."

"I don't give a damn about that," he snapped. Then Ramsey's tone turned petulant. "You're proud of the stats because you're the one who's been making the speeches."

"On your behalf." The black Suburban in front of her moved down the hill at a snail's pace. Must be a granny behind the wheel. "Go," Kelsey encouraged the driver. "Can't you see it's green?" The light turned yellow light and the black vehicle braked. "Floor it, then we can both get through."

"What are you talking about?"

"There's either an old granny in front of me or the driver is scared of the Dunkirk-Monroe intersection."

"It's one of the busiest in the state," Ramsey reminded her. "No shame in being cautious."

"The driver started braking on green, if you can believe that."

"Nothing wrong with driving safely." The light turned red and the disgustingly cautious driver slammed on the brakes. The tires left a trail of black and stopped several car lengths behind the white line. "Oh for crying out loud. Kelsey braked hard to avoid rear-ending the timid driver. Her foot slammed to the floor.

"Maybe I should have hired a grandma as my chauffeur, then maybe Abby and Jen would still be alive. Or at least I wouldn't spend every waking moment reliving how I was the one driving and how my actions killed them. I can't go on without them," Ramsey whined.

Kelsey pumped the mustang's brake pedal. Nothing happened. If she didn't get around the Suburban, she'd hit it. To her left, was a solid line of oncoming traffic, to her right, a curb, a metal guardrail, then a twenty-foot-drop into Dead Man's Gulch.

Kelsey looked for an opening in traffic.

There was none.

Had the black tire mark over Ramsey's campaign sign been an omen for her?

Kelsey dropped the phone, grasped the steering wheel in both hands, braced herself and stood on the brake with both feet. The pedal flopped lifelessly to the floor, while the car surged down the hill like a run away racer. The phone slid off the seat and Ramsey's complaining became distant.

The hair on the back of Kelsey's neck stood on end. She laid on her horn and glared at the black Suburban. "Move. You have to move." Even as she screamed at the driver, heavy east – west traffic starting across the intersection made that option impossible.

The idea of rear-ending a Chevy Suburban with a convertible seemed risky, possibly even deadly. "Stop, dammit," she shrieked at her mustang. Kelsey yanked on the emergency brake. With a screech, the steering wheel jerked toward the gully. "Augh!" She fought to keep her car out of the deep, rocky ravine, which had claimed Abby and Jenny's lives.

The mustang continued too fast toward the black Suburban.

"Kelsey, what is it? What's wrong?" Ramsey's panicked screams spewed faintly from the phone. With a terrible pop, her car shuddered as if it had broken free of its fetters. "Oh, God, it's your car! That's how mine sounded! Oh, no! Oh, God! Get off that road! No, don't! If you do, you'll end up in the gulch. Oh, God, I can't bear this. Oh, God, oh, God, it's the nightmare all over, again."

Desperately hoping that friction would reduce her momentum, Kelsey wrenched the wheel to the right; her front tire scraped against the curb. Ripping metal sounded like banshee screams. Kelsey screamed with it, as she hung onto the steer wheel and held the position.

A bang vibrated through the car and the front right corner dropped several inches and the speed slowed a bit. The steering wheel whipped out of her hands. Oh, no, she was heading toward the gully.

Sparks flew from the right front quadrant and sailed over the roof. Kelsey ducked, as if the embers could seer through the windscreen and threw every ounce of her strength into keeping the car next to the grinding curb without leaping into the fatal chasm.

Perspiration bathed her body and a red curl stuck to her forehead. "Please, please, please stop!"

Horrible thuds hammered the mustang's underside. Her feet bounced on the floorboards and her teeth collided so hard that it sounded like a pile driver was working overtime in her mouth.

An eighteen-wheeler loaded with newly sawn wood lumbered across the intersection. When she hit the Suburban, she'd knock it beneath the semi's wheels and kill the little old driver. No, she couldn't do that. She wrenched the steering wheel toward the gully and certain death. "Please God, let me be the only one hurt." One tire jumped the curb. Then the front fender bounced off the metal guardrail and the wheel jerked from her hands.

Kelsey grabbed for the wheel while she yanked the shifter into park. Amid howling gears, the Mustang's rear whipped back to the right. Her forehead hit the steering wheel. Half conscious, she hoped her prayers had been answered. A split second later, she hit the Suburban. Her head whipped forward. The airbag billowed in her face and a terrible stench burst over her.

Her spine hit the seat with an explosion of pain. Metal shrieked until her marrow reverberated.

Squealing brakes joined the profane chorus and howling made her ears cringe.

Darkness swirled around her.

Horns blended their indignant voices in a bedlam of sound. Children screamed in terror and agony. Kelsey's blood turned icy at the thought of hurting innocent children.

Over the clamor of doom, Whitney Houston started singing about how love would save the day. Kelsey's last thought before her world turned black was that love had never saved her days.

ooo

Doran slammed his suburban into park, and pulled on the emergency brake. Still, the momentum of her car pushed his heavier vehicle toward oncoming traffic. How fast had she been going? Horns blared. He gritted his teeth and prayed that he'd calculated the proper amount of space to stop both vehicles.

His tires screamed as the locked vehicles slid toward the thick white line.

Over it.

Toward the traffic.

The slide seemed to last a lifetime.

And then, mere inches from smashing into a heavy load of pine logs, he realized the movement had stopped.

Heart hammering, Doran slammed his suburban into park, vaulted out and sprinted back to her mustang. It's engine roared as if she still had her accelerator floored. No wonder it had taken father to stop than he had calculated. He yanked her door open, reached across the steering column and

42

turned off the ignition. "What the hell were you doing?" he shouted. "You sure as hell weren't driving." Then, he whipped out his knife and stabbed the airbag. "And are you insane to keep the damned car floored?" Kelsey lay collapsed against the tan leather seat, her left temple was covered with blood and her face looked impossibly pale. Dear God, was she dead?

He convulsed backward, as if she's slapped him back to reality. "Ohfuckme." Doran screamed out his fears for her safety and horror at how horribly wrong the plan had gone, without thinking about what he was saying. Then, her lashes fluttered to reveal a leaf-green flash of color and a tear trailed down her aristocratic cheek.

What had he done?

What had he said?

What would she remember?

"Hey, don't cry." Scalding tears poured down her cheeks. "Oh, hell." Doran wished he could yank out his tongue, but all he could do was try to perform damage control. "Ma'am, your car might catch fire." He made his voice as gentle as possible. "I need to get you away, from it. Do you hurt anywhere?"

"Ev-ery-whe-re."

Hands moving over her body, he searched for broken bones, but found none. He whipped off her safety harness, picked her up and sprinted around the back of her car, to place her on the pavement near the curb, then he raced back to her car and grabbed the navy and black buffalo print fleece blanket off the floorboard. "Talk to me," a voice bawled.

He jerked in surprise, then saw her cell phone lying on the car mat. He snatched it. "Hello?"

"Who the hell are you? Where's Kel?"

"Devlin Doran. The lady just rear ended me."

"Aaaaaaaaaaaaoh, God. She's dead. She wouldn't listen. First Abby and Jen, now Kel." The sounds of misery emanated from the phone. Doran held it away from his ear.

"She's not dead," Doran shouted. She couldn't die.

"If you're lying," the voice said, "I'll have your guts for garters."

"We're at the corner of Dunkirk and Monroe. Call an ambulance." Doran cut the connection and started to toss the phone back into the mustang, then realizing he'd be wasting a prime opportunity, he slipped it into his pant's pocket.

He wiped away the blood on her forehead with a corner of the blanket, then finished tucking it around her shivering form. The gash was still bleeding profusely, as head wounds generally did. It would need stitches, but her hair should hide the scar.

She should only have gotten scared, not hurt.

Sitting back on his heels, he studied the face he'd only seen in photos and watched on surveillance footage or from a distance, through binoculars and from under her vehicle. She looked more human. More vulnerable than she had looked the night before. More innocent. More tempting. He winced at that unwanted thought. Beauty and wholesome looks were a great camouflage for a felon and he couldn't afford to forget that fact.

He told himself that his only concern was what he'd feel for any other fellow human. But he didn't completely believe it and he knew he couldn't let that feeling grow. He gritted his teeth and counted to ten, then twenty.

Doran touched her wrist, trying to count the racing beats of her pulse, but his attention kept coming back to her blood-streaked face. She should have followed her normal morning pattern, been on time and putted along five miles below the speed limit, instead of playing Indy 500 and scaring the shit out of him.

Doran took a deep cleansing breath and began a calming routine that had helped him through far worse situations. As a bit of serenity trickled in, he pressed the skin at her temple into place and applied gentle pressure; the flow of blood slowed to a seep. Once the head wound stopped bleeding, her shivering intensified. He had to salvage this dismal beginning and recoup the situation. For the case and the lives of future victims; not because she looked appealing lying on the hard asphalt between the back bumper of her totaled mustang and the front bumper of Quinn's van. With his partner watching every move and listening to every word, Doran controlled his reactions as he sat on the ground with his back to the Quinn's van, picked Kelsey up and cradled her on his lap.

ooo

Kelsey didn't know how long she stayed in the peaceful midnight velvet place, but when she left its cozy cocoon, heat scorched her. With difficulty,

Kelsey opened her right eye. A gentle golden luminescence surrounded her.

I'm dead.

In the distance, a man's angry voice shouted, but it took too much effort to listen to him. Instead, Kelsey focused on the featureless haze enfolding her. She'd expected to end up in heaven, not this odd nowhere.

It was worth it, if no one else got hurt.

Air moved across her left shin. Strange. She'd never thought of the afterlife having wind. Abruptly there was a fetid whoosh and the airbag crumbled. Too startled and sore to do anything else, she stared through at the cracked windshield through her eyelashes. The guardrail for Dead Man's Gulch had broken free, curled up over her car and pierced the Mustang's hood. That sight could only mean one thing: she was alive.

It hurt to breathe.

Judging by the furious gray eyes glaring at her, survival might be temporary. The dark, angry man leaned into the car and stared at her. He had the hardest, angriest expression she'd ever seen. Had she hurt him? Anyone he loved? She tried to form the question, but he started talking. Her heart skipped a beat.

"I'm s-so s-s-sorry," Kelsey said. It hurt to look at him, especially since he was so furious.

"You should be."

"Th-the brakes failed."

Intense emotion snapped deep within his gaze. "I'll just bet they did."

The dark haired man leaned closer until his

broad shoulders blocked the door. He had a lethal looking switchblade in his hand and every rugged plane of his face seemed to be etched with fury. "The way you were speeding, you could have gotten us both killed."

Tears burned her eyes. Kelsey looked from the man's blazing gray eyes to the knife and couldn't hold back a sob.

He jerked back out of the car, as if he'd been slapped. "Ohfuckme." For the first time, the man sounded human. "Hey, don't cry." She couldn't help it. Scalding tears poured down her cheeks. "Oh, hell."

Kelsey felt for the steering wheel, then laid her aching forehead against it and sobbed.

"Ohfuckinghell, I'm screwed." She sensed frantic movement over her body, something that should have concerned her. But it didn't.

"I'm s-sorry," she whispered when the verbal barrage ended.

Dizziness overcame her and again, her world turned dark.

Kelsey didn't know how much later it was the next time she tried to open her eyes, but they felt glued shut. She smelled hot metal mixed with gas and blood. She tried to regain her grip on reality without throwing up, but she started shivering so hard that she thought her bones would rattle free from her skin. A warm spot grew across her back. She envisioned a bone protruding from her body and blood saturating her beige linen jacket.

"Lady, I'm sorry, too," a gentle baritone voice said. "You scared the shit out of me. I'm checking your back for injuries. Okay?" Soothing heat melted over her.

"How bad is it?"

"It doesn't seem like there is anything is broken." She could listen to this wonderful man's voice, forever.

"Smell blood."

"You hit your head. It'll need stitches, but the scar shouldn't show."

A lump of tears blocked her throat, but the sweet man didn't seem to mind. "Lungs burn."

"Probably from the air bag." He held her close. "What's your name?"

"Kelsey."

"Pretty name for a pretty lady." He cleared his throat. "Well, Kelsey, I don't feel anything fractured in the spinal area, but your left shoulder might be dislocated."

If it had been, he had a magic touch. In fact, everywhere he placed his hands tingled with health, vitality and something more, but his hands never stayed anywhere long enough for her to identify the elusive element.

"I'm checking your arms and legs." The lovely, intimate, comforting warmth migrated over Kelsey and settled around her like a soothing sensual haze. She moaned with pleasure. "Please don't cry." She couldn't focus on anything, except the man's tender touch and tone. Thank God that horrible angry man had left.

A distant wailing reached a crescendo. Kelsey burrowed deeper into the reassuring heat and prayed that the deep, protective drum, which resonated against her ear, would stay there forever.

The siren suddenly stopped. She breathed a sigh of relief and cuddled closer to the steady, enduring beat that seemed to enfold her in a tender embrace and shield her from the background pandemonium.

Running footfalls became louder. "What happened?" a woman's high-pitched voice asked.

"She lost control," the gentle voice crooned. "I think she's in shock."

"Lucky she didn't jump the guardrail and kill herself in Dead Man's Gulch," the woman said. "Last month, we lost three people there."

"I heard," the man said.

Ramsey, had crashed in The Gulch. As fear coiled tentacles around her, Kelsey began gasping for breath.

Something cold clamped over her face.

"Place her on the ground. Flat on her back," the woman ordered. The safe, secure bond melted away and hard roughness replaced soothing warmth. Kelsey moaned in protest. "Now, step aside and let me examine her." Kelsey had never heard anything as irritating as that high-pitched tone ordering her comfort away.

A cold, hard surface replaced the soothing warmth and something frigid was pressed over her heart. Again, Kelsey moaned in protest. But instead of receiving relief from the harsh treatment and the return of the wonderful warmth, her right arm was yanked sideways and pressure began increasing around it. Though she knew help had arrived, she missed the sweet man's warm, soothing support.

"Sir," a man with a rough voice said, "did you

witness the accident?"

"Yeah," the nice man said, "I felt it, too. She lost control about two-thirds of the way down the hill."

"Curt," the woman said, "keep everyone out of my way."

As if through a thick layer of water, Kelsey endured her body being pushed, prodded and pricked. Though it was uncomfortable, it became easier to breathe.

There was a soft click. "Laceration near the hairline." Even when the woman murmured, her tone was harsh as splintered glass. "No major loss of blood, possible concussion, low blood pressure, clammy skin, rapid heartbeat, shallow breathing, and dilated pupils. Definite shock." Another click then the woman said, "Ma'am, I'm going to elevate your feet. Tell me if this hurts."

"Mmmmm," Kelsey agreed.

"Steady, now. Try not to move."

The hard pavement stank of tar. Kelsey fought nausea.

"No apparent broken bones," the woman said.

The sunlight burned hot against her face and she saw red blobs of movement through her closed lids. When she ran the tip of her tongue over her lips, she tasted blood. "Am I going to die?" she whispered.

"No." The conviction in the woman's voice helped Kelsey regain a measure of control.

"Why did my brakes fail?"

"I don't know."

"Do you think he tried to kill me?"

"Who?"

"I saw tire tracks on the sign."

"This may sting." Kelsey felt another prick. A moment later, she returned to the impersonal darkness.

ooo

The Mecklenburg County Officer motioned for traffic to continue moving, but people seemed more interested in rubbernecking than in getting to their destinations. Finally, backup arrived. Relieved of traffic control, the cop stalked toward Doran and flipped his notepad open. "Okay, you ready to start?" Doran nodded. The cop scowled at his pad. "Name?"

"Doran. Devlin Doran." He handed over his driver's license to the officer. "I need to make a phone call."

"This will only take a minute." The officer began scrawling down information.

"I have a mobile in my car." He gestured to the Suburban.

"Make it fast." The tip of policeman's tongue protruded between his teeth, while he concentrated on writing Doran's height of 6' 2" in the correct slot.

Under weight, the officer wrote 180.

As Doran walked toward his Suburban, he assessed the damage. Long skid marks marred the asphalt where he'd braked for both vehicles. A slash of deep hunter green smeared his rear quarter panel, and the right side of his Suburban's rear bumper was bent down into a scowl. Underneath, the ragged corner, laid a red shard from his taillight.

In contrast, the Mustang looked like a trash compactor had mauled it and then the guardrail had tried to pummel it to death. Kelsey looked as bad as her car and grayer then the concrete curb. Worse, her blood saturated hair and the tiny lines of pain near the corners of her eyes and mouth made her appear close to death.

She shouldn't have gotten hurt. Wouldn't have, if she'd followed her normal, methodical pattern instead of acting so erratic. Perhaps she'd gotten a snoot full of her product. He shook his head in disgust, but wasn't certain if he was more dismayed by the suspicion that she was a user, or by his lack of anticipation of her unpredictable behavior. In truth, he was most appalled by the intense sensation of protectiveness he'd felt when she cuddled against him and the loss, when he'd been forced to lay her on the pavement.

He sighed. Thus far, nothing had gone as predicted. He'd certainly never expected to feel compassion and guilt for anyone who was part of Ling's cartel. Doran straightened his spine and turned away from her. "You might look angelic, but I know what you really are," he whispered. Infatuation, his mind supplied. A dealer, he corrected.

He turned his back to Quinn's van, pulled Kelsey's cell phone out of his pocket, and dialed. "What is it?" Quinn snapped.

"Well, good morning to you, too."

"She looks dead. You get ahead of yourself and kill her?"

"She has concussion, so they'll probably keep her

in the hospital for observation." He grimaced. "That'll put us behind schedule, but a couple days shouldn't matter. We can use the time." Quinn made an indecipherable noise. Doran pinched the bridge of his nose to forestall the threatening headache. "I'm speaking to you on her mobile phone. Think you can bug it before I give it back?"

Quinn snorted. "You called me to ask such a dumb question?"

"No." Doran casually glanced back at his partner and gave him a subtle smile. "I called to remind you that you agreed to cover my meeting with Frederickson."

Quinn growled something that sounded suspiciously like bigoted jackass.

"Look," Doran said, "I know you don't like our esteemed senator, but he pays on time and he's on the committee that keeps Wes funded." An uncomfortable coincidence, which he'd never fully accepted. But one that made him suspicious enough to try to keep the senator's trust. At very least, if he was a happy client, he'd help give validity to their cover op.

"I did say I'd do it," Quinn grumbled.

Doran made a sound of sympathy. "Break the contract, if he bothers you so much." Quinn snorted at the thought. "Or we could send Trent."

"The prissy turd would love Trent's redneck Confucius routine," he said sarcastically.

"Particularly if he introduced himself like he did to our Vegas connection." Doran cleared his throat and mimicked Trent's 'aw-shucks' accent, "Have you ever noticed that the severity of an itch is inversely proportional to your ability to reach it?"

Quinn laughed out loud. "You're bad."

"Of course, you'll have plenty of time to scratch any little thing you want before you take my appointment," Doran promised. After a few more comments, he turned off the phone and slipped it back into his pocket, then adopting a concerned expression, he went to give his version of the accident to the trooper.

Chapter 3

The Mac-truck of a nurse pushed Ramsey aside and thrust a thermometer in her mouth. Her brother's lips flattened with anger at the disrespect, but instead of protesting, he hobbled around the bed and sat on the mustard colored vinyl seat of the visitor's chair. Hoping her brother would forget the point he'd been harping on, Kelsey smiled at the woman.

The nurse slapped a blood pressure cuff around her arm and pumped it up. Then, she wrote numbers on the chart and without so much as uttering a word, the door swooshed shut behind her. "Obviously a descendent of Attila the Hun," Ramsey said.

Kelsey adjusted her uncomfortable I.V. then smoothed her faded yellow hospital gown before she turned to Ramsey. "Just because she keeps her stethoscope frozen doesn't make her Asian." Whispering made her head throb.

He snorted. "You know what I meant." Vinyl squawked as Ramsey rose from the chair. His shoulder brushed against the vertical blinds, thrusting the ivory vinyl ribbons against the glass shrouded night scene. Their sound mimicked the tapping of his cane. "Sure is different when you're the one in the bed, isn't it?"

She inclined her head.

He squared his shoulders, staring at her over the footboard. Ramsey preferred a position of power while delivering blistering lectures and undoubtedly, the foot of the bed was one. He straightened the knot of his maroon tie. This wouldn't be good. After the horrible gray-eyed man, she didn't think she could survive another angry verbal assault. Kelsey held up her hand. "Before you start, let me point out that I didn't realize how unpleasant some nurses were. Sorry for anything unsympathetic I said, while you were in this position."

He glared at her. The uncompromising set of his jaw confirmed that a belated apology wouldn't be enough. "We're both lucky to be alive." Ramsey used the conciliatory tone he favored when delivering closing arguments to juries. Whatever her brother was about to pontificate on would probably be self-serving. Kelsey stifled a groan by clamping her teeth together. A jolt of blinding pain swelled inside her skull, so she quickly relaxed her jaw.

"Now that you know how it feels to be the injured one," he gave her a penetrating look, "you'll have a lot of time to lie there and think. At least you don't have to bear the guilt of injuring anyone." Trust Rams to bellow so loud that thought became impossible. 'Or killing your loved ones' hung unsaid in the antiseptic air.

Kelsey exhaled a breath of relief when he did not continue the expected tirade. "I'm thankful for that."

"Now that you are the one in their sights," he tapped the metal top of his cane against the hospital bed for emphasis, "do you still think I should continue to run for office?"

She blinked in disbelief. "Why do you really believe my accident has anything to do with your election campaign?"

He stared at her as if she had become impossibly stupid. Kelsey plucked at the thin blanket, which would not protect her aching head from the rant she saw in his eyes.

"I'd have thought a murder attempt would have knocked some sense into you and made you realize why I quit." The brass ball on top of Ramsey's cane hit the bed's footboard harder with each new word. The sharp sounds sent jabs of pain between her eyes and the room seemed to shrink.

"Stop that!" Her shriek throbbed in her temples worse than his bellow. Kelsey placed her fingers against her aching scalp. She hadn't shouted in years, obviously the accident had scared her more than she'd acknowledged. She swallowed. "Loud noises hurt worse than these stitches." She fingered her temple.

"Apologies." He actually looked appropriately contrite.

"Only cowards quit." She didn't realize she'd said it aloud, until he blanched. "Rams, I'm sorry. I didn't mean that."

He looked at his feet for several heartbeats, then raised his head. His hazel eyes shimmered with tears. "Don't apologize. It's true." He sadness etched his face and beneath the shimmering pools, his eyes looked like bottomless tombs. "I don't have the energy for politics. Not any more. Not without Abby. My love. My life." He heaved a miserable sigh. "And Jenny, my wonderful, beautiful baby girl." He leaned heavily on his cane.

"Abby is half the reason why you must run. Jen is the other half."

"I. Do. Not. Want. To. Run." His cane-top hit the frame so hard the brass bent and thunderbolts of pain split her head. "How can you even suggest that I continue with this damned election, now that you've had a brush with death?" He stared at her. She tried to glare back, but suspected her bandages merely made her look disgruntled. "Is it worth your life to pursue this campaign?"

She inclined her head. "But I still don't believe either of our accidents was about your election."

He looked ready to explode into a rage. "Well they were, and I quit." She shook her head. Ramsey wiped his eyes on the sleeve of his tweed sport coat. "I can't bear for anyone else to be hurt because of me."

"My accident was not about you or politics, it was caused by bad brakes."

"If you're so determined to act naïve, then you run for the damned senate."

"Maybe I will," she said. He scoffed.

Voters in their part of the South rarely elected women. Worse, every male MacLennan would disown her if she invaded their arena and the females in her family would never be able to show their support. Rams was as bigoted as the rest, too. She'd already been unbelievably brazen when she tried to hold the campaign together for him. The fact that she had and he'd continued to rise in the polls probably was one reason why he seemed so furious. God forbid that any male MacLennan owe an election victory to a woman.

Tears blurring her eyes, Kelsey looked down at the shapeless yellow gown, which hid bruises and any hint that she was female. Temptation to take him up on his challenge coiled within her. It'd be worth it, just to show him that a woman could differentiate between poor vehicular maintenance and politics and then win the senate seat. Even if her car really had been sabotaged, it would be worth running for office. If she won, perhaps she could do something to dampen the horrible effects of NAFTA, which had shipped so many jobs overseas and made it more difficult to protect their country. It would be worth winning to change building codes, so buildings and the environment could co-exist in harmony. It would be worth winning just to prove she was not a coward.

Ramsey began drumming his cane on the foot rail. Her teeth clamped together so hard, she thought they'd shatter. If she hadn't been tethered to the I.V., Kelsey would have jumped out of bed and throttled him … at least she would have, if she could find the energy. "Noise hurts," she gasped.

He grasped the cane to his chest, as if he'd just realized he had it in his hand. For a long moment, he just stood there, then he looked her in the eye. "Chet looked over your car." Ramsey limped around to the side of her bed and gently grasped her hand. "There were holes in your brake lines. Not the rusted kind. They'd been drilled, just like mine were." He enunciated each soft word carefully. "You were supposed to die." He gave her a look that normally swayed juries about his confidence in the truth.

She had been immune to that look since grade school, but what really bothered her was the conviction that he was being honest and her brakes really had been tampered with. Kelsey tried to breath despite the lump blocking her throat. "So that's why you're so convinced someone tried to murder me," she whispered. Perhaps it was political, after all. But why? She held her breath as fear clutched her heart as a horrible sense of vulnerability grew.

"The sabotage won't come out in the police report, though." Ramsey looked very tired and old. "Botts will cover it up, just like he did in my accident report."

Why would Sheriff Botts do that? "What do you mean?" It was difficult to breath.

"Figure it out." Ramsey's expression twisted with disdain, but at least he didn't bang his cane against the bed to emphasize his statement. She put up her hands in a helpless gesture. "It's damned convenient to be a criminal when you're the sheriff," he said.

She wanted to protest the ludicrous idea, but Sheriff Botts always stood at Marvin Frederickson's side during political rallies. Could he be involved with Marvin's more nefarious business? Kelsey licked her lips. "If he has corrupted Botts, he can do just about anything he wants in this area."

Ramsey nodded. "Now you're starting to see the whole picture." He gestured to the hospital room. "Too bad you had to get hurt to figure it out."

Tears of frustration at such a hopeless situation burned her eyes. No wonder Ramsey was so determined to quit. If he was right, instead of just paranoid, anything else was suicidal. "Is Jake Botts really one of Frederickson's puppets?" Ramsey glared at her. "What if he was just getting back at you for insinuating that he's incompetent in that interview?" She referred to the article, which her brother had given the previous year. In it, he'd implied that he'd lost a murder case due to police incompetence.

"He is an inept cop." Ramsey's tone sent shivers of dread up and down her spine. "And I'd bet my trust fund that he's also one of Marv's most skilled lackeys. For a long time, I've noticed that he seems to work hard to ignore certain bits of evidence." A chill rippled over Kelsey. Her brother's expression turned grim and she suspected this might not simply be due to losing any court cases. "Jake mislabeled certain crucial pieces of evidence prior to that court case and he certainly tampered with details from my accident. Fact is, I can think of several situations, which seemed shady, but I could never figure out why."

"Why haven't you said or done something?"

"Who should I talk to - another reporter?" He scowled. "That comment was supposed to have been off the record."

"Obviously not her, but someone."

"What should I say?" He ran his hand through his curly auburn hair. "I don't have any evidence, just a gut feeling and lots of suspicions."

"For how long?" she asked.

"Since Sam Reynolds suicide." Kelsey blinked, as she tried to recall why that name sounded familiar. "He was Marv's tax accountant a few years ago," Ramsey added. She nodded, finally able to place the name with a person. Her brother gave her a sober look. "I saw Sam at the country club a few weeks before his death and he mentioned that he'd given Marv three months notice to find new representation." Ramsey wet his lips. "Accountants don't dump their high-prestige clients without a good reason and the best one I can think of is that they don't want to become an accomplice to something illegal."

"Perhaps you're right, but maybe he was just depressed. After all, he did commit suicide."

A tiny muscle jumped in his temple. "Did he? Should someone who falls through a window and cuts their jugular vein in the process be labeled suicide? ... No one every found the glass shard that supposedly cut him... I could buy accidental death, but... Would you label it suicide?"

She stared at him, as he willed her to respond, then she remembered to shake her head. If her brother's information was correct, Mr. Reynold's death didn't sound like suicide, but it didn't necessarily mean Marvin had murdered him, either. And with Frederickson in D.C. so much, it could have been as simple as Mr. Reynolds disliking the geographical problems associated with working for someone so far away. Or disliking the man and his 'for me' politics, as much as she did. Just because Ramsey knew of one person who might have wanted him dead, that did not mean there were not others. Others who could have had the opportunity to kill him, if he had been killed...

"Having Botts as a partner would be perfect," Ramsey ranted on, "particularly when you're trying to kill off the competition and establish a billion dollar empire for illicit activities."

"You think he was the one who-" Ramsey nodded. She gulped down a gasp.

"Botts tells his deputies what to write, then files their reports." His expression hardened. "Want to bet that the report about your accident states that you were at fault?"

"But I was," she said.

"Jake will probably tell reporters that you were either high or drunk." Again, the tic, next to Ramsey's eye, jumped.

"Sit down. Relax." If he didn't, he could have a stroke.

He ignored her. "It'll be in confidence, of course and he'll only be listed as 'a reliable source'." Ramsey's mouth flattened. "Botts started the rumors that I was drunk and that I had an extensive criminal history as a juvenile."

"Prom night?" She frowned. The railroad track of stitches across her scalp pulled, making it feel like she was being scalped. "If he's making a mountain out of that mail box, that's all the more reason for you to run for Senate."

"I've already told the Party that I quit for health

reasons."

"Rams, you have to take it back." He shook his head. Kelsey stared at him. "You'd let someone get away with murdering the two people you loved most?"

"He's already has gotten away with it." Ramsey swallowed then continued, "But what's important now is protecting you. If you hadn't started doing the speeches for me, you wouldn't be in that bed."

He couldn't know that. At least not for certain. "I want justice," Kelsey said. "Now. This year. Not at some unspecified point in the future when divine intervention finally miraculously delivers it." He shook his head. Unbelievable. "How can you wait and hope that maybe some day, some year things will come out right if you aren't willing to fight for fairness, now?"

Tears glittered in his eyes. "I laid in a bed just like this for two weeks." His cane pinged against the foot rail; he snatched it back. "I didn't know if I'd ever walk again, but I knew I'd never see Abby and Jenny again. Ever. Every morning, when I wake, I still wish I'd died." The knuckles holding his cane whitened. "If I'd had the chance to kill Marvin when I first found out that Abby and Jenny were dead, I would have strangled him." Sobs wracked him.

"But not now," she whispered. He shook his head. Kelsey heaved a tired sigh. "Fine, we'll do it your way." She swallowed. "I'll run."

The door to the room banged open. Ramsey whirled around, tripped on his cane and stumbled backward against the bed.

Zoë Lancaster burst into the room. "You can't run," Zoë exclaimed. Kelsey glared at her. How typical of their illegitimate half sister to eavesdrop, then burst in, as if she had a right to be part of a discussion, which didn't concern her.

Her brother wiped his eyes on his sleeve. "She's right," Ramsey said. For the first time in their lives, her brother and illegitimate sister were allies.

"Someone has to try to beat him," Kelsey said.

"Not you," Ramsey said.

"You said-" Kelsey began.

"It was sarcasm."

Zoë grabbed Kelsey's hand. She winced as the I.V. jabbed deeper into her flesh. "Marv is your uncle, don't-"

"Step uncle," she corrected through gritted teeth. With her free hand, Kelsey grabbed Zoë's garishly bejeweled fingers and tried to loosen her grip before she screamed with pain from the pressure on the I.V.

"-do this." Zoë's chest heaved, emphasizing the too-tight sequin-covered maroon shirt covering her huge silicon breasts. Ramsey looked at the ceiling. "You're tearing up our family."

"Running is ridiculous," Ramsey said.

"You're hurting my hand," Kelsey gasped. When Zoë ignored her, Kelsey pinched Zoë's finger. She jerked back, in surprise. Finally free, Kelsey heaved a sigh of relief.

"Mother knows Marvin for the dishonest crook he has always been," Ramsey told Zoë. "Furthermore, the only family the accident tore apart was mine. And I'd bet my last dollar that dear

Uncle Marvin arranged it."

Zoë leaned toward Ramsey, virtually thrusting her artificially enhanced bosom in his face. "You are wrong. Your decision to run hurt everyone." Her skin-tight V-neck dark red shirt's sequins flashed pulsated with each breath.

Ramsey's Adam's apple bobbed as he stared at the phony cleavage.

"Why did Winston and Jacqueline leave town?" Zoë glared at Ramsey as if he should know why his father and stepmother did anything. "Why aren't they coming back until after the election?" With every syllable, her ludicrous chest inched toward Ramsey.

Kelsey stared, fascinated to watch Zoë use her artificial attributes to quell her brother. She glanced down at her own modest bosom and wondered if Zoë understood how effective her ridiculous melon-sized breasts were against males. Of course she did, just like she knew certain men would do anything for phony blonds, which was why she bleached her hair to near white. Manipulative as she was, it was probably why she spent so much money to look fake.

Ramsey shuffled back to the visitor's chair. He sat down heavily on the mustard colored vinyl, then turned his head and stared through a crack in the vinyl blinds.

Without anyone to argue with or a male to enthrall with her phony breasts, Zoë sat on the bed, next to her and leaned close. The heavy scent of her sickeningly sweet perfume made the air seem suffocating. "You can't do this." From years of experience, Zoë obviously knew her artificial enhancements wouldn't distract her half sister, so she used a soft, compelling tone. "Marv has to win."

Kelsey stared at Zoë, amazed that she'd take the jerk's side. "I'm sure Marvin has to win to save his hide. However, voters need him out of office so-"

"Quit saying that," Zoë interrupted.

Kelsey closed her eyes. When she reopened them, she noticed the clock on her nightstand. "I have to give a speech at the Masons in an hour."

"It's been canceled," Ramsey said tiredly from the chair. "Just like the entire campaign." He rose, shuffled to the end of the bed, then gave her a commanding look. "Stay in that bed until the doctor says you're well enough to go home. And pray that you're here long enough for Frederickson and his cronies to get the message that I quit and that he has won by default."

Kelsey glared at him. "I will run and you can not stop me."

"You can't," Zoë shrieked.

Ramsey looked at Zoë, his expression speculative, as if trying to understand how he and his illegitimate half sister could possibly be on the same side of any issue.

Too bad they couldn't have agreed on something that favored revenge for Abby and Jen's deaths or team up on some other useful issue, instead of fight her when she was bedridden. Kelsey shoved the self-pitying thought aside. "I am exhausted." Kelsey enunciated each syllable clearly, then gave them an innocent smile. "Maybe if you two quit arguing with me and let me get some sleep, I'll change my mind."

Ramsey nodded and walked toward the door, his pace hurried, but Zoë studied her as if looking for deception. Her eyes narrowed. "I guess you really don't look so good. No wonder you're saying such stupid stuff."

Kelsey allowed her eyelids to flutter, as if she was completely exhausted. "I need rest."

"Fine, I'll be back tomorrow."

"That won't be necessary, I'll get out and be home."

"Then, I'll drive you." Zoë looked pleased with that thought. "Until then."

After the door whispered shut behind her, Kelsey listened to the departing tap of her stiletto heels. Then, she sat up in bed, grabbed the phone and dialed campaign headquarters.

Chapter 4

Mandy popped into the hospital room, baby Merry secure on her hip. Her three boys trooped silently behind her.

"It's great to see you, but I'll be home later, today," Kelsey said.

"That's good to hear," Mandy said. Mark, Mattie and Mike nodded vigorously; even little Merry seemed to smile. "The boys were convinced you'd been abducted by aliens."

"They certainly have great imaginations."

"But we saw it," Mark, the eight-year-old, blurted out. Mandy shot him a 'look'. "I'm sorry, Ma, but we did." Mattie and Mike nodded vigorously.

Mandy sighed. "I warned them that kids weren't supposed to visit people in hospitals and that I'd have to sneak them in." She, again, gave them 'the look'.

"It's okay. If anyone asks, I'll introduce you as relatives." She smiled at the boys. They grinned back. "So, tell me about this alien."

"We was up in our tree house," Mike said. She loved to listen to them play in the old magnolia. Sometimes she wondered if she would ever have children and if she did, if she would be half as great a mom as Mandy.

When Merry got older, would the tree house turn into a fort, as Ramsey's secret hideout had, or would these three boys be accept a tiny girl and her playmates into their lair?

"Sleeping," Mattie added. Kelsey tore her thoughts from what might be to the present and tried to pay attention.

"We was wide awake," Mike corrected. "And then we saw that black thing sneaking from shadow to shadow."

"Yeah, sneaking," Mark said, "but it didn't move like Smigel or nothing; it was more like Princess Leia when she dressed up in that bounty hunter getup."

Kelsey blinked. Mandy grinned. "Star Wars."

"And Lord of the Rings." She should have caught on right away. The boys were mega-sci-fi fans.

"Yeah," Mike said. "It was bigger than a Princess and really good at hiding in shadows."

"It acted like is could see in the dark," Mattie added.

"And I thought you said that side door in your garage was busted," Mark said. Kelsey nodded. She hadn't been able to open it since a key had broken in the lock ages ago. "Well, it went in that door."

"Stayed until after Miss Zoë got home. She was in there with it for a while," Mattie said.

"We don't know that," Mark said. "We couldn't see if she stayed in the garage with it or not."

"Yeah, that is right," Mattie conceded. "Did ya

fight off that bounty hunter okay?" Mattie asked, his expression deadly serious.

"I've had so many," Kelsey said, playing along. "Which one are you referring to?"

"You know. The one we was just telling you about, the one dressed up like the Star War's bounty hunter with the mask-thingy on his face."

"Oh, that one." Kelsey nodded, as if she knew what the boy's over-active imagination had concocted. "I'm here, aren't I?"

"We sorta thought he was really after Miss Zoë," Mark said. "After all, he met her in the garage."

"Really?" Kelsey said. "Did they do anything interesting?" She knew she shouldn't have asked that question the moment it slipped out.

"Only if you call parking the car int'restin'," Mark shrugged. "He shore did scare us."

"I can imagine," Kelsey said.

"It went back the way it'd come, so I think its spaceship was in the forest across the road." Mark's eyes were round as marbles. "Ma won't let us go over there and look for it." He gave Mandy an excellent imitation of 'the look'.

"Well, that is truly interesting," Kelsey said. "Perhaps when I feel better, we can all go over there and look for evidence." The boys all nodded eagerly. Mandy grinned. "We could make a picnic of it."

"What if it's still there and dangerous?" Mattie asked. His brothers both shoved him. "Well?" the four-year-old huffed. "It could be."

"Miss Zoë is okay. I saw her this morning. If it didn't hurt her, I don't think it'd hurt us." Kelsey wondered if she, Ramsey and Zoë had ever been as imaginative as the adorable M & M kids.

ooo

The hot afternoon sun glared against the hood of Zoë's candy apple red Porsche and blazed through the windshield as Zoë parked next to the brick sidewalk, which led to Kelsey's front door. Ruby-red lips pressed into a flat line, Zoë glared straight ahead. "Sorry about letting you out here. I can't seem to find my garage door opener."

Her opener? More like the spare one, which she'd confiscated, after finding red paint a small dent marring her Mustang's dark green passenger door. "Mine is still in my car, but I'm not exactly sure where it is." Envisioning her last glimpses of her poor car, the banged door seemed insignificant, but that did not mean she was ready to discuss the remote she'd reclaimed. Let Zoë think she'd lost it. Though every muscle wailed in protest as she eased out of the low-slung passenger seat, she said, "This is fine."

The afternoon sun blinded her; she staggered, grabbing the Porsche's hot roof for support. A wave of nausea surged through her, she closed her eyes against the hot, punishing light. The metal's heat tingled all the way from her fingertips to the railroad track of stitches paralleling her hairline. "I will not faint," Kelsey whispered, "I will not faint, I will not faint." Though the mantra soothed her stomach and strengthened her resolve, her head still throbbed like the drum of doom.

Worse, she smelled death.

"I will not faint." Not now, not when there was

72

so much to do. Ramsey could feel sorry for himself and bleat about self-preservation, but someone had to save the constituents from their self-serving step-uncle. Now she had Party approval and freedom from the I.V. that had held her captive, all she needed to do was make it inside her home and close the door to get sanctuary from the sun and anyone who wanted to harass her. Kelsey promised herself that as soon as she was inside, she would lock the door, unplug the phone and reclaim control of her life. She could start making calls, scheduling speeches, and form a strategy to win the seat for herself. Once elected, she would start giving their constituents the kind of representation they deserved.

She took a deep breath, stood upright and let go of the hot metal. Her doctor had wanted her to stay in the hospital at least one more day for observation, but in her opinion, doctors were usually after more money for less work and lower premiums on their liability insurance. Kelsey snorted. "I hate being watched."

"Yeah, I know." Zoë slammed the driver's door. "Your goal is to be a first class wallflower."

Through the heat waves rising from the Porsche's crimson roof, Zoë appeared to waver. Kelsey tipped to her left and grabbed back onto the car. Perhaps she should have stayed in the hospital and let Attila the Nurse continue her sadistic games. Kelsey blinked. Zoë's face stabilized. "Not since I began campaigning for Rams."

Zoë sniffed. "Politics is for nerds."

"It's better than modeling underwear." Kelsey

forced the fingers of one hand to release the scorching metal. Zoë tossed her phony-looking bleach-blond mane. When she kept her balance, Kelsey cautiously leaned forward and tugged her briefcase from the backseat.

Ignoring the heat, Zoë draped herself across the hood in a provocative pose. "I love lingerie." She twisted into an even more lewd pose and simpered at Kelsey. "Don't you?"

Kelsey glanced at the street, grateful that the houses were far away. Hopefully, none of her neighbors could see Zoë's latest performance. She didn't have the energy to figure out what was actually bothering her childhood friend, so she turned her back on the car, squared her aching shoulders, and then limped toward the shady relief of her front porch. With ever step, her ankle protested and the rancid scent grew worse. "Maybe something crawled under the porch and died."

"Jeez, it does stink."

Kelsey climbed the front steps and hobble-marched into the porch's shade. Something dark and ominous seemed to be emerging from the door's pale blue surface, where the knocker should be. She stopped and squinted at the apparition.

Blood and words.

She gasped and dropped her briefcase.

Feathers.

Zoë bumped into her, knocking her toward the revolting carcass. Kelsey grabbed the siding next to the door, barely avoided falling into the oozing mess. Hundreds of flies rose in a buzzing cloud, but the fetid, decapitated chicken hanging upside down from her brass doorknocker didn't budge. Rivulets of blood oozed down the door's pale blue paint.

Kelsey's teeth clinched so hard her entire head throbbed.

Zoë shrieked and leaped backward, staggering on her four-inch heels. "Who did that to my door?"

"My door, not yours." A wave of nausea passed over Kelsey and her world started to spin. She stood very still and hung onto the wall until she could study the message.

Drop out or dye.

Hadn't Ramsey received a chicken advising something similar before one caused his accident? There were already too many parallels between their situations for Kelsey to believe that the chickens were a coincidence. The stitches across her forehead pulled. She quickly relaxed her brow and reminded herself not to frown. Her stomach knotted with the putrid proof that Marvin Frederickson must have heard about the switch and was either trying to frighten her out of running against him or kill her.

Sick as she felt, the fly buzzing around her head could finish her. A drop of perspiration rolled down her spine. Kelsey took a step backward and focused on the sloppy red threat.

Drop out or dye

"All that blood." Zoë's squawk conveyed horror mixed with melodrama. "They've ruined my beautiful door."

Her door, indeed. Blistering resentment surged through Kelsey. She relived coming home three weeks earlier and discovering that Zoë had taken the liberty of painting the elegantly understated hunter green surface that putrid shade of blue. She tilted her head and squinted. Now that she really looked at it, the dead bird looked almost as good as the sickly hue Zoë had chosen.

"It's not all blood," Kelsey muttered. "Mostly it's red paint."

"Blue doors are supposed to bring good luck," Zoë wailed.

"Maybe you should have painted your apartment door blue."

"Must you always bring up Bryan?"

"Oh? Did I mention him?" Zoë was fortunate Kelsey hadn't joined the rest of the family and ostracized her after the incident with Bryan. "You should never have done that without asking."

"You expected me to ask you if I could fuck your finance?"

"I wasn't talking about Bryan." Kelsey clenched her teeth against the torrent of anger and her nails dug into the cedar siding. "You were lucky I didn't paint you blue." Or better yet, harlot red.

Zoë looked away, as if embarrassed, then her attention centered on the door. "Are you going to drop out of the election, now?"

"Not for a chicken. Even if it's the third one."

"Third?" Zoë's voice hit high C. "You mean you've had others?"

"Ramsey had two." Zoë wailed. Kelsey put her palms over her ears until the nerve wracking sound ended. "The first was frozen solid and hurled through his kitchen window. Rams swears the second ran in front of his car and that's when he lost control."

Zoë started crying.

"I hate chickens," Kelsey growled. "I hate eating the darned things. I hate them on my door and I hate the ones who run for office and are so damned afraid of losing that they'd rather intimidate and kill their opponents then run a real race."

"Quit." The fake gems on Zoë's fingers flashed as her arms gesticulating wildly between the alternating shadows and streams of sunlight coming through the climbing roses, which shrouded the porch. "You need to quit."

"Not now. Not later. I'm in this to the end."

"Do you have a death wish or something?"

"No."

As Zoë stared at the carcass hanging on the brass doorknocker, a sheen of perspiration condensed on her upper lip. The droplets trembled as she inhaled through her mouth. "So whoever is trying to get you to quit only succeeded in convincing you to run harder."

Kelsey shrugged to dismiss the conversation. "Go find the garden hose."

Zoë's too high shoes wobbled dangerously as she dashed down the front steps.

Flies were swarming over her burgundy leather briefcase, so Kelsey moved it farther away from the mess then stagger-stepped to the railing. Head spinning, she grabbed a rounded white column and leaned her forehead against it for support. It took several restorative breaths of clean, rose scented air before she could cross the grass to the line of large magnolias, which defined the south border of her front yard. She pulled a fallen branch from the periwinkle, then resolutely returned to the porch. By the time she returned to the pulpy, reeking mess, she felt as if she'd run a hundred-mile-marathon.

Her first two attempts to dislodge the clenched talons from the twining metal vines of the brass knocker were futile. She paused for of moment until the dizziness passed. Gritting her teeth, she tried a third time.

"I found it," Zoë said. "But-" She held up a two-foot section of mangled hose, which had apparently been mowed.

"Great."

Kelsey closed one eye, lined up the stick with the doorknocker and jabbed for the third time. The carcass slithered down the desecrated door and landed in the rank puddle of drying blood and gore. Flies swarmed upward in a buzzing cloud.

Zoë took a deep breath, her complexion turned olive green, and then her eyes widened; she dropped the piece of hose, slapped her hand over her mouth, kicked off her heels, leaped down the steps and sprinted around the corner of the two story colonial house.

Oh, to have had a camcorder! "What's wrong, did you swallow a fly?" Kelsey called after her. There was no answer. Kelsey turned her attention back to her front door. Since she had lost the key to the garage's man-door years ago, this and the garage's car door were the only ways into the house. She looked beyond the porch, to Zoë's car. If Zoë hadn't slammed her car door into the mustang and left a six-inch scratch, she wouldn't have taken the spare remote away. And if someone hadn't sabotaged her car's brakes, she'd have her own remote.

Ifs had never gotten anyone anywhere. Kelsey eased the tension in her back, then fitted her key into the now accessible dead bolt. Bits of debris dropped onto the slate floor of her foyer as the door swung inward. "Darn," she muttered, "I was afraid that would happen." Kelsey slammed the door and stomped up the stairs to find her nastiest clothes.

Later, clad in a pair of tattered jeans and a faded moss colored T-shirt, which said 'Save the Rainforest', Kelsey downed two aspirins. Before she lost her resolve, she snatched a can of bug spray and a trash bag from under the kitchen sink. Outside, in the backyard, a secretive movement behind a butterfly bush caught her attention. Kelsey squared her aching shoulders, unlocked the kitchen's sliding door and stepped into the hot, humid air.

Could it be the person who'd left the mess? She gripped her bug spray tighter and headed toward the hidden watcher. Halfway there, she identified Zoë as the individual sitting on the ground and holding her stomach while she rocked back and forth. Should she comfort her unwanted guest or deal with the mess?

The longer the blood dried, the harder it would be to clean and any comfort she gave Zoë would only convince her to prolong her visit.

Kelsey limped back to the house, past the now open garage door. Back straight, she marched onto the porch and sprayed every fly in sight. While the flies dropped, she put on rubber gloves and bagged the reeking carcass, then started scrubbing the door. Finally, muscles protesting, she squatted down and began working on the floor. By the time most of the mess was cleaned, Zoë plunked a splattered quart size can among the dead flies on the porch floor. When she put an aluminum foil wrapped paintbrush on top of it, Kelsey glanced up at her deathly pale face. "You don't look so good."

Zoë shrugged, as if her looks didn't matter to her. "We might not have enough left over paint."

Darn, if she'd known there was more puke blue, she'd have taken the can to the dump or at least taken it to work and hidden it in one of her greenhouses.

Zoë stared at the door and shuddered, then abruptly pulled off her skimpy silk top to reveal a lacy black bra. "What are you doing?" Kelsey demanded.

"What's it look like I'm doing?" Zoë tossed her shirt over the railing and shimmied out of her tight skirt. "I'm getting ready to repaint my damned door."

"My house. My door," Kelsey snarled.

Zoë shrugged and jammed a screwdriver under the edge of the lid. An awful thought sent a chill through Kelsey. "Did you paint it dressed in your underwear before?"

"It saves my clothes." Zoë smiled at her.

The chill turned icy. Kelsey looked up and down her quiet street. She couldn't see her neighbors' residences to the North and East, because of the woods surrounding their houses, but their children usually played in a fort they'd built in her largest magnolia, so any number of kids could be gaping at the spectacle Zoë was making. She squinted at the tree, trying to see through its thick foliage, but all she could hear was a singsong countdown, which seemed to be coming from a different direction.

"The outfit is a Versace." Zoë waved her hand toward her discarded clothing. "With him dead, it's irreplaceable. This," Zoë snapped the elastic of her skimpy black thong, "is a Frederick's. It's expensive, too. Perhaps I should go down another layer." She started to pull down the thong.

"No!" Kelsey glanced toward the road, grateful for the lack of traffic. Knowing Zoë would do whatever she pleased, wherever she was at, Kelsey hoped the porch's deep shade would hide any exhibition Zoë made and she prayed no irate mothers would blame her for Zoë's immodesty.

Zoë laughed and plumbed her ridiculously enhances breasts so hard that they nearly leaped from the skimpy black lace. "You're redder than your hair. What's the matter? Still the virgin princess, afraid to enjoy life?"

Kelsey fingered her aching temple and wished she could scratch the cut above it. "I need to clean the foyer."

"You are! I don't believe it. You're still a fucking virgin." Zoë grabbed her arm. "Isn't it about time you grew up?"

Kelsey shook free and took a step backward. "Maybe being grown up means something different to me than seeing how many guys I can screw."

Zoë's expression hardened. "You should try it sometime." Zoë thrust out a hip in a disgustingly provocative pose. "Or are the rumors that you like pussy true? Is that why you hate it when I'm naked? Hmm? Afraid you'll blow your cool over me?"

"Hardly." Kelsey gestured toward the road. "Your mother said she'd drop by with my dry cleaning, this afternoon. With all the problems you two have, I don't think Martha needs to see you making a spectacle of yourself on my front porch."

Zoë arched backward. "I get paid big bucks for this."

"You aren't modeling now. Why don't you be quiet for a minute and listen." Zoë glared at her. She glared back. "If you listen, you'll hear kids playing hide and seek in the woods and others playing starship in the magnolia. Do you intend to give them a peep show?"

"I passed up a Caribbean shoot to be here for you, 'cause Ma said you were grieving over Jenny and Abby and you needed me." Kelsey rolled her eyes to heaven. To the best of her knowledge Zoë hadn't spoken a word to her mother in years. Seeing her doubt, Zoë seized her hand in a crushing grip. "Don't you dare try to suggest that I can't get work."

"My porch isn't a studio and I certainly hope there isn't a camera focused on you right now, because if there is, this will turn into some sort of crude smut for Marvin's mud slinging campaign." Zoë's eyes widened. Kelsey removed her hand. "Like I said, Martha is due soon." Kelsey looked

Zoë up and down. "Who are you trying to impress? Or are you after negative attention?"

"So … Ma is still doing your errands."

"She offered. Just like you volunteered to drive me home."

"Ma always makes time for you." Zoë had visibly snubbed Martha at the dual funeral.

"Yesterday, Martha dropped by the nursery to pick up some plants. Amber told her what happened." Kelsey looked Zoë in the eye. "She came by the hospital and asked if she could help." Kelsey paused, alarmed by Zoë's furious expression. "Look, if you insist on painting, at least wear some of my grunge clothes. Otherwise, forget it. I'll get someone to redo it later." And it will return to being a beautiful hunter green.

"I'd never fit into your clothes; you're too darned short and flat-chested." Zoë caressed her bulky breasts. Kelsey looked away, grateful that at least Zoë's back was toward the sound of children playing. A gust of hot air grazed her flushed face and shifted some of the flies. When the silence became painful, Zoë sniffed. "I'll paint the door, then I'll wash the floor and if I see someone coming, I'll hide. Okay?"

Kelsey nodded, amazed by the unprecedented meekness.

Zoë lightly touched her hand and gestured toward the annoying message with the brush. "Whoever wrote this is serious. Deadly serious." Zoë prodded the pool of dried paint with a red enameled fingernail. A welcome mat would cover the mess until she got more gray paint. "Do you think the same person who sabotaged your car did this?"

Kelsey inhaled sharply and instantly felt queasy. "Maybe I hit a rock and that broke my brake line."

"And I'm the Easter bunny." Zoë's mask of concern dropped and she made a lewd pose. "I'd make a better Playboy bunny, don't you think?"

"I wouldn't know." Kelsey took a step sideways. Zoë grabbed her upper arm.

"You'd better get serious and face facts," she hissed. "Marv wants to win that stupid senatorial race and he'll have his bootlickers make sure he gets what he wants. Right now, he sees you as an obstacle in his path and I don't think he'll hesitate to kill you. I don't think someone as coddled as you can possibly understand what he's capable of."

"Women don't belong in business or politics; they belong in the kitchen and bedroom." Kelsey mimicked Calhoun's senatorial tone and arrogant stance.

"Why are you quoting your grandfather?"

"Because I think he had someone leave me this warning to let me know how angry he is about me, a lowly female, entering politics." She raised her chin. "I'll show him."

Zoë's grip on her arm tightened until it crushed. Kelsey tried to pull free, but Zoë was stronger than she looked. "I don't want to go to your funeral and I don't think Calhoun did this. He's too sick."

"Of course he didn't do it himself. He can spell. He had someone do it."

Zoë closed her eyes and appeared to fight for control. Kelsey glared at her, then closed her own eyes and started to count to ten. When she got to eight, Zoë said, "More than half the guys I know would sell their own mothers to get what they want and Marv is one of them. Believe me, I know the type."

Kelsey blinked; confused by Zoë's continuing flip flop between the serious concern of a real friend and the flat out bullying of an obnoxious bimbo. No matter which one was the real Zoë Lancaster, it didn't say much for the people Zoë associated with. Kelsey frowned and wondered what it said about her.

Zoë's dark glare looked cold and lifeless. "Listen to me, I know what I'm talking about. I like men, and I don't just enjoy them, I watch them. Keep out of Marv's way or you'll end up as dead as that bird."

Kelsey jerked her arm free. "You know what this stupid threat tells me?"

"I bet it isn't something smart." Zoë's hands were shaking. For years, Zoë had only shown up when she needed a safe port during some real or imaginary crisis in her life, so Kelsey suspected the funerals were coincidental timing for whatever Zoë's primary motivation for coming actually was. Kelsey wondered how long a sister should force herself to tolerate the actions of an embarrassing sibling. Particularly, when the sibling was illegitimate and no one knew they were related or understood the bond, which had been forged when Martha had brought Zoë home from the hospital. At three, she had thought Martha had brought home the greatest doll in the world. In some ways, she still felt as if Zoë belonged to her. But they were no longer young; Zoë had changed from her best toy into a childhood playmate, then transformed into a self-centered pre-teen, who oozed rage and anger at everyone who cared about her. The grownup Zoë with her in-your-face sexuality, lack of moral values and filthy language was the worst personality change, yet. Kelsey shivered with the thought of how many more appalling makeovers could take place if Zoë lived to a ripe old age.

"Well?" Zoë snarled. "Spit it out. Tell me how this stupid threat backfired."

Kelsey massaged the back of her neck, wishing they could go back twenty years to a simpler, closer time. But time travel only existed in books. "Obviously, someone thinks I have a chance of winning this election."

Zoë blinked. "You just now figured that out? I could have told you that. Your fucking grandfather made the MacLennan name a household word in this state."

"Can you communicate without cussing?"

Ruby lips flattened and black eyes hardened. Even her long, bleached curls seemed to stiffen. Zoë made a palpitating motion with her hand over her heart causing the fake jewels in her rings flashed. She pouted. "Oh, dear." She fanned herself; a caricature of a Southern Belle about to faint. "I don't know what made me say that about such a sainted person as Calhoun."

"Cut it out. The sweet act doesn't become you." Kelsey took a deep breath then slowly exhaled. In a calmer tone, she added, "I'd like to think I could win this election on grounds other than my last name."

"Not a chance." Zoë peeled aluminum foil off the paintbrush, as if she was a vulture tearing flesh from road kill. "You should drop out now, before the piranhas eat you alive." She looked up and smirked. "Of course, if you're lucky, they'll settle for raping you."

"I'm thrilled you have so much faith in me." Kelsey closed her eyes and breathed in the mingled scents of Pine Sol, roses and Raid. "I forgot to thank you."

"For what?"

"Picking me up from the hospital." She gave her a gracious smile. "Thanks, Zoë."

Zoë appeared confused. "You're welcome." Obviously, she didn't remember Grandma Rose's cardinal rule about politeness. Zoë shoved newspaper under the door, then slapped blue over the D in Drop. "You should have phoned the sheriff." She continued painting. "This is criminal vandalism, you know."

Kelsey bit her lower lip until she felt confident that she could manage an equally calm tone. "I'd never call Jake Botts. I can't prove it, but I know he's one of Frederickson's lackeys." Kelsey gave an internal shudder at the thought of giving Frederickson or any of his carefully placed, corrupt pals, an opportunity to invade her home. "He'd probably imply that one of us hung the chicken up for a decoration." Zoë swiftly turned to stare at her, shock in her expression. Kelsey shrugged with a nonchalance she didn't feel. "Or worse, tomorrow's newspaper would have headlines screaming how I practice voodoo and killed chickens for my rituals."

"Voodoo? You?" Zoë snorted, as she turned back to the door and continued slopping paint over the offending message.

Kelsey pushed a wayward copper ringlet out of her eyes. When her fingertips grazed the stitches near her hairline, it felt like the top of her head had exploded. She took a deep breath then slowly exhaled. "Even if I wanted to report the crime to someone, it's too late. We've tampered with the evidence."

Zoë stopped daubing and stared at the door. Paint dripped down the brush handle and oozed onto her hand "Oh, shit. We did, didn't we?"

"Don't worry, it won't matter. The police are so incompetent that they couldn't solve a crime if they caught the felon red handed." Her lips quirked up, wondering if the perpetrator hands were red-smeared.

Paint trickled onto the heel of Zoë's hand, then fell and landed on her thigh. Zoë swirled it into an abstract pattern and gave Kelsey an odd smile. "Don't you think blue skin looks fantastic on me?"

"Oh for-" Kelsey bit her tongue and turned to leave.

Zoë snickered.

Kelsey abruptly realized the threat had given her an opportunity. She paused, then turned back. "In light of the threats, I think you need to find someplace else to live." She gave Zoë a pointed look. "At least until the election is over." And by that time, she sibling should have found someone else to freeload off of. Maybe she could even find a decent way to support herself.

"Are you kicking me out?"

"You'll be safer."

"You're serious." Zoë ran her perfectly manicured nails over her abdomen, leaving a trail of blue stripes. "You must realize whoever left that bird is serious. So, you should drop out. Instead, you tell me to leave?"

"Zoë, I'm going to stay in this race. But I don't want you to be in a position where you might get hurt because of my decision. You need to go. If things get uglier, at least I'll know you're safe." And embarrassing someone else, who is hopefully far, far away from me.

"As if you give a royal shit." Zoë jammed the brush into the paint can. "I came here to support you. I even went to the damned funeral. All you've done is ignore me." She looked angry enough to spit. "You're right. I should leave."

"It's for your own safety." Kelsey bit back adding, 'and next time you want to do something for me, ask if it's something I want. And don't stay for six weeks.' Instead, she made a mental note to call a locksmith in the morning and have the dead bolts rekeyed. Perhaps he could even fix the garage's man door.

"Sheesh." Zoë's rage hardened her face. "You never cease to amaze me with your stupid bullheadedness."

Kelsey held up her hand. "Listen to me. Despite what some reporters wrote, I know Ramsey was sober because I was with him for most of the evening before the accident. Frankly, I don't care what Jake Botts put in his official report or what he told the paparazzi, because half of what gets written is more for sensationalism and that leaves out a ton of fact. I think someone tried to murder Rams and I've thought that since I heard about his accident. I thought so before I started campaigning for him and knew I could be in danger because of that, but it didn't matter then and it doesn't matter now."

"Saint Ramsey. To hear you yap, he never drank. Well, little sister, I've got news for you, he drinks. He likes Wild Turkey best and when he indulges, he'll down a whole fifth straight from the bottle. He gets so plastered he forgets his name and who he's supposed to be screwing."

Kelsey gritted her teeth and wished she knew why Zoë always made such crude allusions. To the best of her knowledge, Rams had been true to Abby. "Ramsey is only human, but he does not drink than drive."

"Dream on."

Kelsey stared at Zoë's smug expression and remembered the mailbox her brother had sideswiped on prom night. "Not since high school." Their grandfather had been furious that a MacLennan, especially a male MacLennan, would do something so stupid in public where voters, who thought Calhoun's family were perfect, could see they were merely human. They would have seen just how human Calhoun was if they had seen his reaction to Ramsey's silly accident. Kelsey, who had been watching from the stairs, had expected her grandfather to have a heart attack right in the middle of Beja Flora's foyer.

Zoë sneered. "Know everything, don't you?"

"About the night of Abby and Jen's death, I know as much as I need to know. It was Sunday and we'd all been at Beja Flora for dinner." Zoë jerked at the mention of Kelsey's ancestral home; the home they'd shared in their youth, but where Zoë was no longer welcome. "We each had one glass of cabernet sauvignon with dinner. That wasn't enough to get Rams drunk." Zoë opened her mouth to argue. Kelsey put up her hand for silence. "And he didn't leave until two or three hours after dinner. Before you say anything, he didn't spend the time drinking. He didn't stop anywhere to pickle himself, either. He hasn't done anything that stupid since high school. Furthermore, his car crashed within a few minutes of when he left. I'm not sure why Rams lost control of his car, but I know for a fact that it wasn't because he was plastered."

'The car crashed within a few minutes of when he left'. Her car had crashed moments after she'd left home, too.

"Accidents happen," Zoë said.

'The car crashed within a few minutes of when he left'. Chills raced up and down her body. Kelsey tried to swallow the lump of terror in her throat and the suspicions it was telling her. "I think Rams' wreck was planned." And hers had been, too. They'd both crashed near Dead Man's Gulch. Both crashed shortly after leaving a place where their cars had been unattended ... Ramsey had said the brakes had been tampered with, but how could

91

anyone have gotten onto Beja Flora's grounds or
into her locked garage? Even more worrisome, how
could anyone have gotten past Beja Flora's guards
and security system? Abruptly, she recalled the kids
telling her about the alien. A cold chill ran down
her spine. She cleared her throat. "It wouldn't
surprise me to learn someone had shot out his tire
or done something to his car."

"You really think someone tried to kill him."
Zoë's expression looked so incredulous that it
would have been comical if they were talking about
something else.

Kelsey nodded. "What's worse is that our
worthless sheriff is letting whoever did it get away
with homicide and now I'm the next target." She
took a breath, then gestured to the door and added,
"They've made that fact quite clear." Ramsey could
be right about Jake Botts being involved in both
accidents, but somehow she couldn't see anyone as
fat and lazy as Botts managing to squeeze under
either car to drill brake lines. She glanced at the
tied trash bag. She could certainly see him doing
something as anal as hanging a dead chicken on a
door, though.

"Right, the chicken. So how come the only thing
that upset you was the mess you had to clean up?"

Kelsey sighed. "Zoë, are you ready to die for
something I believe in?"

Zoë gulped and shook her head. "Quit."

Kelsey shook her head. "I have to run for myself,
for my family, and for the constituents." She
paused. "And for you." She lowered her voice.
"Did you ever wonder why Frederickson wants his

political position?"

Zoë looked surprised by the question. She opened her mouth, as if to answer, then snapped it shut and shrugged.

"I've heard rumors that he deals dope," Kelsey confided. "I believe Frederickson wants to keep his Senate seat so he has official protection. Think about the political protection his office provides." And the additional protection Botts could add. "Without the senate seat, Marvin Frederickson would be at the mercy of whoever could arrest him first."

"Who told you that?"

"Soon after Frederickson hired on with Grandfather, there have been rumors."

"We were in junior high, then!" Her brows arched and her gaze narrowed, then understanding dawned. "Oh, the Great Calhoun MacLennan and his pompous dinner conversation." Zoë chewed her lower lip. "Rumors usually aren't true."

"Grandfather's idea of conversation might be boring as dirt, but it's usually accurate."

"Is it true?" Zoë swallowed. "About Marv?"

"Grandfather thinks so, but could never find proof. That's why he didn't fire him."

"Oh." Zoë looked as devastated as if she'd just found out her implants were shrinking.

With nothing left to say, and a raging headache to medicate, Kelsey picked up the trash bag and went to the garage. As she dumped the vile refuse into the trashcan, she noticed a wrinkled bit of paper next to the utility cupboard. Cautiously, she bent over and picked up the small rectangle. When she turned it over, a young girl beamed up at her. Kelsey smiled back at her infectious grin, then looked around the empty garage, wondering how the photo had gotten inside. Faint giggles came from the area outside the man door. Perhaps one of the neighborhood kids had dropped it when they had hidden in the garage during a game of hide and seek. Or perhaps the M & M kids had been right about someone being in the garage. Gooseflesh shivered over her. She shook her head. If someone had been inside, they'd have done more than leave a photo. Kelsey went to find the kids.

Mattie was halfway up to the tree house when she came around the side of the garage. As she eased under the stately magnolia, Mark's curly head peeked over the side. "Hey'ya Ms. Kelsey. Wanna come up for a peanut butter and raspberry jam sandwich?"

"Sounds good, but not today."

Mattie wrapped his legs around the tree trunk, halfway to their platform and stared at her. "Are you better enough for a picnic?"

"Not quite yet."

"You sure?" he asked. She nodded

"Did 'ya ever see Star Wars?" Mattie asked.

"Course she didn't," Mark said. "She don't have time for stuff like that. She does 'portant stuff like grow plants."

Kelsey grinned. "I'm glad that you think my plants are important, but I came out here to ask you if you know this girl." She held up the photo. The boys scrunched up their faces in concentration, but neither indicated any recognition.

"Is she someone 'portant?" Mark asked.

"Perhaps." Kelsey shrugged. "Perhaps not. I'm not feeling too well today, but if I'm feeling better tomorrow, I think I'll make some chocolate chip cookies. Do you think you two could help me eat them?" A chorus of eager agreement burbled around her. "Good. I'll see you tomorrow, then."

As she secured the garage and went into the house, she checked the man door, which was still locked. The only other way the photo could have gotten here was Zoë, but it seemed illogical that she would carry around a child's photo. Kelsey studied the girl's bright inquiring eyes and laughing expression. Did it really matter how the photo had gotten into her garage? The girl looked a few years older than Jen, but like someone Jen would have liked to look up to. The longer she looked at the photo, the more her headache receded. She'd told Ramsey that he needed to win the election for all the faceless children and make the world better for all kids. This nameless girl was the reason she had decided to run for office. "Whoever you are, once I'm elected, I'm going to make the world a better place for you to live in." Kelsey carefully smoothed out a wrinkle in the upper corner of the photograph, then carried the new symbol of her campaign into the house.

Chapter 5

Thick navy curtains blocked the hot afternoon glare and turned Doran's home office into a shadowed retreat. Though he had a mountain of paperwork to do, he sat in the darkness watching the chrome yellow tang tease a candy-striped cleaner shrimp in the 150-gallon salt-water aquarium, built into the floor to ceiling bookcase across from his desk, meanwhile both bright orange and white clown fish stroked their anemone. Despite the dim lights and steady, soothing drone of the tank's bubbler, his fingers drummed on the polished black lacquer top of his immaculate desk, and cold sweat beaded his brow. The only other time Quinn had been this insistent about aborting a project, had been two years ago. He'd ignored those warnings, confident that he could handle Pia Chen. How wrong he'd been.

Doran's breath came in ragged gasps, as he relived the waking nightmare of Pia's lifeless body lying beneath him, the hole from Quinn's bullet perfectly centered in her forehead. The worst part was feeling Quinn's unresponsive form on top of him. He would never forget his frantic efforts to get his best friend to the hospital before he bled to death and the agony of fearing he'd die on the operating table.

The phone rang. Doran jerked. "Yeah."

"The early bird may get the worm, but the second mouse gets the cheese." Trent paused, then added, " MacLennan left AMA before I could sneak it back."

"Trust a MacLennan to go against medical advice," Doran muttered. The oak paneled walls felt like they were closing in on him.

"Maybe they wanted to take more x-rays. The colder the x-ray table is, the more of your body is required on it and she's so damned cold already, that she-"

"Does this have something to do with getting her cell phone back or are you working up to another of your convoluted Confucius sayings?"

"Sorry. I'll be serious. I couldn't plant the phone like you wanted, so, what should I do?"

Doran sighed. "Bring it by my house. I'll figure something out."

"Thanks, Boss." Trent hung up.

For close to twenty-four hours, he'd thought that finding Kelsey's phone provided an alternative to seduction. Perhaps it could still work, even though the bug Quinn had installed provided limited information. Not that romance was much better. Why should he have thought this plan would suddenly start going right when nothing had so far?

Doran leaned back in his navy-leather chair, closed his eyes and contemplated the seduction scenario. How in Hades could he pull off a cool-headed affair when he couldn't get close to the woman without getting a hard-on? Quinn was correct about which head he was thinking with, but unless he could figure out a way to get the phone back to Kelsey, he would have to try another idea. Doran picked up his phone, encoded the scrambler, and dialed Quinn. "The bird has flown. And my new love is on her way home without means of communication."

Quinn's silence spoke volumes. "So, you're back to the damned plan you used on Pia. Didn't you learn anything the first time?"

"Yes, and that's why I figure I know the pitfalls, this time."

"I've still got a bad feeling about it."

"I know, but I don't see an alternative."

"There are so many holes in your scheme that you're liable to end up Swiss cheese."

"Have you got a better idea or just more complaints?" At least his voice didn't sound as terrified as he felt. "This is the best strategy I've been able to think of."

Quinn made a negative sound. "Let Trent get in her pants. He's superficial enough to pull it off." Quinn sighed. "You hate everything she stands for. You'll never be able to convince her you've got the hots for her."

He wasn't worried about convincing Kelsey of his feelings; he needed to persuade his damned body that she wasn't the most desirable flesh in the world. And he sure as hell wasn't about to trust Trent with such a delicate assignment. "I can't see her going for his humor or the redneck routine. Can you?"

"You have a point."

"I'll do it, but I need you to run one last check on Kelsey MacLennan's business." Maybe saltpeter would work.

"Look it up, yourself."

Doran gave his computer a distrustful glance. "Please, pull up the file."

"I'm not your damned secretary." Quinn sounded even more pissed off than he had an hour earlier. "Dev, get past your fear of computers."

"Right now?"

"No, yesterday."

Doran sighed. "Fine, I'll try to access the damned files. Satisfied?" He swatted the mouse. A log in screen appeared. Carefully, he typed in Marnie, then hit enter. "Okay, I'm in. Now where did you store the file?"

"Under Mac." Quinn cleared his throat. "I can't stop comparing MacLennan to Pia."

Neither could Doran. The memory of Pia smiling up at him while he made love to her, then his shock when she jammed the handgun against his temple was still vivid after all these months. The cold sweat on his forehead got so thick, that a drop trickled into his eyes. He typed in Mac and hit enter. A long list scrolled across the screen. "Now what?"

"If it's business info you want, type in flower." Quinn paused. "Or you could just pull the hard copy I printed out for you last week." Quinn's tone sounded like he was resigned to the inevitable. "I don't think I've added anything to that file since then."

99

"Why didn't you remind me about that first?" With a sigh of relief, he turned away from his adversary and unlocked the bottom drawer of his desk. Pushing aside the fat MacLennan files labeled Ramsey, Winston and Calhoun; he pulled out Kelsey's folder and plucked out the thick manila envelope. As Doran fished out the report, a newspaper clipping fluttered to the floor. It was a grainy print of Kelsey taken at some formal society event. The straight dress made her look flat as a preteen and the tied-back hair gave her a harsh spinster air.

He tried to equate the bitch-queen in the photo with the trembling, apologetic woman he'd held in his arms or the spitting mad woman in the skimpy silk nightgown. The memory of the way the fabric had caressed her tender flesh made his flesh tighten. Doran smacked himself, tossed aside the photo, then started speed-reading the report. Halfway through the second paragraph, he reread the paragraph. "Are you kidding?"

"About what?"

"That she hasn't had a date in three years." He frowned and backtracked through two pages. "Not since Byron Bainbridge broke their engagement when she was a senior at Duke."

"That's a fact. Lots of rumors around it, though." Quinn sounded as if he was smiling. "Everything from Granddaddy Calhoun telling her she couldn't marry out of party, to her finding Byron in the sack with Zoë Lancaster. But the one I lean toward is that Byron found Kelsey in the sack with Zoë. If she's a lesbo, like I suspect, you'll could tap-dance on your own head before you ever get anywhere near her bed." Quinn sounded pleased.

It wasn't as if he intended to seduce the woman for pleasure. He had to do it for the public good. "Like that thought, do you? Let's assume she is heterosexual," Doran said. "Dollars to donuts she's eager for male companionship."

Quinn snorted with derision. "She'd have to be desperate to look at your ugly mug."

"Thanks, pal."

"Seriously, the woman spends her time working, has dinner with her family every Sunday and attends about one charity event per month." Quinn paused. "Since she started standing in for her brother, she's been doing a lot of public speaking engagements, and she's been attending just about every benefit and social function in the state."

"The MacLennans do hang tight."

"Zoë Lancaster is known to be AC/DC, and her permanent residence is in New York. The hitch in your plan is that whenever Lancaster gets a chance, she's back here shacking up with MacLennan. Has been doing it off and on for years." Quinn paused significantly.

"Which is why I figure the plan has a damned good chance of working. An attentive male escort will allay a lot of rumors."

"At least you didn't call yourself attractive." Quinn laughed at his own joke. "Fact: the two of them have been shacked up since Ramsey crashed his BMW and wasted his wife and kid. Couple that with the fact MacLennan doesn't date and is never seen with men other than members of her family and I'd bet the farm that you won't get to first base. Even if she isn't a lesbo, she's way outta your league."

"So what's your plan?"

"Forget her."

Doran closed his eyes tight and shook his head. This was turning into the same argument they'd already had a dozen times. He stifled a groan. "No can do. I know in my gut that Kelsey is our ticket to nailing that slime-ball family."

"Gain her trust. Protect her life. But forget fucking her."

"I planed to romance her. I never said anything about screwing her."

There was silence from Quinn's end, then he mumbled something unintelligible.

"What?"

"Check out page 56." Quinn paused while he flipped through the report. "Take her an orchid as a peace offering."

Doran read some dull information about Kelsey's degree in botany and her early effort at hybridizing orchids. It felt good to finally have his partner on his side, but he didn't see how this dull information could be of any value. Then he read the final sentence; he realized the significance of Quinn's suggestion. Doran smiled. "Good idea. I'll find one."

"Go to The Flower Shop." Quinn chuckled. "You've been fixated on her greenhouses, but she owns a couple florist stores, too."

"So you do think I'm right and she's pushing dope along with plants."

"Let's just say that you've made some plausible arguments."

"Is it the one near her greenhouse complex?"

"Bingo."

"I checked it out the night I tried to get into her secret lab."

"If she'd had a low budget security system, you could have dropped her as a suspect weeks ago."

"Or already nailed her," Doran said. "The fact that she has a secret laboratory tells me that she's in the cartel right up to her prissy pearl earrings."

"Labs can be used for things besides illegal drugs."

"Not secret labs."

"Lots of inventors are cautious. Stands to reason someone who hybridizes plants could be, too."

"We should have gotten a search warrant months ago."

"I will not put any unsubstantiated rumors in my files," Quinn snapped, "but I do see how compelling the information is and I do see that the hearsay seems to form a solid pattern, which might hold up in court, if the circumstantial evidence was for any other family than the MacLennans." He paused for breath. "Dev, if I was going to bet, I'd wager that my informant is right and the lab is at the PBCO plant. But hunches and bets aren't enough for a search warrant."

Doran understood how Quinn had arrived at his conclusion, if he hadn't discovered the state-of-the-art security system at the greenhouse, he would have been betting along with his partner. "You think she's the innocent victim of my 'lust for revenge'?"

Quinn made an indecisive sound. "Getting back to that note on page 56, Kelsey supposedly developed the Blessed Promise in honor of her engagement and I hear it's her best seller." He cleared his throat. "Scuttlebutt says she attaches a lot of sentiment to that plant, but rumors are divided between if it's positive or negative emotion. If you're game, getting her one might carry a subliminal message."

The knot in his gut eased. "Thanks, pal." Though they disagreed, they were still a team.

"Since you're willing to listen to alternatives, I have an idea about how to get close without having to touch her." For the next half-hour, Doran listened to Quinn's proposal.

Later, he stepped through the door of the Flower Shop and looked at the extravagant selection of expensive imported gifts intermixed with exotic blooms. Flaunt your wealth while you can, MacLennan. He studied an ornate arrangement of roses, which seemed to overpower one corner and wondered why anyone would buy something so vulgarly pretentious. Then, he reminded himself why he'd come. He squared his shoulders and surveyed Kelsey's store, as he looked for a white moth orchid with exceptionally glossy, dark green leaves. At first he didn't see any orchids, then he spotted waxy leaves peaking out from behind a four-foot-high wooden giraffe. Intent upon finding out the botanical name, Doran ignored the graceful bloom stalk covered in frilly, butterfly shaped flowers and read the nametag.

Success.

He carried the Blessed Promise to the teenage clerk and gave her his best good-ole-boy smile. "Could you put something around this to pretty it up? It's a gift."

"Sure thing," said the gum-popping girl. She picked up the orchid, then gestured toward a small gilt basket. "Want a card? They're free."

He snapped his fingers and winked at her. "Good idea."

She carried the moth orchid to a worktable and added garish gold metallic paper and a gaudy white bow. Doran thought the frou-frou made the plant look cheaper and out dated but honorable, which was perfect for his plan.

He smiled.

Picking out a simple white card, he tried to decide what to write. Finally, he simply wrote Kelsey then underlined it with a flourish.

The girl returned to the counter and glanced at the card. She stopped popping her gum and choked back a laugh. "You aren't buying this for Kelsey MacLennan, are you?"

"As a matter of fact, I am." Doran assumed his most innocent expression. "Do you know her?"

"Of course." The girl gave him a wide smile and resumed bursting bubbles. "I bet no one ever bought her one before."

"Why?" He hoped his expression was as innocent as his tone.

She shrugged and giggled while she rang up the sale. The gum popped. "Wish I could see her face when you give this to her." The girl continued snickering.

"Doesn't she like orchids?" He started taking the money out of his wallet, then hesitated and looked worried.

"Oh, she likes them, all right. Thinks they're the greatest thing ever." The girl laughed. The bubble burst, leaving a sticky spot on the tip of her nose. Still laughing, she rubbed at the goop.

Doran smiled and handed her the money. "I certainly hope you're right."

The girl began choking and pounded her chest with her closed fist.

Though he was tempted to draw out his performance, Doran didn't want to press his luck too far, so he picked up the pot and left.

He placed the foil-covered pot on the Suburban's passenger seat, which he'd already protected with a thick pad of newspapers and secured it with the seat belt. The kid's intense reaction indicated that Quinn was right about the plant's emotional value, but he had a really bad feeling that his partner was setting him up to fail. Luckily, Quinn didn't know his entire plan and all he needed the stupid plant for was an excuse to get in the door. Positive or negative, it should at least do that. He patted the pot and whistled Notre Dame's fight song all the way to Kelsey MacLennan's driveway.

Though the MacLennan family was as paranoid about security as any other drug lords, Kelsey's drapes were wide open and lights blazed from the downstairs windows. Doran could see all the way across the main room and if he'd been a sniper, he could easily have shot her from a kilometer away.

Fortunately for MacLennan, she was more valuable to him alive. He plucked the transceiver from his shirt pocket. "Ready to back me up?"

"Have been," Trent said. "Hey, Boss, have you noticed that a day without sunshine is like, night?"

"Not in Alaska." Doran grinned, pleased to finally have a comeback for one of Trent's odd sayings. He turned the unit off and wondered if he was being overly paranoid to believe he needed backup for such an apparently innocent errand, but bedding Pia, should have been safe, but it hadn't been. He placed the unit on the Suburban's seat, then grabbed the pot, walked up to the front door, grasped the brass knocked and tried to ignore the prickles of apprehension, which usually meant he was being watched. He told himself it was only Trent, but he didn't believe it.

After a minute, the porch lights came on. After a pause, the lock clicked, then the door opened an inch. A bruised face with pain in her eyes peered over a flimsy safety chain. He gave her a sheepish grin and held the plant toward her. She stared first at the waxy white petals, then raised her green gaze to lock with his look. Consternation flooded Kelsey's expression, then the door slammed shut.

What had he miscalculated? Why did it feel like anger had been directed at both him and the plant? With everything lost and knowing nothing could get worse, he gently tapped the knocker.

After a moment of silence, there was a scratching sound, then the door whooshed open. Kelsey's expression looked as thunderous as her bruises looked painful. Had she somehow managed to figure out his plan? She raised her gaze from the plant to his face. Suddenly her body stiffened even more. "You. What are you doing here?"

The pure venom in her tone chilled him. Surely she couldn't know that he'd sabotaged her brakes. Doran resisted taking a step backward, and gave Kelsey his most apologetic smile. "My name is Devlin Doran." He used a rueful tone and tried to look embarrassed. "I've come to return something I inadvertently took when I got the blanket out of your car." He handed Kelsey her cell phone, but she didn't move to accept it. "I keep mine in my pocket. In all the confusion, I didn't realize I'd taken yours." Doran gave her his sheepish look. "I wouldn't have touched it, if your brother hadn't been screaming from the receiver." When the truth didn't soften her glare, he inched the plant a bit closer. "Please accept my apologies."

Her expression flushed with anger. "My brakes did fail."

He'd seen that look when he punctured the airbag. Apparently, she hadn't gotten past the initial impression. Perhaps the situation could still be saved. Doran focused on his feet and tried to wrap himself in an air of contrition. "I know."

"You do?" Her voice cracked.

He nodded and risked a peak at her face. "I'm sorry I screamed at you. I don't usually shout obscenities at people. The truth is that you scared the shit out of me." He looked pointedly at the railroad track of stitches near her hairline and told her the truth. "There was so much blood and I didn't know how to help you. I panicked."

She stared at him as if weighing his words on some internal scale of honesty. Her clinched fist relaxed and she smoothed the faded denim covering her thigh. He played the meek role, as he never had before.

After an excruciating moment of hesitation, the right corner of her mouth tilted up and she took the plant. "I got the brown stuff scared out, too. I was so afraid that I'd hurt or killed someone else." She swallowed. "I heard children screaming."

"I vaguely remember a school bus going by afterward, but I was trying to help you, so my memory could be playing tricks."

Tears welled, enhancing the suffering look, already deep in her gaze. He looked down. They were both wearing jeans and sneakers. She sniffed and stepped aside. "Come in, but don't touch the door. The paint might still be damp in spots." She grimaced. "My friend was pretty sloppy with it. Once she leaves, I'll have it redone."

"Nice house." Doran stepped onto the foyer's slate flooring, then leaned over and placed the cell phone on an ornate antique table.

"Thanks." Kelsey shifted from one foot to the other and held the pot away from her mint green shirt as if she had a dirt phobia. Odd conduct for someone who supposedly hybridized plants and must work in dirt all day long. If Quinn could see how afraid she was of soil, perhaps he would stop defending the woman's nonexistent honor.

Kelsey smiled. "Can I get you a drink?"

"I don't drink."

"Really?" He nodded. Kelsey studied him.

"How'd you find me? I don't recall us swapping insurance information."

Doran tried to make his body language and voice seem as non-threatening as possible. "My partner and I own an investigation service."

"So, you're a super sleuth."

He laughed. "Nothing that glamorous." She closed the door. It was all he could do not to heave a sigh of relief. "Our firm primarily deals with deadbeat dads and compensation cheats." One of her elegant eyebrows started to raise, but the movement ended with a wince of pain. Doran cleared his throat. "You've probably heard of the type - people who file phony disability claims, other fraudulent stuff."

"I saw a newscast about one gentleman who couldn't work. They showed video clips of him spending his days rock climbing and water skiing." Mouth flat, she shook her head.

"That's the sort." He gave her a quick, shy smile. "You wouldn't believe how many people are trying to find a way to bamboozle their way into million dollar payoffs."

"Actually, I would. That's one thing I'd like to change about our legal system."

"Wouldn't we all." He gave a depreciating laugh. "Of course, if that happened, my partner and I might be out of a job."

"There would still be cheaters, no matter what." She gestured toward her living room. "Would you like to sit down?" The archway framed the same cozy garden-style motif of peace and blue tones that he'd seen from outside. He gratefully entered the room and walked in front of the window, so Trent would get the message. Antique wicker furniture was surrounded by silk plants and piled with comfortable pillows.

Since Kelsey had a botany degree, the theme appeared appropriate to her mindset, but the fact that she chose to live with fake plants surprised him. Add the fake plants to her apparent aversion to dirt and the greenhouse looked like more of a front. Doran wondered if these facts would alter Quinn's convictions about why she needed a fancy secret laboratory. "Nice room." He settled on the sofa, which faced the window.

"Thank you." She avoided eye contact with him as well as the orchid.

Footfalls clattering down the stairs heralded Zoë Lancaster's arrival. He glanced toward the archway as Zoë stopped on the bottom step and thrust her chest forward until the small ruby triangles threatened to rip over her protruding nipples. Kelsey stared at Zoë's skimpy red bikini top, and skin-tight, semi-transparent white shorts as if unable to look away. Hmm, what had he interrupted? He cleared his throat. "Obviously, I came at an inconvenient time." He started to get up. Kelsey tore her attention away from Zoë and blushed crimson as she glanced at him. Zoë jerked when she realized they weren't alone, then her smile widened "Hi." Zoë thrust her chest forward and batted her lashes at him as she moved across the foyer. "It's so good to see you again."

Doran frowned. "Have we met before?" What kind of mascara did she use? The closer she got, the more it looked like she'd glued tarantulas to her lids.

"You don't remember?"

He shook his head. Surely she she'd been too drunk to see him under Kelsey's car, much less recognize him as the man beneath the face paint.

Zoë shrugged, then glanced around as if looking for something to talk about and spotted the orchid in Kelsey's hands. She jerked in surprise. "Where'd that Blessed Promise come from?" Zoë asked.

"Mr. Doran brought this gift." Kelsey held it even farther away from her conservative camp shirt.

"You did?" Zoë's smile widened to reveal perfect teeth, but her eyes remained mistrustful. "What a lovely gesture." She smirked.

Kelsey put the plant on the coffee table. "It's a great gift." She wiped her hands on her faded jeans and gave Zoë a look he couldn't interpret.

"I've got to go check the kitchen." Zoë bolted back into the foyer. Once out of sight, he heard muffled sounds that sounded like an odd hiccupping laugh.

"Make yourself comfortable." Kelsey gestured nervously around the room, then hurried after Zoë.

ooo

"Have you finished packing?" Kelsey soaped her hands at the sink.

"Getting there." Zoë nodded toward the foyer's archway. "Where'd you dig him up?"

"I banged into him."

"You banged him?" Zoë's startled whisper reeked of disbelief. "Well, go girl! It's about time you started learning how to live." She snickered. "But it's funny how he brought you the plant you grew to commemorate your engagement to good old Byron."

"That subject is taboo. Go any farther into it and I'll have Mr. Doran throw you out."

"Mr. Doran? You don't need to copy your grandma. It's okay to refer to a man by his first name after you've had him."

Kelsey blushed scarlet when she finally understood how her remark had been interpreted. She opened her mouth to correct her, then realized that Zoë was going to believe whatever she wanted because she simply couldn't understand anyone living by a more upstanding set of moral values. She rinsed her hands. "I promised him a glass of ice water."

"I'll get it." Zoë knocked over two other glasses in her haste to grab one.

"Be my guest." Zoë threw ice into the glass, then overfilled it with water and slopped as she tossed a lemon quarter into the glass. Kelsey tilted her head, amazed at Zoë's urgency. Then, she realized that her stepsister thought she was involved with the man, a situation guaranteed to make him irresistible to someone who wanted everything she had. For a moment, Kelsey felt sorry for the man, then she remembered the vulgar way Mr. Doran had initially screamed at her and figured he deserved a good case of Zoë and whatever diseases she had. "Take your time. I'm going to make up a snack tray." She dried her hands, then leisurely reached for her cookie jar.

Chapter 6

Ice cubes clinked as Zoë handed Doran a sweaty glass. "Here's your water." When he took it, she perched on the edge of the love seat and leaned toward him. The suffocating stench of Opium enveloped him. He clamped his jaws together to keep from gagging. "So, what part are you playing tonight?" she whispered in a conspiratorial manner. Her come-on rivaled a street-corner whore's. Too bad he didn't have any doors to lock or windows to roll up as a barrier against the vulgar behavior.

"Excuse me?" He took a sip of the water, grateful that it didn't require any acting skills to appear confused. "What game might that be?"

"Politics." She tugged at her top's straining spaghetti-straps causing silicon to jiggle like jello in an earthquake.

"Politics?" He repeated, as he tried to focus on the topic instead of the crude woman. Doran lowered his gaze. Zoë's lacquered red toenails dug into the peach-toned oriental rug.

"Maybe control." She made an expansive gesture that sent a rainbow of light across her feet from light reflected off her rings. "Possibly power. Or maybe just manipulation of the facts." She licked her upper lip. "Call it what you want, but Marv just calls it politics."

Doran recalled a rumor claiming Frederickson, not the MacLennans dealt drugs. Was Kelsey's girlfriend setting the stage for that scenario? If so, why? Had she somehow made him and honed in on in essential elements of the investigation? He decided to play naïve until he could figure out the facets of the game she was playing.

"You really don't remember me." Her abrupt shift from casual conversation to challenge caught him off guard.

"If we'd met, I'd remember." There was no way he'd have forgotten those tarantula eyelashes or that ridiculous bosom.

Her dark gaze shifted to look past him. She grinned and leaned forward. "I remember you," she breathed. Her lips twisted into a character of a smile. "I know who you're working for." Her clandestine singsong tone reminded him of kindergarten conspiracies.

Doran kept his expression quizzical. How had this bimbo identified him as a DEA agent? He blinked. Perhaps she could bluff better than he suspected. Well, two could play that game. "And that is?"

"Marv, Marvin Frederickson, Senator Frederickson."

Oh, so she knew the cover story, but not his real identity. His heart rate slowed and he relaxed. "Is there a reason it bothers you that we did a job for him?"

Zoë blinked as if confused by his casual

acceptance. She tugged harder at the top's strap. "Men always remember me."

"Is it important if we've met?"

"Just to my ego." Zoë pouted. She might have been cute, if she weren't lying about her motive. "Kel believes Marv will do anything to keep his senate seat. She thinks it gives him power and money to control things and she thinks he's a drug smuggler or dealer or something." She shook her head over that piece of information. Hmm, the woman was slicker than he'd given her credit for and definitely had an unusual way of twisting rumors. "He's not," Zoë whispered. She gave him a pleading look. "He's a good man, but Kel's whole family hates him and they brainwashed her." Perhaps she should be an actress.

Two could play this game and he had a heck of a lot more practice than she did. Doran took a sip of water and tried to determine the point she wanted to make. In order to play his part, he had to be certain if her ploy was geared to support the character-smearing rumors about Frederickson that had begun a few weeks before Ramsey MacLennan declared his candidacy or not. Doran frowned and gave her a confused look. "I don't understand. Please explain."

"Kel believes Marv tried to have Rams killed and tried to kill her, because she campaigned for him and now that she's actually running -"

Doran put his hands in a T, for time out. She immediately clamped her mouth shut. "Who and what are you talking about?" This time, he didn't need to fake his confusion.

"Kelsey." Zoë gave him an exasperated look and

pointed toward the wall, where he could hear faint sounds of someone chopping something. "And Marvin Frederickson."

Doran nodded. "I figured out that much." But she seemed to have a whole new slant to the script. He massaged his temple, giving her the picture of bewilderment.

"I've known them both all my life," Zoë whispered.

"Them who? Kelsey and the senator? What in the world does that have to do with anything? And why are you so concerned about the subject?"

Zoë looked at him as if he was dumber than dust. He gave her his most befuddled look. Zoë leaned back and stared at him, as if he was an alien. "Kelsey is my half sister." The decade of undercover work was the only thing that saved him from laughing. "My mother is their housekeeper." Her tone said that her mother was much more than the housekeeper and added credence to her claim of paternity.

Quinn, who was listening to verify the bug's reception, would love that detail. Had Zoë and Kelsey cooked up this sister story to hide the lesbian relationship that Quinn suspected, or could it be that the master of trivia had missed this bit of information. Doran made a non-committal sound, uncertain how laudable or believable the idea of them being related seemed.

"And Kelsey's step-mom is Marv's sister." Zoë gave him a patient look. "Marv is Marvin Frederickson and Senator Frederickson is your boss."

"Client, not boss. It's an interesting coincidence that you're aware of that case and I guess it does show how small a world this is." He tilted his head. "I must admit that your genealogy lesson was fascinating, however, I really don't understand what bearing that could possibly have on this situation." Doran gestured to the cell phone lying on the table, then massaged a kink developing in the back of his neck. "Is the contract our office has with the senator what has you so concerned?" Disbelief tinged his tone.

Zoë stared at him. "You actually have something in writing?"

"Of course, though our client list is confidential." He didn't need to fake his confusion.

"I know who you really are." She enunciated each syllable distinctly. Zoë's eyes shifted to check every shadow, and the tip of her tongue darted out to moisten her lips.

Doran fingered the droplets on his sweaty glass and decided she must be putting on this show to check him out for some unknown reason.

"Kelsey needs to quit this stupid election. I want you to warn her that the chicken was no joke." She gave him a significant look. "Kelsey needs to listen to someone. Maybe she'll listen to you."

How had he gotten into such a ridiculous dialogue? "You expect her to listen to a stranger, when she apparently won't listen to you?" Doran laughed. Zoë's face registered embarrassment. "I'm just here to return her phone and apologize for being a first-class jerk when she crashed her car into mine. I really don't understand what our car accident has to do with politics or anything else."

"She banged into you?" He nodded. Zoë's gaze narrowed on his face. "If you work for Marv, why would you be stupid enough to-" She snapped her mouth shut.

"Are you suggesting I did something to cause the accident?" She widened her eyes at his tone. "If I'd known her brakes were going to fail, do you seriously think I would have gotten hit?" He shook his head. "Frankly, I don't know why you're so obsessed with the job we were hired to do for the senator, but I gather that Ms. MacLennan is the MacLennan running against him. Is that accurate?"

"Yes." A suffering look suffused Zoë's lace. Without warning, she vaulted to her feet and fled upstairs.

Doran took a sip of water and tried to decide if he'd won or lost the strange verbal match. Moments later, Kelsey carried in a tray filled with cookies and sliced vegetables. The fine lines around her eyes and at the corners of her mouth indicated pain. An upstairs door slammed. She glanced toward the stairs, her confusion comical. Back straight as a saber, Kelsey bent her knees and placed the tray on the coffee table. With a slight sigh of relief, she settled onto the chintz cabbage rose covered cushion of the chair facing him. Feet together, she folded her hands in her lap, Kelsey silently studied him.

How could two women – particularly ones that could be some sort of siblings, be so opposite?

Doran sipped the lemon-flavored water and wondered if he'd met his match or if the woman was too medicated to show emotion.

"How much do you want?" Kelsey said.

He glanced at the cookies, which looked great, but he didn't need the carbohydrates or sugar. He chose a small handful of broccoli stalks and celery sticks. "These are great, thanks."

Kelsey made a dismissive gesture at the laden tray. "I meant to repair your car. That is why you're really here, isn't it?"

How could he have overlooked such an obvious scenario? Doran pointed at the cellular phone. "I'm just returning your property." He gave her his most apologetic look. Kelsey's expression became disbelieving. "My car only suffered minor damage," Doran assured her. "My insurance will cover it." She looked to the ceiling, as if expecting lightening to strike him. Doran cleared his throat. "My partner and I do a great deal of work for insurance companies. One benefit is great coverage."

"It was my fault." Her chin rose a fraction. "I should at least pay your deductible."

Doran studied her and took a bite of broccoli. Even after he chewed it thoroughly, her aloof attitude remained intact. Time to alter that. "Are you suggesting you were the one who drilled your brake lines?"

Her posture stiffened; something he would have thought impossible. "I beg your pardon?" The color in her complexion faded to chalk white. He took a bite of celery and chewed while she gripped the chair's arms for support, her knuckles whitened, and her gaze seemed to block out everything but his face. "How would you know that unless you did it?"

Doran choked. Damned but the woman was quick to see through the b.s. He cleared his throat. "Yesterday, one of our people was at the impound lot checking on-" He cleared his throat. "Something else." Doran kept his tone calm. "Ever since I overreacted, I've-" He grimaced as if admitting personal failure was too painful to verbalize. He hoped he wasn't overacting. "On a hunch, I had my investigator check out your car."

"So Rams was telling the truth." She looked ready to have a stroke. "Someone tried to kill him and now they're trying to kill me."

"Rams? Was he the guy on the phone?" Doran gestured toward her phone.

She nodded, then smiled. "Mr. Doran-"

"Devlin."

"Mr - " She paused and tried to smile. "Devlin, do you happen to know where I can hire a good bodyguard?"

It wouldn't do to look too eager. Doran scratched his ear. "Quite a few of our clients employ them, and we've vetted a number of references, but I can't think of anyone who isn't working full-time, at the moment." Kelsey put her face in her hands, a portrait of defeat. He sighed. "If you like, I can check out some sources when I get back to the office."

"Could you, please?" He nodded, when she glanced up. "Dear God, this is rough. Do I drop out like Rams, or hang in there and hope I can survive long enough to improve life for everyone?"

"Ms. Lancaster mentioned politics. I hadn't realized you were the MacLennan on the posters." Doran hoped his ignorant act looked convincing.

Kelsey took a calming breath. "My brother was initially running, but his vehicle was sabotaged." She swallowed. "Just like mine, except his involved fatalities." She cleared her throat then wiped a tear from her cheek. "His wife and daughter died." Her tears welled.

Doran exhibited the surprise he genuinely felt for her obvious emotion.

Kelsey fought for control. "With Abbey and Jenny dead, Rams is willing to allow a child killer to represent us instead of face another murder attempt." Her jaw stiffened. "I know that Marvin Frederickson is behind the sabotage." Doran shifted uncomfortably. "When Rams quit," she added, "the party agreed to let me run."

"I beg your pardon?" This time, his surprise was genuine.

Kelsey looked him in the eye, as if he should know what she meant.

He blinked. "I read something about the wife and kid of a candidate dying." Doran frowned and if trying to recall the article that had infuriated him. "When his family died, the candidate's rating soared and he became the leading contender, even though his drunkenness caused-"

"I know exactly what piece of garbage you read," she interrupted. "It was so-called journalism at its most libelous. Rams was sober." Kelsey's eyes widened, as if she was surprised by her harsh outburst. "He ruptured some disks in his back, crushed his leg, fractured a hip and was in a coma for twelve days. Believe me, he suffered more than a sprain." Kelsey closed her eyes and took a deep breath. "Don't believe everything you read, Devlin Doran," she concluded in a slightly more controlled tone.

He inclined his head, as if chastened. "I didn't realize politics could be worse than mud slinging."

"Only when the incumbent is desperate to keep his office so he can continue making a mockery of the legal system."

"Mockery?" He frowned, blatantly showing his confusion.

"Outside the capitol, Senator Frederickson functions more like a Mafioso Don." Her fury appeared genuine. Either the lady was one hell of an actress or his gut instinct about her family was one-hundred-percent wrong. And he was rarely wrong.

"Meaning?"

"Organized illegalities like murder, drugs, prostitution and all the garbage that goes with that. Payoffs, so that he owns the law or else he sets colleagues up with hookers, and makes tapes – tapes which he threatens to share with wives and voters. Of course, the philanderers don't want that, so they vote with him and help protect him from prosecution."

It looked like she could give an inspired emotional lecture on this topic indefinitely. " Do you have proof?" Lips pressed together, she shook her head. He had to get her back on the subject that benefited him, but when he got back, he'd read over Frederickson's file to see if anything appeared out of order. "And now that you're running, you feel it's necessary for you to have a bodyguard to guard you until the election." Kelsey nodded. "So, unlike most executives, you'd only need protection temporarily." Doran noticed a movement in the shrubbery outside the window. Without being obvious, he watched the window.

She nodded, again. "Until now, all I've been doing is making campaign speeches on my brother's behalf." She swallowed. "Obviously, Frederickson's camp thought that my efforts were threatening enough to eliminate me." She wet her lips. "Fortunately, they didn't succeed in killing me, but Rams was so spooked by the attempt that he quit." She gave a tired shrug. "Now that I'm officially running, I'll be more of a target." As if to underscore her words, a tongue of fire flared behind the shrub and a bottle's ghostly shape appeared.

The flames blazed higher and moved outward, as the unseen person prepared to throw it. Doran lunged to his feet. The streak of light rocketed toward the picture window. He vaulted over the coffee table and tackled Kelsey, chair and all. She gasped in shock as they somersaulting backward. The bottle smashed through the thick plate glass with the sound of two freight trains colliding. Glass shards rained down as the wicker back struck the floor. She shrieked, then his weight landed on her, turning her scream into a cry of pain. "Sorry." He covered her with his body.

Cutting shards created an explosion of tiny knives. Gas fumes stung Doran's nose, when he looked back at the sofa. With a whoosh, a blinding pillar of flame exploded across the coffee table.

Thankfully, the chair protected them from the worst of it. Kelsey shrieked. As the flames streaked to the ceiling, Doran jumped to his feet, keeping the chair between him and the fire he yanked Kelsey upright. She stumbled, but caught her balance, then turned and stared transfixed at the blaze. Placing his body between her and the flames, he half-carried her toward the foyer. "You have a back door?"

"Yes."

"Where?"

"Kitchen. One slider to the backyard and a door into the garage."

He altered course toward the kitchen's archway. After he shoved her into the comparative safety. "Get into the garage. It should be safer, since the sonofabitch is outside. But don't stay in there. Get outside, away from the house." He drew his handgun from his shoulder holster and dashed toward the front door.

"Where are you going?"

"To catch the fucking arsonist." The smoke detector began squealing. "Get to safety, but don't let the asshole see you." Kelsey gave him a dazed look, as she nodded and moved toward the kitchen.

Doran rushed out the front door, hoping against hope that Trent had stayed on the job long enough to ID the perp, better yet, if he was still watching his back, he could help him catch the sonofabitch.

ooo

As soon as Doran sprinted out the front door,

Kelsey recovered her wits and sprang into action. "Zoë," she screamed. "Get out of the house… Now!" With that, Kelsey grabbed the fire extinguisher from its bracket on the kitchen wall, where she kept it as a precaution against cooking disasters and ran back into her living room. Intense heat enveloped her and smoke choked her as pointed the nozzle at the center of the flames. She held her breath and tightened her finger on the trigger. Nothing happened.

Dark gray smoke curled upward while flames licked across her favorite rug in a wave of destruction.

Tears streaming down her cheeks, Kelsey squinted at canister, then yanked out the locking pin. This time a stream of white sediment merged with the dark smoke. The flames leaped high around the powdery haze. Kelsey steadied her aim and moved the stream to thwart the ever-expanding circle of fire.

"What the hell are you hollering about?" Zoë shouted. "Jesus H. Christ! What the fuck!"

"I think it was a molitov cocktail." Heat clawed at her exposed skin and her stitches felt like they were on fire. Kelsey held her breath until her lungs threatened to suck in the entire cloud of dust and smoke. Still, she fought the blaze. Slowly, the flames subsided, but as they winked out, the smoke turned black as coal and cloying as death.

As the extinguisher spat out its last blob of talcum-like dust, she whirled away, fell to her knees, her lungs burning for air.

The tarry smoke blotted out all visibility. Kelsey

frantically pulled her shirt up over her mouth and a took a shallow breath. Her lungs felt as if she'd inhaled acid. Her eyes stung and it felt like one of her stitches had torn.

She crawled to where she hoped the kitchen door was located. "I will not panic," she thought, "I will not panic. I will-" Her skull butted a solid surface. Pain radiated to her toes and she fell backwards Dizziness and searing heat enveloped her.

She wanted to lie down and die, but she had to keep going. Inch by inch, she crawled to her right. Cookies crunched beneath her weight. Thorns of hot glass dug into her palms and knees. Smoke filled her lungs. After everything she'd been through in the past few days, it would be anticlimactic to die of smoke inhalation in her own living room. "I will not panic. I will not panic. I will not panic." She focused on the thought while she made steady, painful progress forward.

Time lengthened. Her starved lungs felt as if she was burning from the inside out. Each movement felt more sluggish than the one before. Kelsey opened one eye for a peek and noticed gentle movements of gray amid the black. Convinced that she was hallucinating because of oxygen deprivation, she blinked, but the phantom shapes continued to drift and twine.

She could barely find the energy to move her left knee. "I will not panic. I will not panic…" She toppled forward and landed face-first. Stitches ripped. She gasped with pain.

A gust of fresh air fanned her cheek. She cautiously inhaled, then coughed so hard that it felt like her lungs were trying to turn themselves inside out. She inched her right knee forward, then the left, and again the right, until she was out of the smoldering black fog, and then, drained of energy, she lay down on the cool slate floor.

A soft breeze caressed her skin, bringing more life-giving air.

She opened one eye. A foot of clear air lay over the floor. Above that, shades of darkness swirled above her like phantom vultures in dark mist. Over it all, an acrid black smoke hung like the cloak of doom. She rolled onto her back and watched the dark movement with morbid fascination. Another gust of wind wafted through the open front door causing the shadows to swirl and the dark birds of prey to disperse.

The slate beneath her back felt like a welcome caress against her aching muscles. Devlin Doran had saved her life, but why had he run away? Why had he told her to escape instead of save her home?

Light from the distant streetlight painted streaks on the porch floor. Kelsey wondered why the house's lights were off. Had a circuit breaker tripped or had Devlin Doran turned the lights off? If he had done that, why?

With ever breath, inhaling became easier and her thoughts became more coherent. It took longer for strength to return to her aching body. Kelsey lay still, content to watch the eddying smoke and contemplate how much Marvin had paid this latest hoodlum.

Her palms and knees began to ache. "I did not panic," she murmured. She levered herself onto her

128

hands and knees. Forehead pressed against slate, she whispered a new mantra, "I can get up. I can get-"

"What the hell is going on down there?" Zoë clattered down the stairs; a bulging suitcase in each hand. "What happened? Did the orchid guy try to kill you?"

"He saved," she paused to breath, "my life."

Zoë dropped her luggage, grabbed Kelsey's upper arm and yanked her upright. Kelsey's legs wobbled. She grasped Zoë's waist to keep from falling. Pain streaked out in fiery rays from her palms and knees.

Zoë touched her forehead and her finger came away bloody. She moaned as if she were the injured one. "You have to quit." Zoë started crying as she tugged her toward the kitchen.

"We need go outside." Each syllable came from her throat in a raw, painful rasp, as she tried to guide Zoë back toward the life-giving air.

"Marv has terrible friends. You have to quit." Zoë sobbed and yanked Kelsey off balance, half dragging her out of the doorway. "You have to hide. He'll kill you when he finds out you're still alive."

Zoë's surprisingly strong grip propelled Kelsey into the kitchen. She paused to grab a damp towel and ice, then continued across the room, Kelsey clung to Zoë despite the tearing pain of having the makeshift icepack pressed against her head. They were going out the kitchen's sliding. Not good. Doran had told her to go into the garage. If she'd done it, she wouldn't have hurt herself. But if she'd done what he told her, she would have lost her home.

Zoë stopped. "What happened?"

Kelsey took the lead as they inched across the kitchen. "When someone threw a molotov cocktail through the window, Devlin pushed me out of the way, and told me to go into the garage. I think Devlin went after them."

"How come all the lights are off?" Zoë, who had been afraid of the dark since Junior High, shivered.

"I don't know for sure, but it's sort of good because no one can see us." Kelsey stretched her free hand forward into the darkness, feeling for the wall.

"So he didn't start the fire?"

"No. He saved me."

"How convenient." Her voice trembled.

Her questing fingertips touched the back door's handle, it moved. Kelsey gasped and yanked her hand back.

The door whisked open. Zoë screamed.

"Stay inside and keep down," Doran ordered. Legs already weak as noodles, Kelsey plopped to the floor. Zoë began hyperventilating. "I'll be back in a minute." Though Doran had initially seemed either terribly shy or embarrassed, he now appeared totally competent and in command of this horrid situation.

Kelsey recalled the aftermath of her car crash, the angry, scared man, and the tender gentleman. Could they be aspects of the same person? Could a crisis make Devlin Doran blossom? Zoë continued moaning. What had made Zoë so afraid after the accident? Zoë's trembling fingers touched her; Kelsey gave her a reassuring squeeze. Jolts of searing pain took her breath away in a gasp.

"You have to q-quit."

"Never."

Suddenly the lights came on. Zoë gasped. In the split second before she shut her eyes, Kelsey saw Devlin Doran holding a lethal looking handgun.

Kelsey waited for the click she always heard on television.

Time dragged while Zoë howled. Would this be the last thing she heard, or would she hear the gun fire a moment before she felt the bullet?

"Are you all right?" His soft, concerned tone was achingly familiar. She wanted to curl up in his arms and listen to the steady beat of his heart. She wanted to feel his arms wrap her in another protective cocoon and shut out the din of the world.

She squinted though her lashes. Doran had holstered his weapon. His black silk jacket draped over the armament as if it was made for wearing weapons. Kelsey opened both eyes and stared at him. How much more did his perfectly tailored jacket hide? It reminded her of her first glimpse of him, holding that lethal-looking switchblade. Except this time he seemed calmer.

What sort of person needed to carry a switchblade and gun? And appear calm after a molitov cocktails burst through the window? How could he act like this be an every day event? Interesting that he'd been there for her twice in the past three days and each time she had nearly lost her life. A bit too interesting. Was he some sort of guardian angel with perfect timing or did he have a dark agenda? Doran hunkered down in front of her, grasped her chin in one hand then gently washed her forehead with a damp corner of a kitchen towel. "Know anyone who owns an older model Ford?"

"No," Kelsey said through clenched teeth.

"I think it was red." Doran sat back on his heals to survey her face and appeared satisfied.

"Did you see who it was?" Zoë's pitch sounded strained. If it got much higher, her voice would shatter glass. Doran shook his head. "Male? Female?"

"Probably male, but not enough light to be positive," Doran said. He picked up her hand, gently caressing her inner wrist with his thumb. "You're hurt."

Without a word of warning, he scooped her into his arms and carried her to the kitchen sink. Despite her doubts about him, this felt right. After placing her on the counter, he tenderly rinsed her injured hand. Gentle as a mother tending a babe, he extracted a shard of broken glass, then rinsed the wound and applied pressure.

Relief seeped through her arm. She smiled up at him. Zoë lurched up, went to a cupboard and poured herself a stiff drink, then downed the whiskey in one gulp.

"I can use a bit of that here," Doran said.

So much for the man only drinking water.

Zoë grabbed two more glasses and poured hefty slugs into each, then put the bottle to her own lips. Kelsey took the one that Zoë thrust at her, and set it next to her on the counter, because it was easier to do that then explain that she couldn't drink while on antibiotics. Doran set his aside, also and maintained pressure on her palm, with one hand, while he tenderly washed the blood off her knee with the other. When he removed a long splinter of glass, blood ran down to her ankle. Zoë slammed the bottle down on the counter and looked ready to either faint or throw up.

"It might have been a Taurus," he said in a conversational tone, as he drizzled the liquor over her knee. It burned so badly that she had to clamp her jaws together to avoid crying out, and that set off another set of pains.

"A red Taurus?" Zoë yelped, then gagged and sprinted from the room.

Doran studied Zoë's retreating figure for a moment before he turned all his attention back to her. "Know anyone who has one?" he asked.

"I wouldn't know a Taurus from a Sagittarius or a Capricorn," Kelsey joked, to take her mind off of the pain.

He blinked and stared at her, then something infinitesimal changed and suddenly the reticent man returned. Doran dropped his gaze and continued to check her knees, but now, as he felt for shards, his touch felt like business instead of a gentle caress. Darn, she preferred the compassionate man, who could handle frightening situations like everyday events.

Doran set aside another sliver, rinsed the new area, then applied pressure to it. "It isn't as bad as it looked." His smile seemed reassuring.

"You saved my life, twice. You're really a good

doctor."

"Just standard military training." His mouth flattened in concentration as he extracted another shard. "You were lucky, so far, nothing has hit a vein."

The tone, the touch, Devlin Doran was definitely the gentle man who'd saved her, not just the knife-welding maniac. "You're good at keeping people safe." Her intuition answered the question of whether he was a guardian angel or something darker.

Kelsey swallowed hard. "I want you to protect me."

Doran gave her an odd look. "I'm not a bodyguard."

Yes he was, he just didn't know it, yet. "I'll pay you."

He shook his head.

"I didn't know anyone could react as fast as you." She put her fingers on his wrist and silently willed him to look at her. "You're the only one I trust with my life. Please say you'll do it." He peeked at her, but shook his head. "You can name your price."

"You can't afford me." He nearly blushed.

She would have laughed if she'd felt better. "How about a hundred-dollars-per-hour as a beginning bid or is your rate higher?" He looked at his wrist, where her fingers still clung to him, then peered back at her. His face was definitely flushed.

"You mean I'm not just some sort of jinx for you and this sort of thing happens to you a lot?"

She stroked his forearm; it was the most brazen

thing she'd ever done in her life. "Marvin Frederickson wants me dead, so what I'm offering you isn't a safe job." He rubbed the back of his neck, in a familiar gesture, which her father made when he was trying to say no politely. Tears blurred her vision. "Please."

"If I do," he said, "you have to trust me and do everything I tell you without question."

He'd do it! The breath she didn't know she'd been holding rushed from her lungs in a burning blur. "Anything." She wished she dared hug him. "I'll do whatever you say." She smiled at him. His neck and ears turned beet red. With her own personal guardian angel at her side, she could handle whatever Frederickson's goons threw at her.

Doran dropped his gaze and plucked a sliver of glass from her left palm, then one corner of his mouth tilted up. "Anything?" She nodded and meant it, as she held out her hand to shake on the bargain. He engulfed her hand in his larger one, his attitude professional. How many more faces did this man have? "First, we need to find a safe place for you to stay."

Kelsey swallowed hard and looked around. The kitchen doorway framed wisps of smoke, which still hung in the air. Where her hands and knees had been, drying splotches of blood marred the floor. She looked from the trail of blood to the shard of glass Doran had extracted. In his own lethal way, Devlin Doran was like the fragment, which appeared innocent and oddly beautiful.

"I'm sure a hotel would be safer than here," she admitted. He frowned and she remembered that she'd agreed to let him make the choices. "Do you know of someplace better?" Kelsey took a deep breath, then coughed as the horrible smell gagged her.

He daubed her forehead. "Would you prefer to spend the night at my home or the hospital?" As if suddenly hearing the invitation he'd just offered, his eyes widened until the whites were visible. The poor man was absolutely endearing.

"Your house sounds fine," she said with a confidence that astounded her.

His stared at her as if wishing he could rephrase his previous comment. Apparently he didn't sleep around either. He swallowed hard. "Go pack whatever you need. While I call-"

"No police."

"But-"

"I'll agree with you on anything else, but not that.

He raised a brow. "Fine. Would it be alright if I call in my crew and have them secure your window and clean the mess?" His embarrassment made her trust him with her life. "They'll make certain they keep any evidence they find."

"I'd appreciate that and I'll certainly pay them, too." What would she have done if he hadn't brought back her phone? Would she even be alive to wonder?

Chapter 7

Zoë stomped on the brake pedal as her Porsche skidded across the gravel parking lot, sending up a cloud of dust into the first light of dawn. Her car halted two feet short of the ruby Taurus, which was parked next to her guy's silver Lexus. The dust billowed across the parking area and shrouded the bleachers. Zoë squinted at the joggers, which populated the local high school's track at sunrise. She spotted her quarry as he rounded the far turn of the track. Her mouth flattened with the effort of holding back the torrent of angry words, which had been building inside her since the firebomb attack.

Zoë grabbed the beach-bag she used for a purse and whipped her door open. The knowledge that slamming her door into the side of his car would scar her beloved Porsche was the only thing that saved his precious red paint.

Instead, she kicked the Taurus' tire. Though her foot ached, she felt better. Zoë put on her sunglasses and with purposeful strides, marched toward the bleachers. Next to her guy's distinctive athletic bag sat a shabby one, her hand balled into a fist. How dare the bastard attack Kelsey!

She settled primly on the weathered aluminum

seat behind her guy's gear, crossed her legs, and demurely adjusted the ankle-length skirt of her conservative black dress to conceal her high heels then she pasted a serene smile on her face and waited. While she pretended a tranquility she didn't feel, a group of senior citizens power walked past. Next came a middle-aged couple, who held hands and looked more interested in each other than the exercise they were getting. The man gave the woman such tender smiles that Zoë's heart ached with envy.

Next, her quarry jogged past, his head tilted toward her guy as if he was memorizing whatever he was saying. The next lap, her guy was alone, and jogging as if in deep thought. Tension filled her and she tried to appear casual as she looked around the area. A downward glance confirmed that the old black nylon bag was still there. Though her guy didn't look up, she knew he'd seen her. She fought to control her breathing and overcome the raging emotions she felt whenever his attention focused on her. Trying to appear casual, Zoë pulled a candy bar from her bag. He began doing his cool-down workout without glancing her way. But she knew he was watching her.

She did the thing guaranteed to attract him: she ignored him.

Exercise done, he sauntered over to the bleachers. Perspiration gave his skin a vital sheen and his muscles looked taut. Zoë re-crossed her legs and concentrated on the elderly couple. He got a bottle of flavored water out of his bag and sat with his back to her. Safe from his stare, Zoë noticed that gray roots were visible beneath his damp hair. Though mere inches separated them, he appeared unaware of her. Zoë looked past him. The lovers stopped, then hugged and kissed. Her stomach did a flip-flop of envy.

He leaned back, held the bottle to his forehead and hissed, "What the hell is so all fired important that you had to see me before evening?" Ever the consummate actor, he looked carefree and totally oblivious to her presence as he took a long swallow of water.

"Where's your damned buddy?" Zoë hissed through clamped teeth. "I want to throttle him for nearly killing me along with Kelsey

Her guy snorted and stared at the rising sun. "You weren't in her car. You were in my bed."

So he was behind Kelsey's brakes, she had hoped she was wrong. Zoë hid her quivering hands in the folds of her skirt. When the fabric jostled, like cats fighting, she clenched her fists so hard that her fingernails bit into her palms. It took every ounce of acting skill she possessed to appear relaxed and indifferent. She raised the candy bar, as if nibbling it. "I meant last night." Good, her tone was steady. She studied him out of the corner of her eye. "When your buddy torched her house. He failed miserably, you know."

He didn't blink, didn't even glance at her. "Lower your voice, surveillance could be anywhere." He raised the bottle and took a long swallow.

Public opinion was all that mattered to him; that and having a chance at the White House four years hence. "Marv, are you trying to have me killed?"

"Don't be stupid. No one can suck dick like you."

"Answer me, dammit."

Marv's mouth eased into a false smile, but he didn't look at her. "Why? You getting wet?" He shaded his eyes with this palm and looked out over the field.

The rising mist gleamed like spun gold in the early morning light. "Such a romantic view." She sighed. "Once you divorce Helen and we're married, we can watch the sin rise every day."

Marv's posture stiffened. "I never made you any promises."

"Yes, you did." He snorted. "If you hadn't, I would have screamed the first time, when you snuck into my bed!" He sneezed. She suspected it camouflaged laughter at her naiveté. Zoë's anger grew. "I was nine years old! Nine." He made a slashing motion with his hand. From experience, she knew she'd better quiet down or else. That hand had been the one he'd silenced her with the first time. It was the hand she alternately loved and hated; the hand that she saw in her nightmares and the one she wanted to hold in her waking dreams.

Zoë gulped. "I thought someone finally loved me." Despite what he kept promising, she realized he'd never leave his ticket to society. Bile rose in Zoë's stomach at the thought of his perfect, rich, society wife, who always wore a perfect string of pearls around her skinny neck. "But you didn't then and you don't now." Her pitch rose and cracked.

"Keep your voice down, dammit." Marv took a

deep breath then added, "Why have I spent the past fifteen years fucking you?"

A scalding tear rolled down her cheek. Others blurred her eyes. "Because I'm stupid and easy."

"Keep making a scene and I will have you killed." He glanced back at her, his eyes gleaming. Marv's eyes always shone with delight when he heard details of gruesome death or saw photos of violent crimes. Brutality aroused him.

Zoë grabbed her bag and stumbled off the bleacher. He surged to his feet. Forgetting all resolutions of propriety, she broke into a run.

"Hey Lady," he called. "Hey, did you forget this?"

Zoë ran faster. The toe of her high heel caught in her hem. She tripped, but when the fabric ripped, she caught her balance. The sound reverberated in her ears. She was sure everyone had turned to stare at her. It didn't matter. She hiked up her skirt and ran for the parking lot.

She heard Marv running behind her.

Zoë stumbled as she rounded the bleachers and pain shot up her ankle. His footfalls were closer, but her car was only a hundred feet away. The Taurus was gone, so she wouldn't have to fight them both. She gasped for breath and ran for her life, oblivious to the gravel turning under the impossible heels.

"Hey, lady, hold on a minute." He didn't sound winded.

Zoë dodged around the concession stand. Her car was only forty feet away, just beyond the gate.

A hand clamped on her shoulder and yanked her

off balance.

She tried to catch her balance, but Marv grabbed her waist with his free hand and hauled her into the bathroom. With a muted bang, the door blocked most of the light. Without pause, he threw her toward the dark rectangle of an open stall door. She gasped. The stale smell of urine gagged her as she fell toward the toilet.

Her scream turned to a gasp when he grabbed her hair, then his hand slammed over her lips in a stinging blow.

ooo

Doran glanced sideways at Kelsey. Her rigid posture and the way her fingernails dug into the Suburban's leather seat made him wonder what she was thinking. "Either you're not a morning person or you don't trust my driving," Devlin said. She grunted. Since waking, she'd given him driving directions, as if he was some sort of machine, instead of the man she'd clung to for support and comfort. Perhaps she'd expected him to sleep with her instead of give her his bed, while he slept on the sofa in his home office. "If I did something to offend you, I apologize."

She grunted and indicated he should make a left hand turn. The silence lengthened. As he eased the Suburban to a stop beside the back door of her greenhouse complex, her attention fastened on the rearview mirror. He glanced in his, but only saw parked cars. He'd had enough of her brooding. "I laid awake half the night trying to figure out why you hated my peace offering." He tilted his head toward the building. "You must be sick of plants if

142

you work with them all day long." He gave her a shy smile. "Why didn't you tell me you worked here?"

She turned to him, tension etched in the tiny furrows at the corners of her eyes. Either she hadn't had any more sleep than he had, or she needed to take some pain medication. If anyone other than a MacLennan were looking at him like that, he would have hugged her and told her that everything would be all right, but Kelsey was a MacLennan and he didn't dare let himself actually care about the woman. Not when he intended to use her to infiltrate her misbegotten family, so he could shut down their corner of Ling's drug empire.

"I own The Flower Shop and the adjoining greenhouses." Her tone dared him to make something of it.

Doran arched a brow. "Does that mean you were serious about paying me to protect you?"

"Don't worry, you'll get a check." Her tone sounded final.

"What changed overnight?"

Kelsey stared down the skirt of her moss green suit. "I hybridized the Blessed Promise. That's the name I chose for the plant you bought. I originally thought it represented some sort of golden future." She shook her head and winced as if the movement were painful.

Quinn had been correct; the flower symbolized something, but nothing happy. "Boy was it dumb to buy you a gift you already owned." He put on his stupid-me face. "Why do I get the idea that whatever expectations it symbolized never materialized? Isn't it a good seller?"

Kelsey couldn't hold back the pain-riddled guffaw. "It's my best."

"So it must have come to mean something else to you," Doran said. "Is that part of the reason why you seem so troubled?"

Her eyes widened, then she turned away from him, and hopped out of the Suburban. "Thanks for the lift." She leaned inside and whispered, "It was really nice of you to go out of your way for me, but I can't continue to endanger your life." She swallowed. "I'll send a check to your home." With that, she slammed the door and hobbled toward the building. He'd never had anyone shut him out so effectively. Each limping step ground his plans into the dust. Suddenly, light flashed.

A quick glance at his rear-view mirror showed a skinny man with a big camera. He took two more photos of Kelsey as she moved toward the door. Doran didn't think. He slammed the door open and went after the photographer. The man jumped into the open door of a faded blue Pinto and sped away.

Realizing that he'd lost the race, Doran switched directions and caught up with Kelsey outside the glass door. "You hired me to be your bodyguard." He tilted his head toward the receding car. "Do you get a lot of jerks like that?" She nodded. He put his hand on her upper arm. He felt the flesh beneath her thin silk blouse become rigid. She yanked her arm away as if he was an attacker.

"It was a dumb idea made in a moment of fear." She said. "I think we both know that." She glared after the Ford. "The paparazzi are everywhere;

always an annoyance, and always misconstruing things."

"So you don't want to be seen with me."

She looked away from him. "Don't worry, you'll be paid."

"I didn't agree to do this because of the money you offered."

"Last night, I hired you out of fear. This morning, I'm unhiring you, because I don't make choices based on negative emotions."

"I don't hire on as a bodyguard, either, but it seemed like the only thing to do."

"Regardless, I won't need your services anymore. I'll send you a check for your time and add extra for lodging." She lowered her voice, "You can never tell anyone what happened."

"The fire damage is pretty obvious."

"Not that. The fact that I went home with you," she hissed.

"Nothing happened."

"The paparazzi would never believe that nothing happened. If they figure out that you're the one I rear ended, they'll probably tell the world that we'd had a lover's spat and that the accident was my way of getting back at you."

"That's ridiculous."

"It doesn't matter to them. The more lewd the story, the happier they are." With inbred dignity, she turned away from him and went into the building.

Doran watched the Flower Shop's door swish closed. Why was the woman more worried about tabloids than saving her life? What had he figured wrong? Why had she rejected him, just when he was making progress and gaining her trust? Things had been fine the previous evening, after he'd tended her knee. Doran rubbed the back of his neck. Could it be that she was attracted to him and either that scared the shit out of her or she was upset because he hadn't tried anything?

Judging from her injuries and the pain she must be in, being upset because he had behaved like a gentleman seemed highly unlikely. Was she afraid a reporter would find out she'd spent the night with him? More likely. If so, perhaps he could change her attitude. With nothing to lose, Doran squared his shoulders and followed Kelsey.

Chapter 8

"Let me go." Zoë yanked her arm, but his hold was too tight. Blood welled where his nails cut her flesh.

Eyes bright with lust, Marv shook his head.

Zoë took a breath to scream, but his hand clamped over her mouth and he jerked her hard. She kicked his legs, beat his chest and tried to bite the soft palm that was suffocating her. He laughed and grabbed her by the throat. Her lungs screamed for oxygen and her surroundings turned gray than black. She heard a distant, heavy thud. His laugh deepened as her world reduced to a pinpoint of light.

Zoë couldn't move, could barely think. As her life drained away, the texture of the concrete block wall imprinted itself on her back. Dying wasn't as bad as she'd expected. In fact, it was sorta nice.

When she accepted her fate, the pressure slacked off and oxygen began trickling into her ravenous lungs. With every molecule, the blackness receded. Her gaze focused on Marv's face and his satanically exultant expression. Was he prolonging her death for his own preserve amusement or simply to show her that he could?

His pelvis rammed against her with an unmistakable significance. He took his hand away from her mouth and assaulted her with a bruising kiss as his pelvis repeated the message. He smelled of sweat and arousal. Nausea curdled in her stomach. Hatred kindled in her soul.

Feebly, she tried to push him way.

Marv laughed with excitement and bit her lower lip. She tasted blood; the taste of Marv's kind of passionate love. But she didn't want that, not since he let his buddy try to burn her too. No more. Zoë pushed harder at his chest and kicked his shins. He grabbed her breast and twisted. She gasped with mixed pain and passion. He ripped her skirt then used the torn strip as a binding for her hands.

Next, he tore off her silk thong, his nails scratching tender flesh. Zoë gasped in pain. He chortled in delight. His fingers jabbed into her. Despite herself, she felt excitement kindle. Why did it always end up like this? She moaned.

"Want me to stop?" he asked. She nodded. His mouth flattened and his nails bit into her most tender part.

He only wanted two things from her, but would never give her anything she wanted. "You don't need me to spy on Kelsey, not with Doran there." Her voice sounded raspy.

Marv let go and backed up a step. "What are you talking about?" His eyes reminded her of the way a cat watched its exhausted prey for a twitch. She tried to smooth her skirt, but bound hands made that impossible. He nonchalantly rubbed the shin she'd kicked.

148

Zoë wet her bruised lips and tasted more blood. She tried to swallow, but it felt as if a hot ball of hatred on blocked her throat. "After the fire, Kelsey hired Devlin Doran to be her bodyguard. He belongs to you, doesn't he?"

"His firm has done work for me." His face appeared to merge with the room's shadows, while his body appeared ready to attack at the slightest provocation. "How's she hook up with D. Q.?"

Zoë shrugged. She had been in this situation a thousand times before and knew the immediate threat was gone. Zoë looked past him to the filthy urinals. Previous impromptu couplings had been in worse places. Somehow, the setting seemed appropriate for the way she'd lived since he'd raped her the first time. She tried to control her breathing, so she didn't have to inhale the foul stench. Illogically, she felt like laughing.

"Why the hell did she hire a milquetoast P.I. for a body guard?" he demanded.

His furious question sobered her. "I guess because he was there." Zoë allowed herself to appear defeated. "I figured you'd set it all up." The night had certainly seemed choreographed. Marv's amused expression suggested that he didn't trust her with the truth. Apparently Jake didn't mind killing Doran or anyone else, if it meant killing Kelsey; the question was whether his 'kill 'em all and let God sort 'em out' attitude came from Marv. Zoë risked a glance at him. His lack of faith in her hurt more than anything he'd done in the previous seventeen years. And this time, it made her angry. Fortunately, she knew better than to show her fury

149

and give him a reason to beat her.

He smirked. "I'm good, babe, but I'm not that good."

She'd seen Jake reporting to him. Why was he trying to pretend he didn't know about the attack? Had he lost trust in her when she refused to help him kill Kelsey? Exactly what had gone on the previous evening and what part did Doran play? Had he defied orders and put out the fire? Or had he done it as a ploy to get Kelsey to trust him? Pretty damned dangerous, if it was the latter. Perhaps the studmuffin was as disposable as Marv made her feel.

Marv's hands twitched as if he wanted to wring her neck. Zoë forced herself into her most seductive pose. "Marv, you're the best." Despite the bindings, she ran the tips of her nails across the front of his athletic shorts and felt an instant response. This time when he grabbed her, she didn't fight.

Vaguely, she heard footsteps outside the door. Someone said something about a leak. Marv thrust her away from him. Her shin connected with the toilet and she tripped. Terrified of the darkness, tears flowed down her cheeks. "Don't cry, you damned bitch," Marv hissed. "Or I'll cut your eyes out, so it'll always be dark." He slammed the stall door closed and she was alone. Her knees gave out, her chin hit the porcelain, and she sat down hard on the fetid floor. The odor suffocated her, the pain of lost dreams tore her heart and Zoë was certain she'd shattered her jaw.

As darkness shrouded her, she heard water start running and Marv greet someone in his best politician's tone.

If she lived, she was going to pay him back for this.

ooo

Ashley, who was filing paperwork, looked up as Kelsey entered the reception area of her wholesale business. "Good morning, Kelsey. I didn't expect you in this morning."

"Is there anything urgent that I need to deal with?"

"Jade has been covering wholesale for you."

What would she do without her cousin? She'd have to find time to cover retail for her. "Well, then, I'll be in my office." Each step took her farther from the temptation of Devlin Doran, her proverbial knight in shining armor. And while each footfall made her stomach ache a bit more with loss, it steeled her resolve to protect him.

The door behind her opened with a resounding boom. Ashley dropped several invoices. As the papers fluttered downward, Ashley spun toward the door. Her expression changed from alarm to animation as if a switch had been flicked. Only a gorgeous man could do that.

Kelsey hastened toward her office, praying she could get there and slam the door before Doran caught up with her and she had to explain her decision.

His footfalls were gaining fast. A large hand caught her shoulder and spun her around. She gasped a lung full of spicy aftershave and her resolve started to melt. She squared her shoulders against his magnetism. He leaned close. "Get this through your hard head," he said softly. "I make the rules, not you." Her heart fluttered. She shook her head. Determination hardened his features. "You agreed to do as I said, when I said." His domineering tone sounded just like all the male MacLennans she'd spent her life fighting.

She felt herself stand straighter as her will strengthened. "I most certainly did not," she hissed.

Mere inches separated them as Doran put his hands on his hips and raised a brow. Had a man ever smelled so good? "Didn't you?"

"Well, maybe I did," she muttered. He smiled. Something fluttered in her stomach. Even if she weren't trying to protect him by firing him, she'd have to remove this man from her life because being around him made coherent thought impossible. With him around, she'd never be able to concentrate on anything. More papers dropped as Ashley stared at them. Doran was giving her gossipy secretary enough fuel to bend ears for the next year. "But-" she began

Doran lowered his head and kissed her.

Heat rushed through her. Her legs trembled. Doran tenderly drew her closer, until every hard plain of his body met one of her curves. When he drew back an inch, his breath caressed her lips. "I've wanted to do that since the first time I saw you."

"But-"

"No buts." His soft tone sounded sensual, as he lightly brushed her lips with his. "Are you going to continue arguing with me?" He leaned back to look at her. She shook her head. His head tilted a fraction of an inch closer, as if to seal the deal with another kiss. There was a loud crash. As she jumped, Doran shoved her behind him, while his right hand disappeared under his gray tweed jacket.

Kelsey peeked around him. A pool of papers surrounded Ashley, whose face was red with embarrassment. Kelsey wondered if Ashley had done it intentionally to get Doran's attention. When his hand came out from under his jacket, empty, she realized just how quick and controlled his reflexes were.

Ashley lower lip trembled as she looked from Doran to the mess. Kelsey had seen her secretary's charms turn otherwise macho men into mush. She ducked behind his back, certain that he would be on his knees any second and knew that when he did, it would help her past this unexplainable attraction.

Doran glanced from the papers to Ashley's face, then ignoring her stricken secretary, he turned and gently stroked her upper arms, finally placing a warm hand on each shoulder, he stared down at her. Kelsey's heart pounded. Doran smiled at her with such heat that she knew she'd never have hired him had she seen it before.

"I need to-" she gestured toward her office. He smiled and ushered her toward the gray fire door. It closed behind them. As she neared her desk, the deadbolt snapped into place: the sound of entrapment, which her stepmother used as her preferred method of control; the sound of safety, which her grandparents had spent a fortune on.

British Sterling wafted through the room. The same compelling scent had infused his bedroom and her dreams. The hairs on the back of her neck trembled for a new reason.

She had felt out of control before. The first time was when Byron had entered her life. Kelsey clutched the front edge of the antique rosewood desk, which her grandmother had bequeathed to her. The wood felt solid beneath her grip, reminding her that she was a successful woman, not a baby. She gritted her teeth and turned to Doran. "You are fired," she enunciated each word separately, and hoped that he couldn't sense how she felt or how much that terrified her.

He gave her a smug smile. "You're arguing." Behind the shy mask, the man had audacity enough for a family of four. Courage enough to be a MacLennan.

"No, I'm firing you." She inhaled and squared her shoulders against his irresistible scent and killer body. "Just who do you think you are and who gave you the right to touch me?"

"I am the person you hired to keep you alive." Doran appeared unfazed by her anger, but the bags under his eyes suggested that she might not have been the only one plagued by lack of sleep. The memory of the erotic dreams, which had continually woken her, made her blood pressure rise and her head throb.

Fighting the temptation to touch the stitches at her hairline, Kelsey mimicked his posture, "And you think that gives you the right to touch me? Maul me? In public, no less?"

He smiled. Her stomach did a flip-flop. "I can't help it if you're one of the most desirable women

I've ever seen. While we're on the subject, I'll point out that last night I gave up my bed for you and slept on the sofa. Not that I got much sleep." His gaze savored her. "I was awake all night thinking about you in my bed. Did I do anything? No. All I did was give you one measly kiss this morning."

She gulped at the idea that he'd consider that toe-curling kiss measly. She'd lain awake, breathing his smell, afraid to move, because with every tiny movement his male scent brought her body alive with need. No, it would never do to have Devlin Doran around. Never do to have him know how deeply he affected her. Never do to let him know how much she needed him. Kelsey backed into her desk with a thump and sat down on its edge.

Doran closed the distance between them, put his palms flat on the polished wood, one on each side of her hips and leaned down so he was at eye level with her. Fiery heat radiated through her. Kelsey couldn't have moved it her life depended upon it, and deep in her soul, she didn't want to.

Slowly, his mouth inched nearer. As their lips touched, she wrapped her arms around his neck as if he was a lifeline, and she was going down for the last time.

Doran's arms enfolded around her. She molded her body against him. His hands moved over her; heated flesh against chilling memories of the last time she'd felt such closeness. She needed to push him away, yet wanted him closer. Her hands moved under his jacket and stroked the sensual silk of his shirt.

He groaned with desire.

His hands roamed over her, first bunching up the fabric of her shirt, then sliding over her skirt.

She sighed.

He broke the contact and tucked her head beneath his chin. His ragged fanned her forehead. "I'm sorry for whatever I did to upset you earlier and I'm sorry for going too far, now." His thundering heartbeat matched her own. "Please forgive me."

The tenderness in his tone brought a lump to her throat.

How could something that felt so right have such lousy timing? Even her infatuation with Byron had never been this confusing.

"Are you angry at me?" he asked.

Was she? "I don't think so."

"Then why did you fire me?"

Fear of her desires. "To protect you." Kelsey couldn't articulate the confusion of being torn between never wanting the contact to end, and knowing that she didn't have time for this, her tears began spilling over.

"I am good at protecting myself and I think I can protect you, too." He hugged her tighter, reminding her of the man she'd trusted with her life. Weeping released buried demons and she sobbed until there were no more tears. He simply held her, more concerned about her than anything else in the world.

Finally, she rubbed away the tears. "I'm so sorry." She pushed away from him. "I think I've ruined your shirt." His chuckle was a warm, deep sound and he pulled her closer.

"I like holding you. Touching you," he said. The thought of what her mascara and tears had done to the black silk, which he didn't seem to care about made her eyes water, more. "It's only fabric. It'll dry." His thumb moved over her cheek. "Things don't matter." Doran stroked her throat, while she listened to his heartbeat and his gaze caressed her lips. "People matter." He tilted her head back until he looked into her eyes. "Tears matter." He kissed the bridge of her nose and regretfully removed his hands. "You ready to give me that tour now?"

"Not until I fix my face." Embarrassed by her response, to Doran, Kelsey averted her eyes as she hurried into the small half bath. She shut the door, exhaled, and leaned back against the door's solid steel surface. Eyes closed, her heart hammered while her mind sorted through the tumult of mixed emotions Devlin Doran inspired.

She inhaled and detected his spicy aftershave. Her eyes opened. The oval gilt-framed mirror displayed a face with clotted rivulets of brown mascara on her checks, red-rimmed eyes and a line of stitches across her forehead. What did a nice, intelligent man like Doran see in her other than the hundred dollars an hour she'd promised him?

Kelsey touched her lips and grimaced. Strange how good it had felt to be kissed by him. For the first time, she realized how inept Byron had been.

Stepping to the sink, she wet a paper towel and washed away the marred makeup. Kelsey studied her reflection. Bruises in assorted colors remained; the outer edges remained purplish, while the inner portions had healed to an unflattering olive tone. Not a face to attract a handsome, virile man. She stared at herself. Doran must have sick taste when it came to women.

Why hadn't he made any sort of physical play for her until he knew she owned this business?

Worse, why wait until he had an audience? She glanced at the connecting door to the lab, where she hybridized orchids. Tempting as it was to feed the code into the security system and escape, it was also the coward's way. And she wasn't a coward; she was a MacLennan. But what was Devlin Doran?

He seemed changeable as the Carolina's weather; hot one-minute, chilly the next. A raving monster one minute; a saint the next. Could he be some sort of gigolo?

Kelsey studied her reflection in the small oval mirror. The railroad track of the stitches paralleling her hairline were strained. She gripped the cold white porcelain of the pedestal sink until the pain passed. Perhaps he felt sorry for her. She reapplied her makeup, but still couldn't decide on a course of action. With a sigh, she squared her shoulders and walked out to deal with the man, who both mystified and attracted her.

ooo

When Kelsey came out of the bathroom, her carefully combed hair and makeup covered most signs of the accident as well as her possible humanity. She went straight to the main door, unlocked the deadbolt and marched out head high. Doran followed. The blond secretary eyed them as if she had a million questions and laryngitis, but Kelsey ignored her.

Apparently Kelsey's hips hadn't gotten the message that the woman they belonged to wanted to be an emotionless automaton, because they swayed enticingly as she leaned against the thick metal door that connected The Flower Shop's reception area to the hothouses.

From blueprints filed with the county, Doran knew that the door they were going through went into a long corridor that connected all ten half-acre growing chambers to the office and hidden lab. Various parts of the passageway served as potting sheds, tool storage and an employee break area, but over half was devoted to shipping and receiving.

A month before, he'd attempted a clandestine visit to the lab, but the effort had uncovered more security installations than the blueprints specified, so he hadn't had the proper tools to deal with the unexpected problems. That foray had convinced him Kelsey MacLennan was a key player in her family's drug processing facility. Following that sortie, he'd spent weeks covertly monitoring the five acres of greenhouses. The more he watched how customers, workers and freight came and went unheeded, the more he realized what an ideal cover her setup made. Watching Kelsey from a distance, he'd come up with his 'savior plan'. And now she was escorting him into the area she guarded like Fort Knox.

Doran pushed through the heavy metal door, in the light of day, as an invited guest and silently congratulated himself on winning Kelsey's confidence. Entering the main hall, thousands, perhaps millions, of orchids filled the half-acre area. And all were in full bloom. Doran stopped, stunned by the view of the long connecting greenhouse that ran perpendicular from the main hall.

The door swung back, softly grazing his arm.

Kelsey stifled a chuckle.

Doran blinked. Neither night-vision goggles nor hours of peering through whitewashed glass had prepared him for this sight.

A hard thud against his ankle brought him back to reality.

Instinctively, he went for his Smith & Wesson 9 MM, but Kelsey grabbed his hand in a death grip. Doran looked down.

A brown and white rabbit with floppy ears worthy of a huge bloodhound stared up. "This is Lucky." Kelsey awkwardly picked up the creature. Despite dirty paws and fur, she hugged him to her chest. "He was Jenny's." Her voice broke. She swallowed and caressed the rabbit behind its ungainly ears. "When my niece died, I brought him here." The rodent snuggled to her and nuzzled her neck. Her arrogant mask cracked as she blinked away a tear. "Sometimes I think he's more trouble than he's worth, but he's a living, breathing connection to my niece. Please don't shoot him." Doran squinted at the rodent. The creature seemed to grin at him as it cuddled to Kelsey. One ear cocked out, like an airplane wing, while the other hung down, like a basset hound's, giving it a comical appearance.

"I thought rabbit ears were supposed to stand up."

"He's a French Lop, their ears droop." Kelsey tickled it under the chin. "Fortunately, he doesn't eat orchids." She gave the rodent a hard look. "Irrigation hoses, electrical wiring, rabbit cages, plastic pots," again, she tickled the beast under the chin and raised her gaze to him, "Lucky eats those … but not orchids."

"Interesting." Doran focused on the building's glass walls. "If I was going to assassinate someone, I'd wait for them to stand right here." Kelsey's back stiffened and she stared at the semi-transparent surface, as if seeing it for the first time. "People feel secure when they're indoors, but the target would probably be visible to a sniper on the outside." Kelsey stepped behind him. "It's impossible to secure an area like this."

"But-"

"Until whoever is after you is in jail, avoid this area." He turned around and looked down at her. "It'll be hard enough to protect you in your office, don't come back to this area until after the election."

Kelsey blinked. "Just who do you think you are? Telling me where I may and may not go."

"The man who intends to keep you alive."

"I fired you."

"Prior to that you agreed that you would do whatever I said – without question."

"Are you after more money?"

Doran caressed her under the chin and shook his head. "I have plenty of that."

Unwilling to meet his look, she focused her attention on her armful of rabbit. "If not money, what?"

"Want another kiss?" Kelsey shook her head and moved a step backward, her heel thudding against the wall.

Her eyes widened; Lucky frantically fought to get free. When Kelsey let him down and he bounded across the hall, into the greenhouse and under the orchid-laden table.

Doran chewed his upper lip while he calculated his next move. Either her innocence was a damned effective act, or she was one hell of a natural kisser. If simply kissing her could make him forget she was a MacLennan, he needed to heed Quinn's advice and forget pursuing a sexual relationship. Her body language supported the celibate strategy: body guard, yes; lover, no. Doran didn't know why he felt a sense of loss over that decision.

He smiled. "I've never forced myself on a woman, but I've never felt about anyone quite the way I feel about you, either." At least that was the unvarnished truth. Her shocked expression eased, as she chewed her lower lip. "This isn't about money. It's about holding you." He cleared his throat. "While you were bleeding, I held you and tried to help you and I never wanted to let you go," he truthfully admitted.

"Will I at least be able to work in my lab?" Kelsey pointed to a distant white door. "That's where I develop new hybrids."

"Show me." To his shock, she immediately walked toward it.

ooo

Doran studied the construction of her lab as if every dab of paint, every unseen nail and every globule of mortar mattered. Until today, she'd taken the white enameled concrete blocks for granted and had thought fire doors and a triple security system would protect her tender plantlets from incineration or any other ordinary phenomena; now she squinted at the walls, and wondered if they could shield her from Marvin Frederickson's megalomaniac plans.

Kelsey looked around the large rectangular room. Under the upper cupboards along the wall, lights bathed her tools, computer and notebooks, which were precisely laid out on the steel countertop. Except for the computer, books and varied plants, the room looked as it had when her grandfather had it built as a graduation present. White enamel walls, made clean up easy and gave the room a pristine feeling. Two long thin growing tables, one for hydroponics and the other for potting, dominated the center of the room and were spotlighted like a stage. Kelsey viewed this development area as the place where she created rising botanical stars. Could Marvin be as twisted as a terrorist and willing to do anything to win the senate seat?

Doran turned his attention from the door and started studying the general layout of her lab. Would her protector deem the room safe and allow her to work? She held her breath and awaited his verdict. This was her sanctuary from the disappointments and harsh reality of life. This was the one place on earth where she was in control and could create beauty. Being in this room was as important as oxygen.

Kelsey wondered what Doran saw when he looked at the room. Did he see the cupboards as a place for a murderer to hide or a location to conceal a bomb? Would he tell her she couldn't come here? A sudden chill rushed over her. Kelsey rubbed her upper arms. If he told her that, would she choose him or her first love? If she chose him and his methods of protecting her, who could she entrust with her valuable hybrids?

Doran studied the ceiling, which was two feet of solid concrete. She tried to relax. "When my grandfather had this area built, he modeled it on World War II bunkers." She shrugged and tried to smile. "Some of his best pals were generals, so he's very security conscious. Too much so. I don't think he ever got over the Cold War."

He arched a brow at her. Her mouth went dry. He made a sweeping gesture. "Do you have to come through the hothouse to get here?"

"No." Kelsey gestured toward door opposite the one that they had come through. "That leads to my bathroom, which leads to my office." Wetting her lips, she asked the crucial question, "Will I be able to work in my lab?"

He gestured to her office door. "It shouldn't be a problem since you have that access. I'll secure the other door."

With the click of the locks, the glistening white windowless walls transformed to a prison. Great. First she decided to stand up for her beliefs and offer society the choice of honest representation, now she'd become a captive.

Kelsey bit her lower lip as she watched Doran study the door's hinges. Over and over, her memory replayed the words, which had devastated her: 'people feel secure when they're indoors, but here, the target is visible to an outside sniper. It's impossible to secure an area like this. Until whoever is after you is in jail, avoid this area'. Would she ever feel safe again?

Having finished his inspection of her hinges, Doran turned to face her. "You should be safe here and my house has state of the art surveillance, plus the Suburban is bulletproof, so w-"

"Surely, you don't think I'm going to continue staying with you."

Judging by his surprised expression, that was exactly what he'd thought. Macho as he occasionally acted, she suspected people rarely cut him short. But then she'd been raised in a family, which thrived on testosterone.

"Afraid I'll kiss you or afraid of what people will think?" Afraid? Yes. Afraid of what she'd do if she tasted him, again. Afraid she'd never get any sleep alone or otherwise in his bed. And yes, afraid of what the tabloids would print. "You can't stay at your house."

"And I will not stay with you." Not after that sleepless night and a reporter taking their photo. Journalists were horrendous snoops and she could just imagine the incriminating headlines if they discovered she had spent the night at a man's house after knowing him a couple hours.

"I can't think of anywhere safer, can you?"

"A motel."

He shook his head. "The keys are way too easy to duplicate. If not my place, somewhere safe; preferably with a good security system or maybe man eating guard dogs instead of a bunny rabbit." The corner of his lips twitched.

He thought he was amusing, but he'd unknowingly described her family's ancestral home. Kelsey rolled her eyes heavenward. The security at her grandfather's palatial home made Alcatraz seem like a mere jail. She rubbed the gooseflesh on her arms. Since childhood, she'd hated that house and its sense of imprisonment.

Doran's home security system was almost as bad, but the claustrophobic feeling of his two-bedroom townhouse with the thickly covered windows seemed ten times worse than the estate. Kelsey barely managed to suppress a shudder. "How come you have such a high tech security system for your townhouse?"

"I've earned a lot of enemies." He leaned against her stainless steel hydroponics tank. "Suppose someone claims they've been robbed and I prove it's a hoax." He tilted his head. "They lose the payoff from the insurance company and sometimes the insurance companies prosecute, so the cheating liar ends up in jail." He rubbed the back of his neck. "Along with my percentage, I earn another person who wants me dead." He gave her an apologetic smile.

No wonder he seemed so practiced at protection. "I didn't know anything could be more cutthroat than politics."

He shrugged. In the distance, a phone rang. "You mentioned your family had a good security system. Are they nearby?"

"Close enough, but I don't want to go there."

"Fine, we'll think of somewhere else."

"That's just it. There is nowhere else. Beja Flora is the safest place in the state." Disgust filled her tone.

"Must be a delightful place."

Kelsey grimaced, then feeling contrite added, "My grandmother named it Beja Flora; that's beautiful flower in Portuguese." Gooseflesh rippled over her arms. He looked ready to caress warmth into her; she stepped behind a hydroponics table, well out of his reach. "I always though the walls had eyes and ears. I think I was twelve when I found out that instead of being haunted, there was a huge security system."

"What's more important, staying alive or sleeping in a haunted house?"

"Vanquishing childhood fears?"

His brow arched, then he grinned. "Phone your parents and see if it's okay for us to move in today."

"Us?"

Doran tilted his head to one side and gave her an odd look. "Is there room?"

She nodded.

He gave her a 'well then' look, that normally saw on Lucky's face. It was so comical that Kelsey forgot her outrage. "Actually, it's my grandfather's house." He crossed his arms, obviously confused.

"I'll phone Martha, she's the housekeeper."

As Kelsey dialed, she assured herself that she could tolerate all the inconvenience, the feelings of entrapment and even having Doran under the same roof as long as she could work in her lab and know that the situation was temporary.

After the election, she would face the confusion he'd brought to her life and decide if he might be the man or her dreams or another opportunistic gigolo.

Chapter 9

Doran lifted a finger off the wheel of his Suburban and indicated the sky. The sunset painted the clouds peach and gold. "Can't ask for a better welcome than this."

She shivered. "It reminds me of my living room… How it looked before the fire." She pointed to the upcoming intersection. "Take a right, there."

Doran inhaled deeply as he turned the suburban onto Beja Flora Lane, which curved across a flat pasture. Today could well be the high point of his career. First, he'd gained MacLennan's trust, then he'd learned the codes to her lab, so he could return to check it out for hidden areas; now, he was being invited to stay at their private fortress.

And Quinn had called his plan foolhardy.

Kelsey glanced at him. He felt heat rise under his collar. She gestured toward the mowed pasture, on the other side of the deep, barren ditches and birdhouse posts, which bordered the two-lane road. "Ramsey hates it when they mow the fields, but grandfather insists that it must be done for safety." Her lips compressed. "He's the most paranoid person you'll ever meet."

"Why so?"

"Years of public service and hanging out with way too many political types. If I get elected, I hope I don't start thinking that I need an open area to expose infiltrators and a forest to cover the defenders." She pointed to the woodland, as the first shadows caressed the Suburban's hood. As if afraid of the woods, Kelsey wedged backward into the leather seat, her complexion white against the gray.

Spotting a glint from the woods, he slowed. There was another flash. It was too early for fireflies. The twinkles were the height of the bluebird houses. The third glimmer came from the nesting hole. As he passed, he saw glass reflecting the sunset instead of a hole. Hats off to whomever had camouflaged the surveillance system. He checked his rearview mirror and calculated that the birdhouses were spaced at four or five hundred-foot intervals along the curving road. The question was whether they encompassed the entire five-hundred-acre forest or not.

At the border, the forest was a thick mass of twining briars. Bravo to the landscaper who had made the access to the house appear grand, yet simultaneously made it impossible for an uninvited vehicle to arrive unseen.

Lucky for him, he was invited.

An aerial photo of the property had shown that the circular woods covered roughly a quarter mile. What other technology and natural hazards did the boughs conceal?

Rounding a curve revealed a high brick wall topped with spikes and an ornate iron gate. He stopped at the guard booth. Two cameras were evident; Doran suspected more were hidden. He pasted on a friendly expression and rolled down the Suburban's tinted window. A man wearing a light brown shirt and slacks stepped out of the enclosure. His hand was on his unsnapped holster and the fit of his shirt suggested that his stocky frame had Kevlar protection.

Why would anyone need to invest millions in security if they weren't guilty of something?

Kelsey, exuding a sweet, fresh aroma, as she leaned across Doran. The guard nearly clicked his heels and saluted her. "Evening, Ms. MacLennan. I didn't recognize you."

She placed her palm on his shoulder. "This is Devlin Doran. He's my temporary bodyguard. We'll be staying here for a while. Let him come and go as he needs, okay?"

"Right." The gate opened on well-oiled hinges. Kelsey settled back in her seat, her spine looked so stiff that he wondered what sort of horrors this place held for her. He nodded to the guard and drove through the gates. Oak trees edged the curving, ditch bordered road. Sunlight reflected from an overhead branch. Passing into the gloom beneath the branches of the spreading oaks, he saw several more brief flickers above the winding road. If he hadn't been looking for the security system, he wouldn't have noticed. The blueprints for Beja Flora's security system hadn't done justice to the real thing, worse they'd only shown a fraction of it.

Across the barren ditch, a gardener pretended to clip a well-manicured hedge; something else blueprints couldn't show. Doran wondered how many visitors were gullible enough to believe hedges needed clipping at sunset.

Kelsey stared straight ahead, face rigid as her body. Was she afraid of what he'd find? Did she suspect his real interest in her?

A sprawling four-story mansion appeared to dwarf the trees and surrounding formal gardens. Thick black metal grills between the white shutters gave the redbrick building the appearance of a genteel prison. Soon, he'd give the MacLennans even stronger bars over their cell windows.

Doran gaped at the imposing facade, as if he'd never expected this. "When you said your folks had a good security system, I figured you were talking about top of the line, off the rack stuff." Only the guilty needed such extensive security.

"Why do I get the idea you don't approve of money?" she asked.

"My approval doesn't matter."

"Go around back," she pointed to the left, "we can take in our things, than you can park in the garage." Doran stopped the vehicle, turned to her and took her hand between his. "Will you be okay here? I sense bitter memories or something."

Her fingers curled over his. "You don't like it here, either, do you?"

He sighed. "I detest the way some people get rich at other's expense." He gestured toward the palatial house. "I don't know how your family came by their money, so I'm not in a position to judge, but it does seem safe." When she nodded, he resumed driving to the back of the house, where he opened the door and stepped out of the comfortable air conditioning into a hot, humid parking area large enough to handle the crowd of most fast food places. Rosemary and sage, reminiscent of his grandmother's tiny backyard plot, scented the breeze.

Before he could walk around the vehicle, the passenger door slammed. A flock of birds exploded into the air. He dropped into a crouch and went for his gun.

When he straightened, Kelsey stared at him over the Suburban's hood. "Despite the ambiance, we're safe here."

"When a person feels safe, they're most vulnerable." Doran opened the back hatch, slung his navy duffel bag over shoulder.

Kelsey rolled her eyes to heaven. "You and my grandfather will certainly hit it off."

"Where did the molitov cocktail land?"

She snatched the handle of her flight-attendant-style suitcase, whirled away from him and stomped toward the screened in porch.

Doran keyed in the Suburban's security code then followed.

He caught up with her as she entered the house, which smelled of roast beef and chocolate. Kelsey turned to her right and marched down a wide hallway, her footfalls muffled by thick maroon-toned oriental carpet, and her height diminished by mahogany-covered fourteen-foot high walls. Ornate gilt frames encased large paintings of militaristic men and vapid-looking women. Elaborate moldings separated the walls from the ceiling and decorative plaster circled the chain of a hanging chandelier.

Kelsey placed her bag under the gaudy chandelier and waited for him. Back stiff as the general's in the portrait-laden cave, she looked every inch a MacLennan. "I need to let Martha know we're here."

"Didn't the guard notify her?"

"He should have." Footfalls sounded in the distance. "Come on, we'll meet her in the main foyer."

The rogue's gallery of a hallway ended in at a large two-story foyer, with dual circular stairs joining together overhead. A round cherry table large enough to seat eight sat at the foyer's center and supported a scentless silk floral display, big as a Roman fountain, yet perfectly proportioned to the area.

Doran didn't need to feign awe as he looked over the area. The foyer was three times larger than his home office and if the technology report was correct, the elaborately carved moldings contained twice as much hidden technology. He bent forward, pretending to sniff a huge burgundy gladiola and noted the microphone nestled into the silken throat. Perhaps he'd discovered the reason for artificial flowers, when Kelsey owned so many greenhouses.

Kelsey rushed around the table, her shoes clicking on the black marble floor toward a tall, thin woman, wearing an expensive gray suit. The woman's stern expression melted into a smile. "Martha." Kelsey threw her arms around the woman.

"It's good to have you home." She hugged

Kelsey, with obvious affection.

Kelsey pushed back from the embrace. "This is Devlin Doran, the man I told you about."

"Ah, the mystery man from the paper." She looked him up and down. "The photograph didn't do you justice, and it's certainly created quite a fervor of interest in Kelsey's private life." Doran raised a brow, wondering what she was referring to. Martha hitched up her chin and turned her attention back to Kelsey. "I've prepared your room and one for your friend." The woman gave him a look that guaranteed bed hopping would be considered an offense punishable by dismemberment or worse. Doran gave her a shy smile and nodded his thanks. It seemed to somewhat mollify her. He followed them, as they went back to where Kelsey had left her luggage. Martha touched a bit of molding. A moment later, there was a soft ding and a wall-panel slid aside to reveal an elevator. Kelsey's steps dragged as she entered the six by four-foot mahogany lined elevator. Her expression looked like she was getting into her coffin instead of a conveyance.

Once inside, Doran glanced at the control panel: B2 B 1 2 3. He swung the duffel off his shoulder and hit B2.

"Enter security code," a baritone voice said.

Doran pretended to look for the man.

Martha studied him with expressionless eyes, and then pressed 2. "While here as a guest, you will only be authorized on the first and second floors."

He gave her his warmest smile. "Your wine cellar must be impressive if it needs this much protection."

Martha raised a regal brow. "I beg your pardon?"

"You're primary objective seems to be protecting the basement," Doran said. "In an old house like this, the lower levels customarily contain wine. They're too humid for anything else."

"We have a wine cellar," Kelsey said, "but mainly my grandfather stores old files down there." She wrinkled her nose. "You're probably right about the mildew, but then grandfather hasn't been all that logical since my grandmother died." Martha glared at Kelsey, whose expression became rebellious. She added, "It's a lot easier to humor grandfather than argue. Besides, he can do as he pleases, after all, this is his house."

"Loose lips," Martha murmured.

Doran pretended to study the grain of the dark paneling, which made the elevator feel like a mausoleum.

Kelsey sighed. "Martha, Devlin saved my life."

"That's a favored way for a man to get into your bed."

"Martha!"

"They pretend to save your life, earn your gratitude, than use you for whatever they want." Martha glared at him, as if she'd like to thrash him for every indecency man had ever done to woman.

Worse, the spinsterish looking woman was too close to the truth for comfort. Doran cleared his throat. "It seems to me that you need to meet men who have more integrity. Not all of us think bedding a woman is our top priority."

Martha snorted.

Fortunately, the elevator doors opened to reveal another hallway. If it hadn't been for the gilt pedestal across from the doors having cherubs instead of a flower motif, Doran would have thought he was on the same floor.

The wheels of Kelsey's suitcase clattered off the elevator then she went directly to the third door on the right. She stopped and took a deep breath then twisted the knob. Doran glimpsed pale blue walls and white eyelet. Dropping his duffel at the door, he pushed past Kelsey and entered the room. Martha made an outraged sound. Doran wondered if his offense was entering the room or his apparent lack of trust for the security. The icy tones of the room and the fact that the room looked ready to be photographed for some posh decorating magazine didn't surprise him. So this was where the ice queen had lived as a teenager. He could definitely understand how growing up in such an environment could give anyone a skewed outlook on life.

Kelsey wheeled her suitcase to the closet, then sat on the window seat and picked up an old ratty rag doll that had been camouflaged by the thick white curtain.

He checked the widow bolts, then inspected the large walk-in closet. The last door revealed a spacious bathroom with peach-toned marble floor. Beyond the white claw-footed tub, there was the dark oblong of another door.

Martha followed him into the bathroom. "That will be your room." She pointed to the closed door. "But don't get any ideas about hanky-panky. If I'd had my druthers, you would be sleeping in the carriage house."

He didn't doubt her for a moment. "I'm not here to seduce you, Kelsey or anyone else. I've been hired to keep her alive. Period. She requested this arrangement so I could be close enough to save her if she was attacked."

Martha snorted. "Surely you can't believe anyone would attack her here."

"Since being hired, I've done some checking. Her brother's accident happened moments after he left this house." Her eyes widened. "Furthermore, the brakes on her own car failed within twelve hours of her leaving here." Martha's expression suddenly registered dread. "Don't tell me you never put two and two together."

"That's not possible," Martha whispered.

"Isn't it?" Doran demanded.

"No," Martha said.

"Isn't it possible that someone employed here could be trying to settle a grudge?"

"No." Something in her eyes told him that she was far less certain than she sounded.

"If you knew that then why did you agree for us to come here?" Kelsey stood in the doorway.

"You don't have a decent security system in your house and-" She frantically motioned for him to hush. He sidestepped mentioning the fire. "Besides you were occupied supervising that painting." She smiled her thanks. Doran added, "And you didn't want to stay at my place a second night."

"What?" Martha looked ready to do bodily harm.

"Not to worry, I slept on the sofa," he assured her.

Martha whirled to confront Kelsey. "What if the media get wind of this?"

Since when did maternal figures concern themselves more with publicity than pregnancy and VD?

Kelsey hugged Martha. "Don't worry. If anyone had noticed, it would have hit the front page by now. And like Devlin says, we didn't do anything." She looked over Martha's shoulder at him. "Of course, I wish he'd pointed out the coincidence in the brake failures before we decided that this would be the safest place."

He gave her a reassuring smile "My Suburban has anti-sabotage security."

"Is that why you insisted on driving me?"

He raised an eyebrow and let her draw her own conclusion.

Martha straightened. "I must check on Mr. Calhoun."

"And I have to run some errands," Doran said. "Do I need a pass for the guard or anything to get back in?"

Kelsey shook her head. "Will you be gone long?"

"Probably. Don't leave the house unless it's on fire, and if it is on fire, do not stop to put the fire out." He glared at her.

"You're worse than my father."

"Is that good or bad?"

"Good," Martha said.

Kelsey looked heavenward and shrugged.

ooo

"What is it with you?" Quinn demanded. "Talk

about jumping straight into traps!" Headlights from a tractor-trailer flashed through the van's windshield and highlighted tiny white stress lines radiating from Quinn's compressed lips. "Wasn't it bad enough that you nearly got killed for sitting in her fucking living room?"

Did Quinn see a pattern that he didn't? Doran looked away from his best friend. Beyond the white and blue handicapped card, hanging from the rearview mirror, a semi-trailer eased into a parking slot. The silent tension radiating from his pal increased to funereal magnitude, while the stench of fuel coming from idling diesel engines churned Doran's stomach.

Was Quinn right? He'd been correct about Pia except that he hadn't foreseen that Pia Chen had inherited Ling's taste for murder and preferred to get blood on her own hands instead of permit minions the fun.

Was he the hunter who had Kelsey MacLennan in the crosshairs? Or was he the prey?

Quinn fingered the van's manual accelerator. Was the gesture an intentional reminder about the last time he'd ignored his advice, or a subconscious movement at the memory of losing the use of his legs?

Doran tried to breath despite the oppressive guilt, which hounded him day and night. The big rig's driver slammed the door of his ride and stretched before heading to the all-night-diner.

"Damn, Dev." Quinn sighed. "You don't phone in for over twenty-four hours, then call and tell me to meet you here. No explanation. No 'how are ya', just instructions. It'd serve your sorry ass right if I shot you."

"You should have said-"

"I have to do the PBCO stakeout because of you. Damn your rotten hide."

"Your points are valid and my actions were wrong."

"Shit."

Doran smiled. "I'm staying at Beja Flora."

"Beja Flora as in the MacLennan's personal Fort Knox?" Quinn asked. Doran nodded. "Damn!" Quinn guffawed and slugged him in the shoulder. "Way to go, buddy."

"I take it that you believe it's relatively safe."

"Better'n her living room."

Doran knew he should have paid better attention to the instinct, which had told him that he was being watched. "They've got security cameras everywhere and it's way too sophisticated for me. We need to figure out a way to get you in."

"Well, shit!" Quinn squinted at him. "What'd you have to do?"

"Get hired as her body guard."

Quinn laughed. "Don't you mean burn down her house?"

"That wasn't me."

"So it was Trent, on your-"

"Wasn't him, either."

"Who?"

"My best guess is whoever did Ramsey's car." Quinn frowned. Doran sighed. "I got a tour of her damned lab."

"And?"

"She really has plants in it."

Quinn hooted with glee. "Told you so. While you're busy getting yourself invited into all the MacLennan secret spots, I don't suppose you got a gold plated invite to PBCO." Doran shook his head. Quinn sighed dramatically. "Put it on your agenda, okay? It could save me days of stacking out that stinking dump." Quinn's brow furrowed. "Why the hell are you staying at Beja-whatever, when they already have half a platoon guarding the place?"

"I told you, Kelsey hired me to be her bodyguard." Quinn laughed. "I'm serious," Doran said. "I'm being paid a hundred bucks an hour to stay there."

Quinn laughed so hard that his eyes welled with tears. It took a while for him to realize it wasn't a joke. He cocked his head to one side and studied him. "What is it with you Irish? You've got more luck than anyone I've ever seen."

"Are you ready to hear the details and help me work out a way to get you inside? You need to get into the basement and snoop through the files and whatever else they have down there." He sighed. "I'd give my last nickel to get in there to study their files and procedures myself, but -" Doran shrugged

Quinn patted his useless legs. "Right-o, I'll just tap dance down those steps."

"They have an elevator." Quinn studied his face, and grinned. "Do this for me and I'll do all the night surveillance for the next year." Lights flashed through the windshield. They both raised their forearms to shield their faces.

"I'm getting too old for this clandestine stuff,"

Quinn said. "I should apply for a transfer to a desk."

"I thought you loved field work."

"I wanted a chance at Ling. Then Wes changed his tune and we got shuffled to this backwater berg instead." Quinn shook his head and raised a fisted hand. "But we'll get Ling, yet."

Doran nodded. "If Wes finds out that Ling has an actual part of his operation here, he'll transfer us … again."

"Don't look at me, I haven't whispered a word about my suspicions in the weekly reports." Quinn punched the dashboard. "My chariot is fine, but I want revenge."

More lights flashed as a semi pulled into the truck stop. Neither the brightness nor a woman's high-pitched laugh did anything to lighten the heavy silence within the surveillance van.

ooo

Bright lights flashed behind the drab earth tone drapes that shut out the hot pink neon glow from the bar across the street. A car door slammed, then another. A woman laughed.

Several heartbeats later, the door to the next room thumped shut.

Zoë rolled onto her side and squinted at the red numbers of the alarm clock. Ten more minutes. She sighed, rolled back onto her back and stared at the boring rerun on the motel's chintzy little television. She punched the remote, again and again, but nothing caught her interest.

Next door, the woman laughed louder. Her sexual tone sent ripples of expectation through Zoë.

Another car drove up. With a lithe move, she hopped off the bed, grabbed the pillow, plumped it, then propped it against the imitation walnut headboard. She adjusted her new silk negligee in a provocative way, which still hid the crotch-high slit.

A distant door slammed.

Nine more minutes. He'd better be on time. Zoë sighed and readjusted her crimson silk so that the navel-deep neck merely gave a glimpse of cleavage. Then she adjusted her legs to conceal the cigarette burn on the puce bedspread. After fluffing her black Cleopatra wig and arranging her arm over the pathetic pillow, she flipped through several more channels. Something bumped the wall behind her. The woman gasped. Zoë ground her teeth.

Whoever was next door wasn't concerned about the décor, comfort of their accommodations or lack of interesting shows on the television. They were here for the same reason everyone came to the Zzzzz's Motel.

Six more minutes.

Zoë paused at scene showing a bride and groom cutting their cake. Next the still happy gray-haired lovers were strolling along a beach hand in hand and gazing tenderly into each other's eyes. Envy hot and acid clawed at her gut.

Two more minutes.

She changed the channel. Marv's face smiled at her. Her breath caught. "Vote for Frederickson for Senate," the commentator said. "A man who stands for family values." The video switched to Marv with his arm wrapped familiarly around his horsy wife's waist. Tears stung the back of her eyelids. Zoë threw the remote at the television, but it hit the wall and exploded in a shower of batteries.

Outside, thunder boomed.

A door slammed and the sound of a man's tread made her brush away the hurt. In one minute he'd be here, with her, not posing for some stupid commercial with the sexless bag he was stuck with.

The steps got nearer. Maybe one day the two of them would be able to walk openly on white sand instead of live for clandestine moments.

ooo

Doran tossed and turned beneath the covers of the high four-poster-bed. When he'd returned from his meeting with Quinn, Kelsey had been taking a bath and hadn't thought to lock the door to his room. Until today, he'd never viewed a suds-shrouded woman, with only her face visible as sensual. But, now, hours later, the occasional whiff of her floral soap brought a wave of arousal.

Finally, he lay on his back and stared up at the ceiling trying to spot hidden cameras and microphones in the ornate crown molding without appearing to do anything more than count wood. He'd feel one-hundred-percent better about this place if he knew the monitoring schedule and which cameras were active. Perhaps Quinn could find that out if and when he figured out a way to get the technical wizard into the house.

His cell phone cheeped. He grabbed it halfway through the chirp. "Need help?"

"Nope but maybe your luck is rubbing off." Quinn sounded better than he had since the bullet smashed his vertebrae. "I just taped MacLennan going into the building." Smugness permeated his tone. "Got some great footage when lightning illuminated his face."

"So you don't need backup." Anything would be better than lying here, inhaling Kelsey's fragrance and trying to remember because Marnie lay in her coffin because of Kelsey and her family.

"According to our informant, tonight was a distribution meeting."

"Maybe so, but something doesn't feel right about him." Doran scowled at the ceiling.

"The way he hates MacLennans, I'd think you'd love him."

"He's almost too good to be true and that worries me." Doran's Irish intuition wasn't as reliable as Quinn's gut feelings, but it had been right on more occasions than it had been wrong. "He and Winston used to be pals," Doran reminded Quinn. "Makes me wonder."

"Whatever. I taped the gimp and his car sneaking into the factory lot in the middle of the night. Owner or not, there's no reason for him to be here, now."

"We can't prove that. There could have been a problem we don't know about or he might prefer to work at night so he can have the place to himself." Doran preferred that, himself. "We need more evidence than a midnight stroll across an empty parking lot to get a conviction."

"Sleeping under their roof making you go soft?"

"Hardly." If that wasn't an understatement, he didn't know what was.

"Incoming…. more company just arrived for the party." Thunder boomed and static crackled. Doran closed his eyes and listened to the faint sounds of Quinn adjusting the equipment.

"Christoncrutches!" Quinn exclaimed.

"What?" Doran sat up so fast that he felt dizzy.

"I gotta be wrong," Quinn muttered. "Dev, come by the office tomorrow morning and look at this."

"Look at what?"

"Gotta get back to work. Come by the office first thing tomorrow." Quinn cut the connection.

Heart racing for a new reason, Doran stared at the cell phone. In the distance, thunder boomed. Would the storm soon encompass him? If so, it might give him an opportunity to check out the house and grounds. He got out of bed and quietly dressed in black.

Chapter 10

Kelsey came down to the den, turned on the gas fire and some soothing music, then settled onto the loveseat's navy and yellow shantung strips, with her feet tucked up, she leaned against a fat cushion and opened a history book on the Byzantine Empire. Outside, a storm approached, and upstairs, Devlin Doran slept in the next room. 'He reached Byzantium by the inland route, choosing the Bosporus crossing…' If this didn't put her to sleep, nothing would. Thunder rumbled and a distant door slammed shut. Kelsey burrowed against the pillow and concentrated on the book.

The den's sliding doors slammed open and Ramsey stalked into the room. Kelsey jerked in surprise, then ran her finger down the page, to find the paragraph she'd been reading. After, she noted it, she looked up at Ramsey, but he stood spine stiffly toward her, hands to the flames flickering in the fireplace. She couldn't tell if the tension he exuded was due to anger or worry.

The last thing she needed was Ramsey's negative emotions, but even one of his diatribes about the accident was better than the frustration of imagining a replay of her bath – one where Devlin had shed his clothes and joined her beneath the bubbles instead of back out of the room as if his eyes had been assaulted.

A Bach fugue began playing softly in the background, underscored the harshness of her brother's breathing. She inhaled deeply and caught the scent of the nearby arrangement of white roses. Memories of her grandmother and relaxing summer days spent in the garden edged into her consciousness.

Someone cleared their throat. Martha stood in the doorway. Ramsey turned, his expression just as disgruntled as she felt. Martha's face was even sourer as she carried Grandmother Rose's heirloom serving trap onto the room and plopped it onto the coffee table hard enough to rattle the three porcelain cups. "I guess no one could sleep tonight," Kelsey said. "Martha, is something bothering you?" She knew better than ask her brother the same question.

Outside, thunder boomed. "No," Martha snapped.

Kelsey peered over the ornate silver coffeepot flanked by matching sugar and creamer to see if Ramsey knew what was the matter with Martha. He gave a slight shake of his head, then sat down on the opposite loveseat and poured himself a cup. A drop of water in the damp hair over his right ear shimmered, as it reflected the firelight.

"Is it decaf?" Kelsey asked.

"Yes," Martha growled. Oblivious to the soothing flames and arrangement of pewter frames, she began pacing in front of the fireplace.

Without being asked, Ramsey filled all three cups. Kelsey twisted a napkin and wondered how long it would take the two of them to tell her whatever was bothering them. Through the window, lightening illuminated the garden and Kelsey shivered. Thunder boomed; for a fraction of a moment, the lights dimmed. The storm must practically be overheard.

Martha paused long enough to close the thick curtains.

"What's wrong?" Kelsey asked.

Martha bit her lip and shook her head. What if her parent's boat had sunk? Dread crept through Kelsey. What if Grandfather had suffered another stroke?

"Did someone die?" Ramsey demanded, as if reading her thoughts.

Kelsey held her breath. Martha shook her head. With her handkerchief, she dabbed at a tear in the corner of her eye. Kelsey exchanged a concerned look with Ramsey. He motioned for her to give it a try. Dear Lord, last time Martha had been this bad, Grandma Rose had died. Kelsey swallowed a lump of rising terror.

"I should have said something sooner." Tears tingeing Martha's tone and she shuddered. "I didn't think it was important. Not then, but when Mr. Doran said –" She put a hand over her mouth, unable to go on.

Kelsey rushed to Martha. While uttering soothing sounds, Kelsey hugged her surrogate mother. She ushered Martha to the sofa. It felt odd to have their rolls reversed.

As Martha's tears saturated her left shoulder, Ramsey staggered to his feet. Even the collapse of the World Trade center hadn't had this devastating an impact on Martha. What could Devlin possibly have said in the brief time Martha had been around? She tried to recall his comments, but the odd cadence of Ramsey's pacing made it impossible to concentrate. Finally, he stopped, but he stood looking down at them, weight balanced on his good leg, cane gripped in a white knuckled hand.

"Martha, you're more than our housekeeper," Ramsey said. "You're our proxy mother."

Martha straightened, wiped her eyes and looked up at him. Without Martha's body heat, Kelsey's shoulder felt chilled.

Ramsey glanced at Kelsey, willing her to speak.

She took a deep breath. "Exactly." Kelsey hugged Martha. "We love you. We don't know what we'd have done if it hadn't been for you. You're the one we relied on. You helped us through losing our mother, first day of school jitters, puberty and learning to accept Jacquelyn." Ramsey's expression told her she was blathering and to get back to the point. Kelsey softened her tone. "Please tell us what's wrong. We want to help."

Instead, Martha surged to her feet. For a moment, it looked like she was going to sprint out of the room, but she dodged around the coffee table to the fireplace, then grabbed the mantle and held on, as if she needed the cherry wood's support. The clock chimed the half hour. Kelsey glanced at it

12:30. Inwardly, she groaned at the thought of how little sleep she'd get. But, like Grandma Rose always said, 'people came first'.

Martha put her hand to her heart. "It's Zoë."

"What is it this time?" Ramsey's tone sounded resigned. Since getting his law degree, he'd been the one Martha called to bail Zoë out whenever she got arrested for: drunk driving, indecent exposure and everything else, which embarrassed Martha, which explained her brother's presence and his mood. "Has she been arrested for soliciting, again?" Ramsey glanced at Kelsey. "Just asking." He colored.

Of course the charges would probably be legitimate, but they'd never say so to Martha. "Ramsey MacLennan, how could you suggest such a thing," Kelsey played her well-rehearsed part. "I know Zoë dresses in a less than sophisticated manner, but it's her style." Kelsey cleared her throat. "I've always wished I could be more like her. More carefree."

"I didn't say it would be a valid arrest," Ramsey protested.

Martha sighed. "You don't need to make excuses for her. Zoë is what she is ... She's a product of her heredity." She daubed a tear. "Long ago, I realized that I couldn't change her genetic heritage and if I kept trying, I'd completely alienate her." The admission seemed to wring every ounce of starch out of Martha. She staggered back to the navy and yellow striped sofa and slumped onto the seat, as if she wished it would consume her.

"But Martha. She's your daughter." Kelsey knelt

in front of Martha and took her hand. "Your genetics are wonderful. Do you know how many times I've wished you were my mother?" Kelsey paused, but Ramsey motioned for her to continue. "I always thought Zoë was lucky to have you. Jacquelyn is so shallow." She felt her nose wrinkle with distaste. "I don't know what father sees in her."

Ramsey shook his head as he limped behind Martha's seat, where he traced exaggerated curves in the air. Then leaning over, he messaged Martha's shoulders. "What Kel said goes for me, too. You've always been here for us, when we needed advice. Let us help you."

Martha covered her eyes and shook her head. "This is hard. So hard." She blotted tears with her soggy handkerchief, then turned and grasped Ramsey's hand and bowed her head. "I never told you, but Zoë came to see me the night of your accident."

Kelsey took a deep breath. "I'm glad something positive came out of that." She wet her lips. "Maybe now she'll accept our family for what it is instead of what she wishes it was."

Ramsey gave her a quick nod, as he patted Martha's fingers.

"Not your accident. Ramsey's." Martha's voice was barely legible.

Kelsey blinked in confusion. Hadn't Zoë come the day following the horrid wreck? Her gaze locked with Ramsey's. His look held a warning to let him handle this. "Surely, you can't believe Zoë caused my accident," he said.

Martha made a miserable sound that told them that was exactly what she thought. Ramsey looked as if he'd been blindsided.

"She's a lot of things, but she loves us and she'd never do anything to hurt us." Kelsey glanced at Ramsey for confirmation. He gave a curt nod. "Besides, she doesn't know anything about cars and she sure wouldn't get greasy or risk breaking a fingernail." But it was unnerving to discover she'd been around each of their cars before each of the accidents. More unnerving than the fact that Devlin had been present at her two catastrophies.

"You're right, she'd never get dirty," Martha said. "At least not that way." Martha dabbed her eyes, but it did nothing to stem the flood of tears. "I can't believe she'd allow her jealousy to—" Martha shook her head and closed her mouth.

"Zoë isn't easy to understand." Kelsey sighed and perched on the arm of the yellow loveseat. "She never was." She twisted her fingers together and wished she'd been the one to think of rubbing Martha's back. Wished Ramsey would rub a few kinks out of her own aching spine. Martha's shoulders shook so hard that Ramsey nearly lost his grip. His expression urged Kelsey to say something to calm Martha. What could she say? What would make things right? "I wish father had made things right." Kelsey cleared her throat. "I've always thought he was wrong for not marrying you."

Tears poured silently and unheeded down her cheeks as Martha stared at her. "Do you mean that you think Winston is Zoë's father?" Martha's tone sounded incredulous. Kelsey nodded. Martha looked over her shoulder at Ramsey. He nodded, too. Martha shook her head, her expression suffused with amazement. "All these years." She shook her head, again.

"Are you trying to tell us you and Dad didn't, uh..." Ramsey paused, as he tried to think of an appropriate word. His eyes begged Kelsey to find a polite way to phrase the impression they'd always held.

"No," Martha said, vehemently. "Never."

"But you two have always loved each other," Kelsey said. They had, hadn't they? Or had her childish wish for a normal family made her see something that wasn't there?

"Not in a romantic way." Martha chewed her lower lip, then sighed and looked her in the eye. "It's a symbiotic relationship where both of us benefit." Some of the starch went back into her spine. "Winston didn't father Zoë." She took a deep shuddering breath, then slowly exhaled. "I was raped."

"Jesus!" Ramsey's face paled. "Do you know who it was or were you mugged?"

"This isn't something I want to talk about or think about." Martha looked everywhere, but at their faces. "And after all these years, it doesn't matter." She sniffed and dabbed her eyes. "I mentioned Zoë because I think she's involved in this." Her voice cracked.

"I hope you're wrong," Kelsey said. But Martha was probably right. Zoë always did stupid stuff because she wanted people to like her, though it never did any good. Worse, she always got caught.

Kelsey cleared her throat. "Annoying as Zoë can be, and paternity aside, I've always thought of her as my sister and I'm not going to change now. I can't believe a sister would try to kill her brother." Not that she couldn't understand someone considering it.

Ramsey pursed his lips and blew her a kiss. "I love you, too." He turned to Martha. "What makes you suspect Zoë?"

Martha tweaked a rose from the arrangement next to the sofa, and twiddled it between her fingers as if the most pressing problem in life was finding the perfect spot for the flower. Martha picked off a less than perfect petal, twirled the stem, then picked off another petal. Zoë had spent her life on the edge. At eleven she broke into the liquor cabinet and got drunk. When confronted, she'd thrown up all over the front of Grandma Rose's favorite Chanel suit. Martha picked off two more petals. At her prom, Zoë had stripped and danced naked on the banquet table. And most recently she'd stripped nearly naked on her front porch.

Embarrassing as Zoë's behavior was, it didn't make her a murderer.

Martha yanked the rest of the petals off the rose and tossed the stark stem onto the serving tray. "Something someone said."

Kelsey frowned. "What did Devlin say?"

"It wasn't so much what he said." Martha swallowed audibly. "It was the connection I made. Until then, I never thought about the fact." She looked at Ramsey, pain and misery in her expression. "Your car went out of control just after you left here and you left just after Zoë."

If Zoë had been at Beja Flora, why hadn't she said so when she showed up the following afternoon? Why had Zoë specifically said that Martha had phoned her and told her to come, if she was already here? Something simply wasn't right. But what? Zoë always stayed with her, appearing without warning. If she had been here, then left, where had she spent the night? "Surely that was just a coincidence," Kelsey said, though she didn't believe it any more than Martha obviously did. "Why don't you try some of the advice you gave me? Just cry it out. It really does help."

Martha looked like she wanted to disagree, but the tears cascading down her cheeks, made it impossible. She covered her face with trembling hands. Kelsey moved over to her and stroked her back. "That's it. Let it all out."

Ramsey shifted from foot to foot, looking as if the tears were harder to bear than anything else he'd recently endured.

Martha cried until there were only dry sobs. Eventually even those ended and her breathing evened out. By that time, Ramsey was long gone. Kelsey settled Martha on the sofa and tucked a blanket around her, then took the serving tray and tiptoed out of the room. As she walked past a window, she saw lights glistening off rain-washed foliage, but the storm was past.

When she entered the kitchen, Ramsey was seated at the round oak pedestal table, a cobalt stoneware cup half full of chocolate sat in front of him. If he'd put any marshmallows in the brew, they were long since melted.

"I thought you'd gone up to bed," she said.

He shook his head. She placed the overloaded tray down on the green marble counter next to the stainless steel sink. "Want some company?"

He gestured to the vacant seat across from him, with a 'take it or leave it' flip of his wrist. Kelsey sat down across from him and studied his haggard expression. "Still can't sleep, huh?"

He shook his head. "How about Martha? Did you get her to bed?"

"She fell asleep in the den." He nodded and twisted his mug between his fingers. "Do you believe-"

"No," he interrupted, "I think you hit bulls eye when you said she'd never break a nail."

Kelsey blinked twice. "I was thinking about the rape thing. I think she knows who, but won't say."

Ramsey grunted then raised his mug and took a hefty swallow. When he plunked the solid cobalt mug down, semi-gelled chocolate clung to his upper lip like a stale mud mustache.

"I had the oddest phone call today," Ramsey said. "Mandy Caruthers –

"My nutty neighbor?"

He nodded. "Mandy called to make certain I was okay. She said that Mattie, Mike and Mark had camped out in their tree house and seen the boogie man sneak into your garage."

Kelsey shook her head. "Kids. They told me about that at the hospital, too, except then, it was some alien monster."

"They must have seen Zoë come home."

"Could be." Kelsey shrugged. "Mark told me, 'He was big and black all over 'an had a big-ole thing over his eyes like he was either blind or he was 'protectin' people from his laser vision'." Ramsey chuckled at her imitation. "Poor Mattie sounded like he was still scared." Kelsey shrugged and added, "Mark thought it was like one of those bounty hunters from Star Wars." She grinned. "I think Mandy needs to control how much time they spend watching TV.

"Jen used to dream of things like that." Ramsey sighed. "I miss her so much."

Kelsey put her hand over his and squeezed. "We all do."

An hour later, Ramsey still rotated the half-full cobalt stoneware in slow circles. The only difference was that the chocolate's surface had developed a shiny sheen.

Kelsey sighed. "I don't know what to think."

Ramsey pushed his mug away. "I always thought Martha and dad had a thing going, too."

Kelsey chewed her lower lip. "But Martha never lies." Ramsey tilted his head to one side as if wondering whether this conversation was going to be a replay of the one they'd already batted around. Kelsey didn't want to go there. "Who do you think raped Martha?"

Ramsey opened his mouth as if to answer, then frowned. "Perhaps a better question is why she let him get away with it."

A zing of shock surged through her. Martha had never let either of them get away with anything, no matter how confessing embarrassed them. Why would she allow someone to get away with such violence as rape? "What makes you think he did?"

"Just a feeling."

Kelsey sighed and nodded. "So, what do we do, now?"

Ramsey looked perplexed. "About what?"

"Zoë." His expression suggested that the conversation had truly escaped him. "If she's not kin from the wrong side of the sheets, I don't have to put up with her disgusting behavior, but I still feel I owe something to Martha for raising us." Even though she didn't have a familial obligation to put up with any more of Zoë's nudity and vulgar sexual remarks, it seemed wrong to totally shut her out. And it still felt like she was a surrogate sister.

"Just because we found out there wasn't a genetic link is no reason to toss her away." His tone suggested otherwise.

ooo

Doran entered Beja Flora's back door and paused for a moment. Faint strains of classical music drifted from somewhere deep within the house. He quietly closed the door. It amazed him that while the perimeter was so well guarded, he could move around the grounds with relative freedom, courtesy of the snoring gate guard made.

The lock clicked. "So much subterfuge," Kelsey said.

Doran froze, sweat beading on his spine as he tried to think of a good excuse for sneaking into the house so late. "You know," she continued, "if we'd had a different father, one who'd talk to us, we'd know the family secrets and not spend half our lives believing a lie."

Huh?

"Lies, not lie," a man said. Doran rubbed his temple and told himself he was ten kinds of fool for jumping to conclusions. "Dad must have known what we thought. Makes me wonder."

Made Doran wonder what they were talking about, too.

"I never thought father cared what I thought or felt." There was a quick rustle of fabric. "He cared about you. You were the son. I was just the girl-child."

And what a girl.

The conversation drifted from the direction of the kitchen. Doran moved quiet as a cat toward the soft light. He paused long enough to determine that Kelsey and a man were alone. When the man turned his head, Doran recognized Ramsey MacLennan. Hot damn, he'd been trying to find a way to meet him for five months.

Doran melted several feet down the hallway, then returned, making enough noise to advertise his arrival.

Blinking rapidly, he entered the kitchen. Ramsey turned around and Kelsey straightened. Doran smiled, He offered his hand to Ramsey. "Hello, I'm Devlin Doran; Kelsey's bodyguard."

"Ramsey MacLennan, her insomniac brother." The soft grip could have belonged to a woman.

Doran stuffed his hands in his pockets and cleared his throat. "My condolences on your loss."

"Apparently you understand why I dropped out." Ramsey gave him a forceful look, which belied the soft palms. "Think you can help me convince my sister to step down and save her life?"

Kelsey surged to her feet and leaned across the polished oak. "I told you then I'm telling you now, I will not quit. Period."

Ramsey looked at Doran, as if trying to enlist his aid. Doran turned a chair around backwards and straddled it.

Kelsey's eyes narrowed on Ramsey. "Why should I quit?" she demanded. "He wants me dead whether I run or not."

"That's poppy-"

"My brake lines were cut before I entered the race."

"You were the one making speeches."

"So, I might as well run and try to win. That way, I stand a chance of seeing him and his merry band of creeps prosecuted for Abby and Jenny, but better yet, if I'm elected, I can help everyone by giving them honest representation." She gave a defiant nod.

"They weren't trying to kill you." Ramsey's voice sounded whisper soft, but certain.

"What do you mean?" Kelsey sat down.

"Don't you remember?" She tilted her head to one side and thought hard, then shook her head. He sighed. "The previous weekend I'd borrowed your car. You almost died in their second attempt on my life."

Doran looked at Kelsey, wondering if she'd buy her brother's theory.

"He's not worth it," Ramsey said.

"Justice is worth it."

"Haven't you heard?" Ramsey's face contorted. "This is America, everyone is innocent until proven guilty, since he'll never be tried, there will never be any justice."

Doran cleared his throat. "What - who are you talking about?"

"Marvin Frederickson," the two MacLennans said in unison.

"A criminal, who poses as a perfect citizen," Kelsey added.

Gooseflesh rippled over Doran as their sheer conviction touched something deep within him. He'd never liked working for the pompous Senator, and hadn't listened to Quinn's insistence that PBCO, not Kelsey's greenhouse, was the site of the clandestine laboratory. Now, he wondered if failing to acknowledge what his subconscious was telling him might had put them all in danger.

Chapter 11

Doran felt like he'd pulled an all-night stakeout, instead of a half night. He settled onto the stiff-backed office chair and sipped coffee thick enough to cut. Quinn raised the remote control, which he'd specially built so he could rule his domain. Pointing it, he pushed a button; the thick, ivory drapes closed to block the morning sunlight. Lowering it, he keyed in the video player. As the picture came into focus, wind gusts from the approaching storm bounced a Styrofoam cup across PBCO's shadowed parking lot. Lightening flashed in the distance. "One-thousand-one, one-thousand-two," Quinn softly counted. Doran glanced at this partner. He grinned. "I was timing the storm. Thunder hit at 7 seconds." Doran nodded and watched the vacant parking lot. As promised, thunder rolled.

"That was thrilling," Doran said. "You got anything interesting off the tap on Kelsey's phone, yet?"

Quinn grinned and paused the tape, then keyed on the audio system. "Rams, get over it," Kelsey said."

"The nights are the worst." Ramsey's voice sounded slurred over the speakers.

"I've noticed."

"I can't live without Ab-n-Jen."

"Yes, you can. You just need to realize that you can, decide that you will and quit drowning your sorrows. Lucky needs you."

Quinn flicked off the recording and gave him a triumphant look. "They're cagey, but we'll crack the code."

"What code?" Doran asked.

"The drug names for one abengin has to be an anagram for something and she tells him that the cartel needs him."

"You think Lucky is a code, too?" Quinn nodded. Doran laughed. Quinn glared at him. Doran sobered. "Lucky is a pet rabbit with big enough ears to make belong to some sort of retro elephant."

"You going soft of the MacLennan's?"

Doran shook his head.

Quinn reactivated the image of the closed factory with the remote in his hand. He pressed another key. 11:59 appeared in the lower corner of the screen. "My informant mentioned that the meeting would take place at midnight. With the storm that close and no one there, I'd decided to give it a half-hour; if no one showed, I was going to go home and get a decent night's sleep."

Headlights flicked off as a white Mercedes crept into the parking lot. Like a ghost, it moved from shadow to shadow then finally disappeared in the deep darkness cast by a magnolia. Over the recording, Quinn hummed softly as the angle of the camera shifted and focused on the license plate. As the numbers came into focus, Doran leaned forward. Even without checking his list, he knew the plate belonged to Ramsey MacLennan.

"Gotch'a," Quinn chortled.

A man stumbled out of the driver's seat, tugged his wide brimmed hat down to combat the wind and turned up the collar of his trench coat. The furtive figure peered into the gloom. Satisfied that no one could observe him, he limped toward the building, relying heavily on a brass-topped cane.

Lightening flashed.

The man lurched, twisted, knocked his hat backward and landed hard on his injured leg. Thunder boomed just as the residual light dimmed. The man shuddered and the first large drops smacked the asphalt. He hurried to the building and disappeared inside.

Quinn whistled softly. "Was that worth getting up for or what?"

"Oh, yeah." He wondered why Quinn seemed inordinately proud of the tape.

Happiness sparkled in Quinn's eyes. "This is the point when I phoned you."

The gimp let himself into the factory. Clouds skimmed across the sky, as if fleeing from the wind. Doran's eyelids felt heavy, but he fought the urge to close them and looked around the room Quinn had created for himself. A long U-shaped work area, perfect height for Quinn's wheelchair, clung to the wall on three sides of the room. Monitors and cork-boards covered the wall above the white Formica countertop. The lower half or the cork was covered with printouts and photos.

Underneath, the counter, dozens of drawers contained the tools electronic bits that Quinn used so effectively.

The speakers in Quinn's surround-sound system rumbled. Doran looked back at the screen. Another vehicle was moving through the parking lot. He sat straighter and took a sip of the mud-thick coffee.

On the screen, the dark van moved deep into the shadows. Quinn vibrated with anticipation. Doran scratched the back of his neck and wished he'd had another hour of sleep. The screen brightened and thunder boomed.

Quinn paused the tape, turned and glared at Doran. "Don't act so excited. Here I catch MacLennan sneaking into PBCO in the middle of the night – this is a company they own through a whole string of fronts, so obviously don't want themselves associated with it." His lips compressed into a thin line."

"Sorry, I was out scouting the hedges until about 2 a.m."

"If the tapes haven't rung your bell so far, this should." Quinn pressed play. On the screen, a dark van stopped. Doran feigned interest, then a diminutive passenger with a distinctive gait got out. He jerked. Coffee slopped on his wrist. He moved toward the screen for a better look. "Dear Lord," Doran exclaimed, "that's Ling!"

Quinn beamed. "I knew you'd love my film." When Quinn stopped the tape on Ling's face, they both stared at the image. The only contacts Ling made personally were with the top echelon of his operation. Had Wilting Wesley suspected or even known this backwater berg was a major entry point for Ling's poison when he transferred them here? A thousand questions circled like vultures through his mind, but he couldn't articulate a single one. Doran, still speechless, turned to Quinn. His partner gripped the denim covering his now useless legs, lifted, then let the shrunken limb fall.

Quinn's smile was sheer malice. "I want Ling more than I want my next breath. Who'd of thought your damned bullheadedness to get the MacLennans would net us the Godfather of Drugs. If it hadn't been for your insistence about them, I'd never have followed up on that lead. Okay, now that Ling and his two thug-appendages are inside, I'll fast-forward it." He restarted the tape. The time read 3:14. Doran looked watched the screen, while Quinn gloated. "Damn." Quinn hit his useless leg. "I take the tip and see Ramsey-boy arrive and think my day is made. Then Ling comes and it's like we've just won a hundred-million-dollar lottery."

Doran's racing heart stilled. "Ramsey left after 3?"

"Yeah, Ramsey." Quinn looked at him as if he had the intelligence of a rock. "Ramsey MacLennan."

His bad feeling was getting worse. "When did you see him arrive and how long did he stay?"

Quinn consulted his notes. "Arrived 11:48 p.m. left 3:48 a.m. Shit! Dev, what's wrong?"

"It wasn't Ramsey."

Quinn's mouth flattened. "Of course it was." Doran shook his head. Quinn grabbed the remote and rewound the tape.

"Trust me," Doran said. "I know for a fact that Ramsey MacLennan was sitting in the kitchen of Beja Flora two-fourteen a.m."

Quinn shook his head.

"I was talking to him and he'd been there so long that his cocoa was petrifying." Quinn rewound the tape and stopped the picture on the lightening-lit face. "Can you magnify the face?" Quinn hit several buttons as if they were the enemy. Doran suspected the hard plastic was a substitute for his skin. Slowly, the murky face took up the screen. Quinn smacked several more buttons and the black and white image began to clarity. Both men leaned toward the screen, unwilling to believe their eyes as Senator Marvin Frederickson's face materialized. "Crap," Quinn said. "What the hell was he doing there?"

"Either setting us up or setting up the MacLennans. Maybe both." Quinn looked like he was torn between murder and mayhem. To relieve suppressed energy, he propelled his wheelchair back and forth through the tight space. "Did you find it odd that he picked us to get the goods on his wife's supposed affair?" Doran asked. Quinn frowned then shrugged. "I mean, all she does is sit home night after night and drown herself in scotch."

"Your point being?"

Only one scenario made sense. "What if the senator heard about the bounties Ling has on us and has been stringing us along until he figured out a way to collect it."

That stopped Quinn's fidgety movements. They

stared at each other; possibilities and scenarios tumbled through their minds so fast that verbalizing them were impossible. "Fine," Quinn said, "lets say that Frederickson somehow meets Old Ling and hears your scalp is worth five mill. It doesn't take too much of a leap to realize the Senator is money hungry, but how would he learn about PBCO or get a key to it?"

"His supposedly estranged sister?" Doran ventured. An 'ahha' feeling tingled his spine and he had to move, so he got up and went to the coffeepot. "I got the feeling from Kelsey that there was no love lost between her and her step-mother. Assuming Jacquelyn and Winston knew what could be going down, it'd explain their sudden interest in sailing the South Pacific. Can't beat that for an alibi." Yet it didn't explain everything.

Quinn scowled. "You make sense, but there are way too many holes. Like does she hate her step kids enough to sail off and let them take all the heat? If so, she's gotta know all about the drug lab." Quinn's mouth flattened and he pressed some buttons. A moment later a printer hummed to life and began printing Frederickson's face. "What about Winston? Does he know his kids are being set up?"

Doran pursed his lips and frowned. "Beats me." He drank the last gulp of the vile coffee, then filled his cup. "What if the MacLennans learned we'd discovered their drug operation?" His fingers drummed against the Plexiglas pot as he tried to recall when he'd first heard the rumor that Frederickson, not the MacLennan's was the power behind the local drug operation.

"Frederickson versus MacLennas aside, my guess is that whoever is pulling the strings knows exactly who we are because they're part of Ling's network," Quinn said.

"Agreed."

"The question is: what's really going on."

"True, again." Doran scowled. "For the case of debate, let's assume it's still the MacLennans." Quinn raised a brow and looked at the monitor. "I know, but they're smart and I've never liked asshole politicians, so it's too easy to see him as scum."

"You mellowing toward MacLennans after spending one night under their roof?"

"No." Doran slugged down a gulp of Quinn's so-called coffee. "Since Ling is part of this, there's a good chance he's here to personally pay off whoever cashes us in."

"That's a bet I'd make, too."

Doran grabbed the still-damp print. "Okay, are the MacLennan's setting us up to get millions tax free or do they want to end our investigation?"

"Why not both? Whatever their plan, it's not working - you're Ramsey's alibi and I'm there to finger the senator."

"True, except you were supposed to do exactly what you did: identify Ramsey. I don't think that bolt of lightening or my walking into the kitchen was expected," Doran said. He frowned. "Okay, how about this: MacLennan's rumor about Frederickson is true. He's the one who contacted our firm." He scowled. "And Kelsey's lab proved to be a red herring."

"Go on," Quinn said.

"I'm trying to think this through." And he was getting more confused by the minute.

"I've always accepted the fact that the MacLennan's could simply be dups. You're the one that's been fixated on them." Quinn gestured toward the printout. "Can we assume that the good senator has known Ling for a while?"

Doran sat back down. "What are you getting at?"

"Can you think of any other reason why 'the wise one' would leave the door open?" Quinn ran the tape forward, then slowly played the portion where Frederickson went inside. He tapped the screen. "If you don't know someone and plan to meet them somewhere in the middle of the night, wouldn't you wait in the parking lot? Or at least by the door?" Doran nodded. "But he went in, acting like good ole Ling would know exactly where to go." Quinn fingered the fabric covering his thighs. "I don't want to get ambushed again. We need to weigh everything before we do anything. Frederickson virtually ordered me to go to PBCO last night."

"The question is did he know for certain you were there."

Quinn shook his head. "I was careful."

"But we can't be positive," Doran said. "What if Frederickson is the link and he's using his sister to set up the kids without Winston's knowledge? What if Frederickson wants two things: the money and an uncontested election?"

"The plates on the car were Ramsey's if the lightening and wind hadn't-"

"Exactly!" That's an incriminating bit. Either Frederickson swiped the car, switched the plate or somehow had duplicates made. For certain, Ramsey didn't loan him the vehicle. "Faking the limp was a nice touch." Doran frowned. "Do you recall which car MacLennan totaled?"

"The white Mercedes."

"That's what I thought, so he is starting to make mistakes."

"He'd have gotten away with it, if you hadn't been so determined to nail them." Quinn snickered at his own pun.

"I am not sleeping with her," Doran said. "I'm using your plan and it's working brilliantly. Oh, and Ab-n-Jen were Ramsey's wife and kid. He was whining about them dying, not talking about drugs."

Quinn raised a brow. "While trying to expose them, you seem to be exonerating them."

"I want the real pushers. I don't care who they are." He wanted the streets and school playgrounds safe for kids.

"As long as I get to even the score with Ling," Quinn said.

"Agreed."

"Okay, then. What's our next step?"

ooo

Dressed in black sweatpants, a gray T-shirt and his favorite sneakers, Doran arrived at the local high school track fifteen minutes before sunrise. He was finishing his warm-up routine when he spotted Frederickson swaggering toward the bleachers. From the bottoms of his obviously new running shoes to the spotless green sweatband at his brow, the Senator looked like an Adidas advertisement.

Doran jogged over to him. "Morning, Senator." Frederickson gave him a cursory up and down look, his expression of disgust increasing as he tabulated every article of Doran's well-worn clothing. Though the feeling was mutual, he hadn't woken up this early for a debate about attire. Doran schooled his features into a bland expression, while he adopted his most conciliatory attitude. "You're a hard man to track down."

"This is the one time during the day when my constituents don't besiege me." Frederickson began his stretches, posing as if hoping a camera could be nearby. When Doran lounged against the bleachers instead of leave, he cleared his throat. "Who told you where to find me?"

"I have my sources."

"My sources tell me you're in bed with my opposition."

"Like her brother, Ms. MacLennan had some attempts made on her life." He paused significantly.

"Surely you don't think I'm behind it."

"She hired me as a bodyguard."

The senator straightened and looked him in the eye. "The yo-yo nature of their campaign has shot me ahead in the polls," Frederickson said. "It'd take a miracle for her to win and winning is the only problem I have with the frigid bitch."

Until this moment, he'd had doubts; now, Doran knew the truth, but he still needed evidence. He gave the senator a lazy smile. "Whatever problems you have with Ms. MacLennan are irrelevant to my reason for being here." A pair of elderly joggers approached. "After all, that's not what you hired our firm to research."

Frederickson finished his stretches and began to jog in place. When everyone else was out of earshot he grinned. "Did you finally find out who Helen is boffing?" His harsh, quiet tone seemed out of sync with his friendly smile.

"In quite a hurry for that divorce, aren't you?" Doran easily matched the senator's pace. "From what little I understand about politics, something like that could be disastrous to your political future."

"Not since Bill Clinton." Frederickson's smile reminded him of a shark. "I should never have married her so soon after Bernice died. Can you believe the lousy luck I have with wives? Two died accidentally, now I'm married to a tramp."

The statement had so many inconsistencies with what they'd uncovered that Doran made a mental note to look into the circumstances of the other wives deaths. He shook his head. "The only thing Helen seems to take an interest in is Scotch." Frederickson looked ready to punch him. "As I previously told you, I believe your wife is an alcoholic and needs help."

"I suggested it." Frederickson's mouth thinned into an angry line. "She refused."

"You should insist."

The senator's glare told him to mind his own business. "I can not force her to do something against her will." Frederickson jogged toward the track.

Doran watched him for a moment. The senator was slick, but just how sharp was he? Furthermore, did Frederickson suspect that he'd been photographed entering PBCO while disguised as Ramsey MacLennan? Doran stretched the tense muscles in his neck. With Ramsey out of the senatorial race, what was his motivation for the charade? He set out at an easy loop and quickly caught up with Frederickson. "Actually," Doran said, "the reason I'm here is to ask why you were at PBCO last night."

Frederickson stopped as if struck. Doran jogged a couple paces, then turned. Face pale, the senator stared at him. "Whoever told you I had anything to do with that is lying."

The man was guilty as sin. Had he realized that his trap would come up empty and he'd lose millions? Doran clenched his hand to hold back the punch. "Based upon information you passed on."

"What information?"

Doran continued on, as if the senator hadn't spoken. "We had an operative film th-" His calm tone seemed to terrify the Senator.

"Film it?" Frederickson's voice cracked like a teenager. "You got into the building?"

Doran went to full alert, but outwardly adopted a casual stance. "No." He shrugged, as if the senator's poorly concealed terror wasn't an admission of guilt.

"Too bad." Frederickson visibly relaxed. "If I'd known your man was around, I'd have gotten him in."

"Yeah." Doran signed. "Too bad." Despite his

216

outward nonchalance, Doran went to full alert over the easy way the man made up plausible-sounding lies in a split second.

Confident of his deception, Frederickson began running in place. Doran matched him step for step, while he tried to decide how much to reveal. Side by side, they began a slow jog around the track. Frederickson kept a self-assured smile pasted on his face, as if prepared for a photo shoot. Running for Congress gained new meaning. Frustrated by the crawling pace, Doran turned around and began running backwards. Frederickson's eyes widened, and he picked up the pace, but his poster-boy smile didn't falter.

"So, why were you there?" Doran asked.

"I owe them for a smear campaign."

Doran adopted an inquisitive tone. "And you thought verifying the rumor would balance the scale?"

"Something like that." Perspiration beaded on Frederickson's upper lip and they hadn't even made a whole lap around the cinder track.

"So, what'd you find out?" This was going to be good.

"Nothing." Frederickson tried to hide the fact he was short of air. "I heard someone coming and hid in a closet."

Doran let his disappointment show. "Too bad you didn't hear what was going on."

"Yeah, too bad." Despite a flushed face and a saturated sweatband, the senator acted like neither the speed nor the lie bothered him, but the tic by his eye and shift of his gaze belied the relaxed facade.

They continued at the annoyingly slow pace for a second then a third lap. Doran could have walked faster than Frederickson ran, so he continued jogging backwards. When it became evident that Frederickson had no intention of saying more about the previous evening, Doran launched into a casual summary of the previous two-month's of surveillance they'd done for him. "In conclusion, Quinn and I think it's a waste of your money and our firm's time to continue the investigation of your wife," he finished.

"Fine. Send me the bill."

Doran inclined his head. "You're getting along pretty good." Despite his flushed face, Frederickson raised an arrogant brow in question. "On the tape, you looked like your leg was bothering you."

"Old injury. It acts up when it's damp." With that, Frederickson stumbled. Doran caught his arm. The senator yanked his arm free and glared at the bleachers. Doran glanced back in time to see a familiar head duck behind the field house. Why was Zoë Lancaster here? Was she following him? The senator faked a turned ankle and headed for the bleachers. By the time he reached his athletic bag, his limp was as pronounced and false as his story.

Though Doran remained solicitous, he found the fake limp more incriminating than anything he'd discovered about the MacLennans. After Frederickson assured him that he would be fine, Doran ran two more laps, then collected his gear. He then drifted into the bleacher's shadows, where he quietly stowed his duffel bag, then settled down to watch Frederickson continue making a big show

218

about messaging his ankle.

Doran thought back to the night he'd mistaken Zoë's arrival as a trap. Though she'd reeked of booze and Opium, how drunk had she really been? When she'd jiggled down the stairs in her skimpy attire, she'd kept insisting that she recognized him. Had she identified him as the man tampering with Kelsey's car? If so, why hadn't she made any attempt to stop him or call the police? Instead, she'd given the impression that Frederickson was as close a friend as Kelsey. He frowned and remembered Zoë's words. 'Kel believes Marv will do anything to keep his senate seat. She thinks it gives him power and money to control things and she thinks he's a drug smuggler or dealer or something. He's not. He's a good man, but her whole family hates him and they brainwashed her.' Doran messaged his temple. What if Zoë had been telling him what she figured he wanted to hear, because she somehow knew he worked for the senator? He winced at the far-fetched nature of that theory. Still, the girl had seemed sincere. Could she have been somehow brainwashed? The senator was certainly slick enough to dupe him and Quinn. What if Zoë was one of Frederickson's conduits for misinformation? What if Frederickson had been irritated with him for showing up because he had come for a clandestine meeting with his informant, not for exercise? It would certainly explain the pristine clothing and the lack of wind, which he would have expected to habitual jogger to have.

If he wasn't here to run, why was he here every morning? Doran scrutinized the other walkers and runners as they moved around the track. This would make an ideal place to pass information. Which made the fact that Zoë was here even more interesting. When Zoë had accused him of working for Frederickson, it had seemed like her allegation carried a hidden meaning.

People always suspected others of doing what they were doing.

Damn, this mess was convoluted. Of course, anything involving Ling Chen always was a tangle of lies.

If the MacLennans were innocent, he was after the wrong person.

After posturing and preening for several more minutes and giving anyone who noticed the idea he was into physical fitness, but injured, Frederickson grabbed his gear and hobbled toward his Lexus.

Unless Zoë had seen him duck under the bleachers and was avoiding the senator because she didn't want to be pegged as the mole, he could kiss the theory that Frederickson was actually at the field to rendezvous with Lancaster good-by. He watched the Lexus depart, but stayed concealed in the shadows. Doran saw movement behind the field house. He froze, ready for anything. Looking haggard as a bag woman, Zoë emerged from behind a dumpster. Eyes focused on the exit, where the senator had departed, she adjusted her too-tight tiger print jumpsuit. Doran silently moved behind her. Mouth flat, she kicked a soda can, then stumbled as her too-high heel connected with the uneven ground. As she teetered, Doran caught her elbow. She screamed yanked her arm free and whipped to face him. When she recognized him, her expression became wary and uncertain.

"Hello, Zoë. We meet again."

"You remembered, this time."

Doran glanced at the dust left by the Lexus and decided to test his theory. "And I remember the other time we met." He smiled at her and allowed his look to pass over the straining tiger print fabric. His glance ended at the fire engine red toenails encased in four-inch-high-heels. He raised his head and smiled at her. "Interesting choice of bed partners." Her guilty look spoke volumes. Doran smiled. "Especially considering where you officially spend the night when you're in town."

"You have no right to criticize."

Score one for deduction. "Valid point." Doran intensified his smile. "However, I'm not screwing one and pretending to be a friend to the other. Both employed my firm, but when I realized there could be a potential conflict of interest, my partner and I decided to drop Frederickson as a client. We'd concluded that his issues lacked substance, anyway." Whenever possible the truth was always the best.

Zoë's eyes narrowed. "The way I understand it, you're one of Marv's hired goons. Kelsey was supposed to die or at least get the message with her accident. You were there." She shook her head, but didn't look confident about her conclusions. He doubted if she was certain he'd been the one under the mustang.

"No conflict? I'd call simultaneously kill her and protect her a major conflict. Furthermore, DQ's contract with Frederickson had nothing to do with murder. Lastly, I am not his goon or anyone else's."

Her bright red lips pursed. "So what is your contract with him?"

"That's privileged information, which I can't divulge." She snorted. "Ask him. I assure you that it didn't have anything to do with you or Kelsey."

"Why should I believe you?"

"You have to believe someone. It might as well be me." Doran studied her and wondered if the trashy clothes were a mask or if Kelsey really considered someone this tasteless a friend. "Think about this: you seem to believe I was hired to kill her. I must conclude that you are referring to the way someone sabotaged her car." Zoë's eyes widened. Doran nodded in confirmation. "I met her when she crashed into me. If I'd damaged her car, why would I risk having her crash into me?"

She gave him a confused look. "That was when she banged you?"

"According to your theory, I would have known her car didn't have brakes."

"How - when did you find that out?"

"I told you, my partner and I are investigators."

"So they really are trying to murder her."

"Perhaps." Doran shrugged. "It would have been suicidal to stop in front of a car that had enough velocity to push both of us into the intersection. I am not self-destructive."

"So you didn't have someone toss the firebomb through the window, either?"

He shook his head. "Sheer luck that I saw the flash in my peripheral vision. With the line of work

I'm in, it's best to stay alert 24/7 - I never know when someone is going to want a piece of my ass or where they'll chose to take it." He gave her an embarrassed glance. "Until Kelsey told me about Ramsey's accident and all the other threats, I thought the Molotov cocktail was meant for me." Zoë studied his face. Doran pressed his point. "I acted without thinking. If I hadn't, I'd have been hurt, maybe killed. So would Kelsey and maybe even you. Saving her was pure reflex. Whoever wants Kelsey dead doesn't care who else gets hurt."

Zoë's gaze shifted to the exit the Lexus had taken. Her unstated implication was clear. Where did her loyalty lie? With the family she'd been raised in or with her lover? Doran studied the expensively vulgar outfit and knew where his bet lay.

She chewed her lower lip until her front teeth became streaked with red and her lips showed pale through the gloss. "What you're saying is that whoever this person is would just as soon kill me, too. Right?" Her look begged him to be honest. Doran nodded in agreement. "Why do they hate Kel so much? What'd she ever do?" The childish, plaintive tone sounded odd coming from Zoë.

Doran tilted his head to one side. "I was hoping you could tell me."

Zoë gave an exaggerated shrug, which shoved her artificially augmented breasts against the already straining fabric.

He glanced at his watch. "Shoot. I'm late." Zoë looked as if he'd slapped her. In case he could somehow use her in the future, he added, "I'm really sorry, but I have to leave." He fished one of DQ's cards from his pocket. "If you can think of anything that would help me protect Kelsey, call me. Okay?" She nodded. He eased a tense muscle in his spine. "I'm really beginning to hate politics."

She nodded vigorously. "Me, too. You gotta help me convince her to drop out before he kills her. Please?"

He patted her bejeweled hand and nodded.

ooo

Feet tapping to the jazz playing from the lab's speakers, Kelsey bent over the hydroponics table and, using special tweezers, carefully separated the roots of the young plants. When the weather report came on, she took off her gloves and rubbed her lower back. "What do you think, Lucky? Are you tired of keeping me company in here?" He peaked at her from under the counter, one ear straight out, the other drooping, as if he wasn't quite sure what she'd asked. The polished steel counter showed bags under her eyes. She gently pulled back the skin at the corner of her eyes, but the stress of the past two nights still showed. She let go of the slack skin and squinted at her reflection. She must have looked this bad when Devlin Doran had come into the kitchen last night, yet his eyes had glistened when he'd spotted her. Kelsey trembled with the memory of his look, and her belief that his eyes conveyed the message that he wanted to sink into her warmth and remain there forever.

She'd yearned for that hot, wet union, too. Had craved him since his heat had enfolded her after the horrible crash. Had desired him since her soul had

224

been captivated by the rhythm of his heart. Had been too ill to do anything about her yearnings and had been terrified of the intensity of her need.

Did he know how his kisses had enflamed her? Did he realize she wasn't accustomed to the feelings? Unlike Zoë, who seemed to view sex as a recreational sport or hobby, she'd always needed love and commitment.

Her stomach growled. A glance at her wristwatch confirmed that it was nearly lunchtime. If she hadn't promised Doran that she'd stay locked in, she would have gone over to the gym and exercised away the cloying tension. Instead, she tilted her head back and slowly rotated it, then she touched her chin to her chest and counted to ten. The stretch helped, but not enough because she still wanted him to touch her. Hold her. Kiss her. She sighed and wondered if Zoë's values were rubbing off on her or if she'd virtually fallen in love at first heartbeat.

Kelsey looked around her lab. Both doors were dead-bolted from the inside; there were neither cameras nor windows. Kelsey stepped out of her navy pumps and placed them near the chair, which held her navy jacket. Then she took off her lab coat, hung it up, hiked up her skirt, put her feet shoulder width apart, her arms straight out to her sides, she started the deep muscle toning routine she'd practiced for years. With a bounce of joy, Lucky sat next to her.

Hand firmly placed on her hip, she reached overhead with her opposing arm and lengthened the bunched muscles in her side. Within moments, she began to feel better. After doing fifty, she switched sides.

Strange that she'd never thought to exercise here. While, the lab lacked a shower and steam room, it had a privacy that a locker room could never hope to achieve. Not having to compare herself against tall women with perfect curves made up for a lot.

Kelsey slid out of her navy blue skirt and folded it across her jacket. Clad in pantyhose and ivory tank top, she bent over, grasped her ankles and elongated her leg muscles for a twenty count, while Lucky leaned against her shin. Five. Six. Seven. Something thudded against the connecting door to her office.

If Doran caught her like this, she'd die of embarrassment.

Kelsey straightened so fast that she felt dizzy. She darted across the lab, grabbed her skirt and scrambled into it.

Someone pounded on the door. Amber should have used the intercom to warn her. Kelsey snatched her lab coat, then a horrible thought struck her. What if Amber had been mugged and was lying unconscious in a pool of blood? Icy fingers of fear spread through Kelsey's stomach and breath caught in her throat.

Someone pounded on the door. "Kel, are you in there?" Zoë yelled.

What the heck was she doing here? Had Doran really meant everyone, when he told her not to open the door for anyone except him? Surely not.

"Hang on a minute," Kelsey called. "I'm coming."

"So you are in there."

"Where's Amber?"

"Beats me. Everyone must be at lunch."

12:08, yes, they would be gone. "How'd you get in?"

"The door was open. What'cha doing in there, playing with yourself?"

Debating if pursuing friendships with sluts, who weren't actually kin, was necessary. Kelsey bit her tongue on a remark she would have loved to make. "Why are you here?"

"I thought we could go out for lunch." Zoë's voice held a plaintive tone. Had she spoken to Martha? Learned that the truth about her paternity was known? Kelsey unlocked the door. "It's about time." Zoë strutted in on four-inch metallic gold heels. Her skin-tight black lace strapless top probably had more fabric than her black leather skirt. Black pantyhose and a wide gold belt somehow made the outfit seem briefer.

Her top and hose had been modest by comparison.

"I can't go out," Kelsey said.

"You never like spending time with me." Zoë pouted. Her fire engine red lipstick made the action appear lewd. "Everything is more important than I am. Why don't you just say you hate me and that I should leave you alone?"

Oh, the temptation, but would it be true? Kelsey sighed. "I think of you as a sister." Even now, when I know we aren't. "When we were little, we were the best of friends. I don't know what happened. Maybe we both changed when I got sent away to

227

school."

"Always the right thing ... You always say the right thing." Zoë's mouth flattened. "Did they teach you that in your fancy boarding school?" Zoë clutched the end of the hydroponics table as if she wanted to hurl it, or do something drastic.

"Zoë –"

"Don't you Zoë me."

"What is wrong?"

"Nothing." She turned toward the growing table.

Kelsey darted between Zoë and her work. "Don't lie to me." She grasped her arm. "Something is obviously wrong. Talk to me." What had gotten into her?

"It's everything." A sob shook Zoë.

Kelsey maneuvered her toward the chair. Tossing her jacket onto the counter, she helped Zoë sit. What had Martha told her? Had she just learned that she was a product of violence? Did she know that her own mother distrusted her so much that she even suspected her of murder?

Zoë wiped away her tears. "Why are you running for senate?"

Kelsey blinked at Zoë's serious expression. "Because it's the right thing to do. Marvin Frederickson is an evil man and having him in office is detrimental for everyone."

Zoë's hair whipped back and forth over her shoulders as she disagreed. "He's your uncle."

How could anyone be this dense? "Only if you want to get technical. Assuming I viewed him as family, every family has a least one black sheep. In my opinion, we MacLennans have a lot more than one, but that's another topic. Bottom line: Marvin Frederickson is not my family and voters deserve honest representation."

"Marv is honest."

Kelsey laughed at such a ludicrous thought. Zoë glared back, her look serious and defiant. "Do you know why Grandfather had him thrown out of the party?"

"Marv didn't get thrown out. He left because he couldn't stand Old Calhoun dictating to him."

"Where did you hear with that nonsense? Political advertisements?" Kelsey laughed harder, then realizing Zoë was serious, she sobered. "That's what Marvin told anyone who'd listen, but what he says and what he does are two different things." Kelsey rubbed a wrinkle and thought back to conversations she'd unintentionally overheard. "Grandfather discovered Marvin was impersonating my father."

Zoë's features contorted into a 'get real' look.

Kelsey nodded. "He got arrested while buying drugs. The DA's secretary recognized the name and called grandfather." Kelsey closed her eyes and condensed the details from several scraps of conversation and angry comments. "Grandfather was ready to wring dad's neck, but when he discovered it was Marvin he decided to have him prosecuted for drug possession, forgery and anything else he could think of."

Zoë snorted. "That never happened." Her expression proclaimed that she didn't believe a word of it.

"Only because the next day Grandmother died

and Grandfather had his stroke."

"Marv hates drugs, everyone who listens to his campaigns knows that."

Too bad that Zoë didn't know the senator well enough to watch what he did instead of listen to the propaganda he spouted. "He was a recreational user when Dad met him in college. From what I hear, he's still one."

"Then how come you haven't told that to the reporters?"

"I don't have proof, and even if I did, I wouldn't use it. I hate campaigns that turn into mud-slinging matches."

"Oh, really? Maybe you don't put it in the headlines, but you do make comments. What about the rumor that he's a pusher? Did you start that?"

"I heard that from you, but it wouldn't surprise me if it was true."

Zoë clinched her fists. "Take that back."

Kelsey shook her head. The lights went out.

Zoë screamed so loud that it hurt Kelsey's ears.

Though power losses weren't that unusual, Kelsey darted to the door and threw the deadbolt, then scooted behind the lab's center island and crouched out of sight.

Zoë continued shrieking Kelsey ground her teeth against the noise, torn between comforting her, as she had countless times while they were growing up and letting her scream herself silly and be a decoy. Kelsey held her breath, listening beneath the high-pitched screeching. Nothing, not even telltale sounds of a lock being picked.

Inch by inch, Kelsey maneuvered around the

island until she could put her ear to the door, but the only sound she heard was the toilet dripping from the tiny hole Lucky had nibbled in the plastic line.

Staying low, she moved to the main door, which connected to the greenhouse. Through the thick metal fire door, she heard the faint hum of the misters.

"Zoë, there's nothing to be afraid of."

"Someone keeps touching me. He's going to knock me senseless then rape me." Her piteous wail made Kelsey wince.

Kelsey crept to the emergency drawer and felt for a flashlight. She swiveled and trained the beam on Zoë, who was cringing and fighting off a furry paw. She dropped the beam and spotlighted Lucky.

Zoë screamed in terror.

Kelsey laid the flashlight on the counter, and then scooped up the playful rabbit. "Zoë, open your eyes and look at the horrid beastie that was attacking you." She held up Lucky, whose ears both stuck straight out from his head, as he stared at Zoë.

She gasped for air while she peered at Lucky as if she'd never seen the French lop before. "It's a bunny."

Kelsey nodded. "I'm sorry he scared you. It sounded like he brought back a horrible memory." Zoë brushed away tears. Black streaks remained on her cheeks. Kelsey wet a paper towel and began cleaning her up, like she was one of the kids in the neighborhood. "This reminds me of when we were kids."

"Like when you found that tube of magenta

lipstick stuck in the sofa and you put it on me and your favorite doll?" Kelsey nodded. "You know something? One tube of lipstick lasts a whole lot longer now days."

"That's only because we've learned it doesn't have to be an inch thick."

"I thought Mom was going to shoot me," Zoë said.

"Dad did." Kelsey chuckled. "I still have the photo."

Chapter 12

Concealed behind the banquet hall's heavy red velvet curtains, Doran surveyed the white linen covered the buffet tables and glanced over the gleaming silver braziers, which emitted a variety of aromas. Waitresses clad in mock tuxedos carryied shiny silver serving trays as they circulated through the room; some loaded with bite-size morsels, others had trays of drinks. False laughter came from one of the small groups, which had coalesced from the two-hundred-people, who'd purchased tickets for this fund-raising dinner; others milled around the room, as if being in a group was beneath them. A few clustered near the waitresses' path, as if their goal was getting their money's worth in booze from the five-hundred-dollar-a-plate meal.

The three who amused Doran the most were an older woman and a pair of artificially developed women who were using the fund-raiser as an opportunity to wear haute couture gowns and be seen in the 'right' circles. He peered around the room, wondering whose mistresses they might be. The elderly grand-dame with intricate lavender hair, bustled around the room, her purple velvet shawl trailing in her wake, as she patted arms and

233

assured everyone except the bosomy duo - that their candidate was a winner.

His attention kept coming back to Kelsey as she stood half-hidden behind the far end of the curtain behind the makeshift stage and licked a crumb from her fingers. Heat raced through his blood. Oh, to be a fleck on her finger and feel her hot, moist tongue wrap around him.

A tall, broad-shouldered woman let out a booming laugh, which temporarily hushed the others. The dapper Master of Ceremonies used the opportunity to step to the lectern and tap the microphone. As the wail reverberated through the room, all eyes turned to him. The distinguished gray haired gentleman placed his hands on top of the podium. "Thank you for coming." A scattering of polite applause and smiles circled the room. The gentleman smiled benevolently. "It's time to take our seats and hear Kelsey MacLennan's views."

A few people moved toward the tables, but the majority stayed huddled in groups. Doran studied the movements, alert for odd actions or suspicious looking people.

The Master of Ceremonies smiled. "Good, since we have plenty of time, I can tell you about my grandchildren. Nan and I have fourteen of them and they're all exceptional. He gestured to the lavender haired lady. "I believe my wife has pictures, if any of you are interested." The tempo of the flow to the table visibly increased in speed. The Master of Ceremonies winked his wife. She smiled back at him, as she tossed her shawl over a chair and settled into the adjacent one. "Does this mean none of you are interested in my photos and stories?" The false injury in his tone brought laughter. He sighed dramatically. "That must mean you're only interested in political platforms, so I'll simply have Kelsey MacLennan, granddaughter of my dear friend Calhoun and his late, lost Rose, tell you how she sees the issues." With a gesture, worthy of a circus ringleader, he brought all attention to Kelsey. Several flashes signaled that the photojournalists had arrived.

She gave the Master of Ceremonies a hundred-watt smile as she walked to the podium. Three people began applauding. Within a heartbeat, nearly the entire room was on their feet clapping for her. She stepped onto the raised platform and stood next to the lectern, hands folded and smiling as she looked out over the room. She scanned the crowd in some sort of pattern, as if she was either looking for someone in particular or making eye contact with as many people as possible.

When her wandering look came to his section of the room, he stepped out from his secluded vantage point and motioned for her to get behind the lectern. She gave him a sunny smile, but shook her head. His teeth clamped together. She'd refused to wear a Kevlar vest under her suit jacket and was making herself a prime target standing there in the open. He took a step toward her. Her radiant smile widened, then she calmly stepped behind the mammoth mahogany podium. A shiver of heat rippled through him. How could he ever have thought of this quiet woman as an ice queen?

As the prolonged applause lowered in intensity,

Kelsey took the microphone off its holder. "Thank you for your warm welcome. Normally, I begin with a joke, but since Ramsey has dropped out, and I chose to run, my grandfather assures me that's enough of a joke."

Most of the members of the audience chuckled, as they settled into their chairs, however, a table-full of women wearing power suits looked insulted by the remark. Kelsey strolled from behind the lectern, to the edge of the makeshift platform near them and gave the ladies and exaggerated wink. "Having grown up in a family that swore the man was the head of the household and thus the only one fit to run the country, at first, I doubted my ability to be your official representative in the Senate." A horsy-looking woman wearing a black trouser suit looked outraged. "Then, I realized that I wanted someone in office who will represent me and my needs; the needs of my family and my neighbors." She paused significantly. "You are all my neighbors. I want the best possible life for each and every person present and for our loved ones. I particularly want that for our children as they go forward into the uncertain future. Since Ramsey does not feel well enough to do this. I will."

"What can you do?" a heckler called.

"I'm glad you asked. For starters, I want to see what I can do to minimize the effects from NAFTA. I think we can all agree that free trade made sense when NAFTA was passed. However, since 9-11 we've realized how vulnerable our country truly is and with so much industry shipped overseas, I now see how NAFTA makes our country vulnerable."

"You gonna bring the jobs back?" a woman shouted.

"If I can, but we all know that things will never be the same as they once were and it takes more than one person to make a change for the good. Times change. People change. Technology change. And hopefully laws change."

"Is NAFTA the only thing you're interested in fixing?"

"Definitely not. I care about people and all their problems. I also care about the earth. This is the only planet we have, so we must learn to live with it in a way that keeps the land healthy." She paused and looked over the audience. "I'll give you an example. Every year during hurricane season, millions of dollars worth of real estate are ruined. I believe we need new building standards – standards that take the fury of Mother Nature into account, instead of alter building standards in the hope that when she does PMS, what we've built will survive. Instead, we humans often build things that make the situation worse."

Several people laughed. But the horsy-faced woman looked outraged and demanded, "What do you mean?"

"About PMS or how we human's make it worse?"

"Worse!"

Kelsey gestured around the auditorium. "Look how large this building is. Think about the acres of asphalt surrounding it." She paused and looked at everyone. "When it rains, where does the water go?"

"Drains," several said.

She nodded. "And the drains eventually dump the runoff in our rivers and creeks… Have you noticed how much worse the floods get every year?" Murmurs of agreement swelled. "Every building. Every parking lot. Every road… it all covers land, which was once permeable. When we humans alter the land, we change it and make the flooding worse. I don't know how we could build in the future to change this, but I do know we have to find a way." Several seated guests leaned forward, intent to hear her ideas. The horsy-looking woman's expression eased from outrage to grudging consideration.

Doran scanned the room for anyone who wasn't listening.

"Too many citizens don't exercise their vote, then wonder why they have lost control of our government." Kelsey paused. "I firmly believe that lobbyists for major corporations control many of our elected officials and if I'm elected, I vow to you that I will not become one of them." Several people clapped.

When the applause died, she smiled. "While I feel that many of the laws have been made to protect us, I also feel that too many laws take away our rights as individuals. Do we really need legislation to replace common sense?"

"No!" a woman shouted.

Kelsey smiled at her. "I'm glad someone agrees with me." She scanned the audience. "I believe that humans are intelligent, but much of the recent legislation takes too much choice from the average individual. I would like to change that trend. If given the chance, I want to return the voice of the people to the Senate."

Another ovation. She stood at the front edge of the platform, making herself an easy target. If she didn't get behind the safety of that lectern, he was going to drag her back there. As if reading his mind, she smiled at him.

"Today, a large percentage of our elected leaders are lawyers." One brazen reporter held a second microphone toward her. "Another large percentage had careers with the insurance industry. Do any of us wonder why such a large percentage of the legislation that gets passed favors the insurance industry and encourages people to file ridiculous law suits?" People shifted to look at each other. "A few days ago, a friend stated that he was trying to understand how the world works." She moved behind the podium and picked up her notes. "I quote, 'If a man cuts his finger off while slicing salami at work, he blames the restaurant. If you smoke three packs a day for 40 years and die of lung cancer, your family blames the tobacco company. If your neighbor crashes into a tree while driving home drunk, he blames the bartender. If your grandchildren are brats without manners, you blame television. If a deranged madman shoots your friend, you blame the gun manufacturer. And if a crazed person breaks into the cockpit and tries to kill the pilot at 35,000 feet, and the passengers kill him instead, the mother of the deceased blames the airline'." She paused and looked over her audience. "Is this the kind of world we want to pass on to the next generation?"

There was a chorus of dissent.

"I didn't think so. That is why, when Ramsey felt that he could not properly represent you, due to his health, I knew it was time to follow my family's tradition and run for office." Several people clapped. She nodded to them, as she came back to the front of the stage. "I've come to believe that now is the time for mothers and future mothers to take up their share of the burden."

Kelsey would make a damn fine mother. Desire to begin such a tantalizing process intensified into rigidity. Doran's hands clenched as he forced the thought away.

The businesswomen stood and gave Kelsey a standing ovation. Red tinged her cheeks and she mouthed 'thank you'. People at several other tables stood and clapped. Then more and more applauded, until noise echoed through the room. If someone had fired a gun, the report would be lost in the clamor. Kelsey simply stood on the edge of the dais, microphone in hand and smiled at each and every person, as if no one had ever considered killing her.

Doran's jaws clenched. When she glanced at him, he gestured toward the lectern and mouthed, "It's impossible to protect you, when you refuse to do anything sensible to shield yourself." She wrinkled her nose at him in a playful fashion that conjured up romps between silken sheets, before she moved behind the podium's marginal safety, with a sensual grace that left him rock hard.

When the clamor subsided, Kelsey finished her speech making short, insightful and sincere points. During the following question and answer session, Doran became convinced that Kelsey was pursuing the office because she felt it was the best way to make her corner of the world a better place. Since getting to know the real woman, instead of the one he'd created from his interpretation of rumors, gossip and misinterpretations, it felt as if his world had been turned upside down and morphed into a constant hard on.

Later, as they walked down Beja Flora's shadowed hall, heading to the elevator, Kelsey sighed. "I can't believe how well it went tonight. Three standing ovations!" Her sigh sounded like an aphrodisiac and he was grateful that he'd worn a jacket that concealed more than the bulge of his handgun.

Amazed by the positive acceptance and desperate to think with the head on his shoulders, Doran chuckled. " People don't pay hundreds of bucks a plate to boo."

She gave him an odd look. "You do have a unique perspective."

"Were you serious about wanting to push for legislation that made elected officials subject to the laws they passed?"

"Absolutely. I'll give you an example. Airline pilots and mechanics have to take random urine tests that ascertain if there are drugs or alcohol in their system. This legislation went through because people could get hurt if they were impaired while performing their job." Doran nodded in agreement.

"I believe that a legislator is equally liable when they cast their vote and they should also be subject to such a test."

"You'd accept that?" he asked.

"I honestly believe big responsibility comes with a person giving as much as they ask of everyone else."

"Valid point," he conceded. "Can I ask another question?"

"Certainly."

"How come so many of your examples deal with the airlines?"

She chuckled. "That would be my opinionated cousin's fault. Kyle is an FAA inspector and is always telling me what's wrong." As they passed the den, a loud, angry baritone voice shouted something indistinguishable. Next, a soft placating male spoke. Kelsey stopped and stared at the door, a look of indecision on her face. Then, she raised her chin and opened the door wide enough to see a slice of navy and yellow striped chintz-covered sofa.

"You need to calm down." Doran recognized Ramsey's voice. "This isn't the end of the world."

"Boy, you're nothing but a lily-livered wimp."

Kelsey touched his arm and leaned close to him. "You're hearing the great Calhoun MacLennan." Each tiny sarcastic breath tickled his ear and raised his pulse. "My grandfather is the king of chauvinists." Her expression mixed irritation with love.

"It's not worth the loss," Ramsey said.

"That's no excuse, boy."

"I meant it as an explanation."

Calhoun snorted with contempt. "That's just a long word for excuse." Something made a dull thump. "I might have known you'd turn out to be as big a disappointment to this family as your father." Doran blinked in surprise. He'd always assumed the MacLennans had a strong familial alliance, yet Calhoun had virtually spat out the term 'your father'. "Of course the pansy is hiding in the middle of some ocean with his two-bit wife," Calhoun added.

There was a long pause. "I'll have you know that I'm proud to be like my father." It sounded like Ramsey's teeth were clenched.

"Winston is nothing but a lily-livered wimp, who makes his money at other's expense." Something thudded twice.

"Whereas your business – politics - was far superior because you earned your fortune at the voters expense." Ramsey's thinly veiled scorn deepened the color of Kelsey's cheeks.

"I never knew he felt like that," she whispered. "If I had, I would never have pushed him." Doran patted the fingers, which clutched his arm and tried to ignore the need throbbing a few inches lower.

"That's enough of your lip, boy." There was a loud crack, which sounded like a whip.

Kelsey jumped, colliding with his side. Reflexively, he grabbed her. Before he could fully appreciate how good it felt to have her flat against him, she shoved his hands away and rushed into the room.

Leaves, broken stems, shards of glass, and white

roses were spread in a dripping arc across the room. Ramsey's expression was a mixture of displeasure and relief as Kelsey rushed over to him. "Are you okay?" she asked. He nodded, then stiffly hunkered down and began picking up shards of glass.

Doran took a step after her, but stopped, when a gaunt, bald man, brandished a cane at him. The old man's eyes looked insane, as he glared at him, and the vigorous flailing movement of the scared mahogany cane could topple the old guy any second. As if fate had read his mind, Calhoun pitched sideways, Doran jumped to catch him, but the old man grabbed onto the fireplace mantle and adverted catastrophe. Without missing a beat, the old man focused on him and waved the brass-toped mahogany as if it were a samurai sword.

As long as he was the focus the old codger's wrath, Kelsey was safe. Doran moved slowly away from her, while keeping the old man's attention centered on him. Old press photos depicted Calhoun as a broad shouldered dominating man with a confident stance and rugged dark looks. Journalists lauded him as humorous, but fair. In reality, he looked pathetic. The stroke Calhoun had suffered a few years before might explain the absence of fifty or so pounds and a misplaced toupee could account for the missing hair, but it couldn't justify the wild eyed rage that burned in Calhoun's gaze.

When Doran got close to the side of the room, he stood still, the old man peered around the room and settled on Kelsey, who was collecting battered blooms. "You!" Calhoun's spittle landed on the damp rug near Kelsey. "What in the samhell do you think you're doing butting into Ramsey's business?" She ignored her grandfather. The cane whacked the sofa's arm. Though Doran leaped forward, Kelsey continued to act as if nothing odd was going on. Doran paused an arm's length from the old man, muscles ready to grab him, if the situation warranted it. "It was bad enough when you set yourself up as his representative," Calhoun snarled. Spittle trickled from the corner of his mouth. "But dammit all, girl, it's one thing to help while a man is laid up, but to take over the entire election is pure bull!" Calhoun grabbed a pewter frame from the mantle and hurled it at Kelsey. She ducked, but continued picking up flowers. The photograph hit the back of the navy and yellow striped wing chair and plopped undamaged onto the seat.

"I should give you the spanking your wimp of a father was always too sissy to give you." Calhoun flourished his cane, but quickly grabbed the mantle to steady himself. His surly tone lowered and his knuckles turned white on the brass knob. "Your penis envy has needed straightening out for years."

Doran's suspicion that he'd misjudged Kelsey deepened to guilty proportions. He cleared his throat. Kelsey furtively signaled him to back off, but he pretended not to notice. "Let me get this right," Doran said, "a MacLennan was only a MacLennan if there is testosterone involved."

"Dammed straight," Calhoun crowed. "I like you boy, you see things right."

Moment by moment, it was becoming highly

improbable that Kelsey was doing anything more than running for office, which had been his suspicion since viewing Quinn's tape. Still, if there was a chance Beja Flora's security protected more than a senile old man, he had to know for certain.

Calhoun leaned on his cane and took a wavering step toward Kelsey. Then he planted his feet wide apart and he raised his cane. Doran moved between them. "Sir, if you so much as touch a hair on her head, you will suffer the consequences."

"Who the samhell are you?"

"Devlin Doran."

Calhoun's eyes glinted with an insane sparkle and he raised his cane as if to swat him out of the way. "Well you listen to me, boy, you are in my house, and as far as I'm concerned, you're a trespasser. One I'd be happy to shoot if'n you wasn't so smart about women." Despite age, infirmity, and wobbly legs, the man's tone sounded intimidating. "So's I guess I jest need to thump you."

When Doran simply stood firm, Calhoun's unfocused gaze became uncertain. Kelsey stood up and gently placed her hand on the old man's biceps. "Grandfather, you can't hit Devlin. He's a guest here." She placed her other hand on Devlin, squeezed his arm and smiled up at him, as if there wasn't any danger within miles. "You must pardon my grandfather, he doesn't think women belong anywhere but in bed or serving the master some other way, like cooking."

Despite a shudder of agreement from his manhood, Doran looked over her head at the men in her life and raised an eyebrow.

Ramsey rose clumsily and leaned heavily on his own brass-topped cane. Ignoring his grandfather, he offered his hand. "Good to see you, again." Calhoun thumped his cane with frustration. Civilities over, Ramsey tilted his head toward his grandfather. "Our grandfather, Calhoun MacLennan."

Kelsey faced the old man. "One of these days you'll learn that women have lots of talents."

Calhoun snorted with disdain. "I've lived seventy-nine years. Tell me that when you have some age on you." He whacked the coffee table for emphasis. "The world was ruined when they gave women the right to vote. Ruined1" His voice crackled with emotion. "Look what you bleeding heart women have done to our country. Food stamps. Welfare. God made the damned poor; they're a natural part of our economy and should be left poor."

Kelsey and Ramsey shared a pained glance. Obviously this was something they heard a lot. Doran raised a brow and tried to reconcile everything he'd read about the esteemed senator with the intolerant man in front of him.

Kelsey looked up at him. One corner of her lips twitched upward. "The 19th amendment ruined our country." Eyes sparkling with mischief, she winked.

"Damned right," Calhoun roared as he raised his fist and shook it at a photo on the mantle. The gesture made him tip backward. In what appeared to be a practiced movement, Ramsey caught his arm.

Before Doran distinguished who the picture depicted, a motion near the door caught his attention. Martha dressed in a sedate navy dress and modest strand of pearls entered. When her attention focused on Calhoun, her mouth flattened with disapproval. "There you are," Martha said. When Calhoun looked her way, she smiled, but warmth never reached her eyes. "I've been looking all over for you. I've got our Scrabble game set up in your sitting room."

Calhoun quit flailing his cane and preened like a dandy. "That what you call it, woman?" He raised a bristly brow. "Scrabble?" Calhoun laughed, but quickly became short of breath.

Kelsey rolled her eyes to heaven as she scooted out the door, her arms full of broken blooms. With a groan, Ramsey hunkered back down to continue cleaning up the glass shards; Doran squatted to assist him. Ramsey sighed. "Damn shame to lose this old vase."

Martha stepped around the mess, gently took Calhoun's cane in her left hand, and clasped his arm with her right. Though the touch looked friendly, Doran knew just how quickly the hold could turn painful, if the subject tried to wander. He suspected Martha knew the possibilities, too. "Yes," Martha said. "Tonight we'll call it Scrabble." She patted Calhoun's stringy biceps and allowed him to escort her out of the room.

Kelsey returned with towels. As she mopped up, she looked at him. "I apologize for grandfather." Embarrassment colored her face and tone. "He hasn't been the same since his stroke."

Ramsey snorted. "Calhoun has always been a chauvinist. An extremist. A diehard. A drama king. A bigot. Take your pick, they all fit." His tone indicated that he didn't want any of those definitions to apply to himself.

Kelsey sighed and nodded. "True, but I don't think he ever got over grandmother's death or finding out his fourteen-carat protégée was nothing but a worm."

Doran felt the tiny hairs at his nape stand at attention and he hoped they would continue with the subject of the political differences between Marvin Frederickson and Calhoun, which had been alluded to, but never detailed.

"This has been one hell of a week," Ramsey said.

While he figured out a way to direct the conversation into more relevant areas, Doran played ignorant. "So, you're father is out of town on business?"

Ramsey gave a half smile. "Dad's life's ambition is avoiding grandfather."

He could understand why. Doran and Kelsey bent to pick up the last bits of glass. For the first time, since entering the room, Doran heard the soft strains of a Spanish guitar playing in the background. An upward glance located the sounds' source at the wooden dog heads, which jutted from the ornate molding separating wall and ceiling.

Ramsey stretched his back, white lines of pain near his mouth. Finally, he picked up the photograph and replaced it on the mantle.

"Father and Jacqueline are circumnavigating the

world," Kelsey said. "It's their way of dealing with our family problems."

Doran frowned. "Then who is handling the business your grandfather mentioned?" He looked at Ramsey. "You?"

"There isn't one." Doran raised a brow. Ramsey shrugged. "When dad got wind of NAFTA, he knew our textile plants would have more problems than they were worth, so he sold out and retired."

"But they do live here," Doran said, as he pointed to the floor.

Kelsey shook her head as she put the last of the ruined vase in the wastebasket. "Father and Jacqueline moved onto the boat just after grandma died. Without her as a buffer, I don't think my father could stand staying under the same roof."

Doran moved over to the mantle and looked at the grainy black and white antiquated print that had outraged Calhoun. Crowds lined a city street as women paraded past. A white-suited woman in the foreground carried the American flag. Behind her, two more women carried a banner proclaiming 'President Wilson declares this is the time to support suffrage'.

Kelsey pointed to the white-suited woman. "That was Grandma Rose's mother. I don't think my grandfather would have married her if he'd known his mother-in-law was such a heretic."

Doran glanced from Kelsey to her great-grandmother. "I can see the family resemblance."

"Thanks." Warmth infused Kelsey's eyes.

Ramsey uttered a loud groan. "Do not let my sister's polite southern belle mask fool you. Kelsey not only looks like Great-grandmother Myrtle, she's a feminist to the core."

"And proud of it." Kelsey gave a decisive nod, then stepped around the wet area and settled regally on the yellow and navy striped chair.

Doran sat down on the sofa. As Ramsey leaned back against the cushions of the opposite sofa and he winked at Doran. "Know what I think? I think that if my sister had realized she'd get a shot at the White House by having me out of the way, she'd have slashed my brake lines herself."

"Rams!" Kelsey sprang half out of the chair before she realized her brother was baiting her.

Ramsey barely concealed his delight as he kept his focus centered on Doran. "She acts like I'm lying, but she has Great-grandmother Myrtle on a pedestal."

Kelsey shook her head, then when neither of them did more than watch her out of the corner of their eyes, she sighed and slumped back into the chair.

"Her real goal is following in her shoes," Ramsey said.

"I could do worse," Kelsey said.

Ramsey got up and limped over to her chair. Awkwardly, he bent down and patted her shoulder. "Yeah, you could." A devilish gleam lit his eyes and he moved out of her reach. "Or you could be a shallow trophy like Jacqueline."

Kelsey's expression turned sour. "I have to live with myself all the time."

"Or you could spend your life biting your tongue, like Grandma Rose."

She smoothed her skirt, then raised an elegant brow as she looked at her brother. "I only have to live with you," she shot Doran a look designed to include him, then turned back to Ramsey, "until I win this election or you move back to your own house."

Doran looked at Ramsey. "You don't normally live here?"

Ramsey shook his head. "This is the last place where I remember my wife and daughter alive and well." He swallowed.

"Funny how we always used to hate the mandatory Sunday dinner." Kelsey stared at the knotted fingers in her lap. "We hated coming here." She shook her head. "Now, we're choosing to live here."

Ramsey nodded. "Amazing how circumstances have a way of changing one's perspective."

Yes, wasn't it? Doran had been undergoing quite a bit of that himself.

Chapter 13

Though some of the evening's sheen had dissipated while she'd listened to her grandfather rant at Ramsey, an hour of cozy conversation and teasing with Doran and Rams had restored her buoyant mood. Amazingly Doran seemed to fit in with her crazy family and enjoy them. At least, he had felt comfortable enough to take off his tie and unbutton the top 2 buttons of his shirt. As the three waited for the elevator, Kelsey stood between the men; one hand tucked into the crook of Ramsey's arm, the other in Doran's.

Doran reminded her of the thread-bare jeans she'd had since high-school; the jeans she still wore when she wanted comfort; the jeans she'd dug out of the trash four times after Martha had thrown them out; the jeans that she packed first, no matter where she was going.

It was hard to believe that she'd only know Devlin Doran for a few days. Doran's gaze centered on the closed elevator door, but his expression looked perplexed. She squeezed his rock-solid biceps. "What are you so serious about?' she asked.

He looked down at her and the corners of his lips twitched. "I was trying to figure out why I was under the impression your family owned PBCO."

"PBCO?" Ramsey looked as puzzled as she felt. "The poultry processing plant?" His tone mixed doubt with amusement. Doran nodded. Ramsey chuckled and shook his head. "Who told you that?" Doran made a gesture with his hand indicating that either it didn't matter or he didn't recall. "If our name was linked to PBCO, it must have been because grandfather tried to shut it down." Ramsey's mouth turned down. "Unfortunately, he had his stroke, and never did get the damned factory regulated, so it's still a major polluter." His forehead furrowed. "The EPA is constantly after them."

Kelsey wrinkled her nose and looked up at Doran. "Have you ever smelled it? Flocks of vultures are always perched on its roof." She rolled her eyes heavenward for emphasis. "The stink can knock you over a mile away." Her expression turned serious, "Worse, the run off has tainted Kramer creek."

The elevator doors slid open. Ramsey pulled free of her grasp and stepped aboard, but Doran stepped into the mahogany-lined space arm in arm with her, his warmth enfolded her. For the first time in her life, she didn't shiver as the silent doors closed and the floor pushed upward.

When the doors opened to reveal the upstairs' hallway, Doran put his hand over hers and patted it in a preoccupied manner as he escorted her to her room. He tripped on the fringe of a long oriental carpet runner and did a quick two-step to regain his balance, but he never let her go. Until she'd gotten used to that blamed rug, it had done the same thing to her. Kelsey smiled. "You're a good dancer."

He grinned. "That wasn't dancing." He pulled her into his arms and waltzed her toward her bedroom door. "This is dancing." His heat surrounded her and desire blazed in his eyes. Kelsey melted against him, wrapping her arms around him, willing for Devlin Doran to lead her anywhere he desired.

He abruptly stopped outside her bedroom door. Reluctant to end the evening, and weak kneed from the closeness, Kelsey opened the door to her room. She looked up at Doran, hoping for a kiss, but his attention centered on the cornice boards, as if he'd rather look at anything but her. A lump of misery choked her. Her hand dropped from Doran's arm, but he didn't notice. Why did men always prefer Zoë? Why did she always fall for the wrong guy? Of course, to him, this was just a job and as soon as she locked her door, he was free of her. Tears burned. Before they burned trails down her cheeks, Kelsey slipped into her room.

Doran followed her and closed the door. Kelsey's heart leaped with excitement, but his somber expression made romance seem doubtful. So what else was new? What was it about her that put men off? Kelsey adopted a neutral tone. "What's eating you?"

He inhaled deeply, then let out a long breath. "Nothing."

And orchids sang opera. "Surely you don't

expect me to believe that." His raised brow indicated that he had anticipated just that. She looked down at the floor. "Devlin, I was teasing you. You're always so coordinated and watchful. I've never seen you so, so, so-"

"Clumsy?" He started to grin. "Thoughtful?" Kelsey nodded. Doran rubbed the back of his neck. "I can't quit thinking about something you said in relation to your grandfather about the PBCO. mess that your grandfather tried to shut it down."

They were alone in her bedroom and he wanted to talk about stinking pollution instead of engage in romance? Misery expanded within her. She went to the window and looked out at the moon-drenched lawn. "That's ancient history." The lump in her throat made her voice tight. She wished she were anywhere but here. Her attention settled on the screened gazebo in the center of the rose garden.

"Maybe." His hands settled on her shoulders. "Maybe not." Gently, he turned her to face him, then his thumb caressed her neck. Shivers of desire radiated up and down her body, making it difficult to think of anything other than unbuttoning his black silk shirt and running her hands over his flesh with the same tenderness he was giving her. "Would you mind telling me about how your grandmother died and when your grandfather had his stroke?"

She blinked several times. He wanted to talk about death and illness? Now? Here? "Why?"

Doran looked up at the ceiling and sighed, then he hunkered down. If he just leaned forward a few inches, their lips would touch. "There are drugs that can create those symptoms."

Kelsey focused on his meaning and tried to ignore the close proximity of her bed. "Surely, you don't think–"

"Actually, only suspect." A new type of lump burgeoned in her throat and a tear fell. He groaned and hugged her tight. The tension in his arms shouted of shared frustration. "Right now," he murmured, "I'm not sure what I think about anything." His male scent enveloped her. Kelsey wrapped her arms around his trim waist and hugged him back. "I knew a lot more last week than I do today." He rested his chin on the top of her head and seemed to focus on something very far away. Kelsey snuggled against him, reveling in the warmth and security of his embrace. Doran sighed. "The more I learn, the less I seem to know."

His heart beat strong and steady against her cheek. His heart rate increased. Bliss bubbled within her. When was the last time something had felt so right?

Doran's hands traced hot ripples of pleasure up and down her spine. Then he nudged her face up and kissed her cheek. Unlike his previous kisses, this was gentle and polite; the sort of kiss a parent would give a child as they put it to bed.

It was the last sort of kiss she wanted. Kelsey slid her hands under his dark jacket and ran them over the sleek surface of his silk shirt. Then, she stood on tiptoe and traced his lips with the tip of her tongue. He groaned and kissed her with the passion she'd dreamed of. Warmth permeated the thin fabric. Doran's arms tightened and heat surged through Kelsey's body.

She needed to touch Devlin Doran's flesh. Kelsey tugged his shirttail free from his slacks. A moment later, his big hands traced the skin of her back.

Kelsey pressed against him harder. His desire was obvious. Doran thrust his tongue in her mouth. Burning with hunger, Kelsey kneaded his body with shocking liberty. Her stifling jacket dropped away. A moment later, her skirt slithered over her hips to puddle on the floor. She moaned and tried to undo the buttons of his shirt. The fabric fought her like it was liquid silk protecting his integrity.

She'd never wanted anything as much as she wanted Devlin Doran.

Something vibrated against her breast.

Doran groaned and tore his mouth free. With a viciousness that nearly tore the inside pocket from his jacket, he yanked a cellular phone free. Instead of turning it off, he pressed the talk button and turned his back to her.

She hadn't felt this rejected since she'd come home and found Zoë in bed with her fiancée.

ooo

Doran took a moment to marshal his thoughts and recenter before he pressed talk. "Yes?"

"Bad timing, huh?" Quinn sounded amused.

"The worst possible." Also, the best: if Quinn hadn't phoned, he'd have taken Kelsey right there in front of the window and the cameras.

Quinn guffawed. "Something tells me that I'd like a ringside seat." Right alongside any guards who'd noticed the show. Could he have chosen a more public place for a seduction? But then he hadn't chosen it, Kelsey had.

"Surely you didn't phone to discuss your preference in entertainment."

"No." Papers crackled in his ear. Doran looked out the window to see if they had attracted an audience. Instead, he saw the reflection of Kelsey shutting the bathroom door. Quinn made a triumphant sound. "I've been digging up old, dirty laundry about Lancaster. Do you know who her daddy is?"

"You phoned to ask me a stupid, irrelevant question like that?"

"Perhaps not completely significant, but it certainly makes for an interesting footnote.

"Fine, I'll bite. Who is daddy?"

"While I'd have bet either Winston or Calhoun donated the sperm," Quinn paused dramatically, "Marvin Frederickson is listed on the birth certificate."

Kelsey emerged from the bathroom; a shapeless chenille robe covered her from chin to toe. From the look of her expression, she'd realized how close they'd come to doing something totally stupid and was furious at allowing unpedigreed swine like him to touch her. He wished he could get over the need for her as easily as she'd obviously gotten over any desire she'd felt for him.

Doran gritted his teeth and focused on why Quinn would view Zoë's paternity as pertinent enough to phone after midnight. "I needed this information because?"

"Martha and Zoë seem to be around for all major

MacLennan events." Quinn paused for effect; it was an annoying habit, particularly now, when Kelsey obviously wanted him to leave. "Dev, I haven't walked since Pia Chan's bullet pulverized my spinal column. Females are vicious. Keep an eye on the Lancasters and watch your back."

"Always have." Except that time with Pia. "Mind your own back and be vigilant about our clever friend."

"I've already ordered a rearview mirror for my wheels." It was an old joke, but Doran laughed anyway.

Kelsey folded her arms her across stomach, her expression looked angry. Now was not the time to share the revelation that Kelsey and Ramsey seemed to think the company was only a pollution problem.

Kelsey's foot began tapping. "Thanks, pal," Doran said. "I owe you." He clicked off the phone and put it back in his pocket.

Kelsey gestured to his pocket. "What was that all about?"

"Some crucial information my partner dug up on another case." Her mouth flattened. Doran wished he didn't still want her. "I was out of line. I'm here to protect you, not –" At a loss for words, he sighed and threw up his hands.

Kelsey looked somewhat mollified. "I started it." She looked at the floor and chewed her lower lip, then straightened and looked him in the eye. "The more I know you, the more I," she paused, "like you."

Doran smiled. "That's progress, huh?" In an

instant, her expression turned hostile. "Well, I call it progress." He felt sick to his stomach. "The threat of a kiss used to terrify you."

"Only because I'm attracted to you," she mumbled while staring at her toes.

He sat down hard on the window seat, as her meaning sank in and he realized how much she disliked what she felt. Doran knew he should be thrilled, but now that he'd gotten to know the real flesh and blood woman, instead of information bits from a file, he didn't want to hurt her in any way. If he were honest with himself, he'd admit that his original plan to seduce her had been based on lust from the start. He sighed.

She looked up, fury making her mouth flat. "The proper response is 'I'm attracted to you, too.'" Her tone sounded bitter.

"And I am. That's the problem."

Kelsey's eyes widened. "What to you mean?"

Doran gestured to the room, then pointed dramatically behind him to the moonlit window. "You felt so good in my arms, that I forgot where we were." He pressed his fingers to his temples. "What kind of bodyguard seduces his employer right in front of a damned window where any sniper worth his salt could make the shot?"

She paled.

Doran raked his fingers through his hair. "You got to me the first time I saw you. Then, when I held you, after I got you out of the car, I wanted you so much that it hurt." He scowled at that admission. "I know it's vulgar, since you were so hurt, but you smelled so good and felt so right in my arms." He swallowed. "I knew I shouldn't take this job." He grimaced. "I knew emotional involvement and business didn't mix." Kelsey took his hand in hers. He twined his fingers with hers and looked deep into her eyes. "I endangered you. If it hadn't been for Quinn's call." Doran shook his head. "I thought I could handle the attraction because there's something about this house that makes me feel like I'm a fish in a tank, but I start thinking about how soft your skin is and-" He clamped his jaws together before he could blurt out any more truths.

She made a sweeping gesture of the room. "All the time I was growing up, I felt like the walls had eyes and ears. I couldn't wait to get out of here. You have no idea how hard it was for me to move back."

"I didn't realize."

Kelsey squeezed his hand. "Don't blame yourself." Her lopsided grin was bittersweet. "Haunted though this house feels, it's safe."

Doran leaned close and whispered into her ear. "I don't think you have a ghost, I think there are hidden cameras in the rooms." She leaned back to peer at the walls. Doran wrapped his arms around her and gave her a quick closed mouth kiss, then lips a hair's breadth from his, he whispered, "My partner knows more about this. Can I have him come out here?"

"Why?" Her breath washed over his, like a hot caress.

"Because when I make love to you, I don't want an audience. Quinn can make certain all the wires to this room fry. He can also find out who is watching, and if there are tapes."

Kelsey gave a startled gasp, then rose and gave him a passionate kiss that tested every bit of his resolve. Doran groaned. Kelsey chuckled, then licked his ear and whispered, "Have him come tomorrow. I'll tell the guards he's okay."

"You drive a hard bargain."

She plucked the phone from his pocket and held it toward him. Doran punched in the code. Quinn answered before the first ring finished. "Hey, pal, could you bring the van out to Beja Flora tomorrow and check out their surveillance system?" Doran hugged Kelsey against his chest. "Ms. MacLennan will make sure they let you in."

"You serious?"

"Definitely." Doran gave Kelsey a thumbs up.

"Damn. You Irish have all the luck." He hoped his partner had this prediction correct.

ooo

Quinn aimed the remote at the drapery rod and pressed a button. The office's ivory, room-darkening curtains moved to block the late afternoon heat. Doran settled onto the stiff-backed office chair, swallowed Quinn's syrupy version of coffee and glance around the long U-shaped work area, which was utilitarian and technology oriented. Blank monitors and messy cork-boards hovered above the tidy white countertop. Quinn's space couldn't be more different from his own peaceful sanctuary.

Quinn flipped open the arm of his wheelchair, plucked out a tiny thumbdrive, then popped it into a black box. The surround-sound system sputtered and numbers swirled as Quinn scanned through the data. Doran glanced at the bulletin board to see if any reports had returned. Abruptly, a vaguely familiar voice came over the speakers, "I never liked Marvin Frederickson, but Calhoun treated him like the son he'd always wanted. So I tolerated him." The tone barely concealed the woman's disdain.

Doran raised a brow. "Ms. Martha Lancaster," Quinn said. He winked. "Patience, Dev. It gets better."

"A few days before thanksgiving, while Calhoun was still in D.C., Marvin brought by a bottle of wild turkey." Martha's tone sounded decidedly disapproving. "Wild turkey was Calhoun's favorite. I put it on the bar." Martha sniffed. "That night, Rose – that was Calhoun's wife was feeling a might poorly and she had a drink. She died of a heart attack, shortly after." A sob emanated from the speakers. "If I'd known she was that ill, I would have insisted on a doctor."

Doran leaned forward and turned off the tape.

"You had me come in to listen to Martha cry? The woman looks reserved, but she's a bloody fountain. If I want to listen to her bawl and whine, I don't need to come here to do it."

"Have you ever listened to what she's actually saying or do you turn your ears off when the waterworks start?" What a stupid question, of course he shut out the caterwauling. Quinn, who knew him well, grinned. "Don't listen to the whiny tone; listen to what she's saying. I spent most of last nigh verifying her complaints." Quinn restarted the tape.

Sobs shuddered around them. Doran gritted his teeth. This had better be worth the aggravation.

"I didn't think anything of it." Martha blew her nose. "I thought it was just her age. And she had been feeling poorly."

"And now?" Quinn sounded like a concerned friend.

"Oh, dear Lord," Martha wailed, "I should have known." Doran's molars clenched at the unholy sound.

"Known what?" Quinn's taped voice asked the question Doran wanted answered. "Known that the lady was ill?"

"That it was poisoned." Doran sat straighter. Quinn grinned and leaned back in his wheelchair. "Ms. Rose died without ever regaining consciousness."

"You believe the whisky was deliberately poisoned?"

He'd never realized how gentle Quinn's interrogations were.

"Not right away."

"When?" Quinn sounded more like he was whispering sweet nothings to the woman than garnering information.

"Later." Martha blew her nose. Doran grimaced. "When Calhoun had a drink. Within an hour he had a stroke." If Martha Lancaster cried much harder, she'd have a stroke, too. "That's when I knew he'd played me for a simpleton. He was wearing driving gloves when he handed me the bottle, but my fingerprints were all over the bottle it because I'd put it on the bar. I'd poured Ms. Rose's drink. If anyone investigated, they'd only find my prints."

"Dear Lady, what did you do?"

"I poured the contents down the drain and broke the bottle into tiny pieces. I thought someone would think I killed them, but I didn't." The tape squeaked and hissed. He envisioned Martha throwing herself on Quinn and sobbing all over his shirt. "I would never do something like that."

Quinn turned off the tape, and gave him an expectant look. "Well, what do you think?"

"That I hope she wasn't wearing makeup when she cried all over you." Doran raised a brow. "Or couldn't she come up with real tears, just lots of noise?" Quinn raised his eyes to the ceiling and shook his head. "Don't tell me you buy her story," Doran exclaimed. "What's her motive for telling you, a complete stranger?"

"I played on her sympathies and loyalties, and inspired her confidence. Martha is a very lonely woman, and she needed to absolve her guilt."

"She could confess to a priest. They're sworn to silence." Doran slugged down the last of the muddy brew, then surged to his feet and began pacing. "I'd bet Martha heard something about our contract with the senator."

"What's her motivation?"

Doran shrugged. "Possibly propagating rumors of past murder and attempted murder to taint the election against Frederickson. Possibly just putting you off balance."

"Could be." Quinn thought for a moment. "But

Zoë is Good Ole Marvin's kid. He and Martha could still be close."

"You think having his bastard makes her loyal to him?"

"More likely the opposite, since he never married her between his other wives. But then, I have no idea what sort of arrangement they do have."

Doran frowned. "Zoë seems to hang around him a lot." Knowing that the man was her father dashed his mistress theory. "So, when it comes to the election, who are Martha and Zoë committed to?"

"Themselves." Quinn fiddled with the remote. "My analysis is that Martha figures if anyone is going to be arrested for anything, it's not going to be her. Zoë seems to be playing both sides, so she can stay on top."

Doran grunted. "I'd bet money that Martha is trying to pin her own past guilt on her old lover." Quinn gave him an expectant look. "Do we know for certain when Frederickson dumped her?" Quinn frowned then shook his head. "So, for all we know, they're still sharing sheets." He fingered the empty mug. "Poison is traditionally a woman's weapon."

"I thought of that, too." Quinn sighed. "I figured she offed the old lady for some reason, then forgot to destroy the evidence and almost killed the old guy, too."

"Sounds possible."

"But can we completely discount her scenario? There are a lot of odd relationships in this bunch."

Doran exhaled noisily. "We'll probably never know the truth about that. Since you served as her confessor, we need to look deeper into the backgrounds of Martha, Frederickson and Zoë."

"Already started."

Doran clapped Quinn on the shoulder. "I wouldn't have expected anything less."

Quinn glanced at his wristwatch. "I need to get out to Beja Flora and continue my security analysis. By the way, there's no drug lab in the basement, just hundreds of old fashioned fire-proof file cabinets."

"You've checked out the both basement levels?" Quinn nodded. Doran frowned. "Think there's another building on the property?"

"Doubt it, but I'm keeping an open mind."

"What's the security like on the second floor?"

"It's got blind spots, but not enough to prevent spotting an intruder."

"Are all the microphones and cameras active?"

"They were. The ones in your room are now on a closed loop tape."

"Thanks. Where do the cameras feed to?"

"Loft over the garage." Quinn wagged a finger at him. "Just because I took your room off line, don't do anything stupid."

"I won't."

"Why don't I believe you?" A muscle in Quinn's jaw twitched. "Stay out of her bed, I can't watch your back this time."

"Tonight I'll be at the big debate. Want to watch my back there?" Quinn shook his head. Doran grinned. "Didn't think so."

Chapter 14

Doran leaned against a wall as he watched Kelsey peer from behind the curtain at the noisy audience. He'd worn his charcoal suit, knowing it would blend with the shadows of the cavernous auditorium's backstage area, like a chameleon. Confident that he could finally watch her without arousing suspicion, he studied Kelsey, who stood several feet away. Though her stance seemed calm, a small mirror hanging near the curtain's ropes and pulleys reflected white knuckles clutching thick burgundy velvet.

Laughter erupted like a tidal wave of noise from the spectators, who were gathering to witness the impending debate. Kelsey flinched. Doran wondered if she'd chosen her dark pinstripe suit to look professional or to hide sweat stains.

A tongue of light from the streetlamp spilled into the dusty area, as the rear door opened. Frederickson's elongated shadow preceded him, like an envoy. Doran switched his attention to the senator. Frederickson's black suit, white shirt, red power tie and dark leather attaché case all proclaimed affluence and power; a definite contrast from the furtive man Quinn had filmed.

The moment the senator's gaze rested on Kelsey's back, his look turned malevolent. Doran silently shifted into a defensive position. Frederickson strolled up behind Kelsey.

"Not the tea party you expected, is it?" he asked her.

Kelsey glanced back at him, her expression calm. Either she'd sensed the man coming or she had nerves of steel. "Half of the county must be out there."

"Only a few civic minded fools." Frederickson made a dismissive gesture.

Kelsey raised a well-manicured brow. "Great description of the constituents."

If Doran hadn't seen her knuckles, he would have thought ice flowed in her blood. But he had seen them, and suspected her icy expression masked terror.

"You can save us both a lot of aggravation and drop out, like your brother did." Frederickson gave her a wolfish smile. "You won't win anyway."

"Perhaps not, but at least I'll know I tried."

"Has Cal realized it yet?"

Kelsey frowned. "What should Grandfather have realized?"

Frederickson's smile widened. "That you'll be the next to die." Doran noiselessly unsnapped his holster and his fingers closed around his handgun.

"Are you admitting that you murdered Abby and Jenny or are you threatening me?"

Of course the bastard was threatening her, yet she acted like they were discussing the weather.

"Would I do such a thing?" His loud, shocked

tone hushed as he leaned toward her. Even when his face was mere inches from her face, Kelsey didn't budge. "No, you fucking bitch, I'm not threatening you. I'm just telling you that certain people want me in office and they'll do anything to keep me there."

Doran put his hands behind his back and stepped forward. "Like Ling Chen?"

Frederickson whirled to face him. For a fleeting moment before he controlled it, his face registered shocked recognition. "What's it to you?"

So, he did know Old Ling. Doran calmly shrugged. "He's an old friend of mine."

Frederickson's gaze narrowed. "He never mentioned you."

"That's strange." Doran smiled. "He usually tells everyone who will listen that I'm worth millions to him."

Kelsey studied him, her expression perplexed. Doran gave her a quick smile, then focused on Frederickson. A flicker of doubt sprouted. A tingle of triumph welled in Doran. "Old Ling and I go way back." Doran casually put his arm around Kelsey's waist. She felt stiff as a mannequin. "I dated his daughter, unfortunately she died." He caressed Kelsey. "Next time you see Ling, tell him that I look forward to our next meeting."

Frederickson's look of confusion intensified. Was it possible that the senator was unaware of the reward? If so, it was the greatest single suggestion of innocence that Doran had discovered. It was also interesting that the only reaction he'd felt from Kelsey was a tiny jolt when he'd mentioned Pia.

Could it be that he'd correct about her involvement
with the drug cartel? No, he wouldn't accept that.

A shout of laughter came from the other side of
the curtain. Frederickson jerked and took a step
backward, where his heel caught on a cable. As he
stumbled, Doran grabbed his arm in a crushing grip
and yanked Frederickson close. "Ling likes
controlling people in power. He doesn't give a
damn whose strings he holds." Frederickson's eyes
showed increasing uncertainty, making him nearly
certain the suspicions about the man were true. But
he had to be certain that Frederickson was Ling's
connection. He couldn't afford to make the same
mistake twice. Doran smiled. So far, the only thing
that had been bad about his lack of judgment going
into this op had been that Kelsey had gotten hurt.
The great thing was that he'd been there to save her
when Frederickson had really tried to murder her.
He looked at the senator. "Fact is, Kelsey is a lot
softer." He caressed her stiff waist, trying to
reassure her. While she didn't relax, he felt better.

Frederickson glared at him, then stalked to the
public pay phone.

Kelsey glared at Frederickson, who turned his
back toward them and mumbled into the receiver.
"What the heck was that all about?" she whispered.

Doran turned her away from him and began
massaging the knotted muscles in her shoulders.
"Putting him off balance." He watched her profile
in the mirror. "Now he feels that his primary backer
doesn't care if he's in office or not."

"I won't work for Ling or be controlled by any-"
He put a finger over her lips. "I never thought

you would," he whispered into her ear. "But think how unsettling it is for Frederickson to think you could be." From a distance a watcher would think he was nuzzling her ear. It took all his willpower not to.

She leaned against him, an amused smile on her lips. "That feels like heaven."

"Thanks."

As he kneaded at the corded tissue, she leaned against his hands.

"Who is Ling?" Her tone was as casual as the languid look on her face.

"Ling Chen controls an Asian drug consortium." He kept his tone deliberately neutral.

"Pharmaceuticals are big business, but that doesn't explain Marvin's reaction. The man has made a career of being perfect and you had him as close to panicked as I've ever seen." Eyes closed and smile soft, she leaned trustingly toward him as he worked the kinks out of her neck.

"So you've never met or heard of Old Ling." He deliberately kept his tone casual.

"No." If her muscles were an indication, she was telling the truth. "What's so special about him?"

"Not all drugs are pharmaceuticals." The flesh beneath his probing hands stiffened. A moment later, she turned and stared at him.

"Are you insinuating that your previous girlfriend's father was a drug lord?"

"Does that shock you?"

Kelsey sputtered.

Doran rested his hand on her shoulders and gave her a quick kiss. "Old Ling's business is very efficient because of his business philosophy." He rubbed his thumbs over her neck.

"Criminals have business philosophies?" Every syllable caressed his lips.

Doran clenched his teeth against his rising need. "Pay your help well and when they cease having value, kill them."

"You are fired!" She tried to break free from his grasp.

"Why?" He pulled her against his rock-hard body.

"I am not going to have you work for me when you work for a drug lord." Her whispered tone rose with thinly veiled panic.

"I never said I worked for him."

"You most certainly d-"

Doran kissed her, until he had to stop or embarrass himself. "No. I told our senator that I was worth more to Ling than he was." Kelsey's eyes glinted with frustration. Doran whispered. "I dated Pia to get to Ling, but I was new to the game and she wasn't the innocent I'd thought. She figured out who I was and set a trap to kill me. You met Quinn. My stupidity cost him the use of his legs." Kelsey stared at him and swallowed hard. "Ling's daughter was killed." Kelsey's eyebrows rose. "Ling has a five million dollar bounty out on each of us - dead or alive." Kelsey swallowed hard.

Kelsey gulped. "Five-million." She swallowed, again. "You mean someone will pay that to see you?"

"Yeah. Ling would like the privilege of torturing me to death, but he'd settle for mutilating my corpse."

Heat suffused her face. Kelsey put her hand over his forearm. "What am I missing?" Her tone pleaded for an explanation while her eyes searched his face for the answer.

He held up a finger. Should he drop the charade now or continue? Doran exhaled, then moved around Kelsey and picked up the phone Frederickson had just used. He dialed the operator. "This is agent Devlin Doran, with the DEA. A call was made from this phone about three minutes ago, would you please look up the number dialed?"

"That is against company policy."

"Ma'am the person who made the call is a suspected drug dealer, who has no compunction against selling at playgrounds, do you want him to go free?"

Kelsey's nails dug into his flesh and her eyes rounded. "Are you serious," she murmured.

"The number was 555-0669."

"Thank you ma'am." Doran hung up the phone, then placing his hand on Kelsey's back he guided her back to where they had been.

"Let me see if I've got this straight. One, you aren't a plain Jane detective, you're some sort of drug investigator." Doran nodded. "Two, you romanced Pia to get to her father, but that apparently ended badly, so now he's after you."

"You could put it that way."

Kelsey glared at him. "Is your entire life a calculated game of lies?"

"Sometimes it feels that way."

Kelsey closed her eyes. "You implied that I'd

help this Ling person." Her voice began to rise. "Marvin knows there's no way on earth I would do anything for a drug lo-" The men's room door began opening. Doran kissed her. For a moment, she responded without thought or hesitation. Hunger, hot and strong surged through Doran. He forgot the assignment, forgot there were ten-thousand-people on the other side of the curtain and reveled in the sweet taste of her. Then, her body stiffened. She pushed him away. "If you admit to lying, how am I supposed to know what's true and what isn't."

He swallowed. "I could ask you to trust me." Her mouth flattened. "I should have told you my real stats to begin with, not the cover story." He winched.

She shoved his hands away. "Did you kiss me to shut me up or are you using physical contact to control me?" Her icy tone and rigid stance sent a new kind of tremor through him.

Doran reached for her, but she slapped his hands away. "This is about survival. Yours."

"Answer my question."

"I've never lied to you."

"As if you really investigate insurance fraud." The anger in her glare made him take a step back.

"Quinn and I have been working undercover and yes, we have done plenty of that.

Kelsey rolled her eyes to heaven. "And this Pia person was one of your covers."

She look fiercely at him. Dear God, was he losing her or was she jealous? It was impossible to tell. "She's dead."

"How convenient." Her sarcastic whisper grated with wrath.

With nothing more to lose, Doran stepped forward and embraced her. She moved to slap him. He secured her arms and prayed she wouldn't scream. Leaning forward, he whispered, "I swear to you on my sister's grave that Pia Chen is dead." He leaned back, hoping that they gave the impression of two people with romance on their minds, which should give Frederickson something to worry about. "Pia found out I was DEA and tried to murder me, but Quinn stopped her." He winced. "Barely." He eased back from her and began unbuttoning his shirt.

"What are you doing."

"Showing you the scars. If you won't believe what I say, perhaps you'll believe what you see." He eased the dark fabric aside to reveal the livid scar at the base of his neck. Kelsey's quick intake of breath above the murmur of the audience on the other side of the curtain was the only sound. "You met Quinn. He's in that wheelchair because of me." Doran swallowed. "He got a bullet in his spine when he saved my miserable life."

"And?" Doran wondered what she wanted to know. "Why haven't I ever heard of this Ling-person before this?"

"He's not someone you'd want to know."

"Right." Couldn't any truth convince her? "But he's someone you know."

"My only goal is to put him behind bars." Her skeptical look deepened. "Kelsey, I am not lying to you. After we were injured, Wes posted Quinn me here and set up our cover – the cover that I told you. It's the story I give everyone."

"When I get elected, I'll find this Wes-person in the DEA and have a chat with him."

"Fine. Do it."

She looked surprised by his quick agreement. "So this Wes-person located you here to arrest Ling?"

"If Wes had known Ling had a distributor in this area, this would have been the last place on earth he'd have posted us."

"Distributor? " Her surprise looked and sounded genuine.

He tried to explain, "Lings bounties on Quinn and me make us major targets in all areas he runs drugs, and that makes our job of collecting evidence almost impossible."

She narrowed her eyes and scrutinized him. "Do you think this Wes or Marvin could be the link?"

"We're not one-hundred-percent positive." He gave Frederickson a significant glance.

Kelsey inched back and looked up at him. "Marvin knew Ling's name." Doran nodded. "I've never trusted him. I always thought he used people and lied." She glared at Doran. "I have zero tolerance for dishonesty."

"If the senator is dealing with Ling, he's playing with sharks and he knows he has to stay in the water or die."

Kelsey stared at him. "Do you mean what I think you do?"

"Ling buys politicians all over the world. If Frederickson belongs to Ling, he has to keep his office or Ling will kill him. If he's a good little drone, Ling will kill off the competition."

Kelsey blanched. "Abby and Jenny?"

"We're investigating that possibility, but haven't gotten a definitive answer or enough solid evidence for a conviction."

The speaker hummed. Kelsey jumped. "Ladies and gentlemen," the announcer said, "it's my privilege to referee tonight's debate."

People clapped. As Marvin moved past them and stepped onto the stage, the applause escalated to thunder.

"Are you telling me that to save my life I should drop out of this election?" Hands on hips, she glared at him.

Doran shook his head. "I'm here to watch your back."

She chortled. "Wonderful. Just wonderful." He raised a brow. "You're worth quite a bit dead. Who is watching your back?"

"Let me worry about that."

She shook her head. "Not when it could mean that I could get shot in the back."

He stroked her cheek. "Trent and Quinn are keeping tabs on me and if I die, they'll take over protecting you." He swallowed the lump in his throat. "Now, get out there and win votes."

Kelsey glanced at the curtain that concealed the cheering crowd and the senator. Her expression changed to the dread he's suspected earlier, when he'd noticed her white knuckles. Doran hugged her. "I thought you were over your stage fright." She shook her head. He kissed her forehead. "I'm not surprised. Most people would rather die than face a crowd and possibly be ostracized."

"Really?"

He nodded.

"Thank you for the wonderful greeting." Frederickson's voice came from the speakers. The cheering dimmed somewhat. "I thought my worthy opponent would be here tonight, but she seems to be missing."

"Don't worry," Doran said. "You'll win the people. For one thing, you're an excellent public speaker because you believe in the issues and people sense your sincerity."

"But Marvin has so much experience."

Doran chuckled. "Something tells me that Frederickson will probably be off tonight."

"How would you know that?"

He wet his lips. "If someone had just told you that your biggest supporter or your most philanthropic secret supporter didn't care if you won or lost, would you be having a good night?" Understanding dawned warm and bright in her gaze. It felt good, probably too good.

"How about you going out there and debating Marvin?" she asked. "You did great back here."

"Face you fears, acknowledge them, then they can't control you … and know that I'm watching over you."

"I'll try." He arched a brow. She squared her shoulders and lifted her head. "No, I won't try, I'll do it."

"Good, now go show the voters that you're worth fifty Fredericksons." When she hesitated, he kissed her.

By the time she walked onto stage amid thunderous applause, her face was flushed.

Doran plucked his cell phone from his pocket and dialed the number Frederickson had called. A recording answered. He hung up before the tape could add a message, then he phoned a familiar number and made a long-due confession to Wes.

Chapter 15

Eyes smarting from the paparazzi's flashes, Kelsey leaned against Doran's solid presence. "Who is your friend?" one journalist shouted. More reporters picked up that line of questioning until she knew it would cause more damage to ignore them, then to answer.

"Devlin Doran," Doran said.

"Are things serious?" another one shouted.

"Have you set a wedding date?" a third demanded.

Kelsey said, "There are lots of serious things in the world. Children growing up without proper food, clothing, education or medical treatment comes to mind." She felt in the pocket of her jacket. "I want to make the world better for all children and give each and every one an equal opportunity. A few days ago, I found this photo near a trash can." She held up the mystery girl's photograph. A tremor went through Doran's solid bicep. "If I'm elected to office, I hope to make certain that no child is thrown away."

"Who is the kid?" a journalist asked, pen poised over a notepad.

Kelsey shrugged as she slipped the old photograph back into her pocket. "She could be anyone. But, for me, her image represents all the children I want to help."

"Mr. Doran," a journalist barked, "how long have you known Ms. MacLennan?"

"Long enough to know she has my vote," he replied. "And now, I hope you all drive safely." With that, he tucked her hand under his arm and steered her behind the stage curtain.

The sudden darkness blinded her, but he continued guiding her toward the rear door without pausing for his eyes to adapt to the dim light. That plus his ease at extricating them from the reporters and their endless questions amazed her. "You have to teach me how to do that."

"Do what?"

"Get away from the paparazzi."

"It's simple: 1) answer a question; 2) give them something to do, and 3) leave." He opened the exterior door part way and silently surveyed the desolate parking lot. Bats swooped through the halo of light, grabbing moths, which circled each streetlight. Though the lights seemed to give off ample light, the shrubbery hugging the auditorium's foundation seemed shrouded in sinister shadows.

After a searching look, Doran stepped outside and visually searched the lot, again. Than, he reached back, took her hand and ushered her toward his vehicle. Heels, clicking with each step, were the loudest sound in the nearly deserted parking lot, but she could hear remnants of conversation and car doors slamming from the front door. Kelsey shivered with a strange sense of being watched and huddled as close to Doran's side as she could get and at the same time making certain that he could reach his sidearm, if needed. With each step the feeling of being spied on intensified. The desire to run to his suburban welled.

While they were at least a hundred feet away, he took his high-tech remote control out of his jacket and tapped a key. The tiny screen flashed scarlet, then red numbers appeared. He stopped walking and scowled at the display.

"Is something wrong?"

"The Suburban's electric shock feature has been triggered." He frowned. "I didn't expect Frederickson to react so fast." He keyed in some numbers and the screen went blank.

Kelsey breathed in the humid air and looked around the isolated lot, wishing that she didn't feel like such a target. "Wouldn't it have been safer to park in the main lot?"

"If I had parked there, we would still be dealing with reporters." Doran smoothed the hair off her forehead. "You did great tonight." He stroked her face, as if the only reason that he'd stopped walking in the middle of the dark parking lot was to look at her. "You made Frederickson look like ground round."

"You're changing the subject."

He grinned. "Stay here. I think the Burb is okay, but there's no need to risk both our hides."

Her knees felt suddenly weak and her heart slammed against her ribs as if it was a prisoner behind bars. As he eased away from her, a chill crept over her. Kelsey wanted to fling herself at him, and bury herself in his safe warmth, but knew that would be the dumbest thing she'd ever done. So, she crossed her arms over her stomach and prayed her over active imagination would stop telling her that the back of her head was in a sniper's crosshairs. "You think there's a bomb there or something?"

"Wouldn't be the first time." The man looked and sounded way too cheerful. "I told you that I'd made a lot of enemies in the past. Truth is most of them are worse than the average insurance fraud and more than one has the ability to build a bomb."

It was all she could do to remain standing as he casually strolled toward his Suburban, hunkered down and looked underneath the frame.

Kelsey focused on inhaling and exhaling.

He chuckled, then did something to the remote that caused a chirping sound. He rose and whistled a jaunty little refrain as he opened the passenger door. A moment later, he tossed a newspaper on the asphalt, knelt and stuck his head under the vehicle. A flashlight beam glinted off something silvery lying near the front tire.

If it were explosives or something deadly, he'd be calling the bomb squad or something, wouldn't he? Gooseflesh broke out over her arms, as she stared at whatever he'd found. His cheerful whistling rose in volume as he reached under the vehicle. It must be safe. Kelsey crept toward the car, while thinking that she should have used the bathroom before they left. She rubbed warmth into her upper arms.

Doran whistled a triumphant tune as he stood up. Using a pair of long-nosed pliers, he held up a foot long metal tool for her to see. "A bit clichéd, don't you think?" He looked and sounded like he'd just won a major victory.

"What is it?"

"A Yankee drill."

He sounded serious. Doran pointed to the thick end. "You hold it here. It operates on spring tension and acts like a sort of corkscrew mixed with a pogo stick. Thus, when you press down, the bit revolves and a hole gets drilled."

Kelsey swallowed. "Are you trying to say that someone drilled holes in your brake lines?" Fear rolled in her stomach.

Doran chuckled. "They tried." He shook open a gallon-sized freezer bag and dropped the drill in.

Great, now they had the privilege of calling a taxi or trying to drive the sabotaged car and wrecking. Kelsey balanced on one foot and pulled off her high heel, then she repeated the process with the other foot. Doran looked from her bare feet to her face and started laughing.

"You don't need to act so pleased. Someone wants us dead and is trying to kill us." And she could still feel their gaze on her.

Still smiling, he held up the bag. "This thing has a smooth handle, Frank should be able to get some great fingerprints off it."

"You treat this like a game."

"It is a game." He caressed her cheek. "Okay, it's dangerous, but still a game." Doran wrapped his arms around her. "You're trembling." His arms tightened. "We all get chances to win or lose. If we're afraid to lose, we automatically lose. Instead of focusing on fear, I allow myself see how close I am to winning."

It felt incredibly safe in his arms. She snuggled deeper into his warmth. "That's the same way I felt about the chicken on my door."

Doran caressed her back. "Having someone try to sabotage the Burb confirms that Frederickson is dirty."

"How?"

"People who are a threat to Ling's 'friends' get killed or at least have attempts made on their lives."

He was right about that, but she should have thought about his safety before she decided he was her guardian angle and demanded that he put himself in danger. "So, you think Marvin phoned someone to come 'fix' your brakes."

"I hope so. The trace might confirm it."

"Don't you think we should call a taxi?"

"The Burb is fine. The electric shock got them before they got it." He stroked her arms up and down, as if intuitively understanding her reaction. "What we need to do is get out of here before you shake to death. And we also need to drop this by Frank's."

Kelsey took a deep breath. "Who is Frank?"

"He's the best fingerprint specialist I know." He helped her into the vehicle. As she buckled and tightened her seat belt, he caressed her under the chin, as if unwilling to leave her long enough to go around the vehicle.

"Devlin Doran, who are you?"

For a moment, she thought he was going to simply close the door. Instead he answered, "I was born William Daniel Dalton. While I was in college majoring in business management, my younger sister died of an overdose. I changed my major to Criminal Justice. After graduation, I started working with the DEA. My goal for the past eleven years has been to track down the slime balls that killed Marnie."

She sensed that very few people knew about this. "You loved her."

He swallowed and nodded.

"Did you ever find them?"

"Oh, yeah. I tracked the poison from the peons up the chain." His laugh was harsh. "Not that it's done that much good in our 'innocent until proven guilty society'."

"Probation?"

"That plus plea bargains and community service. Oh, and don't forget the not guilty pleas that juries believed. But those were the small fish."

"And Ling is the big one."

"Oh, yeah." He closed the door then came around and got in behind the steering wheel.

"So should I call you William, Bill, Will or what?"

He started the Suburban and drove out of the parking lot. "When I found out about the bounty on my head, I legally changed my name to Devlin Doran."

"But you're still with the DEA and you lied about being a PI."

The vehicle turned onto the road, which passed in front of the auditorium. "Quinn and I opened D. Q. Investigations as an undercover op eighteen months ago. It is legitimate, but so is my badge."

The light ahead turned red. Doran turned the radio on. As strains of Beethoven filled the car, Doran watched the rearview mirror. Light from the stoplight accentuated his features. "Quinn is a paraplegic because I fucked up."

Kelsey blinked. "What are you trying to tell me? That I should quit politics and let Marvin and his nefarious friends keep breaking laws? If I get elected, I can vote for tougher laws and try to protect all the kids."

"I hope you get the chance." The light turned green, but he turned to her, ignoring it. "Pia distracted me. She was beautiful, smart and sexy as all get out." The light turned yellow. He accelerated into the intersection, the light turned red, halfway though. "I fell for her and temporarily forgot that my goal was to bring down her old man."

Pia sounded perfect, except for having a drug-dealing father. She'd probably been tall, full-figured, exotic and sexy, everything that Kelsey knew she would never be. She stared out the windshield at the night and wished someone short, flat and sexually incompetent could captivate Devlin Doran enough not to think about security systems and possible watchers. Heat inched up her neck, as she acknowledged how much she wanted him.

"What was supposed to help me bring the bad guys down nearly killed Quinn." He calmly studied the rear-view mirror. "By the way, we're being followed. Hang on while I lose them." With that, he whipped the wheel and the car did a one-eighty. As soon as they passed an ordinary tan sedan, he floored the accelerator. Moments later, the suburban skidded around another corner on two wheels. Where she would have been hanging onto the steering wheel for dear life, he casually drove one-handed. She stared out the rear window, watching the smaller car slide around the corner.

While Doran put the vehicle through a series of moves she wouldn't have thought it was possible for a big vehicle to execute, she dug her fingernails into the soft leather upholstery. For several minutes her heart thundered to the beat of Beethoven's Violin Concerto and squealing tires tore the night's peace.

He finally began driving sedately down the road, several turns after she lost sight of the sedan. She flexed her fingers with relief.

"Sorry about that," he said.

"You need to teach me to drive like that." He shot her an indecipherable glance. "Do you think whoever was in the car was the same person who dropped the drill?"

"That or a journalist who couldn't take a hint."

"They can be pests." She sighed. He grunted in agreement. When he didn't pursue the safe line of conversation, she added, "Somehow, I think anyone powerful enough to make Marvin sweat all over the podium and look like a fool during our debate is smart enough to figure out your name change."

"That's Ling, all right."

"What if Marvin figures out how you're valuable to Ling and tries to cash in?" Kelsey asked. "That sounds like something he'd do." Doran shrugged, as if someone wanting to get rich over his death seemed incidental. "How do you live day in, day out knowing someone is willing to pay millions to have you dead?"

"No matter what he thinks, Old Ling isn't God."

"Does anything ever upset you?"

The Suburban turned onto a quiet residential street lined with overhanging oaks. "Knowing homicidal maniacs are walking the streets and drug pushers are lurking in schoolyards infuriates me." His matter of fact tone assured her that he would do whatever was in his power to remedy the situation. Devlin Doran was a man after her heart.

Kelsey sighed and leaned back against the soft leather seat. "Meeting you was the best thing that ever happened to me."

Doran gave her a swift glance. "Are you trying to tell me you liked rear ending me?"

"No." She groaned. "I liked my mustang without dents. What I meant-"

"I know what you meant." He reached across the console, took her hand and gently squeezed it. "The more I get to know you, the more I like you, too."

"You don't need to look so surprised. I'm not that disagreeable." Just short, thin and flat – everything that men dislike.

"You are shy and sometimes that gives the impression of being frigid. But, you definitely are not cold." He squeezed her hand.

The Suburban maneuvered into the driveway of a brick ranch. Doran parked and grabbed the plastic bag. "I'll only be a minute." He leaned over and gave her a kiss that pledged more when the time was right, then he reluctantly got out, and locked the doors.

Ever since her senior year at Duke, when she'd come back to her townhouse and found Byron in bed with Zoë, Kelsey had avoided dating. Yet Devlin Doran acted different. The first time he'd come over, Zoë had done everything in her power to catch his attention, but he'd seemed more annoyed by the overt attention than anything. Could it be that he felt the same way she did and truly didn't prefer tall women with lush bodies?

While Devlin Doran had always been a complete gentleman, there was little doubt in her mind that he wanted her. If she'd known there were men like him, she would have never bothered with Byron, but at the time, she'd thought Bryon was romance personified. Kelsey ran her fingers over her lower lip. Now, that she had Devlin's kisses for comparison; the difference seemed enormous.

The house's door opened; a rectangle of light bathed Doran in golden hues. What would it be like to become his lover? Kelsey felt anticipation mix with heated longing.

Doran talked to a blond, tousle-haired man and handed over the drill. Then he was coming back to her, a smile on his face. Would tonight be the night?

If it hadn't been for the election and the paparazzi's incredible ability to report scandal, she would have suggested that they register in a motel or go to his townhouse. Heat burned all the way up her neck to the tips of her ears at the uncharacteristically brazen thought.

Chapter 16

Zoë watchfully drove into the rest area and parked her red Porsche in the shadows of a spreading oak, then she waited. The mournful cry of an owl mixed with the rush of traffic on the interstate. During the next ten minutes, her car was the only one at the rest stop. Gooseflesh rippled over her as she remembered the news casts about the string of robberies and rapes, which had occurred here in the past four or five months.

Obviously, she was the only one stupid enough to agree to a meeting here. Zoë rubbed her arms and wished she'd remembered the information earlier.

Something cracked in the darkness. Zoë gulped and locked the car doors. Next, she dug in the depths of her bag, searching for her can of mace and cell phone.

Light flashed off her rearview mirror, as another vehicle turned onto the exit ramp. Zoë held her breath, hoping that the only other person stupid enough to enter the deserted rest stop drove a white Mercedes. The vehicle slowed to a creep at the entrance of the parking area.

Surely the phone call hadn't been a set up. Surely there was a good reason for the furtive tone.

Surely there was some core of maternal love. She wanted to start her car and hightail it away.

The vehicle surged forward and slipped into the slot next to her car, Zoë thought about the call she had gotten an hour earlier. Had it been her mother or someone impersonating her mother? All the traffic noise in the background would have made it easy to fake a voice. Zoë squinted at the driver of the other vehicle, trying to verify that this wasn't a trap, but the dark windows made identification impossible. Was there any reason why her mother would have called from a public phone instead of from Beja Flora? Did she think whomever vetted the phone tapes would give a damn whether Martha Lancaster called her daughter or not?

Slowly, the car door opened. Zoë was so tense, she was afraid she'd pee her pants if the driver didn't show herself or himself soon. Looking more arthritic than ever before, Martha got out of her car. Instead of getting into the Porsche, she limped to the sidewalk, then stared at her, willing her to get out. A smile would be nice. A smile would show that she was here by her own will. A smile would show that she cared. Clutching her can of mace and cell phone, Zoë opened her car door. "I was beginning to wonder if your call was some sort of cruel joke."

Martha straightened her back and changed from a tired woman to her typical starched nails look. "Do you remember the last time you phoned me saying you had to see me?" Martha asked. Zoë nodded. "Abby and Jenny died that same night."

A chill washed over her. "Surely you can't think

I had anything to do with that." How could her own mother think something so awful of her?

"I pray you didn't, but you're the one who knows for sure." It sounded like a condemnation.

Zoë blinked back tears. "You always think the worst of me. Why don't you just admit that you love Ramsey and Kelsey, but hate me?"

Martha looked surprised. "I don't hate you."

"Don't you?" Her mother looked sincere, but Zoë knew better. "You love Kelsey and Ramsey. You always have time for them, but you never had time for me." Her throat constricted and she tried to swallow the lump. "Never."

Martha walked to a nearby picnic bench and sat down heavily. "I was tying to do my job so I could support you."

Food, shelter, clothing, yes, she'd gotten that, but nothing that she'd ever wanted, or at least not unless Ramsey and Kelsey got it, too. If her mother read them a story, it was never her favorite. If someone had a birthday, her mother arranged wonderful parties and had the cook prepare all their favorite foods, but not for her birthday. She had been lucky to get a ten-dollar-bill tucked in a card.

"Why did you call me?" Zoë bit her upper lip and blinked away tears.

"Why did you come to the house that night? Did you need to speak to me because you needed an alibi?" Venom laced her mother's tone. Zoë felt certain that if the clouds had parted, she'd see fury in her mother's eyes. "Were you there because you needed to draw my attention away from something or someone?"

Zoë swallowed. What was wrong? Why did her mother seem to be suggesting she had something to do with Ramsey's accident? "How could you ask that?"

"I had a visitor this morning. Quentin Quinn."

Zoë stared at her mother. "Am I supposed to know him?"

Martha's mouth flattened. "He's Devlin Doran's partner."

"And I care about this because-?"

"Apparently Mr. Doran doesn't trust Beja Flora's security. Mr. Quinn is some sort of specialist, so he came to inspect the system."

"Surely you didn't let him inside?"

"He was very forceful."

"I've seen you block linebackers."

"Mr. Quinn is a paraplegic."

"What'd he do? Ride a panzer tank in?"

"This isn't a joking matter."

Zoë felt her face heat and was glad of the darkness. "Sorry."

"I told Mr. Quinn that Mr. Doran had no right to request a security inspection. He then informed me that he was there at Ms. MacLennan's request and propelled his wheelchair into the foyer."

"But Kel can't schedule something like that, can she?"

"Mr. Quinn was very informed about Calhoun's state of health." Martha took a deep breath. "He even said, 'It's my understanding that Mr. MacLennan suffers from Alzheimer's and the security here hasn't been checked since it was installed.'"

"Unbelievable." But what did it have to do with the veiled accusation her mother had made?

Martha sighed. "It gets worse. Apparently Mr. Doran and Kelsey informed the guard to expect Mr. Quinn, but when he arrived, the guard did not ask to verify Mr. Quinn's identity."

"They didn't ask for mine, either."

"But Mr. Quinn was alone and a stranger. The guard simply checked a list, opened the gate and he rolled himself right inside."

"The guy sounds like a jackass."

Martha shook her head, a gentle smile on her lips. "Actually, he was quite pleasant. Very intelligent, too."

"How do you know he wasn't casing the house?"

"From a wheel chair?"

"Well, why not?"

"Mr. Quinn's concern seemed focused on his partner."

"Devlin Doran."

"Correct."

"You trust this Quinn-guy to see all the security systems tricks because Devlin Doran said it was okay. Did you give him all the security codes while you were at it?" This was unbelievable.

"Ms. Quinn merely verified the safety of the upper level so Mr. Doran could get a good night's sleep."

How could her mother be so trusting? And what did any of this nonsense have to do with the last time she'd gone to Beja Flora?

Martha stared at the passing traffic on the Interstate. "Mr. Quinn's concerns could be warranted. The MacLennans have been having a bad couple of months. First Abigail and Jennifer dying and us not knowing if Ramsey would live or not and if he did, not knowing if he would walk again. I tell you, the sight of Mr. Quinn in that chair took my breath away."

"So the fact he was a cripple got to you."

"I could tell he was a good man. Only a good man would try to help the man who saved his life."

God, had her mother always been this gullible?

"Mr. Quinn reminded me that Mr. Doran had agreed to protect Kelsey. He knew for a fact that Mr. Doran would put his life on the line for her. The least I could do was allow Mr. Quinn to check the system so Mr. Doran could sleep at night."

"Mother, that's the stupidest thing you've ever done. This Quinn must be a primo con artist."

Martha's soft expression vanished. She squared her shoulders and glared at her.

"What?" Zoë demanded. "Just because the man can't walk, he can't lie? How do you even know he needed that wheelchair? He might have been using the damned thing just to get your sympathy." Martha shook her head. "Well, he sure got it, didn't he?"

"Zoë, is there some reason why you're so upset about the system being checked?"

Her mother was acting like she was the enemy. This was unbelievable.

"Mr. Quinn brought up some good arguments. He pointed out that all the murder attempts had been vehicular sabotage."

"Not all. What about the bottle of gas someone

threw through Kelsey's window?"

"It was lucky Mr. Doran was there."

"A little too lucky, if you ask me."

"What do you mean?"

"Think about it, Mom. Don't you find it a bit coincidental that Doran is there to save Kelsey from both attempts on her life? I mean, even I'm not stupid enough to miss that detail."

"You think Mr. Doran is trying to kill Kelsey?"

"Or keep saving her life so he can get close to her for some other reason, yes."

Martha's nostrils flared as she inhaled. "But why?" she asked, faintly.

"Why not?"

"Zoë, why would anyone go to that effort to get close to a botanist?"

"Kelsey is a MacLennan."

"She hybridizes orchids. Surely there isn't a black market for stolen plant DNA."

"This isn't about her damned plants, it's about the campaign."

Martha shrugged. "I assumed that when the brakes lines on Ramsey's BMW were tampered with. There was similar damage on Kelsey's mustang, but how could anyone know she intended to run?"

"They couldn't." Not even Marv could have guessed what Kelsey would decide. "But she didn't have to officially run, just give the speeches and keep gaining points in the polls." Zoë pressed her lips together, afraid that she might have already said too much.

"At least Kelsey made a good choice of

protector."

"Who?" Zoë demanded. "Doran?" Martha nodded. Zoë gave a harsh laugh. "You've got to be kidding."

"He saved Mr. Quinn's life. If it hadn't been for Mr. Doran, Mr. Quinn would be dead instead of in his chair."

That, again. She'd always given her mother more credit than to think a guy on wheels could sway her opinion. "How do you know he told you the truth?"

"He seemed sincere."

Zoë squinted at her mother and wondered just what the guy had done to earn her trust to quickly and completely. "So does any good con artist or actor."

"Mr. Quinn was much to uncertain of what was going on to be conning me. The man was simply trying to help a friend. I have to admire that."

Zoë guffawed. "Unless I'm the one trying to help a friend, then, of course, whatever is being done must be something sinister."

"Mr. Quinn can't seem to understand why Mr. Doran is choosing to protect Kelsey." Martha gave a wistful sigh. "I've seen the way he looks at her, I think he's smitten."

"You call me from a public phone, like this is some top secret thing and asked me to meet you in this God forsaken, rapist infested place to tell me about some damned conversation you had with a cripple and speculate if the ice queen has a boyfriend?" Zoë threw up her hands. "And if that isn't enough, you demand to know why I chose that particular Sunday to came by and try to make amends." Zoë blinked back tears.

Her mother visibly swallowed. Unwilling to say anymore, they both stared at traffic on the interstate.

After several minutes, Martha cleared her throat. "I was picking up my car from the repair shop when I decided I couldn't postpone speaking with you."

"What was wrong with your car?"

"Some strange sounds. I've had it in five times since I purchased it and they drive it for hundreds of miles, but never seem to fix it."

Trust her mother to sound more upset about a damned machine than the feelings of her own flesh and blood. Weren't women supposed to love their kids no matter what? Hadn't anyone told her mother?

Lights washed over them, as a car pulled into the lot. Zoë gripped her mace and hurried to her car, but her mother blocked her from opening the door.

A mini van pulled into a slot near the restrooms. Then, a woman carring a squalling child hurried inside. Zoë stared after them, remembering the last time she'd been in a public facility and shivered. How anyone could go use such an awful place. "I hate public piss pots."

Martha stared at her. "Do you use crude words for attention?"

"No. Are you going to get out of my way?"

Martha shook her head. "We still need to talk about the night you came over to speak to me."

"Get out of my way."

"Why did you really come out to the house?"

301

"That's irrelevant."

"I don't think so. I think you needed an alibi."
Martha glared at her as if she wished she'd never
borne her.

"You think I was part of Ramsey's accident."

Her mother gave her 'that' look. Oh, God, it was
true!

"I wasn't." Zoë's vision blurred with unshed
tears.

"Then you were an accessory."

"How can you say that?"

"I saw the silhouette."

Zoë burst into tears.

"I'd like to tell you everything will work out, but
I stopped believing in happy endings years ago."
She'd never heard her mother sound so tired. "You
have to tell someone what you know."

"Who?" Zoë laughed. It sounded harsh and
condemning. "The sheriff?"

Martha's smile was bittersweet. "Sheriff Botts
would be a good person to ph-"

"Botts! A good person?" Zoë's emotions burst
forth in a flood of tears. It felt like she was
disintegrating. "Oh, God, Mother! Jake would be
the last person I'd talk to."

"Zoë, what's wrong with you?"

"Jake was the silhouette you saw," Zoë said.

"Jake!" Martha's trembling fingers covered her
mouth. She stared a moment then began pacing.

Zoë tried to swallow the lump of misery in her
throat, but it only grew. "Jake told me he'd had a tip
that someone intended to assassinate Ramsey but
he wasn't sure of his source, so he wanted to get

into Beja Flora to check things out." Zoë swallowed hard. "Mom, I thought I was helping Ramsey." He'd helped her so many times in the past; it had been her way to repay him. If Jake had messed with those brake lines, then her mother was right; she was an accessory to murder. Scalding tears poured down her cheeks and she wished she'd died, instead. "I thought." She shook her head. "It doesn't matter what I thought." Zoë buried her face in her hands and sobbed.

Gentle hands caressed her back as they maneuvered her back to the picnic table. "It always matters why you do things."

People could be so deceitful.

Zoë cried harder.

Why did she always believe lies?

Her ribs ached.

Why did she love liars?

Why didn't someone just shoot her?

Why was she so worthless?

She should never have been born.

Her mother caressed her back until she shed all her tears and dry sobs wracked herm then Martha pulled her close and hugged her. It felt wonderful to be held for no other reason than that someone cared. To know that they cared no matter what they thought you'd done.

"You can see the motives," Zoë whispered. "I can't."

Martha sighed. "Not always."

"I'm so damned stupid." It was no wonder her mother couldn't love her. No wonder Ramsey hated her. No wonder Marv refused to commit to her or be seen in public with her. "I'm worthless."

"No you aren't."

"You always see people for what they are."

"Not when I was your age." Martha sighed. "Believe me, I know how easily one can get mislead." Martha smoothed her hair and her voice took on a dreamy tone. "If someone is handsome, smart and a good talker they can make a girl believe she's the woman of their dreams and that they want to give her the world on a golden platter." Martha sniffed.

"Mr. Quinn?"

Martha shook her head.

"My father?" It had been a taboo subject for her entire life, so it was difficult to believe her mother was finally ready to tell her about her love affair with Winston. How difficult it must have been when he married Jacqueline. Had her mother known she was pregnant before the marriage? Had Winston known? Had a powerful man duped her mother, as she had been duped? Zoë tried to focus on her mother's feelings instead of her own sense of complete worthlessness. "You believed he'd marry you."

"No. He was married."

"But-" Why hadn't anyone told her she was a preemie? "I always assumed."

"That you father was Winston?" Martha shook her head. Zoë squinted at her mother. "Everyone thought so, until a few days ago, even Kelsey and Ramsey thought you were their half sister." Martha's eyes watered. "Winston thought it was better that way." She took a calming breath. "If I'd admitted who your father was, I'd have jeopardized his career."

Not Calhoun! Zoë stiffened at the thought of that bigoted old man siring her. No wonder her mother had never wanted to speak about her father! Zoë tried to change the subject, "That sounds like what my boyfriend always tells me." Who would have believed her mother had once fallen for the same line?

"Zoë, take it from me, don't get involved with a married man. And whatever you do, don't believe a word a politician tells you." Martha licked her lips. "Except for the MacLennans, every politician I've ever known has been a lying hypocrite."

Zoë blinked in confusion. Was her mother saying she it wasn't Calhoun? When Calhoun had been in office, politicians had flocked around the house like flies over a carcass. "How have you managed to stay at Beja Flora so long if you feel that way?"

"Tenacity."

Zoë frowned. "Mom, who was my father?"

Judging by her expression, this was the question Martha had been dreading. "Marvin Frederickson," she whispered. Zoë's mouth dropped open and she shook her head. No, this couldn't be. "I thought he loved me and wanted to marry me." Martha's tone was disparaging of the naïve girl she'd once been.

"You're lying." But it all sounded so familiar that Zoë knew it must be the truth.

"I wish I was."

How could she have fallen in love with her own father? Zoë shook her head. "He can't be my father."

305

"He was the one and only." Martha wiped tears from her cheeks. "I wish I'd seen him for what he was."

"Does he know?"

"Yes."

How could Marv have started up with her, when he knew she was his own child?

"I was so stupid."

"Me, too." More stupid than she'd ever imagined. "God, I can't believe this."

Chapter 17

The headlights from Doran's Suburban glinted off Beja Flora's dark windows as he parked the Suburban. When he turned off the ignition, cutting the strains of a Brahms waltz off in mid note. Kelsey stared at the grays and blacks of the landscape and wondered what he planned to do.

Doran stared out the front windscreen, as if he felt as uncertain as she did.

A whippoorwill's lonely call rent the silence and its mournful tones gave a sense of separation to them, as they sat in their cocoon of metal and glass. She'd felt disconnected from everyone, except she hadn't known how abandoned she felt until Devlin Doran had walked into her life and presented her with the Blessed Promise.

"We should go in." His tone was tender as the night and twice as desirable.

Go in and face another sleepless night, knowing that he was so near and yet so untouchable? She's much rather spend the night in the car, watching the sun rise and wash away the shades of gray and night. Unable to speak past the lump of disappointment in her throat, Kelsey nodded.

"But I don't really want to be inside," he added.

"How about a walk, or are the gardens just for show?"

Anything was better than the prison of her bedroom walls. Kelsey got out of the vehicle and walked toward the kitchen garden, where fireflies danced in the air. The soothing fragrance of rosemary washed over her. This was much better than being inside; at least there was the illusion of romance. A door slammed behind her, then she heard him set the car's complicated alarm system. Soon, his quick footsteps approached. A heartbeat later, his arm wrapped around her waist. She didn't resist when he pulled her close against his side and matched his pace to hers. "How come you never wait for me to open the door for you?" He asked.

"You're my employee, why should I?"

He stiffened. "Is that all I am to you?" He released her and all but pushed her from his side. A sense of desolation nearly overwhelmed her and tears blurred her vision. Putting one foot in front of the other, and using sheer determination, she strolled through the herb garden's winding paths; new scents washed over her with each step. Lavender, symbolic of love and relaxation; Grandma Rose's scent. Anise for protection and to cover the scent of whisky on breath; Grandfather Calhoun. The pungent smell of mint surrounded them, and Kelsey inhaled deeply. If her tears wouldn't give her away, she'd have explained the herbs to Doran, as her grandmother had enlightened to her.

"Smells good."

It was hard to keep the pennyroyal from

wandering. She gulped, knowing that her silence condemned her as much as the sound of misery in her voice. "The Ancients believed that if you tied sprigs of mint to your bedpost, it would sharpen your thinking."

"Ever tried it?"

Kelsey shook her head. "Devlin, I'm sorry for what I implied." She swallowed. "Truly, I don't think of you as an employee."

He gestured to the moonlit garden. "So, you know what all these plants are?"

She nodded, while she swallowed the lump in her throat. "Some of their lore, too. Lots of times, that's the fun part."

"Tell me more."

Kelsey stroked a velvety leaf. "This is licorice. The Druids used it to treat sore throats, colds and asthma. Today, it's mainly considered a flavoring, but some people chew the root to help them break nicotine addictions." Doran plucked off a leave and popped it in his mouth. She smiled. "If you have high blood pressure, you'd better spit that out. Historically, licorice roots were believed to bring fidelity and passion to a sexual union and they were chewed to increase sexual vitality." Instead of spitting, he plucked another leaf, and held it toward her lips.

She nibbled it from his fingers.

Surprise flickered deep in his moonlit eyes.

He faced her, and cautiously placed his hands on her waist. "This is awkward."

"What is?"

"Emotions. It's easier to protect someone when-"

He shook his head and looked up at the stars. After a long moment, he wrapped his arms around her and hugged her close. As she hugged him back, his heart drummed against her ear. "Feelings aren't controllable."

True. They could be hidden, but they were as impossible to command as they were inconvenient, and falling in love in the middle of a campaign plagued by reporters and murder attempts was about as problematic as it came. But, that didn't matter when she felt so protected and cherished in his embrace.

She stood on tiptoe and kissed the corner of his mouth. He lowered his head and kissed the tip of her nose.

Kelsey stretched higher, but Doran groaned and tucked her head under his chin. His heart hammered against her cheek. "Let's not make a public spectacle in the middle of the garden."

"But you don't want to go inside." Was there anything more perplexing than a man?

"No."

"When is your partner going to finish checking the security system?"

"He's done and he says the cameras are turned off in my room."

"But you don't believe him."

He stroked her spine. Sensual ripples of pleasure fluttered across her back. "Quinn has a history of designating himself as my protector. While I believe he's got the feed to the guards on closed circuit, I'd bet money that he's watching me, himself."

"What about my room?"

"That's about as public as the auditorium stage."

Her face burned at the way she used to stand half naked in front of her closet, choosing what to wear. She felt the heat of a blush burn her cheeks. "My bathroom?" Were the damned guards getting an eyeful when she bathed?

"No cameras there. You aren't thinking that tile would be comfortable, are you?"

"This is worse than being a teenager."

"Tell me about it. I thought of going to my place, but didn't know who was tailing us." He paused for a few heartbeats. "And I didn't think you'd appreciate another photo in the paper with speculations about who I am and what you were doing with me first thing in the morning."

"But you lost the car following us?"

He made a rumble of agreement. "The one I saw." She didn't know why she was surprised. "A true pro might have managed to match my moves, but it would have been dangerous."

"But not past the gate. I have an idea." Kelsey pushed out of his embrace and twined her fingers through his. Turning down a lavender-lined path, she led him through the cypress hedge and into the rose garden, which surrounded her grandmother's beloved gazebo and several replica Greek statues. The spicy floral scent permeated the air.

"Smells nice," he said. When he acted like she'd brought him here to sniff the flowers, Kelsey pulled him toward the center of the garden, where Grandma Roses' ancient white-lattice gazebo stood, then she opened the squeaky screen door and ushered him into the shadowy interior.

"Watch your step. This building hasn't been used much since Grandma died."

He paused at the threshold. "Can you turn on a light?"

"Sorry. There isn't any electricity out here. No electricity, no cameras."

With a sound of pleasure, he drew her into his arms and started giving her butterfly kisses across the forehead. When he kissed his way down to the tip of her nose, she pulled him toward the antique green velvet fainting couch.

Kelsey edged Doran's jacket off his shoulders and tossed it to where the armchair had always sat. Stealth combined with darkness and heightened the sensation of every touch. As the humid air caressed her skin and their shared kisses increased in passion, Kelsey knew she had never been so ready for anything or anyone in her life. As she edged backward, her shins touched the back of the couch. She pulled Doran down.

He held her and listened to the night sounds, then he began kissing her again and she was kissing him back with a passion she never knew she possessed.

Her heart hammering with a mixture of pleasure, anticipation and momentary misgivings, she sat down on the chaise. He followed her, sprawling on top of her, yet not crushing her as Bryon had the few times he'd crawled on top of her. Kelsey pushed away the unwanted thought and focused on Doran.

Since she'd blatantly shown him how much she wanted him, why hadn't he yanked off his clothes and thrust into her? Of course, she wasn't about to instruct Devlin Doran, not when her toes were curling and he acted as unhurried as if he'd barely begun.

Kelsey wanted to touch his flesh, as she had once before. Her fingers slid to his shirt's buttons and she worked them open, one by one. With a groan, he changed position. She moaned as he drug his lips from hers.

He gave her a quick, closed mouth kiss, and sat up.

Kelsey blinked hard, too abandoned to trust her voice. Instead of fleeing for the door, he shrugged out of his dark jacket and detached his shoulder harness. "Don't want either of us to die for love," he murmured.

How obtuse could she be? Kelsey sat up, next to him and took off her shoes, then her jacket. As she raised her hands to unfasten her blouse, he caught her fingers and brought them back to his own buttons. His fingers moved to her top button. "Christmas has always been my favorite holiday, because I get to unwrap gifts." He paused and looked her in the eye. "But I've never had such a wonderful gift, as the one you're giving me."

Unable to speak, she pulled his dark silk shirt out of his trousers, pressed her forehead against his chest and went with the fantasy of tracing his nipple with her tongue. He shivered. "Sorry, but I've wanted to do that since we were interrupted-"

"Don't apologize and don't stop," he said gruffly.

She tilted her head, trying to see him between the

shadows. "So it didn't bother you?"

"You mean you don't know?" His tone held disbelief. She shook her head. He froze for a moment, then seemed to come to a decision. "In that case, you're going to find out just how it felt." Slowly, and with excruciating anticipation, he unbuttoned her shirt and removed it. Then, he unhooked her bra, lowered his mouth to her breast and gently suckled.

Her body turned into a molten mass of yearning and the reality of the old gazebo dissolved into a heady sensation of mingled touch, smells, heavy breathing and unbelievable sensations. Slowly, he removed her clothing item by item, taking time to nip and caress each new inch of exposed skin.

When she tried to grasp the shredding remnants of thought, she pulled off his shirt and unbuttoned his trousers. His breath went in sharply. "Don't." He stilled her hand. "I'm supposed to protect you." He cleared his throat. "I'm having enough trouble keeping that in mind, already."

Feeling curiously bold, she said, "You're off duty, now and we're safe here." Before he could protest, Kelsey leaned forward and kissed him the same mind-bending way he kissed her when he wanted to win an argument. Heat that had more to do with desire than the humid night coiled through her.

With a sigh, Doran pulled her down onto the chaise and wrapped a strong leg around her. Their bodies fit together as if they were meant to lie together, always, but she wanted more than caresses, kisses and hugs.

Much more.

And Devlin Doran gave it to her at his own leisurely pace, as if he cherished every moment of the sensual torture he was putting them both through. He seemed to anticipate what she wanted before she even knew; he was already filling the ache or soothing the spot with a tender touch. Easing down the chaise, he kissed her belly button, then he worked his way lower, until he suckled a spot that sent flurries of desire spiraling through her. She gasped at the sheer pleasure. When she couldn't take another moment of his tender kisses and gentle touches, he stood up and pulled off his trousers and underwear. Kelsey noticed that all her garments had already been shed, but that didn't mean anything, because she could make out Devlin's silhouette against the inky night and her mind was consumed with sheer, unadulterated lust.

There was a rustle of foil, and a moment later, he was back beside her. Hot as desire and hard as need. "You have no idea how long I've wanted to do this," he breathed. Then he entered her. She arched toward him, wanting more and getting it.

His hands kept wandering, seeking and his tongue tasting. Kelsey had experienced moments like this in her dreams, but never in real life and for ever move he made, she repaid it in full measure, all the while feeling as if she'd been a tightly wound flower bud, which was unfurling into a complete responsive blossom.

Higher and higher her senses spiraled.

Harder and harder her heart hammered.

A moment before she went over the brink,

Devlin kissed her, effectively intermingling and muffling their cries of ecstasy.

In the aftermath, her skin seemed more sensitive than ever before and she reveled at the way their perspiration blended. Hearts hammering in unison, Devlin Doran curled his body around her and held her tight.

Kelsey went to sleep in his arms, more content and peaceful than she'd ever felt in her life

Chapter 18

Waking up to birds singing and dawn rising seemed surreal, inhaling the intoxicating scent of thousands of blooms roses felt sensual as the languid, humid heat. Finding Kelsey burrowed against him, made Doran want hold this moment for the rest of his life.

But he'd scheduled an early meeting with Quinn and didn't want the master of two-plus-two to figure out why he cancelled their late-night appointment. Carefully, he extracted his long legs from Kelsey. Then, he covered her with his shirt. He put on his trousers, grabbed his holster and quickly went to the house for a quick shower.

Anxious to get back to Kelsey, before he'd even left, Doran sped toward the interstate. Luck favored him with green lights and light traffic all the way until the exit for his office. As he turned onto the ramp, the bottom of the hill changed from yellow to red. He braked, but something snapped and the brake pedal slammed to the floor. Damn! He should have checked the lines and not assumed the security system would hinder everyone. The Suburban picked up speed as it hurtled toward the red light.

He grabbed the handle for the emergency brake

and pulled.

Nothing.

A chill ran down his spine as he rammed the transmission into low. As if in slow motion, the cars crawled along the converging road, oblivious of the impending disaster.

Gears howled and sweat broke out in beads, then began to trickle toward his eyes.

Still too fast. Please, God, don't let any innocents get hurt. He'd wanted to believe Kelsey and her family were innocent dupes, but the car had probably been tampered with the same place Ramsey's car had been sabotaged: Beja Flora, with Ling hiding in the background. He couldn't give up and let Ling win. Ling wouldn't stop with one life. Quinn and Kelsey would follow, as would all the innocents Ling offered his poisons to.

One-hundred-feet. Not slowing fast enough. He forced the transmission into park. The tortured gears squealed.

Fifty feet and still moving forward too fast. Doran spun the wheel and did a one-eighty. Horns honked. The car behind him swerved out of the way as the Suburban skidded uphill, then vaulted into the grass.

With a pop, one tire blew.

A moment later, all was silent. Doran laid his forehead on his steering wheel and thanked God for granting some prayers. Then, he asked forgiveness for forcing Kelsey to endure what he'd just been through. He exhaled, grabbed his phone and dialed Quinn.

ooo

Long after dawn broke and she heard Doran leave, Kelsey lay on the chase staring at the peace rose, which had clung to an ancient trellis, which had protected them from prying eyes last night and still hid her this morning.

She inhaled deeply, as her thoughts drifted to the past few hours. Doran's enticing scent permeated every pore of her body. Dreamily, she slipped into his shirt and her own skirt, then she carried the rest of their clothing and hurried into the main house before Martha or anyone else noticed her absence.

Inside her room, the windows muffled sounds of birds singing and a distant lawnmower running. Kelsey padded to the window on bare feet, then settling on the window seat, she picked up her old panda bear, hugged him and looked out at the dew-drenched gazebo. Had it always looked this romantic?

She sat there until the sun rose hot in the clear blue sky. A frown knit Kelsey's brow. He should have been back by now. Unwilling to sit inside and moon over her new love on a gorgeous Indian summer morning, Kelsey reluctantly took a shower, then dressed in an emerald-green silk shirt and dug into the back of her closet, where she'd hidden her favorite jeans. Her nose wrinkled at the smell of smoke, but she hadn't trusted Martha to wash her jeans; for fear that she wouldn't get them back. As she pulled them on, she glanced at Doran's shirt. It wouldn't do to have Martha find those items in her room. Kelsey went through her bathroom into Doran's adjoining room. She inhaled the masculine scent he'd left in the room and wondered what it would have been like to wake a few moments earlier – just enough to watch him dress and perhaps give him a kiss good-bye.

She buried her nose in his shirt and smelled their mingled scents. The aromas seemed right together. Kelsey smiled as she draped it over a chair and smoothed her hands over the comforting fabric.

Quietly, she went back to her own room and slipped the photo of the unknown girl into her pocket. She wasn't quite certain why she never wanted to go anywhere without the old picture, which had come to mean so much to her, but somehow the blue-eyed girl represented all the unknown kids that she hoped to help if she won the election.

When she got outside, the sunlight felt hot as a caress against her skin, but there was no comparison to the way Doran touched her. Kelsey turned to her right, quickly walked through the herb garden, then slowed down when she entered the rose garden. Picking an aimless route, she sauntered from one statue to another, pausing to study each. While she circled the reproduction of Michelangelo's David, thinking that if the artist had wanted to capture perfection, he should have lived a few more centuries and met Devlin Doran. When she walked around Venus, she wished she could compare to the tall, statuesque beauty. With a sigh, she realized that Devlin Doran had made her feel as if she did.

Dreamily, she sat on a sturdy concrete bench, held up by Corinthian columns and breathed in the rich scent of the flowers. Forevermore, no matter what happened, whenever she smelled this lush blend, she would tingle with thoughts of romance and love. Kelsey finally got up and slowly walking from flower to flower, bending over and drinking in the individual perfumes: this one floral, that one exotic spice.

Kelsey didn't realize that the gazebo was her destination until she arrived at it. Her hand caressed the handle for a moment before she opened the door and went inside.

So many of her happy memories had been formed here. She'd sat cross-legged on the wood floor and listened to her grandmother talk about horticulture and expound on the uses of her favorite herbs. Together, they'd painted the floor and woodwork hunter green to honor the happiness and beauty plants brought to their lives.

Kelsey sighed at the memory of her sloppy strokes getting more paint on herself and the screen, instead of the lattice. The paint was worn, but she was a much better painter, now. Kelsey decided that when she could go home, the first thing she would do would be repaint her door as a tribute to Grandma Rose. Or maybe do it as a tribute to new love. Perhaps the lovely green could serve both purposes.

In the distance, a streak of red rocketed up the drive. The idiot drove like Zoë, but it couldn't be Zoë, because she'd been forbidden to enter the gate since Martha had realized she would never be anything but a shameless tramp. If Zoë had learned early on that sexual attraction could be so wonderful, it was no wonder she acted the way she did. Kelsey sat down on the fainting couch and caressed the sun-faded fabric.

Outside, a hummingbird darted among the peace rose's flowers; its ruby throat a striking contrast against the pale petals. Would Doran be like the hummingbird, or would they find a way to stay together? It had taken her years to find the one man she truly loved. "Let him feel the same," she whispered.

In the distance, a car door slammed.

Kelsey stretched out on the chaise on the couch and gazed up at the rustic rafters. The faint fragrance of his cologne mixed with her perfume, the aroma of the garden and the musky tang of love. But would it be love everlasting for him, as it would certainly be for her? She listened to the whirl of the hummingbird's wings and fell asleep to thoughts of her hopes. She dreamed of Doran's lips trailing a sensual path down her neck and his breath hot against her lips as he bent toward her for a kiss. She sighed in her sleep and welcomed the dream with open arms, but moments later, she was startled awake.

Zoë clomped across the room on lethally high crimson heels, while the screen door bounced against the frame. Kelsey sat upright so fast that the gazebo seemed to revolve around her. Zoë put her hands on her hips, where they nearly covered the miniscule red leather skirt. "Kelsey, you need to drop out of this election. I know Marv and he has to win." Her chest heaved against the skimpy white lace shirt. "I don't know why, but he does."

Kelsey blinked several times. "He can threaten

me with dead chickens all he wants. I'm not quitting."

"He didn't leave that, I did." Zoë sat heavily on the corner of the couch, tears welling in her eyes.

"You were responsible for the chickens?" Kelsey stared at her in disbelief. Just when you thought you know someone, you find out that you don't know them at all.

Zoë nodded. Head down, she cleared her throat. "I wanted to scare you off before you got hurt more than you already had been." Tears and mascara created rivulets down her cheeks, but she seemed unable to look her in the eye. Still, Kelsey was certain that for once, Zoë was telling the unvarnished truth. "Jesus Christ," Zoë said, her tone broken by misery, "he had someone cut your brakes, just like Rams' because he wanted Rams out of the way." She swallowed and took a quick peak at Kelsey. "Marv will kill anyone and everyone necessary to get what he wants. I never wanted to see that truth, but I've had to face it. Please, oh please drop out so you stay safe."

Kelsey sat up straight, unable to get past the worst shock. "You put that damned thing on my door?" Zoë nodded. "Were you responsible for both of Ramsey's too?" Though Zoë shook her head, her guilty look said 'yes'. Kelsey gritted her jaw and spoke through her teeth. "Did you deliberately seduce Byron and break my engagement?"

Zoë's expression hardened. "He was bad news. I didn't want you hurt."

She was right and she could keep Byron, but if she so much as looked at Devlin, she'd wring her neck.

Zoë brushed away tears and edged away from her. "I only did Ram's first chicken; the one with the warning note." She wiped her cheeks with the backs of her hands, stark black streaks made her cheeks looked like she was part zebra. "I was trying to save him, too," her tone rose to a whine. Zoë folded her arms across her stomach, as if in pain. "He wouldn't listen to me, either. No one listens to me when I warn them." Zoë suddenly leaned close and grabbed her hand. "If he'd dropped out, Abby and Jenny would still be alive and you'd be safe."

Kelsey looked from their hands to Zoë's desperate expression. If she'd known to warn them, it meant she got her information from somewhere. "How did you know someone tampered with my car?"

She let go of her hand. "I can't tell you how I know, but I've known him and been afraid of him for most of my life." Zoë crossed her heart, as they'd done since she was a toddler. "That's the truth. The honest to God truth." She swiped at her tears and created more smudges. Kelsey studied her, wondering if she'd ever understood her or her motives. Zoë gulped. "I know I'm not worth much to you and you really hate me, bu-"

"I do not hate you." Kelsey took Zoë's hands between both of hers and squeezed them. "I don't like what you've done with your life, but I love you as a person and sister."

Zoë cried harder.

Kelsey drew close and hugged her. Not knowing what to do or say, she let her cry on her shoulder and gently patted her back. "I don't know what to think about the ways you've tried to protect me and Rams, but I appreciate the motive behind your actions." How could anyone have believed a stinking, fly-encrusted chicken would make anyone worth their salt change their mind?

Zoë's tears fell in a hot, wet stream against her shoulder. "I love you, too." She shuddered. "That's why I have to help you." Zoë straightened and grabbed her biceps. "You have to quit."

If she quit, Marvin would certainly win and the voters would lose. Kelsey sighed. "I can't."

"But he'll kill you."

Not with Devlin protecting her. She hoped. "If that's what is meant to be, I'll die for a good cause. Which is more than I can say about staying safe in a laboratory altering orchid genes."

Zoë wrenched free and ran out, sobbing as if she'd lost her last friend. Kelsey lunged after her, then stopped midway to the banging door, which bounced adding percussion to Zoë's wails. Unwilling to follow Zoë, she and began to pace. Physical movement couldn't overcome the emotional baggage Zoë had left in the atmosphere. And it certainly didn't explain why Zoë had been so convinced she needed to be scared safe, that she'd found a dead chicken to hang on the door.

Why a chicken, or all things? Did it represent something particular, or had it simply been easy to get? Kelsey frowned at the memory of the bird's smelly feathers. For certain, she hadn't gotten it from any grocery store she'd ever been to.

Where on earth would anyone get a chicken with

feathers?

Too many questions; too few answers.

Walking had always helped her think. And it was an activity she hadn't had enough time for since she'd stepped in to help Ramsey. She needed a good, long walk to clear her mind and help her find the answers. Kelsey quietly went out and headed toward the trail that wound under an arbor covered with clematis, through the cut flower garden, and then branched, one path circling toward the pond, the other paralleling the main driveway to the gatehouse. Pretty as they were, swan bites left scars. She glanced back toward the house, to make certain Devlin hadn't returned while she'd been distracted by Zoë, but his black suburban wasn't where he always parked. The sun felt hot on her back. Which guard had let Zoë in? It was a question, which could be easily answered. Teeth clenched, Kelsey spun on her heel and walked briskly toward the gatehouse, confident that a good mile or three would bring more than one answer to her questions.

Kelsey ducked behind a broad oak trunk that bordered the driveway and glanced back. Zoë was carrying her shoes and moving fast toward the gazebo. Kelsey looked up in the branches at the surveillance camera and shook her head at the useless technology.

"Kel, where are you?" Though distant, Zoë's voice was too close.

She could either cower behind this tree trunk until Zoë was gone or she could find out which guard was on duty. Without a backward glance,

Kelsey jogged down the trail.

As she trotted around the final curve and the gatehouse came in sight, she heard an engine and saw a white sedan pull up to the gate. The guard stepped out and chatted with the driver, as if greeting a friend.

Kelsey squinted to see if she recognized the friendly guard, but the wrought iron made identification impossible. What she did see was the emblem of the county sheriff on the car door. Perhaps the guard had been smart enough to phone for backup after Zoë got in. When the guard stepped backward, Kelsey slowed to a fast walk. The car door opened and an unmistakable portly figure emerged. Since when did Sheriff Botts come out on nuisance calls?

Kelsey slowed her pace and glanced back. Zoë's distant white and red figure jiggling and wiggling down the path toward her. If the guard had identified Zoë as the problem, she'd bet a month of Tuesdays that Botts had come for the opportunity to frisk Zoë. Kelsey looked in one direction, then the other, uncertain which way seemed less savory. Still, she wanted to know which idiot had let Zoë in. As she studied the man's profile, the guard began making sweeping gestures. Kelsey frowned and wondered why his body language appeared defensive.

Bits of the conversation came to her. "Can't let you n-" Jake pointed to his cruiser then flashed his badge. The guard shook his head.

If the guard hadn't called him, why was he here? Kelsey jogged to the gate. More phrases came to her. By the time she got to the wrought iron, it was obvious that the guard had not phoned for backup.

"Afternoon, Jake, what brings you out?"

Botts looked relieved to see her. "There's been an accident. Someone named Doran is asking for you."

Kelsey gasped. "Devlin Doran?"

Jake eagerly nodded. "Said you were here, but your man refused to phone the house."

Kelsey gulped. "How bad is it?"

Jake shrugged. "He's at County General." He gestured to his cruiser. "You want I should call them and ask?"

She nodded.

The sheriff got into his vehicle and spoke into the microphone. Though she strained to hear the conversation, but his voice wasn't loud enough. After an unbearable wait, while she sweated through the back of her shirt, Jake got out. Face sad, he walked to stand a foot from her on the other side of the gate. "Looks like his brakes failed." Jake looked sad as a sagging hound dog. "He's not so good, but they're operating and hope it'll turn out good."

Kelsey's knees felt like they'd turned to water and she sagged against the gate.

Jake reached through the bars, trying to support her. "You okay Ms. Kelsey?"

Was she?

"You want me ta give you a lift to the hospital?"

She weakly nodded. Jake turned to the guard. "Donny, open the gate." The guard half saluted and touched a button. "Careful, now, just a bit, so's I can get in there to help her."

As the sheriff scooted inside, Zoë screamed. "No!"

Awful as the thought of Devlin being hurt was, at least it had provided an escape from Zoë's whining. Kelsey hung onto Jake's beefy arm and let him support her to the passenger door. "Hop in."

As she got in, a yowl of misery slashed the air. Sheriff Botts turned around as if he'd been attacked from behind. Kelsey slammed the door shut, grateful to have a means of escaping Zoë and her endless supply of confusion. As the door closed, Zoë stopped running toward them, sank to her knees and began crying loud enough to be heard in the next county.

Chapter 19

Doran grabbed his cellular phone, and tapped in Quinn's code number. "Hey, I've got a problem."

"You and me both."

"The Burb lost its brakes."

"Are you hurt?"

"Of course not, but I'm damned determined to get Ling for once and for all." Doran sighed. "In the meantime, I need a wrecker and another set of wheels."

"I'll get Trent on it. Where are you?"

By the time Doran dropped Trent back at the office, he was royally pissed at his lapse of attention to detail and determined to make Ling pay ten-fold.

Quinn was right, if he hadn't been so preoccupied with Kelsey, he would have made a through inspection of his ride before he got in. Instead, he'd been thinking about Kelsey, love and tenderness, just like he'd been doing ever since he saw her photo.

As he drove Trent's old blue pickup toward Beja Flora, he told himself that he had to end it before it went any further. They had a lot of hearsay and some incriminating evidence on Marvin

Frederickson, but no incontrovertible proof and nothing to truly exonerate the MacLennans. Particularly not since his ride could have been sabotaged in their compound. Of course, the damage might have been done at the auditorium, but it didn't seem like it should have taken that long for the lines to leak out.

Still, in his heart of hearts, he didn't want to believe that either Kelsey or her family were involved in Ling's sordid schemes. And if he couldn't be objective, he would jeopardize himself and everyone trying to help him.

It was time to bail out.

Trent's truck rattled up to the guardhouse and he leaned out. The door slammed open and Zoë shot out of the shelter. "I thought you were half dead or something." Her cheeks were a mess of runny mascara and her eyes were red-rimmed.

How the heck had she heard about the accident? A better question was who had told her. He smiled and adopted a casual tone. "Why would you think that?"

Zoë's bosom heaved, as if she'd run a marathon. "Sheriff Botts was here and said so." The guard behind her nodded as he tried to sidestep for a better view down her overstuffed lace shirt. "He told Kelsey you'd been hurt and she left with him. You're supposed to be getting some kinda operation." Zoë looked at him, as if searching for injuries.

"Where am I supposedly getting this done at?"

Zoë sniffed and shrugged.

"Sheriff Botts took her to you," the guard said. "I

think they were going to County General," he grinned. "She'll sure be happy to find out the guy that got hurt wasn't you."

"She left with Botts?" They both nodded. "Shit!" Doran exploded. "They got her." And by using the lamest old trick, too. He should have warned her.

Fresh tears ran down Zoë's cheeks. "He got her for Marv, didn't he?"

"That'd be my guess."

"Marv always calls Jake 'the good sheriff'," Zoë sobbed.

"They left about twenty minutes ago," the guard said.

"I watched her go," Zoë wailed. "And I screamed for her not to, but she never, ever listens to me.

Doran leaped out of the old truck and grabbed Zoë. "Snap out of it." He gave her a little shake. "If you lose it, she won't have a chance."

"Oh God, she's going to die because I didn't stop her, again."

"Think," he shouted. "Where would Frederickson have her taken?"

"I don't know."

"Yes, you do. You must know. Think!"

"Should I call 911?" the guard asked.

Doran shook his head. "Cops protect their own, even if the badge is tarnished."

"I p-put the dead ch-chicken on her d-door to scare her because Marv is always m-making dumb jokes about c-c-chickens and laughing at me b-b-bec-c-cause I don't understand."

That was it!

"Zoë, you're great." Doran kissed her forehead, then let her go. She stumbled backward against the guard. Doran grabbed his phone and punched in Quinn's number. "Botts kidnapped Kelsey. I think he took her to PBCO."

The guard turned an odd shade of gray.

Zoë stopped crying and stared at him. "PBCO? Where I got the chicken?"

"He wouldn't take her there while there were witnesses," Quinn said. "He'd wait until after dark."

Doran turned to Zoë. "What's Frederickson doing tonight?"

She shrugged and shook her head.

"How the hell should I know?" Quinn said.

Zoë wet her lips. "He said something about counting chickens now that they'd hatched."

"PBCO," Doran said. "It has to be PBCO. Quinn, meet me at the truck stop and bring the goodies. I figure this'll be a formal affair and we'll need to wear black."

"I've already got the kevlar in my van. As soon as I get out to the parking lot, I'll be on my way."

"See you in ten."

Zoë grabbed his arm. "Take me with you. I want to help."

Doran gestured for the guard to hold her. "Stay here. The less people to confuse the issue, the easier it'll be to get her back."

Zoë howled in misery, which only served to harden Doran's resolve to keep the noisy turncoat as far away from him as possible. As the guard hung onto her, Doran hopped back into the old truck, gunned the engine and turned around. As he floored it and headed for the meeting he glanced in the rearview mirror and saw Zoë running up the driveway toward the house.

ooo

Zoë blew her nose as she drove slowly through the parking lot, looking for Marv's silver Lexus. When she'd told his campaign secretary she was the personal assistant for the secretary of state, the dumb woman had let it slip where Marv was meeting supporters. Now, she stared up at the posh apartment building, and wondered if the old hag had sent her on a wild goose chase. But with Kelsey's life in the balance, she couldn't give up. Zoë found the Lexus, with its SENATOR tag parked near the rear entrance.

She parked her Porsche in a shady space on the far side of the parking lot, turned off the ignition and leaned back to think about how she could find out exactly where Kelsey was and what she could do to help.

"I can't just confront him," she told her reflection in the rearview mirror. She rubbed her aching eyes and wondered if she should just follow him in the hopes that he would lead her to Kelsey.

A woman's husky laugh caught Zoë's attention. She looked up and saw Frederickson walking an elegant looking woman toward his car. He was smiling down at her as if hanging on her every word and gently caressing her fingers, where they nestled in the crook of his arm. Everything about the pair screamed of the casual intimacy of longtime lovers.

That dirty, lowdown, sonofabitch was two-timing her!

Before she could reconsider her actions or quell her fury, Zoë leaped out of her car and ran barefoot across the parking lot. Marv looked her direction. Halfway into an indolent arc of the brow, his mouth flattened and he motioned her away.

The woman gave a gentile laugh. "That frump looks like she's charging at us."

Marv scowled at her, then smiled gently at the woman. "That's the bimbo I told you about before, the who won't leave me alone. She seems to think that her vote means she owns me."

Zoë screamed with rage. She was going to kill him.

"Obviously she's either drunk or on drugs," he said. "Go ahead to the car and lock the doors. I'll get rid of her then drive you home."

With a final disdainful glance, the woman turned away. Zoë hated the prim walk and sensible suit. Hated the woman for every cell of blue blood, which she obviously possessed.

Marv was walking toward her, anger in every step. If they'd been somewhere less public, she knew he'd be on her like a lust-fest.

"Who is that woman?" Zoë demanded.

"A voter," his soft, harsh tone was filled with suppressed emotion. Marv turned his back to his Lexus and looked her up and down; his expression suggested that he was inspecting a cesspool. Belatedly, she remembered that she hadn't washed her face. She probably looked like a sick raccoon." Specifically, Lynette Pinkney." He let the glorified

Pinkney name hang in the air like a trophy. His expression turned smug. "She just pledged a hundred grand to my campaign fund.

"And how many fucks did you promise her?"

"Vulgar today, aren't you?" He looked as if he never wanted to touch her again.

New tears burned the back of her eyelids.

Marv casually glanced around the parking area. The only other thing within earshot was a fat gray squirrel. His expression hardened. "You dress like a tramp." His words and tone scalded like acid. "You act like a trash. How dare you approach me in public?"

"I lov-"

"What do you think you are? High-class like Lynette?" He snapped her spandex lace top as if it offended him.

"You bought me this. You made me what I am."

"You're a worthless bitch."

Her heart ached as if he'd stabbed her.

"Quit whining after me."

She looked down, amazed that blood wasn't streaming from her wounded chest.

"B-b-b-but I l-l-l-love y-you; you love m-m-me."

"Fool," he spat. "You're good for one thing."

A cold, hard calm settled over Zoë. "You lied when you said you cared and wanted to marry me, didn't you?"

"Why would I tie myself to trash like you? You're lucky you still serve me in bed, or I'd have gotten rid of you by now." His harsh whisper suggested six feet under.

With that, Marv turned his back on her and

strutted to his Lexus.

Zoë stared after him and gritted her teeth. He would pay for every wrong he'd ever done to her. But first, she had to find Kelsey.

ooo

Kelsey tested the plastic tie wraps, which Jake had used to secure her to the metal folding chair with, but they were no looser now, than they'd been when he'd first slammed her onto the hard seat.

If there was any justice in this world, she would get out of this alive. But that thought seemed highly unlikely.

Still, there had to be some way to get out of this room. She carefully looked around at the area. Long tables, covered with more bottles and beakers than her chemistry prof would have ever allowed, took up one side of the large room. That area was bathed in harsh, white light, so the longhaired, tattooed guys playing at being chemists could see what they were doing, but her side of the room was relatively dark. She squinted past the tables and charts pinned to the white wall, but couldn't see any sign of a window.

She looked behind her chair, but couldn't see anything except the large boxes labeled SOAP piled behind her, and on either side.

Defeat choked her, but she knew that there had to be hope, so as bad as things seemed, she would keep looking for a way to escape, until she found one.

ooo

Doran slipped through the late-afternoon shadows of PBCO's parking lot to get a closer look

337

at the vehicle, which was half-hidden by the dumpsters near the freight docks. As he neared the back of the red Taurus, the stench of decay overpowered every other smell. He lifted his binoculars and examined the rear bumper. There were no streaks, or any other sign that a body had been in the trunk.

It wasn't much of a relief, but it was something.

The radio in his pocket vibrated. Doran adjusted the thin plastic tube close to his lips. "Yeah?"

"I ran the tags." Quinn's voice was clear through the tiny transmitter in his right ear. "The car is registered to Botts's wife. Looks like your hunch was right."

Doran grunted. "And it matches the model Trent saw firebomb Kelsey's."

"I noticed the similarity. You think he threw that cocktail at you?"

"I'd bet on it. I'm almost positive he did the brakes on my car, too, but it's only gut instinct." Doran moved closer and peered in the windows: a few dried brown spots, which had probably been coffee or coke, some cheerios and a couple raisins, but no blood or damp spots. Unfortunately, that didn't mean Kelsey was safe, there were thousands of ways to murder a person without leaving body fluid. He touched his pocket, expecting to feel Marnie's photo, but only felt the rapid beating of his own heart. "I'm going in."

"Without backup or a warrant? No way."

Hadn't Quinn figured it out when he left his badge in the van? "You're monitoring me."

Quinn groaned. "I've got a bad feeling about

this. It could be a setup. Worse, we only have a hunch that she's inside."

"Yeah, but I'm still going in."

"At least come back here and -"

"What? Wait for Christmas?"

"Dealing with this bunch, you need to go formal."

Doran suspected Quinn's request was motivated as much by the desire to stall him until backup arrived, as it was by knowing that wearing body armor around Ling was a sensible precaution. Either way, his partner was right and the last time he'd ignored him had been a disaster. He reversed direction and climbed into the surveillance van. The printer was spitting out page after page of paper. Quinn's back faced the bank of monitors, and his expression was grim as he read the printout.

Doran shucked off his holster and dark silk shirt, then opened the locker containing his night gear and vest.

After putting his bulletproof vest over his T-shirt, he dressed and filled his pockets with a tracking device, night-vision goggles, a miniature transmitter, which sent an audio-visual to the van, extra ammo clips and a knife.

Meanwhile, Quinn grabbed pages from the printer as fast as it could spit them out and read them with an enthusiasm that Doran hadn't seen since he'd become reliant on wheels.

When he was ready to leave, Quinn lowered the papers and cleared his throat. "Before you go, let me try to summarize this data." He shuffled several papers, until he found what he wanted.

Oh, no, not another of his delays. Doran cracked open the door.

"In the previous eight years, a total of fifty-three people close to Frederickson died in a variety of accidents and unexpected illnesses, and some very interesting suicides."

Fifty-three! Doran closed the door and stuck his head and shoulders through the blackout curtain. "How many were close to Martha and Zoë?"

Quinn frowned and scanned the document. "Maybe a dozen for Zoë. I'd guess only a couple for Martha. She might be an innocent."

"She gave birth to Frederickson's kid."

"That's what she claims. I'd have bet dollars to donuts that either Calhoun or Winston was the father." Quinn's expression said that he still wanted a blood test to disprove that one. "If Martha offed Rose, I bet it had something to do with the paternity thing."

Doran grunted in agreement. "Zoë does seem close to Frederickson."

"I thought it was sexual until my chat with Martha." Quinn fingered the printout. "She could be mom and dad's go between, but I don't have any motive for that."

"Interesting hypotheses," Doran said. Blood was thicker than water, perhaps his initial assumption had been right except for the guilty family.

Quinn taped a page. "My favorite deaths are the ones labeled suicide." He cleared his throat, then read, "For instance, Ben Galligher died of a gunshot to the back of his head, but the autopsy labeled it suicide."

"You're kidding." Quinn solemnly shook his head. Doran frowned. "Why does that name sound familiar?"

"He's a legend in covert ops. Or was until he went after Ling."

Memories of the rumors surrounding Galligher's disappearance gave him an uneasy feeling. "And he's listed as one of Frederickson's friends?"

With a sharp nod, Quinn looked back at the printout. "Eight years ago, fourteen of Frederickson's friends and acquaintances died: four heart attacks - five if you count Rose MacLennan - five in plane crashes and five due to auto accidents."

"That's only fifteen."

"And it was only one year. He's been busy since then, too." Quinn looked him in the eye. "It seems like someone made an effort at not leaving a pattern." His mouth flattened. "The effort to avoid one, becomes one."

Doran scowled and motioned for Quinn to continue.

"In the past couple years, the casualties have primarily been by gunshot." Quinn lowered the paper and peered over top. "Assuming Frederickson is responsible, one might surmise that he's discovered this method is more efficient or he's got someone new doing his dirty work who likes to shoot."

"Or one could conjecture that once his crony, Botts was in office, it was easier for him to get away with murder," Doran said.

"Interesting point. The seven questionable

deaths, which were labeled suicide, were here in the County." He cleared his throat than read, "Four people fell through windows and were decapitated in the process…. Another seven died by gunshot – that included Galligher."

"If he rigged Ramsey's car, you can add two more deaths of innocents."

"The more I learn about the guy, the more I think he's a plague to society and I can see why Ling considers him a pal."

Doran gritted his teeth. The more he heard about the jerk, the more concerned he was for Kelsey's safety.

"Amazing what the voters will elect to represent them, isn't it?"

Doran grunted in agreement and moved to leave.

Quinn dropped his relaxed attitude and checked the screens, which all showed desolate night landscapes. "You should be clear to go. But, for God's sake, be careful. Ling is involved, so this might turn into a rowdy party." He sighed. "Wish I could come, too."

"I know, pal. I'm hoping that bastard shows up. We owe him. We owe him big time."

"Don't do anything stupid."

"I'll try not to."

Quinn shook a finger at him. "You blink wrong and I'm dialing for help."

He wouldn't have expected anything less and was actually surprised that Quinn hadn't already called in the Marines. Doran stepped through the blackout curtain, then silently exited the van. As he closed the door, he imagined Quinn leaning toward a monitor and testing his heat-signature against the residual heat of the nearby asphalt. Despite useless legs, Doran wouldn't have trusted anyone else to back him. He latched the door and moved toward the building.

Once inside PBCO, he began a methodical search of the main floor rooms. Odd how desolate the building seemed. Normally, in a building like this, someone was working late or at least there was a janitorial staff to avoid. Though the lack of people helped him move freely, it also gave him an even worse feeling than he'd had when he found out Kelsey had been captured.

As Doran entered a large corner office, lights illuminated the window-wall. He went still as a statue and watched the vehicle park. When the lights went out, the room became dark as night. Amazing how quickly things went black after sunset.

He put on his night-vision goggles and adjusted them, then studied the car, which was parked in the murky shade of a magnolia. Though everything appeared greenish, he recognized Frederickson as he emerged from the light-colored Mercedes. When Frederickson headed to the front door, Doran inched the office door open, so he had a view of the reception and waiting areas.

The tidy desk supported a philodendron and a professional phone. Beyond it, three impressionistic paintings dominated the area.

Frederickson came up to the thick glass doors, then opened an inconspicuous panel in the outside wall, which revealed an access to the security system. He held up a flashlight and confidently keyed in the code.

"You recording this?" Doran asked.

"What to you think? The DA will think it's Christmas."

Doran grunted in agreement.

"Notice what he's driving?"

"Ramsey MacLennan's Mercedes."

Quinn made a blaring sound. "Wrong. I did a close-up of the plates. It looks like he overlaid a mockup of Ramsey's plate over another one."

"Good way to mislead witnesses."

"You got it. Did you notice what Martha drives?"

It had never occurred to him that she had a car. "Let me guess, a white Mercedes?"

"Bingo. What's even more interesting is that she purchased it twenty-seven days ago; two days after Ramsey leased his. I'm telling you that those Lancaster women are dirty as sin."

Doran grunted in agreement. When Frederickson finished keying in the code, the lights on the alarm panel changed. He closed the panel then dug a key out of his pocket.

"I'm going silent."

"I'll be watching. The least hint –"

"I know; you'll call in the troops."

Quinn sighed. "Wish I could do more."

The door squeaked open and Frederickson stepped inside. He moved with a confidence that bespoke familiarity with the surroundings. His shoes clicked across the marble entryway, but when he got to the gloomy hallway, carpet muffled his steps. Still, Frederickson didn't falter, as he headed straight for Doran.

Doran fought the urge to close and bolt the door. A moment before an inevitable confrontation, the senator's direction changed and Frederickson passed close enough to Doran's vantage point for him to smell the woodsy scent of his after-shave.

As the hallway bored deeper into the windowless area, Frederickson turned on his flashlight. A few soft footfalls later and the flashlight stopped in front of the elevator bank. Ding. A rectangle of light from the elevator flooded the hallway and illuminated Frederickson's face. He walked in, as if he owned the building and had every right to be there long after everyone else had gone.

Quinn made a sound of intense appreciation and began softly whistle. Now, all they needed was footage of him with Ling or something else incriminating and they had the bastard so good that no jury would let him off.

When the door closed, Doran scanned the area, then silently moved to the elevator and checked the panel. When the elevator stopped at B, he entered the stairwell. Concrete block walls covered with thick chrome yellow enamel paint encased the windowless stairwell, while the metal railings and concrete floor had been left in their natural state.

Doran peaked through the mesh-embedded window at the basement level. A bobbing light illuminated a large fenced in an area containing racks and racks of old files. There was about a ten-foot wide corridor between the stairwell and elevator. Frederickson hunched over, with his back to Doran and appeared to be doing something to the fence.

"Can you zoom in the video?" Quinn whispered over the headset. Doran turned a dial. "There. A little lower and to your right. Good, that has it." Triumphant sounds of appreciation emanated from the earpiece. "Got a good tape of our friend dialing in the combination for the gate. Just how do you suppose such an upstanding citizen came by that?"

"Beats me." Doran whispered, "You'd think with his taste for quality, he'd stay up with the marble and carpet instead of come down here to play with indoor fences and files." Frederickson propped the gate open, the vanished into the tall, long file-racks.

"What's this? A gold-plated invite?" Quinn made an unhappy sound. "Dev, I don't like open gates."

Doran didn't either. He drew his gun and inched the stairwell door open.

Deep within the file storage area, he heard the muffled sound of footsteps. Doran darted across the entrance area and through the gate. His spine prickled and he prayed he hadn't just entered a trap. On soundless shoes, he dashed to the end of the bank of racks where Frederickson had vanished. He leaned back and counted to ten, as his heart calmed, then he peered around the rack.

Frederickson was about a hundred feet down the bank of files and moving with the same casual confidence he'd shown on the main level. When he reached the end of the row, he turned to his left.

Doran mirrored his movement at the top end of the line of open racks. The fifth row down,

Frederickson opened a door marked NO ADMITTANCE. Bright white light and hip-hop music streamed into the aisle.

Doran ducked back out of sight, then moved down the previous walkway.

"About time you got here," someone said from inside the room.

The door started to swing shut. "Marvin," Kelsey said. Doran's heart slammed to full alert. "Somehow I knew you were Botts' puppet master."

There was the sound of slap, before the door clicked shut.

"Dev, see if you can slide the optic lens under the door." Doran forced his frozen muscles forward and threaded the spaghetti-thin tube under the door. "Hmmmm. Interesting selection of shoes. Can you rotate it?" Quinn hummed an annoyingly happy tune. "There!"

"Is Kelsey all right?"

Quinn's tune changed to a non-committal monotone. Doran drew his handgun and clicked off the safety. "Looks like Kelsey is tied to a chair." Quinn snorted. "How cliché can these idiots get?" There was a pause. Doran gritted his teeth and willed his partner to clue him in on how many were in the room and the dimensions. "Botts is there." Big surprise. "He's got a handgun, probably a 38. Three unknowns, they look like lab-rats. I'm getting wonderful resolution on the picture. This'll play great for a jury."

"I'm glad for you," Doran breathed. "Can you confirm five bogeys plus Kelsey?" While Doran was relatively confident that the other room was soundproof because of the music had only been noticeable with the door open, he didn't know what sort of heat, sound or motion technology the racks might hide. "Are Frederickson and the three rats are armed?" There was a beep in the background.

"Looks like more company just arrived," Quinn said, after a moment's silence. Quinn inhaled sharply. "It's Ling." His whispered tone crackled with excitement. "Dev, get out of there." When he didn't immediately retract the mini-cam, Quinn snarled, "Now. I'm phoning our friends. They'll love to join our party." Doran extracted the optics. Though he wanted to barge into the room, gun blazing, he knew better than to put himself and Kelsey in the middle. Over the headphone, Quinn whistled softly as the sound of digital tones played in the background. "Ling brought a couple of our friends for the party."

"Surely you didn't think Ling would go anywhere without Merek and Cedric. That would be equivalent to a bride showing up for her wedding naked."

"Brad, this is Quinn … yeah, I know it's late, but you're gonna want in on this."

Various strains of the conversation were repeated three more times. "Dev, Trent will be here to back you up in ten minutes. Do not do anything stupid before then."

Doran finished removing the video feed and melted into the shadows of the racks. When he arrived near the front of the racks, he readjusted the video feed and focused the tiny camera on the elevator doors. After a few tense moments, there was a ping and the doors opened, discharging a rectangle of light into the basement. The three people standing on the elevator were illuminated to perfection. Cedric stepped into the basement and peered into the gloom, his Uzi ready for anything. When Cedric was satisfied that all was well, he'd moved halfway to the gate, Ling stepped off the elevator with confidence, Merek came two paces behind him, his Uzi only a little less vigilant than Cedric's.

God, but he hated those two mercenaries. Doran's fingers itched for the comforting feel of his gun and he knew that if he was certain which of them had shot Quinn, he'd take the scum out right then and there. Instead, he let training rule his emotions and kept his weapon holstered.

When Cedric entered the racks, Doran pocketed the transmitter and palmed an anesthetic syringe in one hand, a thick cloth in the other. Ling moved into the file section, as if he didn't have a fear in the world. Merek imitated Ling's arrogant posture. When the elevator doors closed, Doran slipped on his night-vision goggles and silently moved in behind Merek. In one swift, coordinated movement he clamped his fabric-protected hand over Merek's mouth and stabbed him with the tranquilizer. The thug whirled, but Doran expected the move. He held him quiet for the count of ten. Then he soundlessly shifted Merek to the floor and grabbed his Uzi. Doran caught up with Ling as he entered the lab.

"Son of a B. Dev!" Quinn's panic sounded palatable. "Get out of there!"

Instead of retreating, Doran ducked behind a stack of packing crates. He laid the video feed on top of somw boxes so Quinn could get a visual of the room.

"Frederickson is bowing to Ling as if honoring royalty," Quinn said.

"He'd probably kiss Hitler's feet," Doran murmured.

"Yeah. Can you rotate the view left?" After tweaking the video angle, Doran placed the backup audio receiver near the camera. "Good, now get the hell out of there."

"No. You make your evidence file, I've got something else to do." Doran crouched below table height and began working his way across the room toward Kelsey, while Quinn ordered him to retreat.

"Ah, my dear friend," Frederickson said. If Quinn hadn't been so busy howling for him to flee, he would realize that the footage he was getting was priceless and start cheering over the implications.

Doran crept behind a bottle-covered table and plotted his next move. Frederickson gestured toward Kelsey, who was wiggling against the tie wraps that bound her to a cheap chair. "In honor of our ten years together, I have a gift for you," Frederickson said.

Ling smiled. Doran shivered. "I recognize her." His laugh sounded supernatural. "Clever of you to eliminate your opposition and call it my gift." He looked around the room then frowned and turned to Cedric. "What's detaining Merek?"

Cedric gave a slight shrug, then leveled his Uzi

at the door and inched toward it. Damn, he'd hoped for more time before the shit hit the fan. Botts wagged his finger at Cedric. "Don't make another 'suicide' look like murder."

Cedric leveled his Uzi at Botts' stomach in a silent threat. "I not shoot friend. You friend?" Botts laughed like it was a joke and raised his hands, but sweat beaded on his forehead. Point made, Cedric grinned and went out the door.

"So, my dear buddy," Ling said, "what else do you have for me? You mentioned a new formula that would make shipping easier."

Frederickson ushered him toward a pimply-faced looking, tattoo-covered nerd. "Thomas developed the process. He should have the honor of presenting it to you."

As the nerd nervously pointed and gesticulated, Doran caught Kelsey's attention. Her only reaction was a slight dilation of her pupils when she saw him. He motioned for her to be quiet, but suspected she would have, no matter what. When everyone focused on Thomas' method, Doran moved behind a stack of dusty boxes and sawed one of Kelsey's hands free. Unable to stay in such an exposed position, he handed her his knife.

Without acknowledging him, she eagerly began slicing into the thick plastic securing her other wrist. A thin streak of blood bloomed on the blade, but her only reaction was to tilt the cutting edge. With a faint pop, the binding dropped away. She held her breath and stared at the others, but when they didn't look back, she carefully bent over and began freeing her feet.

Knowing that he only moments remained to get into position, Doran ducked back behind the table, clutched the Uzi and waited.

The door burst open.

Botts leveled his 38 a fraction of a minute before Frederickson aimed his handgun. Cedric burst into the room, his Uzi leveled. "Merek hurt. Think hit head. No wake."

Ling turned to Frederickson, fury in his expression. "It seems your operation has been compromised."

Frederickson shook his head. Ling nodded, then glanced at Cedric.

With an ear-splitting roar, blood gushed from the chest of first one, then two lab workers. Ling grabbed Frederickson by the ear and hustled him toward the door.

The pimply-faced Thomas screamed and dove under the table where Doran was hiding. He shrieked louder when he saw him. Doran gave him a swift upper cut, but didn't wait to make certain he was unconscious as he surged to his feet and started firing. His first slug hit Botts in the upper arm.

Out of the corner of his eye, he saw Kelsey yank her foot free and dive behind a stack of boxes. A second later, bullets shattered her chair.

Doran roared with rage and peppered Cedric's chest with lead. Though he fell backwards, no blood appeared. Botts lunged at him; Doran gave him a high kick in the solar plexus. Botts staggered. When Doran turned back to Cedric, he'd vanished.

Frederickson fired at Ling, but Ling whirled away. Frederickson fell backward into a lab table.

The table overturned and bottles of chemicals smashed over the floor.

Kelsey darted toward the door, but Ling grabbed her wrist and hauled her up short. She kicked at him, but he moved aside with the ease of a highly skilled martial arts master.

Botts moaned and tried to stand. Doran kicked his groin.

Kelsey tried to stab Ling with the knife, she still held, as if it were life itself.

Frederickson fired. The slug grazed his thigh; he fell next to moaning Botts. Botts struggled to his feet, but before he straightened, Frederickson's gun roared, again. Botts fell, a fist-sized hole in the back of his head.

Doran rolled under a table and tried to get a bead on Frederickson.

He saw the blow coming out of his peripheral vision and rolled out of the way. Cedric roared with rage and dove after him, landing hard on his arm. Hand numb, Doran's Uzi fell to the floor. As it hit, it fired. Someone screamed in pain.

Cedric began pummeling him with a vengeance.

Doran hit back putting every bit of training and rage he'd ever felt into each blow.

They rolled against the table legs; it tipped over. More chemicals crashed to the floor. Flames leaped upward. Thomas, the lab tech staggered toward the door.

Cedric boxed Doran's ear, knocking his head to the left. Through the flames, he saw Ling holding Kelsey by the nape of her neck as he pushed her toward the door, while using her as a shield.

The fire flared.

Frederickson turned toward them, aimed and shot. Doran flipped Cedric into the line of fire too late; it felt like a freight train had hit his side.

ooo

Kelsey knew how helpless puppies and kittens felt with jaws gripping the back of their neck. The small oriental man grasped the tender flesh and tendons with such power that she knew it would take days for the bruise to heal. Still, she watched for a way to break free and an opportunity to use Doran's knife on something softer than plastic.

As Ling shoved her through PBCO's front door, she tried to kick and stab, but the old man swiftly evaded her foot and snatched the knife. Then, in an amazingly nimble move, he wrapped one arm around her waist. Suddenly she felt a knife at her throat and knew it was Doran's.

"Keep fighting and you die," his peanut-scented breath wafted over her cheek. Pain radiated as a hot droplet rolled downward. She gasped and went limp. "That's more like it." Ling's chuckle would make a demon smile. She shuddered. He released her waist, but before she could think of a way to escape, he had her by the collar of her shirt. Only then, did he ease the knife's pressure.

Another droplet trickled down her neck.

Afraid to swallow, Kelsey waited to see what he'd do next.

"Move toward the van." She took a step. The knife connected with flesh. "Not so fast."

What was he worried about? Did he think the shadows were filled with sharp shooters?

Step by painful baby-step, they moved toward the dark van. When they stepped into the parking lot. An unseen man said, "Long time on see, Ling."

Ling jerked; the knife bit into her neck. Out of the corner of her eye, she saw a man sitting in a wheelchair, a rifle aimed in her direction. Martha had said Doran's partner was crippled. She hoped this was Quinn and not some long-time friend of Ling's, as the tone had suggested.

"I thought you were dead." Ling looked Quinn up and down then chuckled. "Well, at least half of you is."

Kelsey's skin crawled.

Quinn made a tiny gesture with the gun. "The rest of me is fully operational."

"Shoot me and the bitch dies."

"Whatever you do with her isn't my concern. One way or the other, I'm going to get you."

Ling laughed as if Quinn had made a joke, but he repositioned her to cover his side, then forced her to begin sidestepping toward the van. "How naïve of you to believe that."

The rifle didn't waver. "I don't see either of your gorillas."

"Not all protection is visible."

"Neither the sheriff nor the senator is here, either."

Ling smiled. "Always so short sighted."

Though the man behind her looked old and wiry, his grip felt like a steel trap. She struggled to break free or at least give Quinn a clear shot, but no matter what she did, the old man with the too-sweet breath kept her between him and Quinn's steady aim. No matter what Quinn had said about not valuing her life, he hadn't fired, so he must have bluffed. As they neared the van, Kelsey realized no amount of wiggling would free her, so she sought another solution.

Quinn's aim followed them the entire way. Kelsey half wished he would shoot. One way or the other, she'd be out of her misery. Devlin Doran had already paid a terrible price for attempting to rescue her; she couldn't expect anyone to rescue her if she didn't make the effort to save herself. Kelsey took a steadying breath and stealthily unbuttoned the bottom button of her shirt. Quinn grinned when her fingers worked the next button free.

She only had the top button to go when they reached the van. Ling's grip changed when they got to the driver's door. "Open it."

She pulled on the handle. "It's locked."

He dropped Doran's knife, but kept hold of her collar.

As the hinge squeaked open, Kelsey undid the button, slammed her arms backward and dove headfirst out of her shirt. Something snagged the back pocket of her jeans. For a moment, she was caught, then the fabric ripped and she was falling, again. A shot rang out. She tucked her chin and somersaulted forward over the rough asphalt in a maneuver she hadn't done since she'd played leapfrog in grade school.

She scrambled to her feet and glanced back as she sprinted away. Ling slammed the van's door. Quinn's second shot impacted against the window.

"Damn, it's bulletproof."

The next shot took out the front tire. Kelsey slowed her pace and stared at the all-too-real drama. Ling gunned the engine. Tires screaming, the van roared toward her. She leaped out of the way moments before it surged past her. The rifle roared, again.

Panting for breath, Kelsey sat down on the dank asphalt, but watched the receding van as if half-expected the van to back and try another run. Instead, it kept going and Quinn kept his weapon trained on it, as he looked for something vulnerable.

Brakes squealed as another car entered the parking lot. Headlights spotlighted her shirt and the photo that had been in its pocket. Kelsey sprinted back and snatched them and jammed her arms into the shirt. She had half the buttons secured before her hands started shaking too much to line up the buttons and the holes. She looked down, and noticed a trail of blood glistening against the parking lot's tarry surface.

Quinn rolled up to her and calmly finished fastening her shirt. "Brilliant move with the buttons."

"Th-thank you," Kelsey said. Her knees began quaking.

Quinn gently pulled her onto his lap, then patted her back and made soothing sounds, as if she was a baby. "You did great." She clutched the photo to her heart.

More vehicles arrived. A slim dark figure leaped from one and ran toward them, but when Quinn pointed behind them and made an odd motion with his hand, the ninja-type silhouette changed direction. A News van skidded into the parking lot. Dear Lord, not the paparazzi circus. No doubt a platoon of cameras had been hidden in the shadows, and footage of her half-naked would flood the networks for several days. The last thing her dignity needed was a picture of her cozying up on the lap of a cripple's emaciated legs. She must be hurting him. Kelsey stood up, holding onto his wheelchair for support.

Quinn put a supportive hand on her back. "Steady," Quinn said. She focused on dignity and balance. If those qualities hadn't been drilled into her since she was in diapers, she wouldn't have succeeded.

The swat team burst from the back of a truck and dark-clad figures fanned out across the area. Another news van arrived. Several police cars and an ambulance roared into the parking lot. The asphalt appeared to shudder under the blue strobe lights. She squinted through the pulsating night, for the one and only face that she wanted to see.

Suddenly PBCo's door burst open and Marvin staggered out. "Arrest her," he screamed, pointing at her, "She murdered Sheriff Botts."

Kelsey gasped.

Unexpectedly, a microphone was shoved in her face and lights flashed. Spots danced before her eyes. "Do you have a statement?" The microphone nudged at her. "Why did you kill Sheriff Botts?"

Kelsey silently shook her head.

Another microphone, thrust at her. "Is the sheriff dead?"

A camera flashed.

Quinn laughed as if someone had told a joke. "Oh, I'll wager Botts is dead all right," Quinn said. "Senator Frederickson shot him in the back of his head. That usually does the trick when he doesn't want someone for a friend any more."

Abruptly the microphones were jammed into Quinn's face; still unsteady, Kelsey clung to the back of his chair. "What's your name? For the Record?"

Marvin shouted, "Officer, arrest that man. He's MacLennan's partner. See, he has a rifle."

Quinn smiled and shook his head. "Senator, Senator, don't you understand?" His tone was infused with amusement, as he flashed a badge. "It's over. I've got the murder on tape and there is no way you will get it labeled suicide."

Now completely confused, Kelsey leaned heavily on Quinn's wheelchair. Since he didn't seem to mind the limelight, she tried to blend into the background, as she tried to figure out how he knew so much about what had gone on in the basement. He didn't need makeup to look ruggedly handsome. He didn't need to worry about how messy he looked after being slapped repeatedly and bleeding all over himself then tumbling across a filthy parking lot and getting abrasions everywhere or having blood all over the front of his shirt ... and he hadn't put his shirt on inside out.

Someone grabbed her. She screamed. "You're hurt." a medic said. "Let me help you."

Kelsey took a shuddering breath, then allowed the paramedic to lead her to the rear of an ambulance. In the background, reporters shouted questions and bulbs flashed. Marvin's tone rose each time Quinn laughed. After she gratefully sat on the back of the vehicle, the medic began treating her throat.

"What happened?"

"Knife." Kelsey looked over his shoulders to where the cameras and microphones moved between Marvin and Quinn like it was a tennis match.

"You're lucky - it missed the carotid by a hair."

"Ling needed me alive, as a shield."

He nodded. "You'll probably have a scar."

"Better a scar than dead." Her attention turned to PBCO's door. Devlin, where are you?

"That's the spirit." He cleaned the wound with something that stung like a nest of bees. She clenched her teeth against the welling scream. The medic made a pleased sound, then swabbed on something that burned like fire. Kelsey gasped and forced herself to remain still.

Was Doran staying in the background because he knew how much his partner enjoyed playing the media game? Her gaze wandered around the parking lot, trying to pick him out from the black-clad swat team. Why didn't he come to her? Was he hurt?

"You're doing great," the medic said. "I'm almost done." If he swabbed another chemical on her neck, her head might come unglued.

Quinn laughed. "I also taped the part about you consorting with known drug lords," he said.

The two reporters shouted questions. Another

one shouted, "$50,000.00 for the tape."

Quinn shook his head. Despite his casual, bantering tone, Kelsey noticed that Quinn's attention stayed focused on Marvin's eyes and his hands didn't leave the rifle that lay, casual as a blanket, in his lap.

"$75,000," The other journalist screamed.

"$250,000."

As the bidding frenzy escalated, a young crew-cut officer approached Marvin and began reciting the Miranda to him. Frederickson turned to the officer and struck him on the jaw. Quinn's rifle rose with the speed of lightening. Marvin tried to snatch the officer's gun, but the officer recovered from his surprise and slapped a cuff on Marv's wrist. Marvin broke free and dashed toward a white car.

Shots rang out.

Frederickson faltered then fell. Someone screamed. Two cameramen stood their ground as they taped the unfolding story.

Kelsey ran to Quinn, as he lowered his rifle. "You shot him!"

"Wasn't me. I only had one left after Ling got away and I wasn't about to waste it by firing through the media." He laid the weapon across his shrunken lap.

Frederickson struggled to rise.

Two more shots rang out. Frederickson jerked, then fell twitching on the ground. Kelsey gripped Quinn's wheelchair for support. Camera flashes illuminated the grisly scene like a floodlight. Another shot hit Marvin between his eyes. He fell face-first against the pavement, then lay still.

Gooseflesh rushed over her. "Dear Lord, they killed him," Kelsey whispered. Weak kneed, she peered through the gathering gloom, wondering who the next victim would be. Most of the swat team members were sighting down their weapons and focused on the shadows beyond the streetlight, but some were darting shadows moving around the vehicles.

"I wanted the bastard for questioning," Quinn muttered, as he slowly rolled toward Frederickson. Kelsey stumbled along behind him, as she hung onto the chair's handgrips for support.

There were several metallic clicks. Quinn stopped. Kelsey tripped and fell against his armrest. Quinn shoved her behind his chair.

A crew-cut officer sprinted in front of them and aimed his handgun at the shadows. "Drop your weapon and surrender." Another click. "Now!" The officer's trigger finger quivered.

Zoë stepped barefoot from the darkness, her arms forward with a handgun balanced on her upturned palms. Oh, no! Was she the shooter? What had she done? Why had she done it?

Lights flashed. Zoë turned toward them, a blank expression in her eyes. "I had to kill him. He was evil." She looked toward Marvin's body and tears fell. "I had to." More lights pulsed as cameramen recorded the event.

"Why?" a reporter shouted.

The officer seized Zoë's gun, wrenched her arm behind her back and cuffed her wrist. Kelsey looked beyond Zoë to where black-clad figures fanned out in the shadows. Zoë snatched his service pistol and turned it on him. Chills ran over Kelsey.

He put up his hands.

"Stay back," Zoë warned. The officer took a cautious backward step.

A reporter shoved past him and thrust a microphone at Zoë. "Why did you kill him?"

She gave the man an incredulous look. "He didn't love me."

"Are you saying you had an affair with the Senator?" he demanded.

Zoë's mouth quivered and her knees buckled. She reached a trembling hand toward Frederickson. "My father... My lover..."

"Which one was he?"

Zoë's confused expression centered on the closest reporter. "My father... was my lover."

"Why did you kill him?"

"He never loved me because I'm nothing." She raised the gun to her ear.

Kelsey gasped and moved toward Zoë. Quinn grabbed her wounded wrist. Pain, hot and heavy ribbed through her. With a gasp, she fell backward. Strong arms caught her, a gunshot shattered the night and the exploding light from the cameras preserved tragedy for eternity. Kelsey fainted.

She didn't know how long she stayed in the black void. When she came to, she smelled disinfectant mixed with vague scents of blood, smoke and jasmine. The mixture was nauseating, but the worst part was the discordant sounds. She clenched her jaws together and focused on sorting out the noise: reporters shouted questions; an officer was reading the Miranda to someone; but the closest sounds were soft assurances that she'd be fine.

The stench of antiseptic suddenly became overpowering, and pain washed over her forearm. She gasped and sat up. White sparkles swirled across her vision, but strong hands supported her.

The spinning images settled into the medic, who had cleaned her wounds, two people hunkering over Frederickson's body, officers forcing reporters away from the crime scene amid flashing cameras, and swat officers in every shadow. "Is Zoë dead?" she whispered, all too certain that she knew the answer.

"The gun went off when an officer grabbed it," the paramedic said.

"But is she alive?"

"Not a scratch on her."

"Is the officer okay?"

"Yes."

"I'll tell Rams to get her a good lawyer."

"Better get her a good shrink," he said. Kelsey nodded. Poor Zoë had probably needed one of them for a long time.

When the medic finished applying the new bandages, she imagined she must look like an escaped mummy. While she was contemplating the medic's gauze and adhesive patches, Quinn rolled up to her.

"You okay?"

She gave a slight nod. "When we were little, Zoë was like a sister, but then she changed, and I guess I finally know why." She bit her lip.

"You couldn't have changed anything."

Quinn was probably right. Before she could ask

him how he knew, an explosion rocked the ground and a section of PBCO's roof shot upward.

People screamed and ran for cover. Quinn's powerful arms grabbed her, then his wheelchair careened across the parking lot. She watched the scene over Quinn's strong shoulder, amazed how the roof disintegrated as it arced back to earth and how the streamers of fire lit the night like fireworks.

Devlin was still in there. "No!" she screamed.

Chapter 20

Kelsey stared in immobile horror as debris rained onto PBCO's roof and the surrounding area. Long tongues of fire erupted from the roof.

As if on cue, a fire engine roared into the parking lot.

Cameramen quickly focused their equipment on the fire, some were so bold that they endangered themselves to a better picture of doom and imperiled the police officers, who tried to save them from their foolish choices.

Kelsey stared at the fire truck. "How?"

"I called them," Quinn said.

"How did you know?"

"Dev was wired." The misery in his tone told her that she hadn't been the only one searching the shadows for Devlin Doran. "I phoned in the fire when the test tubes fell over and ignited. Then, I got out of the van and was coming to help." He looked at the building, his expression saying what he was too polite to put into words, 'but when I saved you, I lost him'.

Tears blinded her. "I should have been in there. Not him." Kelsey tried to wrestle free of Quinn and go toward the building.

Quinn tugged her back. She fought to get free of his grip, but the man seemed strong as an ox. Finally, he yanked her off balance and plopped her back onto his lap. His rifle gouged into her bottom, and must be digging into him, but he didn't appear to notice. With a flick of his wrists, the wheelchair sped away from the building. "Sit tight, we'll find him." Dear Lord, she hoped he was right, but Quinn didn't sound any more optimistic than she felt. "He's not stupid enough to get caught in that mess."

"Oh, God, I hope you're right. I never even got the chance to tell him how much I loved him." She held on for dear life as the wheelchair raced toward the rear of the parking lot at a speed she'd thought impossible. When they were far away from the cameras and pulsating blue squad car lights, the chair slowed. Then they moved off the pavement, onto a sidewalk and from there onto the grass. To think that the paparazzi were probably missing this.

Moments later, they stopped on the hoist of a handicapped van. With a lurch, the hoist rose.

Of course, Devlin would know where Quinn had parked and would go there to find him. Kelsey hugged Quinn. "You're so smart to think of this."

He rolled the chair off the platform and into a gadget-lovers dream. A tall, bony red-haired man wearing black hunkered in front of a bank of small screens and ignored their arrival.

When Kelsey got off Quinn's lap and rubbed her bruised backside. Quinn calmly opened a locker and put the rifle inside. "I can't believe they didn't arrest you or at least stop you for having that."

Quinn glanced at her. "I phoned the regional FBI branch and had them notify the locals that I was armed and on the scene." He gave her a lopsided smile. "I warned them that all hell would break loose if they shot the guy on wheels and that only the jeans and chino crowd was fair game." He looked her up and down. "I didn't know what you were wearing." She stared at him. Who was this man, who could deal with the past situation so lightly? He stared back at her, then focused on her clenched hand. "What are you holding?"

She opened her tight fist and showed him the crumpled photo.

He peered at it, then looked up at her, his surprise evident. "I don't understand."

That made two of them. "I don't know who she is, but she represents why I'm running for office."

"Dev know that?" She indicated agreement. "May I?" Before she finished nodding, Quinn plucked the photo from her hand and gently smoothed out the wrinkles. Then, he snatched a weird contraption off of the only other chair in the cramped van and gestured for her to sit down. He tossed the thing that resembled and odd mask onto the narrow desk.

"How much longer do you think it'll take Devlin to get here?" she asked. The thin man broke his vigil and looked at Quinn, worry etched in his expression.

Quinn shrugged nonchalantly, but his mouth flattened as he looked at the monitors, which portrayed scenes that should have been restricted to Hades.

The slim man gave her a faltering smile and offered her his hand. "Trent Davies."

She shook his hand. "Kelsey MacLennan." He gave her an indecipherable look, before he turned back to the monitors.

"I've heard that to succeed in politics," Trent said, "it is often necessary to rise above your principles. Have you found that to be true?"

Kelsey gaped at him, then quickly shook her head. "Have you seen Devlin on those?" She craned her neck to look over their shoulders.

Trent shook his head. Tears began rolling down her cheeks.

Kelsey didn't know how long the three of them stared at the monitors, but by the time dawn broke, the fire was under control and Quinn's eyes glistened with unshed tears.

Humor no longer danced in Trent's expression. "I'm going out to do a recon."

She sniffed. "He's dead, isn't he?"

Trent gave her a hard look. "Not if it wasn't for you."

Quinn glanced at Trent, but didn't intervene.

"I know." She swallowed a choking lump of misery. "He came after me because he loved me."

Trent snorted. "You were a tool, so don't get all sentimental about it."

Kelsey shook her head. If Devlin hadn't cared about her, he would have stayed outside, instead of coming in to rescue me. Kelsey shook her head, again.

Trent nodded, his eyes glittered with pure anger. "The Boss thought your brother was dealing, he didn't realize the senator was impersonating him."

"Rams would never-" words failed her.

"Yeah, well we finally figured that out, but don't go all soppy about the Boss, you never really knew him. I did. Quinn did. He and Quinn have been together for years and through more than some prima donna like you could ever understand."

"Trent." Quinn's tone held a warning. "Go talk to the firemen. Get their assessment of the situation." His expression looked grim as he tweaked various knobs and studied the faces of individual firefighters, who were packing up their gear. The police cars and swat van were long gone, as were the journalist's vans. Dead fires weren't newsworthy. Soon, only a lone fire truck remained.

Trent paused, hand on the door handle and gave her a livid look. "If he'd gotten out, he'd have been here by now." The door slammed.

A lump of despair grew in Kelsey's throat. "He blames me for getting kidnapped and Devlin caring enough to-" a sob cut her off.

"Dev chose to infiltrate the plant without backup," Quinn's tone sounded grim. He adjusted a few buttons, then tapped the biggest monitor's face. "Watch this." It changed to show the lab.

He hadn't been kidding about having surveillance footage of Marvin kowtowing to the odious little oriental man. Quinn touched the image of the old man. "That's why Dev went in, instead of waiting. He's been out for Ling ever since his sister died."

"Devlin told me about Ling, but I don't think he mentioned his sister."

Quinn gave her a sympathetic look. "There wasn't any need. Wes's plan was to have Dev charm you - seduce you, if necessary."

He'd been told to do all that? "Why?" The word sounded strangled, even to her own ears.

In answer, Quinn touched Ling's image, again. "Dev would have moved heaven and hell to get Ling behind bars so he couldn't ruin the lives of any more kids."

It was a noble motive. Kelsey nodded in agreement. "I wish-" She could barely whisper, 'I'd died instead of him.'

Quinn took her trembling hands in his two large, warm ones. "Kelsey, I've known Dev a long time. He was so obsessed with revenge that he endangered himself. I warned him, that something felt wrong with this op, but he wouldn't listen."

What did he mean?

"The accident was a set up," Quinn admitted. Guilt made it hard for him to look her in the eye. She shook her head. He nodded and gently shoved the photo toward her. "This is Marnie, Dev's sister. He always carried this photo to remind him why he needed to wipe out Ling."

"I don't believe making love was an act." Her voice sounded raw as her nerves.

Quinn raised a brow.

"You were meant to see Dev as your savior and trust him." She swallowed, amazed at how easily she'd viewed him as her guardian angel. Quinn added, "But you were just another innocent victim, just as innocent as Marnie."

Kelsey wet her lips. "His sister chose drugs, I

chose to run for senate. What's the parallel?"

Quinn rubbed his temples. "Wes assigned Dev and me to gain your trust and infiltrate your family's drug operation."

"But as far as I know, we don't have one."

He sighed. "We know that, now, but at the time, we believed the rumors. Dev's way to gain your trust was to romance you."

She closed her eyes and tried to absorb what he'd said, but despite his obvious sincerity, she knew how Devlin had looked at her, how he'd freed her despite putting himself in danger. She looked at Quinn. "It may have started as an act, but it changed." She swallowed. "He changed… I changed."

"Believe whatever you need to."

There wasn't enough air in the van. "I know in my heart that he loves – loved - me as much as I loved him. And I will always love him." She needed air. She lunged out the door and leaped over the hoist. As she landed on the grass, the rising sun blinded her, so she shielded her eyes with her hand and stalked toward the fire truck.

A firefighter's soot-streaked face glared down at her, "You need to go on home. The show's over." She blinked.

Kelsey gulped. "Devlin Doran is still in there." She pointed to the smoldering ruins.

The firefighter shook his head. "I'm sorry, ma'am no one could have survived that." Behind her, the handicapped lift purred.

"He has to be alive," she said.

A strong hand gripped her good one. She looked

through a watery gaze and saw tears in Quinn's
eyes. "I told him he was going to get us both
killed." A tear plummeted. "Instead, he just got
himself."

In a rush of understanding, she realized that
Quinn loved him just as deeply as she did. Her tears
flowed. Kelsey dropped to her knees and clutched
Quinn's fingers. "What he did was for the right
reasons." Even when he'd originally targeted her. If
he hadn't followed orders, she'd never have met
Devlin Doran or understood what true love was.

"Maybe."

"No, I mean it." She knelt down and looked
Quinn in the eye. "I think that the fact that I thought
Marnie's photo symbolized who I was running for
must have been some sort of message." She blinked
away tears. Far across the lot behind him, past a
mound of withered juniper a branch quivered.
Kelsey wiped away her tears and blinked. It moved
again. Kelsey gasped and clutched Quinn's knee. "I
saw something move." She pointed. "There."

"Probably a squirrel," the fireman said. "You
people need to pack up and leave."

The whole shrub shook. Surely a squirrel
couldn't shake that much of a bush and it certainly
wouldn't be in anything as thorny as a pyracantha.
She held her breath and stared. A branch jerked.
This time something round emerged.

"Please God, let it be Devlin." She didn't know
she's spoken aloud until she heard Quinn echo her
plea.

It was a man; a man who was moving slowly.
Kelsey lunged to her feet and sprinted around the

Jeanne Foguth

fireman and Quinn. She dashed across the grass and asphalt, heading toward the apparition. The whirr of the wheelchair and pounding footfalls were hot on her heels. Please, God, let the charred figure be Devlin, not some wino.

Then the figure maneuvered out of the pyracantha and straightened, she was certain that the black apparition was him. "Devlin!" Briars scratched her as she ran straight into his outstretched arms.

"Damned if you aren't the best thing I've ever seen," he said.

The stench of smoke and soil mixed with his spicy smell. "You're alive!" She kissed him with all the love she felt.

He faltered.

"You're hurt."

"Nothing that won't heal."

"You'd better, because I love you, Devlin Doran."

"I love you, too, Kelsey MacLennan, but you may change your mind when you -"

She put her fingers to his lips. "I know about Marnie and your plan." She inhaled. "I understand and I still love you."

"Well," said Quinn from behind her, "this is interesting."

"I'll be damned," said Trent.

ooo

After the firefighter cleaned Devlin's wounds, and Trent helped him into D. Q.'s surveillance van, Quinn followed Trent's battered pickup to the hospital for x-rays.

374

Halfway there, Quinn pulled the van off the road and stared at a smashed section of guardrail, which protected vehicles from Dead Man's Gulch. "You two might think each other is the greatest sight in the world, but I think that's beautiful." He pointed to paramedics struggling to maneuver a body bag into an ambulance.

Quinn looked like he'd won the lottery, but Kelsey's face went white. Her sister-in-law and niece had died in that gully. She didn't need any reminders of that. Doran wrapped a protective arm around her and tried to bury her face against his shoulder, but she jerked free of him and stared at the one car accident with a concentration to equal Quinn's. While his partner smiled at the body bag, she gazed wide-eyed at the nondescript gray van.

Quinn gave her an odd look. "Recognize it?"

Doran's arm tightened protectively around her. "Quinn," he warned, "just drive."

"Last time Kelsey and I saw that car," Quinn said, "Ling was driving it away after my bullet grazed his neck. Looks like he ran out of blood before he got to the hospital."

"Sonofabitch!" Doran felt like he'd won the lottery. "You got him!"

"Looks like it," Quinn agreed. "What'll we do without a price on our head?"

Kelsey cleared her throat. "How would you feel about retiring and opening a real investigative firm in D.C.?"

"Sounds good to me," Quinn said.

Doran narrowed his gaze on his partner. "Why?"

"You don't find a woman worth dying for very

often."

Kelsey looked back and forth at them, simultaneously hopeful and terrified. Doran smiled and said, "Marry me and I will."

Kelsey whooped with joy and hugged him.

Pain shot through his body and he winced. "Careful. I think Quinn is right about the cracked ribs."

Kelsey dropped her arms and bit her lower lip.

He caressed her under the chin. "Don't worry. I heal quick, you have the rest of our lives to hug the stuffings out of me."

Abruptly, she stiffened. He looked back to see what had stunned her. Slowly, she reached for the night vision goggles. Expression tense, she studied them, then looked at him.

"Of course, I should have realized you were the alien boogie man"

"I beg your pardon?"

"Black clothes and skin, thick glasses, like he was either blind or a Star War's bounty hunter." Kelsey swallowed.

"I wanted to close the drug cartel down and save kids. I never intended for you to get hurt." If they were to have a chance at a shared life, he couldn't leave lies in their past.

She held up her hand. "Quinn explained. It's okay." She bit her lower lip. "I have a couple questions: one, did you sabotage my brother's car, too?"

"No."

Quinn lightly touched Kelsey's hand. "Wes came up with that plan. Dev only agreed to it after he made certain he would the one you rear-ended. He thought he'd be able to keep you safe."

"Is that why you slowed down so early?"

He nodded. "I figured the Burb's brakes would stop both of us. You weren't supposed to get hurt. No one was."

"I thought you were the most timid driver." Her brow furrowed.

Doran cleared his throat. "Botts did your brother's car and my Suburban. Everyone was meant to die in the accidents he arranged. I never intended for you to get hurt in the accident or at any point after." He cleared his throat. "But I was using you as a lateral pawn to get Ling's cartel shut down." He waited for the slap that he deserved.

After a heart stopping moment, she inhaled deeply and gazed into the eyes. "I may never understand why my brake lines needed drilling, but the whole mess did result in getting rid of that drug lab and all the pollution that company made." She gestured to Ling's shrouded body. "Killing that odious man made it worth totaling my Mustang."

He nodded. They were silent for several moments. "I thought you had more than one question," Quinn said.

She nodded and cleared her throat. "When we thought you were dead, Quinn told me everything." Doran raised a brow. "Is it me or are there too many coincidences?"

"What exactly do you mean?" Doran asked.

"Your controller relocated you here. He set this thing up. Your funding was approved by Marvin, so they probably knew each other." She swallowed.

"I'm trying to ask if you think there was a conspiracy to keep Marvin in office and cash in a reward."

"I'd bet on it," Quinn said.

"And you can also bet on us getting the evidence we need for court, if we're right," Doran added.

"Assuming I win, I'll give you one-hundred-percent of my support."

His heart swelled with love and warmth. Had there ever been such a wonderful woman? Of course, he owed her. More than she would ever know. And if she'd have him, he'd spend the rest of his life making it up to her. "Still want to marry me?"

She cupped his face between her palms and looked deep into his eyes. Then, with a slight incline of her neck, she kissed him lightly on his parched lips. "Yes." He heard and felt the acceptance, then she deepened the kiss.

Quinn edged the van back into traffic. Kelsey carefully nestled against Devlin. Everything felt right with the world.

THE END

www.ingramcontent.com/pod-product-compliance
Lightning Source LLC
Chambersburg PA
CBHW062002170626
46813CB00001B/12